D1045028

# THE PROFESSIONAL GENTLEMAN

Not until Victoria ascended the throne to put her own special mark on the monarchy were the excesses, inadequacies and indulgences of the Hanoverian dynasty set aside in favour of pride and integrity.

Victoria's accession was a fortunate event for Britain. A darker event, had it happened, might have caused the country and the Empire to endure the rule of her uncle, the Duke of Cumberland, whom some said was born of the devil.

Caroline, the young American widow of Lord Clarence Percival, and a renowned beauty in Regency society, recognised the devil in Cumberland, although her sister Annabelle was blind to it. Both crossed the path of the dark prince, and it was Caroline's hireling, Captain Charles Burnside, a professional adventurer of the times, who delivered them from evil, although not without causing Lady Caroline a deal of confusion and heart-searching.

*Previous titles by Robert Tyler Stevens
available from Severn House*

**THE FIELDS OF YESTERDAY
THE HOSTAGE
SHADOWS IN THE AFTERNOON
THE WOMAN IN BERLIN**

# THE
# PROFESSIONAL GENTLEMAN

**Robert Tyler Stevens**

SEVERN HOUSE PUBLISHERS

This first world edition published 1988 by
SEVERN HOUSE PUBLISHERS LTD of
40–42 William IV Street, London WC2N 4DF

Copyright © 1988 by R. T. Stevens

British Library Cataloguing in Publication Data
Stevens, Robert Tyler
The professional gentleman.
Rn: Reginald Thomas Staples    I. Title
823′.914[F]    PR6069.T442

ISBN 0-7278-1522-9

Printed and bound in Great Britain

# Chapter One

The elegant house in Cavendish Square was pleasingly quiet, the closed library windows shutting out the sounds of passing carriages and criers of wares. Lady Clarence Percival, formerly Miss Caroline Anne Howard of Charleston, South Carolina, seated herself at the handsome redwood desk and read again the letter she had recently received from her father-in-law, the Duke of Avonhurst.

'My dearest Caroline,

'First, allow me to say how *deeply touched* I was when you confided in me some days ago. Such influence as I have was at once yours to command. Although it has not been easy to alight on a suitable confederate, if we may call him that, I am now able to advise you that a promising fellow has been run to earth. He will bring you a letter from me to introduce himself. His name is Burnside, Captain Burnside, and here I must make it clear that his military record is a *dubious* one. Nor is his university background at all impeccable. He was sent down from Cambridge for escapades of a disreputable kind. One might say it is in his favour that he *freely admits* his lack of virtue, and, since you are looking for a man who lives by his wits, I recommend him to you.

'His late father was a bishop, a gentleman who must lie uneasily in his grave on account of the reprehensible qualities of his son. Burnside is undoubtedly an adventurer, but I believe that, once he commits himself to you, you will not find him unreliable. Despite his predilection for knavery, he owns a *peculiar pride* in dealing

1

honestly with a patron, and I am convinced he will do so with you. Beware of any other rogues, for most would betray you by making off at once with whatever monies you might advance, or sell themselves to your adversary.

'Burnside's airs and graces are not unpleasing, and I can well believe him capable of charming ladies to *distraction*. I gather he has fleeced several who have fallen victim to his calculated gallantries. I have no doubt he could pass himself off as a gentleman, despite having long since ceased to be one, and there is every chance he might prove himself an effective rival for the affections of a certain young lady enamoured of the *most dangerous* man in the land. His skill at cards is a challenge to all gamblers who boast a skill of their own, as C does, and I don't doubt he is also an accomplished cheat, which in some men can emulate the skill of a dozen others.

'I trust you will find his wits and disposition suitable to your purpose, and I have instructed him to be at your house at ten-thirty this coming Tuesday morning, and to ask for Mrs Carmichael, as you requested.

'In closing, let me express the abiding affection in which the Duchess and I hold you, dearest daughter-in-law. I am, yours devotedly, A.'

The Duke of Avonhurst had never failed her, although his son had, and miserably. Lady Clarence Percival, who preferred to be called Lady Caroline, moved to the window and pulled the bell-sash. Her footman Thomas entered a few moments later.

'Thomas,' she said, her voice a pleasure to most ears in the lingering quality of her vowels, 'kindly ask the gentleman to present himself.'

'Yes, Yer Ladyship.'

The gentleman was ushered in and the footman disappeared, closing the door with the quiet care of a man devoted to his mistress.

The gentleman advanced. The library, carpeted, had an atmosphere entirely tranquil and cultural. Coming to a halt at the desk, the gentleman bowed.

'Good morning,' said Lady Caroline, still at the window.

2

'Mrs Carmichael? Good morning, marm,' said the gentleman.

She eyed him coolly and discerningly. The gentleman, if he could be called that, had the debonair look her father-in-law's letter had led her to expect. His long, slender frame was clasped by a dark blue coat buttoned above the waist, and cut well back to display a pale blue waistcoat and tight-fitting pantaloons of the same colour. His high cravat was a many-folded triumph, his dark hair had a modish look of slight disorder and he owned luxuriant sideburns. He carried a malacca cane in his right hand, and held his top hat in his left. His countenance was pleasingly masculine, which made her frown. Lord Clarence Percival, her late husband, had shown a similarly pleasing handsomeness, and she, newly arrived from America, had been foolishly blind to the dissolution that lay behind the personable facade.

True, her visitor's healthy complexion spoke more of an upright life than a disreputable one, but she still disliked the fact that his looks reminded her of an infatuation that had cost her dear. He seemed commendably at ease and, although his grey eyes looked to be frankly inquisitive, his manner was deferential. She judged him to be about thirty.

For his part, he could not have been unimpressed. Lady Caroline, daughter-in-law of the seventh Duke of Avonhurst, was a renowned beauty. Mr Creevy, the gossip writer and purveyor of tittle-tattle sometimes scandalous and sometimes trivial, described her as a bosomed goddess of Olympian splendour. In the light of the window, the summer sunshine gently caressing her, she was close to magnificence. Her high-waisted, full-skirted chemise gown of cream silk was backed by a long green train falling from a sleeveless waistcoat, the low square neckline revealing the upper curves of firm, fulsome breasts. Her auburn hair, lushly rich and darkly fiery, was styled in ringlets that danced lightly to every movement. At a height of five feet eight she carried herself in superb, Junoesque fashion, a characteristic complemented by the clarity and fearlessness of her green eyes, framed by lashes dark and long. Her complexion was akin to peaches and cream, for it had always been protected from the ravages of the Carolina sun by a bonnet. In England, she could take off her bonnet on a summer day and let it fly from her hand, for there was no English sun that was as searing as that which blazed over the Deep South of America.

She was an accomplished horsewoman and a gifted pianist. She could claim the maturity and discernment of a woman in her twenty-fifth year, although she had lacked all discernment seven years ago, when she arrived in England at the lovely, eager age of eighteen. Her parents, of English ancestry, were intent on introducing her to the excitements of London's summer season, with the help of the American ambassador, a cousin of her father's. The ambassador had opened the doors of high society for her, and almost immediately she became infatuated with Lord Clarence Percival, only son of the eminent Duke of Avonhurst. Lord Clarence was handsome, witty and amusing. He enchanted her mother almost as much as he enchanted her, although her father had reservations and counselled caution. But caution was the last thing Caroline desired to observe, with the result that Lord Clarence became the first man to discover she had truly beautiful breasts, and legs so long that he declared there was no end to them. Completely taken with this innocent rose from the lush garden that was South Carolina, he conducted a whirlwind courtship and they were married only three months after their first meeting.

It did not take longer than four months for Caroline to realise she had made a terrible mistake. Her husband at twenty-six was already a rake. To give him his due, he married her in a mood of resolution, and certainly with the unqualified approval of his parents, who loved the freshness and unspoiled nature of their American daughter-in-law. They saw in her salvation for their philandering son. She had come into his life like a breath of pure air, and during his courtship she made all other

4

women seem comparatively stale. But his affection and resolution were short-lived. He had known too many females to be capable of lasting love for any of them. He was a compulsive wanderer from woman to woman. His dissolute habits returned, and while vowing himself incurably devoted to his young wife he was repeatedly unfaithful. Caroline quickly began to see him as he was – intemperate, loose-living and, as a husband, a mockery.

She would have liked children. He seemed unable to father any, and nor after a while did she desire him to. Inevitably, there came the time when she kept him permanently locked out of her bedroom. He seemed vastly amused by this, and asked if she would prefer entry into her bed to be the privilege of certain of his friends, all of whom, he assured her, would be delighted to pleasure her. His decadence at least did one thing for her: it helped her to grow up fast.

She frequently thought of leaving him and returning to her family home in Charleston, but England, so green and rural from one year's end to another, had laid its claim on her. Nor was she indifferent to the love and sympathy she received from Clarence's parents, or to the affections of the many friends she had acquired. Also, she enjoyed the atmosphere of London and its endless attractions, and she adored Great Wivenden, an estate in Sussex that her husband had purchased in the heady, early days of their marriage and presented to her. Not far from Brighton, where the Prince of Wales had built himself an ornate Pavilion, Great Wivenden was a beautiful place and a happy country retreat to which she often escaped. Lord Clarence was rarely there himself, except during the hunting season. It was at Great Wivenden, in the fifth year of a marriage that had become a shame and humiliation to her, that he had the grace to break his neck attempting a fence while the worse for claret. Caroline wore black to the funeral, but not thereafter. The London house passed to her, together with what was left of the wealth Clarence had done his best to dissipate.

She might then have returned to Charleston, had she

been able to make the decision. She realised that despite her disastrous marriage she had put down new roots. The pastoral charm and gentle summer beauty of England's countryside were so unlike that which obtained during the fiery summers of South Carolina. She set about the intricate task of rebuilding her late husband's fortune, with the advice and guidance of her father-in-law. She established her own mode of life in London and Sussex, an enjoyable and independent one. She was newly eligible, but had no intention of marrying again unless she could positively trust her feelings and the integrity of any suitor. She had no lack of admirers, the most amorous and arrogant of whom was the Duke of Cumberland, fifth son of King George the Third, the monarch who had foolishly alienated the rich American colonies and subsequently lost them. Cumberland, dark of soul and design, offered her the privilege of becoming his mistress.

'Your Royal Highness,' she had said, 'I do declare that such a privilege is rare, is it not? But how rare, pray? Am I to be your first mistress or your twentieth?'

Cumberland, noted more for his intolerance than his sense of humour, nevertheless roared with laughter and swore that of all sweet creatures she was the one he most desired to bed, and that, by God, bed her he would, soon or late. If he had the looks of the devil, he was still a magnetic and commanding prince, and a man who could discover weakness in the strongest-minded women. He put Caroline in desperate straits on one occasion, six months after she had been widowed. He was one of several guests at Great Wivenden during a long weekend, and on the Saturday night, when she had just retired to her bedroom, he entered without knocking and was arrogant in his assumption that she would take him into her bed. An actual physical struggle ensued, Cumberland confident that such a forceful wooing would excite her into surrender, and Caroline burning and outraged that he should attempt such unforgivable seduction.

Her gown was shamefully dishevelled and revealing by the time she managed to break free and rush to the bell-pull. She threatened to arouse every servant unless he left at once. Cumberland smiled, shrugged, tidied himself, and left.

The Duke was now a new worry to her, and it was him she was thinking of as she addressed her visitor. 'You are Captain Burnside?'

'Captain Charles Wolfe Burnside, marm,' he said, and offered her his card. She made a gesture and he placed the card on the desk.

'Wolfe?' she said, lifting an eyebrow.

'After General Wolfe of Quebec, marm. An uncle of mine was distantly related.'

'Really?' She had acquired the distinctive English way of imbuing that word with scepticism.

'Quite so, marm.' Captain Burnside's voice was warm, mellow and beguiling, and it put her on her guard. She had been trapped seven years ago by a voice just as beguiling. Yet she was not altogether displeased by this trait in the Captain, for she was in need of an adventurer who could be accepted as a gentleman of charm.

'You have a letter for me, sir?'

'That is so, marm.' Captain Burnside, extracting a letter from the tail of his coat, handed it over the desk to her. It was addressed to Mrs L A Carmichael. Caroline examined the flap. It was sealed by a blob of red wax as a precaution against it being steamed open, a natural thing for any rogue to do. She broke the seal and unfolded the letter.

'This is to present Captain Charles Burnside. His production of this letter is a warranty of his identity. A.'

She placed it on the desk and sat down. She looked up at the Captain. He smiled. Deferentially.

'You are a professional gentleman?' she enquired.

'I am, marm.'

'An adventurer of a kind?'

'Of an accomplished kind.'

'A virtuoso?' she said drily.

'I've a variety of gifts, marm.'

'You're willing to engage in an affair of deception and blackmail?'

7

'I'm willing to engage in anything within reason, marm.'

'Within what reason, sir?' she asked, and he seemed intrigued by the softness of her Southern speech. He placed his top hat on the desk. She regarded it as if it had no right to be there. Nor, as yet, had she asked him to sit down.

'Well, marm,' he said easily, 'the devil being my paymaster, as it were, my commissions run well ahead of the acceptable at times, but under no circumstances will I engage to assassinate anyone.'

Lady Caroline looked extremely cool. 'You will not be asked to, sir. I am not in need of a cut-throat.'

'I'm relieved to hear it, marm, relieved.' Captain Burnside was smoothly cordial. 'An affair of deception, then. And – ah – blackmail. Agreed, marm.'

'Agreed?' She was cooler. 'We shall see. You at least come with not unsatisfactory references.'

'True, I did have two or three meetings with a nameless gentleman.'

'You may sit down, sir,' she said, having made up her mind to continue with him.

'I'm obliged, marm.' He drew up a chair and seated himself. She noted the fluency of his movements: his limbs were commendably supple.

'Now, sir,' she said, 'I confess I require the services of an adventurer capable of assuming the manners and deportment of a gentleman, while seeking to make the most of his dubious talents. Although it is something of a paradox, I also require him to be entirely trustworthy. Can you declare yourself so?'

'I ain't averse to cheating an opponent, marm, but I've a professional's honour when dealing with a patron. And for your comfort and reassurance—'

'My comfort and reassurance?' Lady Caroline again raised an eyebrow.

'Quite so, marm. I never, d'you see, enquire into a patron's motives or reasons. I enter only their service, not their private lives.'

8

'Really? How very good of you,' she said sarcastically, at which Captain Burnside assumed the air of a man able to accept every sling and arrow. 'Tell me, sir, is your rank authentic? Are you indeed a British Army officer?'

'I was, marm. I'm now retired.'

'Retired? At your age?'

'Ah, precipitately retired.' He coughed. 'There was an unfortunate incident during a game of cards with fellow officers. I held three aces. Unhappily, the adjutant held two. Most unfortunate, since I was the dealer. More unhappily, I was also at the time under suspicion of having compromised the adjutant's wife, although it was no more than a light kiss or two. The Colonel took me aside, spoke to me about the honour of the regiment and also my mess debts, and I allowed myself to be placed on the retired list – ah, unpaid.'

'You mean you were forced to resign,' said Caroline coldly. 'But you pass yourself off as Captain Burnside, retired. Yes, that opens certain doors to you, no doubt.'

'Only middle-class doors, marm. A retired cavalry officer don't count for much in higher circles.'

'I am to assume, sir, that you live by fleecing the middle classes?' she said.

'Fleecing?' Captain Burnside smiled, and she thought yes, he might very well charm some women in much the same way Lord Clarence had. 'Impossible, marm. The middle classes – tradesmen, merchants and the like – have come by what they own through being industrious, inventive and shrewd. They ain't inclined to part easily with their gains. One must become a family friend, win their confidence, sweeten their wives and charm their daughters – ah, and then borrow from the dear young ladies.'

'And then disappear?' said Caroline with undisguised contempt.

'I make it a rule, d'you see, never to turn up for a wedding,' said Captain Burnside with disarming frankness.

'Sir?' She was not disarmed, not by any means, and she

9

regarded him with frank dislike. Painful experience had made her despise men of his kind. 'Do you say, sir, that you actually propose to innocent and trusting girls, and then make off with such monies as you've been able to wheedle out of them?'

'Not monies, marm,' said Captain Burnside affably. 'Few daughters of the middle classes are able to lay their hands on the family dibs. But some own a little jewellery.'

Caroline's contempt was of a freezing kind. 'Am I to understand, sir, that having deceived a young lady into believing you'll marry her, you are then blackguard enough to decamp with her heirlooms?'

'But don't you see, marm, it's far better for any of 'em to lose a few trinkets than to acquire a husband as worthless as myself. I'd be their ruination, and in faith I can't marry 'em all. But I will say that if the doors of prime society were open to me, I'd gladly marry an heiress and cling most devotedly to her and her wealth.'

Icily, she said, 'I expected to have to deal with an unprincipled rogue, sir, but I did not expect an out-and-out scoundrel.'

Captain Burnside looked pained. 'Marm, I'm a professional,' he said.

'You are also despicable.'

'True, I ain't precisely angelic . . .'

'Be quiet, sir.' She rose to her feet and swept to the window to collect herself, and the sunlight kissed her partly visible bosom with pale gold. She reflected on whether or not she should reject this man, as she was inclined to. But if she let her intense dislike of him discount his suitability, what was left? Interviews with a succession of other rogues, all just as unlikeable, as they were bound to be. It was an impossible venture she had in mind, perhaps, but she could think of no other way to deal with two problems, the problem of her sister's dangerous infatuation with the Duke of Cumberland, and the problem of a dear friend's appalling indiscretion. Such matters were not of a kind to disclose to other friends. In London, one's closest friends talked. The town was a hotbed of gossip. She must put her faith in her father-in-law's recommendation. Without that recommendation she might already have sent Captain Burnside packing. Yet he had the manners and the airs of a gentleman, and he was also a British cavalry officer – retired. He was a Redcoat. Her sister, like their Aunt Marigold, had an eye for Redcoats. When Sir Henry Clinton and his staff quartered themselves in Charleston during the War of Independence, Aunt Marigold had decked herself out in irresistible fashion for one of Clinton's handsomest officers, so the family said. And when the British departed, Aunt Marigold went with them, together with other young and infatuated Southern belles. Aunt Marigold had married her officer in New York, and they now owned a plantation in Georgia, where they enjoyed a contented middle-aged existence.

Caroline reflected further. Perhaps, yes, perhaps she must make do with Captain Burnside. She turned to him. He smiled.

'Marm?' he said.

'I detest deceivers,' she said.

'The natural feelings of any lady,' he said. 'However, I never stipulate that a patron should like me.'

Her resplendent bosom exhibited surging affront. 'I declare, sir, you have an impudence I do not care for,' she said. 'But you may suit my purpose, and I'd not want to interview further scallywags. Now, sir, make up your mind you are to obey me from the outset, and in a manner that will give me no offence. You are to conduct yourself at all times like a gentleman, especially as it will be necessary for you and I to give the impression we are old friends.'

'Be assured, marm, that things shall look precisely as you require,' said the urbane Captain. 'As a gentleman, I shall be faultless, for while I'm no prince or even a baron, I can conduct myself as if I were.'

'Conduct yourself modestly, sir, and not conceitedly,' she said, as imperious as if she had been born of the nobility. She did not intend to relinquish command of their relationship, either now or at any time. 'I'm compelled, I vow, to put my trust in you.'

'You'll not be disappointed, marm.'

'If I am, you shall not receive a cent, sir, a penny,' she said. 'Listen carefully. First, I am not Mrs Carmichael. I am Lady Clarence Percival, widow of Lord Clarence Percival.'

'Ah,' said Captain Burnside, and looked suitably impressed.

'You may discard at once, sir, any thought that as a widow I'm a woman of a helpless kind, for I am not.'

'Be assured, marm, I've never met any woman who could be called helpless,' said Captain Burnside fervently. 'The dear creatures have many subtleties, and can plant the sharpest barbs in Lucifer himself.'

Caroline glanced sharply at him. There were some people to whom Cumberland was known as Lucifer.

'To whom are you referring?' she asked.

'Why, the devil, marm.'

'Well, sir,' she said, 'in this venture you may meet him. But do me the civility, please, of not alluding to my sex as dear creatures. We are not zoological specimens, waiting to be fed sugary buns.'

'Indeed you ain't, marm, none of you,' said the Captain warmly.

'Now, sir,' she said, 'I have faced many problems and resolved them all myself. I come of brave and spirited stock. However, on this occasion, I confess I need help. I am commissioning you to give that help.'

'Pray proceed, Your Ladyship,' said Captain Burnside.

She proceeded. He listened.

12

## Chapter Two

There was a twofold problem, said Lady Caroline. The first concerned her sister Annabelle, who had arrived in London several months ago. Annabelle was twenty, and a little while before sailing for England she had broken her long-standing engagement to a Charleston gentleman. She said she did not love him enough. Her parents, though shocked, were understanding, and helped her to escape biting tongues and acid gossip by letting her go to England for a while. She was accompanied on the voyage by a relative who had business to conduct in London and Manchester.

Once in London, she was received by Caroline with delight and affection. She confessed then that she had broken her engagement because she was fearful of being bored to death by her would-be husband. Caroline not only sympathised with her, she complimented Annabelle on being wise enough not to marry a man unsuited to her. Alas, it was not wisdom in its essence, it was the headstrong act of a vivacious young lady who envied her sister her sophisticated life in London. And once there herself, she was completely captivated by the excitements of its social calendar and the gallantries of the Corinthians, whose gleaming Hessian boots, thigh-clasping pantaloons and colourful coats dazzled her eyes.

She proved even more impressionable at twenty than Caroline had been at eighteen. Received at court, she met a personage of royal rank who quizzed her with a dark and devious eye. He was by no means the most handsome personage of the day, but on the other hand he was so impressive of character and so majestic of bearing that he was a danger to any young lady whose demeanour was that of a breathless, fluttering butterfly. The butterfly, mesmerised, was ready to fly dizzily into the net.

Caroline, aghast, endeavoured to send her back home. Annabelle would have none of it, and Caroline recognised an infatuation potentially more ruinous than her own had been. She knew her parents expected her to take care of Annabelle, to become the watchful chaperone, and to guard her until such time as the emotions and repercussions of the broken engagement had died their death.

Annabelle was only a few weeks away from her twenty-first birthday. At her coming of age she would undoubtedly regard herself as free to do exactly as she liked. She was sweet and engaging, but wilful. Impendent degradation loomed in front of her, for the man in question would not hesitate to seduce her and, later, discard her. As a virgin, she would be an amusement to him, no more.

'You are speaking, marm, of the royal personage?' enquired Captain Burnside.

'I am,' said Caroline, and went on to say that despite being royal he was not a gentleman. The august personage would not himself have agreed with this, for he believed no shame could attach to blood royals, however immoral their pursuits. Her infatuated sister, quite overwhelmed by his attentions, imagined herself becoming the love of his life. She was deaf to what the whole of London could have told her: that she would never be more than just another brief pleasure to him. She was incapable of believing a royal Duke could be a villain. Yet he patently was.

'Regrettably, marm,' said Captain Burnside, 'ladies do have a weakness for villains. My own devious blandishments have, alas, secured the affections of several sweet innocents. In moments of remorse, I've confessed myself unworthy to more than one of them, but without causing any to recoil. Indeed, to be told of my failings only made them declare a loving wish to help me reform.'

Remembering her own weakness for Lord Clarence, and

how she had ignored her father's words of caution, Caroline bit her lip.

'Innocence, sir, is a tender and susceptible thing,' she said, 'and the deviousness of designing men to be held in much contempt. However, pray allow me to continue . . .' And she went on to say that her sister Annabelle must be detached from the man who would almost certainly seduce her. She must become infatuated with another, and in such a way that she would be cured of her feelings for Cumberland.

Captain Burnside raised dark eyebrows. 'Cumberland, marm?' he enquired.

'That is the man, sir, the Duke of Cumberland himself.'

'Your sister, marm, has indeed set her sights dangerously high,' said the Captain. 'Cumberland will take her in his own time, play with her, toy with her, and leave her to her own devices once she's with child.'

Caroline stiffened. 'I would rather you used your tongue less disgracefully, sir,' she said coldly. 'I do not care to have you comment on the consequences of immoral intimacies between Cumberland and my sister.'

'But the unhappy possibility exists, marm.'

'Then it is a possibility you must remove, sir, or does the mention of Cumberland intimidate you?'

'Cumberland is a dark shadow in a thousand corridors, marm, but no, I am not intimidated.' Captain Burnside smiled. 'I ain't as much in his way as his elder brothers are.'

'His elder brothers?' Caroline took serious note of that remark. 'What is this, sir – an imputation that Cumberland wishes himself the only son of the King?'

'He ain't said so to me, marm. I merely made an observation. Favour me by continuing with that which is relevant to my commission.'

Caroline, casting from her mind the unbearable image of Annabelle *enceinte* by reason of Cumberland's lust, said firmly, 'I am engaging you, Captain Burnside, for the purpose of freeing my sister from her attachment to the Duke. His arms have not yet closed about her, but they

will, and perhaps as soon as she is twenty-one. In her
giddiness at coming of age, she will be at her most foolish.
I require you, therefore, to prevent this by inducing her to
transfer her affections to you.'

'Ah,' said Captain Burnside.

'Since you are infamously successful as a ladies' man,
you should not find that too difficult, I presume? You
have the gifts of a virtuoso, have you not?' Lady Caroline
was ironic but hopeful. 'Much as I detest the thought of
my sister transferring her infatuation from a royal
libertine to a conscienceless blackguard, I shall
nevertheless endure it for her sake. You are following me,
sir?' Her green eyes searched his musing grey.

'I am, perhaps, a little ahead of you,' he said. 'Ah – is
your sister of independent means? Comfortably possessed?'

Her eyes became a little fiery. 'Sir?' she said warningly.

'I ain't disposed to fleece her, marm, nor leave her in
tears. If she owns sufficient of the ready or has excellent
prospects, then once I've won her sweet affections I'll not
be averse to marrying her.'

'Marrying her?' Caroline flamed. 'My sister? You?'

'Well, d'you see, marm,' said the Captain reasonably, 'I
fancy that in detaching her from Cumberland, I may
become so much the object of her affections that she'll
conceive expectations.'

'Dear Lord of mercy,' breathed Caroline, 'I vow I have
never known such a scoundrel, nor one with so much love
for himself. Under no circumstances, none whatever, are
you to entertain the idea of marrying my sister.'

'Well, there may be tears, marm . . .'

'So there may, sir, but sooner tears than shameful disgrace. Attend on me, Captain Burnside, and take note
that, if you succeed in this matter, you will at once return
to the disreputable environment you no doubt inhabit. I
will look to my sister and any tears she may shed concerning your disappearance. You will give Annabelle the
attentiveness and consideration of a gentleman
throughout, practising your deception as forgivably as you

16

can, and then depart honourably, as I require you to and will pay you to. You will say, perhaps, that your regiment has called on you for active service abroad. That is as honourable as can be contrived, I suggest.'

'Quite so, marm; all shall be as you wish,' said Captain Burnside.

'And now, sir, to the second part of your commission. This also concerns the Duke of Cumberland.'

'The devil it does,' murmured the Captain. 'The man's a pervasive darkness.'

'He has a letter,' said Caroline.

'Damn me, there's—'

'Sir?' she said freezingly.

'Humble apologies, Your Ladyship. But I was going to say there's always a letter lurking somewhere or other. Who is the dear and unfortunate lady?'

'Do not anticipate me, Captain Burnside, or attempt to take the dialogue out of my mouth. The lady in question is my dearest friend, Lady Hester Russell. The letter is of pale blue parchment and the wax seal, although broken by now, is stamped with a crest appertaining to a swan. Cumberland is using it to command Lady Russell's obedience.'

'Obedience?'

Caroline showed distaste. 'Obedience to his demands, Captain Burnside. I am sure you know precisely what I mean. Cumberland has the devil's own way of bringing the most reluctant woman to a bed. Lady Russell, at a country house party for a week, with her husband and other guests, had the misfortune to see her husband take a tumble that broke his leg. Incapacitated, he was placed in a ground floor room to rest and recuperate. Lady Russell, alone in her bedroom that night, woke up to find Cumberland beside her.'

'Say no more, marm,' said the Captain considerately. 'I quite understand. Ravishment, alas, and yet the sweet weakness of yielding. And so, no doubt, illicit passion was born and indiscreet billets-doux began to spring from the wanton heart. Poor woman.'

'Pray curb your vivid imagination,' said Caroline. 'Lady Russell has no wanton heart. Ravished, yes, but much against her will.' Her lashes flickered. 'Cumberland is all of capable of such a thing. She might have cried out, might have called for help, but there was her husband, sick and suffering with a broken leg in uncomfortable splints. It was not a moment to make her shame known. Further, it was Cumberland she would have had to denounce, and, though he would not have given a fig for it, I vow he would have paid her out in a most unpretty fashion.'

'And so she yielded,' said the Captain.

'Only in shame and anguish, sir.'

'Quite so, marm.'

Caroline frowned. 'You are cynical, sir?' she said.

'Experienced,' said the Captain.

'In ravishment?' she enquired coldly.

'In my observation of human weakness,' smiled the Captain.

Caroline frowned again. The truth was of a shaming kind, according to Hester herself. In desperation and tears she had confessed all to Caroline. Cumberland had indeed ravished her, despite her resistance, a resistance weakened by the circumstances and perhaps, yes, perhaps by the magnetic quality of the man. Hester had blushed vividly in confessing this, in confessing all that had led to her eventual submission, and Caroline remembered all too clearly how Cumberland had attempted to bring her to bed at Great Wivenden. Hester said that after her shameful submission she had begged Cumberland to leave, but he had stayed, he had shared her bed until dawn. Much to her further shame, instead of doing the only obvious thing – slipping from the bed herself and going down to keep her suffering husband company by sleeping in a chair beside him – she had allowed Cumberland to stay and had stayed herself. He took full advantage of this and further ravishment took place during the night, and she was horrified by the extent of her submission. Worse, she conceived a carnal passion for

18

him, a passion that was a quite unspeakable consequence of her shameful night. She became his mistress, his infatuated mistress.

'Yes, weakness did exist,' said Caroline, returning to the subject after her long, reflective pause, 'and I vow it a despairing thing in such a sweet woman as Lady Russell. She did conceive a passion for Cumberland. Myself, I should have conceived only a desire to strike the man dead.'

'We are at the point, marm,' said Captain Burnside, 'where I may assume Cumberland has a revealing letter of hers and uses it to bring her to his bed from time to time?'

'You assume correctly,' said Caroline, 'and she is in utter distraction, for her ardour died after a few brief months and she is terrified her husband will discover her guilt. If you can procure that letter from Cumberland, you will be gratefully rewarded. Since he is blackmailing her, I trust I can rely on you to see that the biter is bitten. You can accomplish this at the card table, achieving such substantial IOUs as to compel him to give up the letter in exchange for them. Such are the debts of all the royal Dukes that they are never in any position to remit payment of heavy gambling losses. Cumberland is an avid, addicted gambler. No sooner will he hear that you are renowned at cards yourself than he will want to set to with you at once. You will ensure he loses very heavily.'

Captain Burnside mused on what was coolly expected of him. 'I shall need money, marm, and luck.'

'I will provide you with funds, sir. But luck, do you say? What need do you have of luck when you own so many accomplishments?' Caroline's softly-drawn vowels were laden with irony. 'You are a consummate cheat, are you not? That is to say, you can palm a card or cause a dice to fall as you wish without arousing the smallest suspicion?'

'Well, it's true I've had moments when all has been won by dexterous sleight of hand,' said the Captain, regarding her with much thought. To Caroline, he seemed to be musing on the feminine appeal of her fashionably low décolleté, which did not please her at all. 'Cumberland,' he murmured, 'ain't known to be a dunderhead, however, and his one sound eye is wickedly keen.'

'Is one sound eye keener than the sharp talents of a virtuoso? Or have you merely been offering me the conceits of a braggart?'

'Substantial IOUs,' said the Captain thoughtfully. 'Very well, marm, consider it done.'

'I hope, sir,' said Caroline with asperity, 'that you don't think me simple enough to accept that particular conceit. The matter will be accomplished when it has been. It will not be accomplished merely by your saying so.'

'We shall see, marm, we shall see.'

'So we shall,' she said, 'and I declare myself hopeful. But I should not be true to my honour if I did not warn you that Cumberland is an adversary as dangerous as Satan. One mistake, one wrong move, and I vow you are like to be discovered in the Thames, drowned and very dead.'

'As a professional hireling, marm, I accept the risks.'

'I commend you for that,' she said. 'Now, sir, what are your present circumstances?'

'In faith, I'm deucedly short of the ready,' admitted the Captain, 'if that's what you mean.'

'Most men who live by their wits own thin purses,' said Caroline. 'Have you never considered honest work?'

Captain Burnside appeared pained. 'God forbid, marm, I should ever become a porter or a shipping clerk.'

'Either might keep you from ending up in prison,' she declared. 'I find it difficult to believe your father was a bishop.'

'Well, so he was, marm, and died in a state of peace and beatitude. I had not then disturbed his soul by becoming the family black sheep.'

'I do declare, you are singularly deplorable, sir,' she said. 'Are you not ashamed that, as the son of a gentle mother and a man of God, you are a self-confessed rake and even a thief?'

'I assure you, marm, I could own finer principles if I weren't so poor.'

'Hard, honest work would lift you out of poverty, Captain Burnside. Now, I shall advance you fifty guineas. It will cover such expenses as you entail. You are to come to this house on Friday, bringing a suitable wardrobe with you. You will profess to be an old friend of mine, lately returned to England from service abroad, and my guest for a period. Do you still own a uniform?'

'I do,' said the Captain. 'I find on occasions it can induce a young lady to regard me as becoming, valiant and deserving . . .'

'Spare me these ridiculous irrelevancies, sir,' said Caroline. 'Bring your uniform. Is the rest of your wardrobe as acceptable as that which you are wearing now?'

'I confess, marm, that part of your advance will sweeten my tailor and persuade him to release to me two new coats, some silk cravats and—'

'Yes, yes,' she said in some impatience. 'Meet the costs out of the advance.'

'I'm obliged, marm, very,' he said.

'So you should be, for in giving you any monies at all I am placing almost foolish trust in you.' Caroline opened a drawer and took out a soft leather bag of coins. She pushed it across the desk to him. 'Fifty guineas in gold,' she said.

'I'm deeply obliged, marm,' he said, slipping the bag into his pocket without opening it, and this at least she appreciated.

'Am I now faced with the possibility that you'll decamp?' she asked.

'You have my word that I won't,' said the Captain.

'I accept the risk that you might.'

'Be assured, Your Ladyship, that there's no risk, for you're now my patron.' He coughed. 'Ah – we haven't discussed the fee. You'll forgive my mention of it?'

'I should have been surprised if you had forgotten to,' she said. 'Your fee, sir, will be two hundred guineas.'

'Marm?' Captain Burnside looked a little put out. 'That's part of the whole?'

'That, sir, *is* the whole, in addition to the fifty guineas for your expenses.' Caroline was firm. 'It's an amount that will keep you very comfortably for more than a year. I consider it very generous, especially as you have implied the venture was no sooner agreed than accomplished.'

'Quite so,' said the Captain, 'which is to say that a professional of my class must command a worthier fee than a bungling amateur.'

'Two hundred guineas and expenses amount to a fee as worthy as you could command from anyone.' Caroline was on her mettle, determined to be in control of the relationship, the man himself and all events. 'Such a sum would set you up in a small business and enable you to earn an honest living.'

'Ye gods,' said the shocked Captain, 'a small business? An honest living? Marm, am I to endure boredom?'

'If you prefer to continue with your dubious practices, Captain Burnside, that is your affair. But very well, since you will be up against a dangerous man in Cumberland, I will raise the fee to two hundred and fifty, and not a cent more.'

'I'm touched, marm. Done, then. Two-fifty and expenses.'

'However,' said Caroline, straight of back and firm of bosom, 'you will be paid only if you succeed. Half if you succeed with one or the other, the whole if you succeed with both. But nothing, sir, if you fail altogether, for you will have proclaimed your gifts dishonestly.'

'H'm,' said Captain Burnside, and smiled. 'I see I'm to serve a critical patron.'

'You are, sir, be in no doubt of that,' she said. 'Well?'

'Your servant, marm.'

'Cumberland will be here Friday evening for supper.'

'Egad, d'you say so?' Captain Burnside looked intrigued. 'Do I take it, marm, that you're on intimate terms with him, that you too find the devil has his own kind of appeal?'

An angry flush suffused her. 'How dare you draw such an inference, how dare you? Be very clear, sir, that I detest Cumberland. But that is not to say I spend my time quarrelling with him. I know him well, and he knows me just as well. I am civil to him, and he is always himself.' She looked up as the door opened. She simulated a welcoming smile, showing teeth that were moistly white and even between her parted lips. 'Annabelle, how nice that you are back from shopping at this moment, for you are in time to meet an old friend of mine, Captain Charles Burnside.'

Captain Burnside came to his feet. Lady Caroline's sister advanced, smiling.

# Chapter Three

Miss Annabelle Howard of Charleston, South Carolina, was in essence a pretty young lady. Her face was round and pretty, her eyes round and blue, her mouth soft and kissable. Her looped-up gown of sky blue showed pretty ankles clad in pale yellow silk hose. Such hose was held in place above the knees by tied silk garters. She wore buckled blue shoes and a white tulle cap from which a tiny silk scarf hung over the back of her fair hair. She looked younger than her age. She was almost twenty-one. Vivacious light shone in her eyes, which were apt to sparkle at the slightest arousal of excitement or merriment. Her complexion was delicately creamy, her bosom plump, its roundness peeping. Her waist could not have been higher. It was a mere fraction below her bosom.

She had wanted to come to London as soon as the family heard Caroline was not returning to Charleston after the death of Lord Clarence Percival, for that told Annabelle of her sister's acquired preference for London and her country estate in Sussex. But there was the problem of Martin Appleby, to whom she had been engaged since she was eighteen. Martin was an undemanding young gentleman of old Colonial stock; he was also handsome and God-fearing. But when pressed to name the wedding date, Annabelle demurred and procrastinated, having gradually come to feel that, while Martin was a good man, he was not much fun. She felt she preferred him as a friend, not as a prospective husband, and so the engagement lingered on.

Her parents worried a little. Caroline, her sister, had married in haste at eighteen and repented almost before the ink was dry on the certificate. She herself at twenty was neither married nor repenting of marriage. With so many beautiful girls in Charleston, all fluttering their eyes at prospective beaux, Mr and Mrs Howard felt Annabelle would soon be too old to be taken to the altar, even by good-natured Martin Appleby. In the climate of the Deep South, girls bloomed far in advance of New England's young ladies, and by sixteen they were sweet peaches ripe and ready for wedlock.

Six months before her twenty-first birthday, Annabelle broke the engagement, protesting she did not truly love Martin. Her mother was shocked, but her sympathetic father let her weep tears on his shoulder and agreed with her suggestion that she quit Charleston for a while and visit Caroline in England.

London, its colourful society, and the brilliance of its grand ballrooms, dazzled her, the more so when the bucks, the young and the mature, gave her so much attention. She was introduced to scions of the nobility, and she even met the Prince of Wales, lately growing portly. She was a trifle confused by his close quizzing of her bosom and the florid nature of his compliments. She also met one of his brothers, the Duke of Cumberland, who was a different proposition altogether. He took her breath with his physical magnificence, with the spectacular width of his powerful shoulders, the defined muscularity of his thighs, the sheer strength of every line of his face and his aura of indestructible majesty. His right eye was blind, palely blind, but his left was dark, glinting and malicious. He was neither suave of manner nor endearing of appearance. The cast of his features was devilish, and his looks were not improved by a facial scar, the legacy of a wound bravely borne at the battle of Tournai a few years ago. A German duchess of Mecklenburg was destined to become his wife. Various other women who found him strangely exciting had hopes, but none had advanced beyond the role of mistress.

He dressed impeccably. His coats paid tribute to his

massive shoulders, and his skin-tight breeches boldly shaped his strong thighs, causing a lady's eyes to linger and her breath to quicken. To some women he was, with his superb physique and dark wickedness, wholly a man, and his reputed kinship with the devil, written all over him, fascinated them and induced shivers.

He had nothing in common with his oldest brother, the effete Prince of Wales, called 'Prinny' by his intimates. Indeed, Cumberland had a great and regal disdain for the effete and all other lesser beings. Under the sensual, peering eyes of the Prince of Wales, Annabelle with her feminine prettiness had experienced a desire to retreat and hide. Under the bold, speculative eye of the Duke of Cumberland, she quickened with sweet excitement. She felt he should have been the heir to the throne, for he was surely made for kingship. Cumberland positively thought so himself.

Annabelle was a monarchist before she was a republican. A royal palace and the brilliance of a royal court had far more magic for her than the businesslike mansion of a president.

At her first meeting with Cumberland, he eyed her, examined her, reflected on her nervous, fluttering curtsey and the unarguable appeal of her décolleté. Then he took her hand, caressed it and said, 'So, you're from the Americas, are ye?' His German accent was deep and guttural. 'Damned if ye ain't the prettiest package that ever came out of them. Are ye acquainted with those radical upstarts, Washington and Jefferson?'

'Sir – Your Highness – I declare!' she breathed in nervous protest. 'I vow myself unacquainted with either. Nor do I wish to be, for of all things I cannot show a polite face to men who were so unmannerly in their resentment of the King and his brave Redcoats.'

Cumberland laughed. 'Ye gods, ye'll not have witnessed their unmannerliness, sweet wench? Or will ye say ye did?'

'Mercy, no! I was not yet born when it all began, and only a small child when the Redcoats departed. Sir, you do not see in me one so old as to have stood and watched that coarse Yankee, Sam Adams, at his brutal business of tarring and feathering the Loyalists, do you? Sir, I do declare myself not yet come of age.'

'But ye've still come of sweet, plump prettiness,' said Cumberland, and Annabelle blushed to her roots.

'Plump, Your Highness?' she gasped in dismay.

The sound eye gleamed, the strong teeth gleamed, and the smile was devious. Cumberland knew her for the sister of Caroline, Lady Clarence Percival, an established and unrivalled American beauty who had resisted his every advance, and he would not have been what he was if he had not seen the chance to win the elder by becoming a menace to the younger.

'Plump?' he said. 'Aye, so ye are, my sweet, but only where ye should be. I vow it a delicious plumpness.'

Her blush deepened. Cumberland laughed again, richly, and there began for Annabelle a royal attentiveness and pursuit that swept her off her feet, and had her enamoured all too soon of the man whom some said coveted the throne, had no respect for his peers, little reverence for God and kept company with the devil. Certainly, he was intimidating in his towering majesty. Annabelle found him mesmerising, and he found her a full-grown bloom of the American South who, re-markably, still owned the freshness of virginity. Because he seemed disposed to suggest assignments of a compro-mising nature, she declared her virginity to him, and begged him not to regard her lightly or carelessly.

His sound eye took on its wicked light. 'By God, a virgin? Say ye so, sweet girl?'

'Sir, I beg, do not embarrass me so. It is said and it is true.'

'Damn me, ye must be the only one in London,' he said, and laughed at her blushes. But there she was, a sweetness to be savoured at leisure, not bruised in haste. If her sister regarded the dalliance with angry frowns and worried glances, so much the better. Let her, Caroline, come into his arms and he would cease his pursuit of virginity. Meanwhile, he enjoyed the teasing manner of his pursuit, and Annabelle was forever suffering quivers of excitement in his presence. In the compulsiveness of infatuation, she acquired and exhibited gowns that were as revealingly arch as they were dangerously provocative. She could not help herself in her desire to catch the eye of a man whose royal arrogance and uncompromising masculinity made him such an excitement to her. Cumberland, quizzing the increasingly arch contours, remarked that if all the roses of the American South bloomed so fulsomely, then it was a lusher nursery than he had supposed.

Annabelle had all the demure mannerisms and fresh looks of a girl no more than eighteen, but knew herself within reach of the age when she could be her own mistress. Accordingly, if at that age she yielded to a clandestine affair with Cumberland, she would be no less responsible than he. She would be unable to make any claim on him in law unless she had his written promise to marry her. Marry her? The thought of being the wife of a son of King George turned her dizzy.

In the library of her sister's London house, her blue gown seemed to swim and float as she advanced towards Captain Burnside. She did not look at Caroline, for there were secrets in her eyes, secrets she could not wholly hide, and she knew Caroline could be discomfitingly observant. She smiled at the debonair visitor, who bowed.

'Sir?' she murmured, extending her hand.

'Captain Burnside,' said Caroline, 'this is my sister, Annabelle Howard.'

The Captain lifted Annabelle's hand to his lips and returned her smile. 'Faith, I'm enchanted,' he said.

'Oh, I surely do think the manners of English gentlemen the last word in gallantry,' said Annabelle.

'A pretty coating over our many imperfections,' said the Captain. In his slender length he was as tall as Cumberland, but without the Duke's bruising weight.

'But, sir, a man without imperfections must be very dull,' said Annabelle, electing still to avoid her sister's eye.

28

'What am I to make of myself, then?' smiled the Captain. 'I'm not only sadly imperfect but also miserably dull.'

Annabelle laughed. 'Sir,' she said, 'by that you have just shown you are not dull at all. Might I ask if you are lunching with us?'

'Alas, I've an appointment with my tailor, as your sister will confirm. I should have been on my way ten minutes ago. You'll pardon me?' He kissed her hand again, lightly, bringing another smile to her face. Her lively eyes took in the suppleness of his physique, his close-fitting pantaloons shaping sinewy legs. How well English gentlemen dressed, she thought, how finely their tailored garments clasped their bodies.

'You all must go before we've scarcely met?' she said, needing the kind of company that would help her avoid Caroline's suspicious eyes and difficult questions.

'Oh, you will meet him again quite soon, I daresay,' said Caroline, 'for he is to be our guest in a few days.'

Annabelle's eyes danced. A handsome man in the house would surely constitute an entertainment. 'I declare myself delighted, sister,' she said.

Captain Burnside made his bow to Caroline.

She said pointedly, 'Yes, your tailor, of course, and do not forget you are expected here on Friday, in the afternoon.'

'To be sure,' he said, smiling in the fashion of an old friend, 'and the prospect is all of pleasurable, as much so as the enjoyment of our reunion.'

He departed with a commendable ease of manner, leaving Annabelle a little disappointed that his tailor had prior claim on him at this moment, while Caroline wondered if his sudden going was related to the fact that he had fifty golden guineas tucked away on his dubious person.

'I do declare, such a pleasant gentleman,' said Annabelle, and turned to leave.

'He's an old friend who has been serving overseas,' said Caroline. 'I am pleased, however, that you met him before he left. A moment before you go, Annabelle.'

'Tra-la-la,' said Annabelle with simulated raillery, 'you

are going to confide in me concerning your old friend? The reunion was sweet?'

'He is a friend,' said Caroline stiffly, 'nothing more.'

'Oh? He is married, I dare say?'

'No. He has been too active with his regiment to find time for marriage.'

'Such a waste,' sighed Annabelle, 'when he's so engaging and appealingly handsome.'

'Do you think so?' Caroline was aloof. 'His looks are passable, perhaps, but one wishes for more than looks in a man. Now, what did you buy in the shops?'

'Oh, I saw nothing that took my eye,' said Annabelle airily.

'Nothing? I thought you set on a new hat at least.'

'I met Elvira.'

'Lady Mornington?' Caroline's eyes held their searching look. Lady Mornington was a confidante of the Duke of Cumberland. 'She took your mind off hats?'

'We had coffee at Beaufort House.'

Beaufort House was the London residence of Lady Mornington.

'Just the two of you, pray?'

Annabelle made a gesture. 'Oh, you surely do plague me, sister, with your questions,' she said, 'and in a way not even our Pa would.'

'Pa would be as concerned as I am about your indiscretions,' said Caroline.

'Oh, hop, skip and fiddle,' said Annabelle, 'I vow myself a model of good behaviour.'

'When do you intend to return home?'

'Caroline, I declare! You are the unkindest sister to so rattle me, and you know I don't intend to return home. I am set on adopting England, as you have, for it is so cool and green, and Charleston is so hot and sticky. But there, dear Caroline, I do not mean to sound vexed with you, only to wish you more indulgent and less critical.'

Caroline stifled a sigh and said no more. Her concerned attempts repeatedly to examine her sister had reached the stage where they were more likely to drive Annabelle into

Cumberland's bed than keep her out of it. She was frankly fearful that her lushly healthy sibling needed only to find herself in the right environment and the right atmosphere for her to allow Cumberland to take her. Intuitively, Caroline was certain it had not happened yet, but just as intuitively she was certain it was not far off. In Cumberland's presence at functions, receptions and the like, Annabelle positively took on the flushed look of an excited and tempted virgin. She had her feminine gifts, yes, her arts and her archness, but within the sophisticated circles of London she was a simple, vulnerable innocent. Women smiled and whispered behind their fans to see her in such susceptibility to the intimidating qualities of Cumberland.

The sons of King George were all voracious lady-killers, and prodigious in the ease with which they brought their mistresses or their fancy pieces to pregnancy. Caroline shuddered at the thought of Annabelle, inherently quite a sweet wench, finding herself with child by Cumberland. She must be saved from that. Dear heaven, Captain Burnside must effect her salvation. She had seemed quite taken with him, and Caroline could not think why he had not stayed to capitalise immediately on that. Had the fifty guineas taken him off, never to return? If so, she would seek him out with the assistance of Bow Street Runners and ensure he spent a miserable term in gaol regretting his sin of betrayal.

In truth, Captain Burnside had departed as a matter of psychology, leaving Annabelle miffed that he had not lingered to savour her prettiness, as so many men did. The attentiveness of the Corinthians quickened her, making her feel that her desirability was such as seriously to affect the emotions of Cumberland. Also, she had felt the Captain's departure left her exposed to Caroline's suspicions. She was sensitive with the guilt of shameless moments. It was true she had met Lady Mornington, but not while shopping. It had been by appointment, at Beaufort House. There, after some gushing words, Lady Mornington had conducted her from the drawing room to

31

the music room, where Cumberland sat at the harpsichord, his long, strong fingers depressing keys to bring forth the lightest and airiest of musical pot-pourri, although to look at him one would have thought his forte was to conjure thunder and lightning from the instrument.

Lady Mornington withdrew after a few moments, leaving Annabelle quite unchaperoned, and Annabelle became bereft of speech as Cumberland, on his feet, took her hands, caressed them, kissed them, smiled at her and then bent his head to place his strong lips on hers. It was the first kiss she had received from him on her mouth, and it robbed her of her breath. It lingered, a kiss of exploration, his lips so audacious and compelling that the dew on hers was gathered like honey.

Weakness enveloped her as his bold mouth repeatedly robbed the freshness of hers, and she could scarcely believe his audacity when, with quick deftness, he released her breasts from the low, revealing bodice and surveyed their shy, quivering plumpness, not with the gleaming smile of an unrepentant satyr, but with the intrigued and deliberate interest of a man discovering delectability hitherto unknown. Annabelle crimsoned, and her uncovered bosom itself took on a rosy flush. Mute, mesmerised and dizzy, her virginal blushes were a sweet delight to the royal roué, her unadorned breasts surely showing the shyness of the untouched. A man who took what he wanted and did what he wanted, though in ways variously subtle whenever subtlety brought more enjoyment than forceful arrogance, Cumberland had no qualms concerning how he might use the virgin sister to achieve conquest of the widowed one. If Caroline thought him intent on bedding Annabelle, she underrated his deviousness. His bedding of Annabelle was only a threat at the moment. If Caroline herself would yield, then Annabelle could go her way still virginal. However, there was the play and the teasing promise of seduction that would, inevitably perhaps, so arouse the sweet innocent that she would recklessly declare to her sister her intent to become his light of love.

Cumberland smiled. A master of the calculated approach to all objectives, he knew Miss Annabelle Howard was unlikely to go home and protest that he had laid unwanted hands on her bosom. Indeed, she stood there in blushing acceptance of his survey, making no attempt to veil herself. Annabelle, further crimsoning under his regard, might have swooned or fled or cried out as his hands reached. But she was too giddy to fly, too enamoured to cry out, and too excited to swoon. Faintly and throatily, she begged his mercy, then experienced burning and palpitations as, in his mercy, he began to caress her breasts as lightly and gently as he had been caressing the keys of the harpsichord. It brought the most alarming, yet the most exquisite sensations to her bosom, and it brought shaking weakness to her limbs. She experienced a wild willingness to be all things to him.

But Cumberland had no intention of ravishing her, and certainly not in Lady Mornington's music room. He merely wished so to condition her for what might be that her emotional state would arouse unbearable alarm in her sister. It was natural and inevitable for him to be in devious seduction of her pretty breasts, for they had been pouting invitingly at him for many weeks.

He seated himself on a chair. He drew the blushing, unresisting Annabelle on to his lap, and there she burned and palpitated and begged him to desist, although her mouth responded to his and her sweetly-used breasts swelled and stiffened. His touch was subtly sweet indeed, gentling the virgin bosom, and she had neither the sophistication to discountenance him nor the will to deny him. Unlearned in the arts of physical intimacy, she did not know whether her bosom was being seduced or truly loved. She only knew that there was such excitement and pleasure that innocence and ignorance were irrelevant. She drew warm breath, she expelled warm sighs, and burned again to see how shamelessly naked her breasts were.

She felt perplexed and confused only when Cumberland, satisfied that she could be taken at a time of his own choosing, eventually restored her bosom to its covering. He did so with such finality that she suspected, in dismay, he had found them wanting.

'Oh, sir, did you not like them?' she breathed.

He laughed, his sound eye mocking. 'Faith, my cuddlesome beauty, d'ye think they lack sweet prettiness? On my heart, no. Ye've a fine pair, by God ye have, and I'll swear they showed the soft blush of the undiscovered.'

'Your Highness, you surely are the first man to put them in such confusion,' sighed Annabelle.

His dark brows arched, and his expression was plainly wicked. 'Is their confusion a reproach to me?' he murmured. 'Ye'll not ask me to be in contrition, for you own a bosom worthy of tender unveiling and loving caresses.'

'But to do so, sir,' breathed Annabelle, escaping from his lap and standing to reproach him as she felt she should, 'to uncover them and render them so very confused, oh, it was a boldness I did not expect. Also, I vow, it was unfair, for how might I in my weakness defend myself against your royal high and mightiness, and your manly strength?'

'Damn me, did I use strength?' Cumberland's smile was amused. 'I thought I gave you only gentleness, and I swear I left no bruises on your pretty pair.'

'Oh, sir, I declare this conversation too immodest,' she protested, 'and cannot continue with same, only entreat you to remember that my parents cherish me. Accordingly, I would prefer noble intentions to further gentleness of that kind.'

'Noble intentions?' The dark eye mocked her. 'Ye gods, what have we here, a blushing rose with a pricking thorn?' He came to his feet, but before he could mesmerise anew, Annabelle found strength enough and sense enough to fly.

And she did not, after all, as Cumberland thought she might, reveal to her sister, by way of agitated emotions, that she was closer than ever to yielding to him.

But she did not have to. Caroline knew that her

susceptible sister was a mere step from his bed. She knew because she recognised an infatuation that more than matched that which she had suffered herself. During their courtship, she had almost given herself more than once to Lord Clarence Percival, and had consequently listened to his proposal with heady relief and all the physical excitement commensurate with virginity.

Captain Burnside's talents were an absolute necessity.

For her part, Annabelle could not help wishing that her sister's old friend would so engage Caroline's fancy as to divert her attention from all affairs except her own. She could perhaps contrive to encourage the handsome Captain to set his cap at Caroline. No one could say that Caroline, with her inherited wealth and sumptuous beauty, was not among the best catches in London.

She wondered how much of a catch she was herself. She thought of Cumberland, and she sweetly burned.

# Chapter Four

Despite the fact that she had hired Captain Burnside, that she had decided to place her faith in his manipulative tricks, Caroline could not free herself of worry or of a feeling that his assistance might come too late in respect of Annabelle. And her dearest friend, Lady Hester Russell, the young and lovely wife of Sir George Russell, was in emotional turmoil as the unwilling mistress of Cumberland. Regularly, Cumberland called for her to pleasure him. He lifted a finger, figuratively, and beckoned, and she had to go or risk what he would almost certainly do: acquaint her husband of the passionate love letter she had written at the height of her brief infatuation.

Caroline knew she must make one final effort to appeal to what was left of royal integrity in Cumberland. The day before Captain Burnside was due to arrive as an ostensible guest, she called at the Duke's house. Cumberland, at home, was happy to receive her.

He, she saw, was his usual dark, satirical self, and that much more physically masculine than any of his brothers. The sleek tightness of his beige breeches might have offended the matrons of Charleston, who would never have approved such revelation.

She, he saw, was a feminine magnificence of such healthy perfection that by comparison her sister could only be thought of as sweetly pretty. The day was warm, and her flimsy white chemise dress of semi-transparent muslin, allowing a suggestion of her delicate lacy pantaloons to be mistily glimpsed, made her look divinely cool. Its shallow V-neckline permitted no more than a hint of her shadowed cleavage to be observed. Her apple-green cap was a lightness on her auburn head.

Composing herself, she confronted the kingdom's most reactionary Duke in no quarrelsome way. She appealed as winningly as she could to his manliness and to his oft-stated regard for her. She ignored the fact that his regard had always been stated in covetous terms. Once, in his effrontery, he had gambled with her husband, and her husband, in his degeneracy, had staked her body against a German hunting-lodge, one of several owned by Cumberland. Her husband had lost, and had coolly informed her that she belonged to Cumberland for a week, that the appointed venue was Great Wivenden. She said nothing to that. She looked at him, she froze him and she ignored him. Cumberland, advised that she had no intention of playing the role devised for her, took it well, permitting himself a laugh, and asked Lord Percival what kind of a husband he was if he could not get his wife to comply with the terms of a wager agreed by gentlemen. Lord Percival replied that some wives came deceptively to marriage, disguising their leanings towards nunnery. He settled in kind, with golden guineas.

Cumberland, standing, feet astride, hands behind his back, listened as his seated visitor embarked on her appeal to his magnanimity. Her choice of words and phrases could not be faulted. She was friendly, reasonable and polite. Cumberland, however, conscious that here was the epitome of lush, American beauty, had his mind more on how she might accommodate his carnal fancies than how he might respond to her requests.

'Of all things, the innocence of my sister is precious to me and our parents,' said Caroline, 'and I would not consider you less of a prince or a man if you conceded that what you might command as a prince or contrive for as a man should be set aside in favour of her honour. Your Royal Highness, you have dazzled her, and unfairly, I think, for she is so new to London and you so over-whelming.'

'Come, virginity ain't more than a condition,' said Cumberland, 'and I dare swear most young ladies don't presume to keep it for ever. I have a notion your innocent sister is hotly eager to dispose of hers.'

Caroline lost her composure and drew herself up in anger. 'That, sir, is not a response I would expect of a prince. Nor is it a response a true gentleman would give. I have called on you to entreat you to end your pursuit, and ask not that you should play a lordly and unyielding role, but to concede as a gentleman would. Is it to be said that the Duke of Cumberland is a lordly prince but never a gentleman?'

'By God,' said Cumberland, malice in his eye, 'ye've a splendid impertinence, that ye have, and damned if it don't make a woman and a half of ye.'

'I do not consider it impertinent to be in concern for my sister, and I know meekness won't avail me. I beg you to exercise compassionate majesty, not only in respect of my sister, but also in respect of Lady Russell, whom you are driving to misery and distraction. Yes, Your Highness, I know of what obtains between you and her, for such is her unhappiness that she became desperate to confide. Her letter, sir: give it to me that I may return it to her. If you seek to increase her wretchedness, I should not hesitate to advise the whole of London that a son of the King has been guilty of unforgivable ravishment.'

The dark, scarred face twisted in a teeth-gleaming smile, and a deep chuckle followed, and then a laugh. 'Upon my soul,' said Cumberland, 'ravishment, ye say? I warrant, dear lady, ye'll not find a word or a whisper of ravishment in the letter.'

Which was what Caroline had suspected, and what made the letter such a self-inflicted wound. Hester, twenty-two years old and married for two, had endured her night with Cumberland eight months ago, had conceived her brief passion for him, bedded with him several times during the following two months, and had then sought to end the affair. But that letter had forced her back into his bed at intervals all too frequent for her, and she was in a turmoil of agitation, for if she became pregnant she might very well not know who was the father, Cumberland or her husband. And her husband, a loving and indulgent spouse, was set on becoming a father.

'You cannot deny, sir, that you are in abuse of a lady both sweet and sad,' Caroline declared, 'and I vow it a horridness that you should continue as you do with her. You have had your pleasure of her. Give up the letter now, and give up also your pursuit of Annabelle. If you persist in your horridness and your designs, be warned, sir, that I am not unknown to the King, and won't lack to request him to intercede. He will not, sir, advance you the kindest of paternal consideration.'

Cumberland's sound eye grew baleful. The other, disfigured by a cataract, glared blindly at her. 'Ye'll ask His Majesty to set himself up as the protector of the innocence of a wench old enough to protect it for herself? Is your sister sixteen? I think not. Is she eighteen? No, not even that. She'll have come of age in a brief while, by God, when she'll command her own actions. As for the other lady, she has a husband. Let him ask for the letter.'

'For him even to know the letter exists would wreck their marriage and her life, sir. You are quite aware of that.' Caroline was cold and very angry. 'I declare, and roundly, that your wickedness is beyond belief.'

'Damn my heart, hand and eye,' said Cumberland, 'ye are a saucy trollop, an impudent baggage. Yet damned if ye ain't also the one woman to outshine all others. Ye've a rare and tantalising beauty. Ye'll recall I once declared a loving interest in ye?'

'I recall, sir, that you once attempted wicked, forceful seduction. I recall, sir, that on another occasion you engaged with my late husband in an outrageous wager, a wager which was a shame to both of you.'

'Outrageous?' He laughed; he slapped a muscular thigh. 'Come, madam, we ain't living among your long-faced American Puritans. Ye'll know I'm disinclined to pursue a reluctant woman . . .'

'No,' she said, fearless enough to interrupt him, 'no, I don't know that.'

'Don't ye?' His eye in its glitter was the mirror of his dark soul. 'Well, I fancy ye'll not deny we were once friends, and that I warned ye Percival had no stomach for real life or responsibility. Ye'd have found far more pleasure in my arms than his.'

'I am not given to promiscuity, sir,' she said, 'and am determined my sister will escape the habit.'

'Ye show proudly determined, I grant.' Cumberland smiled and mused. 'I'm minded to promise I'll see no more of Annabelle, providing ye'll allow me to see a great deal more of yourself.' His survey was insolent. Caroline stiffened. 'I fancy, madam, that out of your pretty gown ye'll show a form worthy of Venus herself. Willingly I'll bed you, dear woman, and leave your sister to her cherished innocence, though I doubt if she cherishes it as much as you do. Well, what d'ye say, does my offer appeal?'

Caroline might have been incensed had she not suspected he would arrive precisely at that compromise. She reacted to it with icy disdain, not anger. 'It has no appeal at all, sir. None.'

'None?' he said, head dipped, eye peering and massive figure looming.

'I came here, sir, in the hope of finding a little compassion in you. I have found only heartlessness, and wish you to understand I would no more give myself to you than the devil. I am not without friends, and should I decide to appeal to the King they will see to it that I reach his ear.'

An inimical smile split the Duke's mouth. 'It'll secure your friends a pretty piece of unpleasantness,' he said, and she knew that such might be the consequence, for the King's behaviour was so erratic that he was capable of reacting ragefully instead of reasonably, and directing that rage at her and her allies. 'Gently, madam,' continued Cumberland, 'be at peace with me, for I tell ye frankly, where ye are concerned I ain't above considering marriage. The truth is, ye've a fine figure, unequalled beauty and a presence as handsome as any royal duchess.'

'Fiddle-de-dee, sir, you will never marry a commoner,

and I would never marry you. I have already sampled the indignities of being married to a rake.'

Cumberland's gleam was malevolent. 'I'm tempted by that remark, madam, to have ye one way or another. But no, I'll not drag ye scratching into my arms when there's the sweet consolation of your sister. It's one or the other of ye, by God it is, and ye may choose, directly or indirectly. However, shall we part on a kiss to show I'm disposed to be forgiving of your unseemly tongue?'

He was bold enough and inconsiderate enough to bend and attempt the kiss. Caroline sprang to her feet and fiercely thrust him off. He stepped back, his face dark with angry blood.

'I am in shame for you, sir,' she said bitingly.

He controlled himself. His suffusing blood receded. He bowed, mockingly. 'Even so, dear lady, it stands, my consideration of marriage,' he said.

'I have no desire, sir, to ask for that consideration in return for your promise to distance yourself from my sister – and, even if I did, your consideration would come to nothing. Also, it is irrelevant, for, as I have already said, I would never marry you.'

'Then good day to ye, madam.'

She departed in pride, but not without feeling she had worsened the situation. Cumberland spent some minutes in scowling irritation. His private secretary, Franz Erzburger, came in. Erzburger was the son of a Hanoverian father and English mother, and in all things was his royal master's most faithful servant. Cumberland's ambitions were his ambitions, and he guarded and protected all the Duke's clandestine activities.

'Your Highness, there's a person wishing to see you.'

'A person?' said Cumberland.

'A man who has information to impart,' said Erzburger, who spoke correct English and perfect German. 'I think Your Highness should see him.'

'Why?' Cumberland was not given to receiving mere persons, informative or otherwise.

41

'He belongs to the Orange Order,' said Erzburger. The Duke was closely associated with this Irish Protestant organisation. 'His information concerns the well-being of the Prince of Wales and—'

'What's that ye say?' asked Cumberland, who seldom interested himself in the well-being of any of his brothers.

'He claims, Your Highness, to have overheard details of an Irish plot.'

'Irish? D'ye mean papist?'

'I fear so,' said Erzburger. 'It embraces assassination.'

'Assassination? Of Wales?'

Erzburger said softly, 'And you, Your Highness.'

'Both of us?' Cumberland, not a man to be in fear of plots, let his teeth show in a hungry smile. 'By God, there's ambition for ye, both of us.'

'I think, Your Highness, that he'll convince you there are certain Irishmen in London who should be apprehended.'

'Why ain't this Orangeman presenting his information to Wales?'

'The Prince of Wales is in Brighton,' said Erzburger.

'So he is, and souring his stomach with pastry and cream, I'll wager. So, then, let this person present himself to me.'

The person, an Irish Protestant working in London as a docker, was admitted. He was a little incoherent in his nervous agitation, but managed to put together an understandable story and to convey truthfulness. Erzburger was despatched on an errand after a while, and returned in an hour. Later that day he took the Irishman to a place of safety, for the man, having overheard an alarming conversation at Wapping Docks, was obviously in peril of his life. He had not thought he was. He insisted the plotters had not been aware of his presence. But the Duke advised him not to take that for granted. Therefore, he must go into hiding until such time as the miscreants had been rounded up and taken into custody. Erzburger escorted him to his hiding-place, telling him he had been sensible to say nothing to anyone except the Duke. He was quite

42

sure he had not? Yes, protested the Irishman, quite sure. And his family was in Ireland and knew nothing of the matter? That was so, said the Irishman.

Good, said Erzburger, and he delivered the man to a house of safety.

'Captain Burnside, m'lady,' announced a footman.

Lady Caroline, in her drawing room, put aside the letter in her hand, the monthly letter from her parents. 'Show him in, Thomas,' she said, 'and have his bags taken up to his room.'

Thomas showed the Captain in and retired. The Captain advanced and bowed. Caroline regarded him critically, but found no fault. He wore a blue coat and light blue breeches, with shining Hessian boots and a white cravat. His appearance was impeccably correct, with no sign of being dandyish.

'Caroline, my dear friend,' he said, 'how good to—'

'Sir!' Caroline came to her feet in a protesting rush.

Captain Burnside cocked a dark eyebrow. 'Caroline?' he enquired.

'I am not your dear friend, sir.'

'I have the scenario wrong, Your Ladyship?'

'This is a moment for the venture to be reviewed, Captain Burnside, not for unwanted familiarities.'

'Ah,' said Captain Burnside, 'then I apologise, marm, for being in advance of the play. I thought to arrive on an appropriate note, to establish at once an atmosphere pertaining to a fond relationship . . .'

'Fond relationship?' Caroline felt again the necessity to be in command of her hireling, or the initiative would slip from her. 'I don't recall making any suggestion that you and I were to be *fond* of each other, only that we were to be old friends.'

'True, marm, true,' said the imperturbable Captain. 'I can only say I am fond of my friends myself, and hope that some, at least, are fond of me.'

Caroline, dressed in a muslin tea gown that was bewitchingly colourful, drew herself up. 'I must tell you quite frankly, sir, that it would be impossible for me to pretend any fondness for you. You all are a blackguard of the kind I most despise, but because the situation is what it is I shall do what I can to sustain a role that compels me to regard you as a friend. Do not look for any fondness, sir; do not look for anything except a recognition that we knew each other before you left England to serve with your regiment abroad. You have just returned and I have been gracious enough to accommodate you as a house guest while you look for a suitable apartment.'

'An excellent expedient,' said Captain Burnside, 'and if you will instruct me in this, that and the other, I'll at once be *au fait* with you. Nevertheless, marm, in view of your peerless looks—'

'Sir?' She interrupted warningly.

'Humbly, marm, and with all respect, I must point out your looks are peerless indeed, and it ain't natural, d'you see, for an officer and a gentleman not to have acquired a fond admiration for you.'

'An officer and a gentleman?' Caroline could not help herself. Her facade as his cool and composed patron broke, and she laughed. Sarcastic though her amusement was, it brought a rich vivacity to her manner. 'Your audacity, Captain, is almost too much for me. But yes, very well, I accept I'm not unattractive and that you admire my looks, but you are here to impress my sister, not me. Therefore, restrain this admiration or the gallantries you are required to bestow on Annabelle will not make sense.'

Captain Burnside nodded in agreement. 'Even so, I suggest cutting a dash in your favour initially, marm, by reason of our happy reunion, and advising your sister I consider you an exquisite American beauty. Then I shall change course by advising her she is even more exquisite, and, faith, she does have sweetly engaging looks. It follows that I shall embrace my role fervently, and you may rely on a performance suitably artistic and entirely successful.'

Caroline quivered at the thought of her sister in the amorous arms of the philandering scoundrel, but conceded even that was to be preferred to Annabelle in Cumberland's bed.

'If boastful declarations could move mountains, Captain Burnside, you would be the first man to move Everest,' she said. 'However, you may sit down. Now, kindly pay attention.'

There were, she said, to be six at supper that evening: their own two selves, her sister Annabelle, her cousin Cecilia and Cecilia's husband Robert, and the Duke of Cumberland. Captain Burnside would find Cecilia and Robert charming, but Cumberland, of course, was an arrogant character and thunderously intolerant of Whigs and like radicals. Was Captain Burnside a Whig, a radical? If so, he must keep it to himself, or Cumberland would not sit down at the card table with him.

'You'd prefer me to be an out-and-out Tory, marm?'

'Yes.'

'Then I am, marm, now and for as long as you consider it necessary.'

'Even though it may be a lie, sir?'

'Oh, any kind of specious prevarication comes easily to me,' smiled the Captain.

'I believe you,' said Caroline cuttingly, and advised him that he, Robert Humphreys and the Duke would be encouraged to play cards after supper. Captain Burnside, as agreed, would ensure Cumberland sustained grievous losses. He was not, however, to take advantage of Robert, an entirely likeable gentleman. He was to play fair with him. Cumberland would cover his losses with IOUs and ask for another game to be arranged to give him the chance to recover them. He never parted with ready money when he sustained heavy losses; he kept on in one way or another until his IOUs were cancelled, either fairly or unfairly.

Caroline said she would see to it that his losses were made public, and Captain Burnside would see to it that at the right time Cumberland must be made to give up the letter for the IOUs. The Captain was to understand, however, that Cumberland was at his most dangerous whenever he felt he was being pressed or disadvantaged. He had no regard whatever for offended husbands or outraged swains. He looked upon them as interfering peasants. As a royal Duke, he was not permitted to engage in duels, but he would not lack to take on any adversary in a boxing match and hammer him almost to death.

'H'm,' said Captain Burnside, 'I ain't too keen on that kind of hammering.'

'You are wise, sir, to fear Cumberland. He has no fears himself, either of God or the devil.'

'Should I come close to being hammered to death, marm, will you take kindly to my asking for compensation in the form of a doubled fee?'

'I will pay the costs of the doctor and the convalescence,' said Caroline. 'Now, sir, are you still willing fully to undertake this venture?'

'As your servant, marm, I'm willing and prepared.'

'Very well,' said Caroline, her beauty complementing the elegant look of her drawing room, with its royal blue motif and its graceful French furniture. 'I hope my confidence in you is not misplaced, and that you can cure my sister of her attachment to Cumberland. No time must be lost. I felt you might have stayed to establish yourself with her the other day, instead of unexpectedly departing.'

'Ah, well,' said the Captain, 'a little indifference in the beginning piques a young lady who has begun to think, by reason of a royal Duke's attentiveness, that she is irresistible to all men.'

'Stuff and nonsense,' said Caroline. 'I shall expect you to contrive more intelligently than that.'

'Faith, marm,' said Captain Burnside, 'intelligence don't always guarantee a satisfactory outcome when dealing with young ladies. They're sweet things, but ain't given as much to commonsense as they are to heartfelt yearnings.'

'Sometimes, sir, your facile tongue takes a very unattractive turn. I will now have one of my servants take you up to your room, and show you such amenities as are available to you. I trust you will not find them inadequate. We dine at six, and I should like it if you will appear at not later than fifteen minutes to.'

'Thank you, marm. Ah, first, when did we meet?'

'Meet?'

'I fancy your sister might ask that question. Shall we say at a ball, perhaps, a while before you were married and I had had some acquaintance with Lord Percival?'

'I cannot deny that the details of our assumed first meeting might be important. Let it be at the Queen's ball in September, seven years ago.'

'Excellent. And may I enquire how I'm to address you? As an old friend, shall it be Caroline or not?'

'Lady Clarence,' she said. 'Or Lady Caroline.'

'Very well, marm.'

'And I shall call you Captain Burnside, to indicate that although we are old friends we are not intimately so.'

'Lady Caroline, marm, I am yours to command.'

'Indeed you are,' said Caroline firmly, 'and do not forget it.'

# Chapter Five

The atmosphere at supper proved as equable as Caroline could have wished. One never knew in precisely what mood the Duke of Cumberland would arrive at any function, private or public, but at least he was more inclined to dispense civility at a small supper party than at a large gathering. At a large gathering, he disliked the possibility of rubbing shoulders with people who might be merely people.

Caroline had not been sure he would put in an appearance following her confrontation with him the previous day. But he did, and he greeted her as if nothing obtained between them but the friendliest of feelings. And with six at the table, the dining room owning a magnificence in keeping with his own, he induced an agreeable atmosphere with his mood of royal benevolence. Nor did he make any attempt to be more attentive to Annabelle than to anyone else. If, from time to time, his eye was a little mocking, and his smile a little satirical, his conversation was most agreeable. He knew each of the three ladies well, and they were all pleasing to look upon.

His hostess, gowned in shimmering jade green, strung pearls clasping her smooth, creamy neck, was undeniably superb, her lightly-powdered bosom a curving splendour. Her sister Annabelle, in delicious, azure blue, came to the eye as a fair young goddess, if with no more worldly knowledge than that of a simple shepherdess. As for Lady Caroline's cousin by marriage, Cecilia Humphreys, her magenta gown gave a vividness to her Latin-like dark looks. She was the daughter of the deceased younger brother of the Duke of Avonhurst, and in her aptitude for radiating gaiety hinted not at all that she and her husband Robert were hard put to maintain their expensive life style.

Robert Humphreys was a pleasant and amiable gentleman who, with Cumberland's help, kept his head just above water. The impoverished third son of the spendthrift Sir Godfrey Humphreys, he had managed to lay his hands on a little property for a nominal outlay, and he had been put in the way of this by Cumberland. He received rents from the tenants, rents necessary to his pocket. Only yesterday, at the request of Cumberland's private secretary, he had turned one of the properties over to accommodate a wish of the Duke. It had meant housing the tenants elsewhere at a moment's notice. The arrangement, Erzburger had assured him, was only temporary. It was also confidential. Robert knew better than to ask questions. Robert was the kind of gentleman who liked people to like him. Why any gentleman should worry about people liking him was beyond the comprehension of the Duke.

Cumberland noted that the other fellow, Captain Burnside, dressed decently enough, as a man should, without lace or fripperies. Aside from that, he was, of course, as much of a nonentity as Humphreys. However, in certain circumstances, a nonentity or two could be tolerated. The three ladies made these circumstances of that kind. Percival's widow was a challenge, her sister a pleasurable toy, and Humphreys' wife an occasional pleasure.

Cumberland's eye caught Annabelle's glance. His dark visage took on a slightly amused expression.

'Well, Burnside,' he said, 'since ye're a Redcoat, what d'ye think of being in company with two of America's choicest blooms? D'ye fancy we can forgive them what the damned rebellious colonists did to the status quo?'

'I fancy, Your Highness, that neither Lady Caroline nor Miss Howard had much to do with that,' said Captain Burnside, consuming a sweet water ice.

'Mere infants at the time, eh?' Cumberland quizzed Annabelle's bosom. 'Babes in arms, d'ye suppose?'

'And quite without the sin of rebelliousness, sir,' said the Captain with easy affability.

'Prettily said, Captain,' smiled Cecilia.

'We're all without sin as infants,' said Caroline, 'and I declare, Your Highness, that both Annabelle and I continue to be perfect. That is, in the eyes of our loving parents.'

'I vow I hope I am perfect in everyone's eyes,' said Annabelle, 'for I cannot think I could be sweeter than I am.'

'Fie to modesty,' laughed Cecilia, 'let all we ladies dare every gentleman to say we are not less than beautiful and not less than adorable.'

'I shall say nothing,' said the Captain, 'for I accept that.'

'Oh, you are surely the essence of a gentleman,' said Annabelle.

'And what do you say, my love?' asked Cecilia of her husband.

'I say, my love, that you are immaculate,' said Robert.

Cumberland's smile had the devil's own gleam of amusement to it. Annabelle, remarking it, shivered deliciously.

Supper over, the company repaired to the room used for cards and other pastimes. Since it was known that Cumberland did not favour after-supper small-talk, no hostess dared invite him to dine without the prospect of the rest of the evening spent at a card table. So the three men played *vingt-et-un*, with the minimum stake a guinea, the maximum fifty guineas, and the three ladies engaged in backgammon at a suitable distance. The light of the low chandeliers, each burning a score of candles, shone on their heads. Caroline's auburn hair glinted with fire. Annabelle's fair hair was touched with gold. Cecilia's hair was a glossy, curl-adorned black crown. Their gowns squarely plunged, and the candlelight shed pearly lustre over gently-breathing curves.

Annabelle fidgeted a little, casting covert glances at the

men, at the commanding, fine-backed figure of the Duke. He had such a dominating presence, although she did not fail to notice that Captain Burnside was so remarkably at ease that he imparted a presence of his own. They were both gentlemen of singular character. Oh, dear, how sweetly exciting it was to be an eligible young lady in London, where the men were so cultured and civilised, and no lady made a fuss if one was not engaged at the age of sixteen or seventeen.

Cecilia cast no glances. She made an enjoyment of the backgammon. She made an enjoyment of most pursuits, for she was easy to please. Thirty years old, she had given Caroline comfort and sympathy in the face of all her marital tribulations, and during her widowhood, although in widowhood Caroline frankly needed far less sympathy than when her husband was alive. Cecilia was on very agreeable terms with her own husband, and they understood each other pefectly. Unfortunately, the splendid dowry she had received from her father on marriage was almost gone, mainly due to Robert's dreadfully bad luck with investments, speculations and cards, poor dear. With three children to bring up and educate, Cecilia might have shown a worried face to the world. So might Robert. But they were both cheerful souls. Neither showed any envy of Caroline's inheritance. It was a blessing to Cecilia that Robert had earned Cumberland's patronage, for the Duke had put him in the way of better investments, and for no consideration at all other than that of sometimes taking Robert's place in her bed. One did not talk about that, of course, and Cumberland never would. Robert said it would be sure to earn him further royal favours, perhaps by way of a Government appointment that would prove lucrative. Cecilia had said, 'Oh, I do hope so, my love, for I'd not yield your place in my bed to Cumberland for a single night if he were not intending to continue favouring you.'

Caroline's friendship with Robert and Cecilia was a warm one, and she was not in the least aware that Cecilia was yet one more woman who enjoyed herself in the arms of the unhandsome but magnetic Cumberland.

Glancing at the men, Caroline was curious to know if Captain Burnside was embarrassing the Duke's pocket. Cumberland's expression told her nothing. But that dark face, with its twisted scar, rarely expressed anything except mockery or deviousness. He sat upright in his chair, his dark grey coat a severity in its cut and its close fit. Captain Burnside seemed thoughtful but untroubled, and Robert was wearing a faint smile, a sign that he was probably winning. The three of them were speaking only in murmurs. When gentlemen were at cards they did not play loudly.

Cumberland regarded the card Captain Burnside had just dealt him. The ace of hearts. A pretty thing. He announced his bet: fifty guineas. He never showed money itself. He received his second card, the ace of diamonds. A crisp gift. He split both cards, betting fifty guineas on the second. Captain Burnside dealt him a third. Cumberland's expression remained impassive as he regarded yet another ace. Spades. Fifty guineas went on that too.

Captain Burnside, knowing the Duke had three of a high kind, placed a card on each. Cumberland took a look at the first. A king. He turned it up. '*Vingt-et-un*,' he said. The card on the second ace was a four. He asked for another.

'Open or closed?' murmured the Captain.

'Closed, for a further fifty,' said Cumberland, and received a six. 'Enough,' he said, and looked at the card on his third ace. A ten. '*Vingt-et-un*,' he said again, turning it up.

'I fancy I'm for it,' smiled Captain Burnside. The Duke had two hands that could only be beaten if he turned up *Vingt-et-un* himself. He looked at Robert. 'Mr Humphreys?'

'Oh, show me one,' said Robert, who held a nine and a three against a bet of five guineas. Captain Burnside dealt him an eight, and Robert's smile became broad. 'I'll stand,' he said.

'I've a feeling of disaster,' said the Captain, and turned

52

up the first of his own two cards. Ace of clubs. Cumberland's eyebrow went up. But the second card proved to be a five. 'H'm,' said the Captain, 'I ain't going to make myself a fortune standing on sixteen. So . . .' He dealt himself a third card, a jack. 'Damn me, an interloper.' He gave himself a fourth. A queen. 'Topped by an unkind lady,' he said.

'Bad luck,' said Robert.

'Who is winning?' asked Annabelle, unable to stay on the outside any longer.

Cumberland disdained the question. Few gentlemen liked to be asked about the state of a game.

'I'm up, I fancy,' said Robert, square of shoulders and open of countenance.

Captain Burnside made a note that he had just lost two hundred guineas to Cumberland and five to Robert. He paid Robert. He now owed Cumberland four hundred and seventy guineas in all.

'Captain Burnside?' enquired Annabelle prettily, ignoring from Caroline a look that told her not to interrupt the men.

'Down,' said the Captain, and Caroline frowned. He was losing? What had happened to his skill, then? Or had she hired herself a mere braggart?

The bank passed to Cumberland. He dealt a series of hands, some at a profit, some at a loss, and the deal then returned to Captain Burnside on his showing of an ace and a jack. Robert received some moderate cards, but Cumberland was dealt three excellent hands in succession. The fourth proved even better. It secured him a five-carder, virtually unbeatable if luck was no more than modest, and his total wager on it was one hundred and sixty guineas. The Captain, having put Robert out of the reckoning, showed his own cards. An eight and a five. Smoothly, he added to them, first with a deuce, then a three and then another deuce, giving himself a five-card hand that capped the Duke's.

Cumberland smiled. 'Pretty,' he said, 'very pretty, and boldly achieved.'

'Oh, something back, sir,' said Captain Burnside. 'To the tune of one-sixty, I fancy?'

Cumberland waved an airy hand. He began to lose steadily then. He remained impassive, although he turned a keener eye on the Captain. The ladies eventually came to watch, to stand in silence around the table. Robert, amiably electing to inform Cecilia that he was comfortably up, received from Cumberland a glance that chastened him. Caroline, making her assessment of the play and the bets, realised the tide had turned for Captain Burnside.

At a little after midnight, a servant entered to announce that the Duke's coach had arrived. At that point, Cumberland owed the Captain four hundred and ninety guineas. He also owed Robert seventy-five.

'Ye've a way of turning the tables, Burnside,' he said. 'What d'ye say, a cut of the cards before I go, to double what I owe ye or conceding quits?'

That was sharp practice on the part of any gambler who made it difficult for a creditor to collect from him. However, Captain Burnside indicated he was willing, and thereby earned himself a sharp look from Caroline.

Robert shuffled the pack with expertise, and set it down. The Duke sat back and glanced at Annabelle. His smile drew a faint flush from her.

'Your honour, sir?' murmured Captain Burnside, and Cumberland made his cut with a careless flourish. He showed the king of clubs. Caroline, disapprovingly, watched Captain Burnside make his own cut with deliberation. Cumberland's smile became wolverine, for the Captain showed the ace of diamonds.

'By God, ye've a talent for uncovering the prettiest pictures,' said Cumberland, and came to his feet.

'You'll oblige me, Your Highness?' said the Captain.

'Ye'll take an IOU and carry it forward for a return game?'

'You ain't possessed of the ready, sir?'

'Nigh a thousand guineas? That I'm not, man. We'll play again in two weeks' time.' The Duke was plainly set on revenge. 'Here? Ye'll allow us, m'dear Caroline?'

'With pleasure, Your Highness,' said Caroline.

'Set the sum down,' said Cumberland to the Captain, who used the table quill and a sheet of paper to inscribe the IOU. Cumberland signed with a rasping scrawl. 'I'll skin ye alive next time, Burnside,' he said, then wished his hostess goodnight, allowing his lips to linger on her fingertips. His goodnight to Annabelle was almost perfunctory, but she did not take offence. She knew his first consideration was discretion.

Robert and Cecilia left with him, accepting a lift to their house in his coach.

With the guests gone, Annabelle said, 'You surely did excel, Captain Burnside, in thinning the Duke's pocket. You all have a profitable way of using cards.'

'Oh, luck tonight,' said the Captain, musing on the blueness of her eyes. 'Misfortune next time, perhaps.'

'I vow the Duke took his losses in generous and manly fashion, did you not think so?' said Annabelle, tingling pleasantly as the Captain smiled. Caroline, standing apart, thought her sister coy and the Captain very self-possessed. 'Any other gentleman might have shown a most unpleasant temper.'

'It ain't too cheerful, being out of pocket to that extent,' said the Captain, 'and I dare swear, Miss Howard, that few gentlemen would have taken it as graciously as the Duke.'

'I declare, you are gracious yourself,' said Annabelle, 'for the Duke is a much maligned gentleman.'

'But sails bravely above it,' said Captain Burnside, and Caroline gave him a hot look. What was he doing in praising Cumberland to the one person he should not?

Annabelle's bosom sighed. Catching her sister's eye, she said, 'I must retire. You all will excuse me, Captain?'

'A little reluctantly,' said the Captain, and Annabelle laughed.

'You surely are very fitting to be an old friend of Caroline,' she said, and kissed her sister goodnight.

Left alone with the Captain, Caroline said, 'What are you about, sir?'

'With your sister, marm?'

'Yes, with my sister, sir. Are you seeking, in your praise of him, to drive Annabelle into Cumberland's arms?'

'It ain't sound tactics, marm, to slander a rival. Preferable to be in praise of him. It'll induce affection in Annabelle.'

'Affection for whom?' asked Caroline.

'Your humble servant, marm.'

'I see.' A slight smile touched Caroline's firm lips. 'But regarding the card play, sir, you risked losing the IOU you held by consenting to a cut of the cards.'

'A matter of running with Lady Luck,' said the Captain cheerfully. 'She's fickle, being very feminine, d'you see, and if you don't—'

'Feminine?' Caroline acquired her cool look. 'Sir, I find it offensive to hear a man associate fickleness with my sex, for I doubt if any man can be trusted to be wholly faithful.'

'You've a point,' said the Captain. 'I should have said sensitive. It means that if you don't run with Lady Luck when she's taken a fancy to you, she'll play the very devil with you next time you need her favours.'

Caroline looked questioning. 'Do you tell me, sir, that it was all a matter of luck tonight, that you did not make use of your vaunted skill or your professional knavery?'

'*Vingt-et-un* requires no great skill, marm,' said Captain Burnside; 'it's a game of pure chance, although one can sometimes sum up what the other fellow holds. The luck favoured Cumberland in the beginning.'

'To what extent?'

'I was down almost five hundred guineas.'

'Five hundred?' Caroline stiffened. 'You take my breath, sir. You expected me to meet this sum?'

'It was, I agree, a trifle excessive.'

'It was a sum, sir, that would be a fortune to many people.'

'Ah, but the game wasn't over at that point,' said the Captain.

'At that point you were almost five hundred guineas down due to luck being against you, if I have it right. You might subsequently have doubled that loss if luck had continued to be unfavourable. I warn you, Captain Burnside, I have not hired you to test your luck against Cumberland, I have hired your professed talents. If you insist, sir, on gambling with airy impunity, don't look to me to settle your debts, for I shan't. I haven't given you unlimited access to my purse, nor shall I.'

'I shan't hazard every penny of your wealth, marm, I assure you,' said Captain Burnside earnestly, 'but should it look as if I am, then I shall cheat my way to the front as skilfully as you could wish.'

'You had better, sir, yes indeed you had better. It occurred to me at the end of the play that the IOU of almost a thousand guineas could have been enough to make Cumberland discharge the letter to you. Now, however, you are committed to giving him the chance to win the IOU back. I trust you will deny him such victory, and that by the end of the next game his further losses will compel him to do what you require of him: namely, give up the letter. Also, by that time, I shall expect you to have fired my sister's interest in you.'

Captain Burnside rubbed his chin. 'It's my opinion, marm, that one can't set fire to a burning house,' he said. 'I shall win your sweet sister, have no fear, but it will not happen tomorrow.'

'Nor at all, unless you show yourself attentive. Annabelle is fond of the river. I've suggested to her that she might like to enjoy an outing with you. She is quite in favour, and wishes a picnic hamper to be taken.'

'Excellent,' said the Captain, 'but you should come too, of course.'

'I've no desire to.'

'But, d'you see, marm, it won't do for you to throw me at her. She'll guess what you're at. Young ladies suffering infatuation don't take kindly to obvious attempts to cure 'em. It's preferable for all three of us to go on the outing.'

Caroline frowned. 'Yes, I see,' she said. 'Very well. In a day or so.'

'Your servant, marm. May I say goodnight?' He bowed,

but she refrained from giving him her hand. She watched him depart for his bed, and as the door closed behind him she wondered if Annabelle might not eventually be in as much danger from him as from Cumberland. In his way, he was, after all, as much of a villain as the Duke.

# Chapter Six

The handsome brown carriage ran smoothly, the pair trotting, Captain Burnside at the reins. Annabelle was perched beside him, her parasol not only protecting her from the July sun but adding the decorative touch that so complemented a lady's outdoor look. Annabelle had expressed a wish for a ride to the park on this fine day, and that had given Caroline the opportunity to arrange for Captain Burnside to escort her and drive her.

Annabelle, having developed a liking for the extremely personable Captain, was happy to have his company, and to talk to him. He was a most agreeable listener. After some harmless sociable discourse, she came casually to that which was so often on her mind. 'Captain Burnside, do you think the Duke of Cumberland an impressive man?'

'Impressive?' said the Captain. 'Cumberland, I daresay, can be accounted a magnificent prince.'

'Oh, I do declare you all of sympathetic,' enthused Annabelle, parasol casting light shade over her prettiness. 'So many people say the unkindest things about him, and even about his looks. But his scar is an honourable one, and gives him, I vow, the mark of a brave soldier. In uniform, he is truly magnificent.'

'A martial lion, Miss Howard.'

'Please call me Annabelle. It's a pleasure to know you and Caroline are old friends, and that I may consider you my newest friend.'

'One could say the pleasure is pre-eminently mine,' said the debonair Captain, wheedling the glossy chestnuts into an adroit passing of a lumbering stage coach. 'I've always been an admirer of your sister, and have already come to the conclusion that you're a sweet young lady.'

'Oh, you all are so gallant,' said Annabelle, and smiled at a lady who fluttered a hand at her from a passing carriage. 'There, that was Lady Russell, a very dear friend to Caroline, and much devoted to her husband, Sir George Russell, who is like you in being charitably disposed towards the Duke of Cumberland. The Duke rendered him much help and kindness when he broke his leg at a country house party many months ago. How I wish . . .' She sighed to a halt.

'Come,' said the Captain warmly, 'confide in me, dear girl. I've noticed your tendency to sigh at times. Count me a true friend. The reverence in which I hold your sister inclines me to lend you a sympathetic ear.'

'Reverence?' Annabelle laughed softly. 'Reverence, Captain Burnside?'

'Well, she comes close to being a goddess,' said the Captain.

'A goddess? Caroline?' Annabelle laughed again. 'She is surely handsome of figure, but a *goddess*?'

'Olympian,' said the Captain, gentling the pair through the rough and tumble of traffic.

'Sir, you stand in awe of Caroline?'

'While you stand in admiration of Cumberland?'

'Truly, he is the most exciting man in England, and I cannot think why your goddess, my sister, should regard him so uncharitably.' Annabelle sighed again, and the carriage sighed with her as it sedately approached the park. 'I confess to an affection for him.'

'Which he returns, I don't doubt,' said Captain Burnside.

'He has declared himself enchanted,' said Annabelle, casting her eyes about, 'but so have many gentlemen who have kissed my hand, and who can say if all of them, including the Duke, aren't merely being gallant?'

'Ah,' said Captain Burnside, allowing the carriage to proceed on a sauntering encirclement of the park, 'but have Cumberland's gallantries been accompanied by his hand on his heart or a squeeze of your waist? Has he, in fact, in one way or another, shown you more than mere gallantries?'

'Oh, because I feel you are already the kindest of friends, I must confess yes, he has even kissed me.'

'Capital,' said Captain Burnside, 'for Cumberland ain't given to bestowing royal kisses on every young lady in London.'

'But gentlemen are apt to steal kisses from all of us,' said Annabelle.

'Well, I ain't,' said the Captain firmly, 'damn me, no. And Cumberland's too high and mighty to rob any young lady unless he has a royal fondness for her.'

'Oh, do you mean, dear Captain Burnside, that you think he could have an especial fondness for me?' breathed Annabelle. 'It's true he has actually declared a loving regard. But I'm not so simple as to believe it an especial regard, or that he would consider marrying me. Do you think he would?'

Captain Burnside glanced at her. Beneath the shade of her parasol and bonnet, her profile showed the musing softness of a young lady living in hope.

'Well, one thing is certain,' he said, 'he ain't yet married to anyone else. Nor need he marry a princess, a woman suitable to become a queen, for he ain't the King's heir. His four older brothers all precede him. So he might marry his own fancy, and a fair young flower from South Carolina might well be his especial fancy.'

'I vow you to be so encouraging,' said Annabelle, eyes searching the environs of the park.

'You're set on him, that I see, even though he's no Adonis. But I daresay he's no wish to be pretty.'

'A gentleman's looks are not as important as a lady's,' said Annabelle. 'A lady prefers a gentleman to be first and foremost a man. The Prince of Wales decks himself out in pretty satins and frills, but isn't half the man the Duke is. Now Beau Brummell dresses to perfection, but never at the expense of not looking a man. And the Duke is of all things manly.' Annabelle sighed yet again as she thought of the sheer masculine nobility of Cumberland's thighs. 'But marriage, Captain Burnside, that is the question.'

'So it should be,' said the Captain, lifting his brown beaver hat to two strolling ladies who had raised flirtatious eyes to him. They at once hid themselves beneath their parasols and giggled. 'Well, Annabelle, you must let Cumberland know that only marriage will bring you into his arms. He may be magnificent, but I'll wager you own enough sweet subtleties to reduce him to frailty. I don't doubt his ardour, so be firm as well as subtle, or he'll attempt to pull you into his bed. To speak plain, he ain't above attempting that with any lady as delicious as you.'

Annabelle blushed. Her eyes alighted on a standing black coach in the near distance. 'Mercy's sake, Captain Burnside, I never did encounter a franker gentleman than you, nor one who advised me better. You are truly a friend, and in friendship will you set me down here while you take several turns around the park? Will you give me fifteen minutes to myself?'

'Ah,' smiled the Captain, observing the black coach and bringing the carriage to a gentle halt, 'I'm to assist you to keep an assignation?'

'If you would be so kind, and in the strictest confidence,' begged Annabelle. 'I'd not want my sister to know, or she will rail at me in the most upsetting way, as if I were a child of ten.'

'Fifteen minutes, h'm,' said Captain Burnside. 'In certain circumstances, even a brief fifteen minutes could be too long, but as your friend I'll rely on you to be firm, not weak, and to make known to the gentleman your determination to consider nothing except marriage.'

'Oh, to be sure,' said Annabelle earnestly. 'You truly believe he might marry me, that the King would not object?'

'The King rarely has all his wits about him, and Cumberland's known, in any case, to be his own master.

62

So don't let him set up obstacles that don't exist. Be delicious, certainly, be teasing, but above all be firm.'

'Captain Burnside, I do declare you a sweet strength to my cause,' said Annabelle, and alighted.

Tactfully, Captain Burnside drove away, but cast a look back in time to see her closing her parasol as she stepped up into the coach. A hand drew the door to, and curtains veiled the interior happenings.

'So ye came,' said Cumberland out of the dimness.

'I whispered to you last night that I would if I could, and here I am, Your Highness,' said Annabelle, and her colour rose to see him frankly contemplating the accessibility of her mouth. 'I am in hope you will speak to me in serious fashion – oh—'

Her mouth was taken boldly and uncompromisingly. If she had arrived in the coach determined to be proudly firm, as Captain Burnside had advised, that determination became a thing of tatters the moment the Duke's lips made audacious contact with hers. Yet she could not say it was not sweet, for although shockingly bold the kiss was neither bruising nor forceful. It lingered, it finished, her mouth opened to draw breath and was captured again. He had an alarming way of inducing response, of making her lips cling to his. But at least she did not forget to bring her hands up in defence of her bosom.

Releasing her mouth and observing her nervous, improvised shield, Cumberland murmured with laughter, his blind eye looking as amused as his sound one. 'What's this? Ye're denying me an acquaintance with your sweet pair?'

Drawing breath, with the coach on the move, Annabelle said as bravely as she could, 'Sir, you made your acquaintance all too intimately with them on the last occasion we were alone. I wish to be treated more circumspectly today.'

'More circumspectly?' Cumberland, sombrely clad, was a wicked darkness in the gloom of the curtained coach.

'Upon my soul, ye jump into my carriage, into my arms, pout them at me and then declare them forbidden? Ye've a teasing innocence, that ye have.'

'I protest, Your Highness.' Annabelle was proudly indignant. 'I did not jump into your arms, and nor did I ask you to buss me.'

'But ye came, I daresay, to be affectionate with me, did ye not?'

'I came, Your Highness, because I do have some affection for you, and to inform you I'm returning to my home in Charleston. My parents are anxious about me, for I've long overstayed my visit.'

Cumberland looked suitably solemn, although someone more sophisticated than Annabelle would have seen the mockery beneath the facade. To Cumberland, this pretty thing was as transparent as daylight, but still a sweet pawn in the game. For all her sister's defiant rejection of him, he was still sure he could win the elder by using the younger.

'Faith,' he said, 'parental anxiety is always a prevailing ailment, but not fatal.'

'You cannot expect my own parents to be indifferent to my welfare,' said Annabelle, sensitive to his nearness in the seclusion of the coach, which was moving at a slow pace around the park.

'Ah, it's your precious virginity they fuss about, is it? Well, God love ye, it's precious to us all. When d'ye sail?'

'I haven't yet decided,' said Annabelle, 'but since my prospects here seem uncertain, I shan't long delay.'

'Prospects?' The lack of light in the coach muted the glint in his eye. 'Prospects, my tender rose, are a mirage, a vision without substance, an illusion. I prefer an objective to a prospect, for an objective is factual, not fanciful, although it ain't always certain ye'll achieve it.'

'Your Highness,' said Annabelle, 'do you see me as an objective?'

'I see ye as a fair flower with delicate petals, and as such worthy of cherishing.'

'Cherishing?' Annabelle experienced glowing pleasure.

'Who could not cherish ye, and lovingly?' murmured Cumberland.

'Your Highness, I do declare, those are the sweetest words you have given me.'

'Well, ye have my affections, Annabelle, that ye have, and since ye haven't booked your passage home yet, I fancy there's time to cherish ye now,' he said, and Annabelle stiffened as a long, strong arm encircled her waist.

'No, I cannot consent to further intimacies, sir, for such should only be between affianced lovers,' she said. The arm tightened. 'Your Highness, I entreat you—'

'My little dove, accept for the moment that we are lovers, and affianced.'

'But we are not – oh—' She could not hold him off. Her lips could not escape his bold mouth, nor her bosom his audacious hand. The warm kiss that weakened her resolve was succeeded by another, and another. Her white bosom, dangerously poised as he loosened her bodice, tumbled free. Annabelle gasped against his lips as his hand teased her, caressed her and brought a rosy hue to her white plumpness. The most alarming excitement invested her, an excitement that was a wild warning to her. Her lips broke free and she gasped, 'No, how can you be so shameless – you must not – I beg you to release me.'

'A cherishing is shameless?' said Cumberland. His dark, scarred face expressed new amusement as Annabelle, vividly rosy, covered her breasts with her hands.

'To kiss me so, and fondle me so – that is dreadfully shameless, Your Highness,' she breathed, and was not sure if it was the moving coach that was swaying giddily or herself. 'And I vow you are making an unkind habit of it.'

'Well, ye're a delicious morsel,' said Cumberland, and then, seeing her seeking agitated refuge for her breasts, he deftly adjusted and secured her bodice, Annabelle palpitating as he rendered her such an intimate service. She scarcely knew where to look. 'There,' he smiled, 'ye're as good as new.'

'Sir,' she gasped, 'I declare – oh, I never did – such attentions are more embarrassing than your caresses.'

'I fancy,' he said, 'that ye'll not come fully into my arms unless we're affianced?'

'I could not, Your Highness.'

'Well, since ye're so enchanting a virgin, damned if I don't find the notion to my liking,' said Cumberland, quite sure that if he had a mind to he could land the virgin far more easily than the widow.

Annabelle tingled. It was indisputable, the Duke's desire for her, his wish to have her. Captain Burnside was a clever gentleman. He knew that if the Duke desired her enough, she could demand marriage. As the Captain had said, it was not as if the Duke would ever succeed the King, that it was necessary for him to have a wife of royal blood. The tingling increased.

'Your Highness, I truly could not surrender except on honourable terms,' she said.

Cumberland's smile was laden with satire. 'Ye gods,' he murmured, 'there's a pretty speech from the prettiest innocent who ever showed herself so roundly to me.'

Her blush took fire. 'I did not, sir. You uncovered me.'

'And covered ye up again in all fairness,' he said. 'Shall ye ride to my house with me now?'

'No, I cannot, and nor could I trust myself with you.'

'Well, I'll be at my town residence on Friday afternoon,' said Cumberland.

'If I can come, Your Highness, I hope you will remember my concern for my future. To meet with you again must mean to talk together, without further intimacies, or I will surely die of embarrassment and confusion. Would you now be so kind as to set me down at the point where you waited for me?'

Cumberland did not argue. He had had his brief moments with her, and all such moments represented an advance towards the real objective, the winning of her magnificent sister. He knocked on the roof, and his coachman brought the vehicle to a halt where Annabelle had joined him. Cumberland did not show himself, and she alighted without assistance. The coach moved off as soon as he had pulled the door to.

Captain Burnside, who had been following on throughout, brought his pair to a halt, and Annabelle stepped up into the carriage. She smiled charmingly at him, and he smiled cheerfully at her, making no comment for the moment on the fact that her face was slightly flushed, her bonnet slightly askew. She opened up her parasol and he began the drive back to Lady Caroline's house.

'A little over the agreed time, young lady,' he said.

'Oh, the minutes flew so fast,' she said.

'And each one was sweet?' he enquired.

'Captain Burnside?'

'Your bonnet's a trifle out of place,' he said.

Annabelle's ready blush appeared, and she set her bonnet straight. 'I beg you won't think the worst of me,' she said.

'Oh, I dare say you teased him a little,' said Captain Burnside, easing the carriage into a stream of traffic, 'which is the way of any young lady set on provoking a gentleman into declaring himself. And if a few kisses were exchanged as well, so much the better. You'll have Cumberland ardent to husband you.'

'Mercy me,' breathed Annabelle, 'you are running ahead.'

'Well,' said the Captain pleasantly, 'I'm interested in this intriguing relationship you enjoy with Cumberland, and am set on helping you. Did you make desired progress?'

'I made up my mind,' said Annabelle; 'that is progress of a kind. And I am quite determined about it.'

'Excellent. Ah, determined about what?'

'About never yielding to him, except as his wife.'

Captain Burnside smiled. Was there ever a young lady more naive? 'Excellent,' he said again, refraining from mentioning that her flushed and ruffled look was hardly that of a female who had held Cumberland off. 'Count on my support and discretion, and regard me as your protector if you weaken.'

'Oh, but I am resolute, I surely am,' said Annabelle, enjoying the open look of this area west of the business city.

67

Favoured for its residential appeal by the rich, the famous and the aristocratic, it brought out carriages from frisky, spanking traps to stately coaches on a day like this, and created an atmosphere both colourful and exciting. 'I vow I can confide to you, Captain Burnside, that although the Duke is very ardent, I really don't wish to – wish to . . .'

'Yes, don't wish to, quite so, quite understood, Annabelle,' said Captain Burnside. 'But some young ladies do weaken, despite their resolution, and should be protected from themselves, especially a delightful young lady like you, the sister of Lady Caroline, whom I so admire.'

'You are so uplifting, Captain,' said Annabelle; 'and such a welcome confidante, although I don't think the Duke would actually . . .' She hesitated.

'Naturally,' said Captain Burnside with cheerful frankness, 'he wouldn't pull you into his bed unless you were within handy reach. Yet he might endeavour to carry you there from the doorstep of your own home if he were in the mood. He's a commanding prince, and you a quite ravishing creature.'

'No, no, you misjudge him,' said Annabelle, 'he would never be as outrageous as that.' But would he not? She wondered. He was of all things audacious. 'I have said his feelings for me are ardent, but no, not ungovernable.'

'Nevertheless, be on your guard, dear young lady. Have you arranged another tryst?'

'We are to meet and talk on Friday afternoon, if possible.'

'Talk? When the fires of love are burning, you expect merely to talk?' The Captain looked grave and shook his head. The parasol moved to hide Annabelle's rising pink from him.

'I expect us to speak about whether or not he might marry me. He has already said he finds the notion to his liking.'

Captain Burnside looked as if he were sighing at such innocence. 'Well, who can tell what such an independent son of the King might or might not do when his affections are so engaged?' he said. 'So, Friday afternoon? I shall take it upon myself to drive you, to keep it confidential and to ensure I stay close at hand, so that if you need to cry for help I shan't fail to hear you.'

'Mercy,' said Annabelle, 'I would not so misjudge the Duke as to imagine he would make it necessary for me to cry for help.'

Captain Burnside might have said that if a lamb entered the lair of a wolf often enough, she would eventually get eaten. But he only smiled and patted the lamb's arm.

Lady Caroline, returning from an outing of her own, found Annabelle at home and asked her if she had enjoyed her drive with Captain Burnside.

'Caroline, I declare him the kindest and most considerate gentleman,' said Annabelle. 'We drove around Hyde Park, where there was a colourful promenade of people, and such gay parasols, quite as gay as in Charleston, but the sun not so dreadfully hot or the heat so exhausting. Captain Burnside was much admired by passing ladies, for I saw them glancing and peeping. He owns a handsome posture when driving a pair and I vow him a pleasure to the eye.'

Ah, thought Caroline, the hireling has begun to impress Annabelle. 'Well, I do count him a friend of several years standing,' she said, 'and can depend on him to keep you reliable company, although I don't see him as much a pleasure to the eye as you do.'

'Oh, at your age I expect you are attracted to older and more mature men,' said Annabelle lightly. 'Such as Mr Simon Hetherington, whom I've seen sighing over you.'

Caroline almost bristled. 'Annabelle, you are absurd. Mr Hetherington must be nearly fifty. At my age indeed. I am only a little over four years older than you.'

'But you have a very mature outlook,' said Annabelle, 'although, for my part, I cannot think why you don't set your cap at Charles.'

'Charles?'

'Captain Burnside. I am sure you could never find a pleasanter or more companionable man.'

Caroline drew herelf up in high affront. 'I have no feelings of that kind for Captain Burnside,' she said.

Annabelle smiled reminiscently. 'He declares he has a reverence for you,' she said.

Caroline eyed her sister very coolly. 'A reverence?' She could not relate that to anything but a moment of impudence on the part of her hireling. 'Reverence?'

'Yes.' Annabelle laughed. 'He sees you as a goddess.'

'He has always had an odd sense of humour,' said Caroline.

'I thought him quite serious.'

'I do not seriously wish to be regarded as a goddess, but I'm at least happy you found him companionable. You haven't given too much time to other gentlemen since you met Cumberland, and it's a relief to find you and Captain Burnside have become friends. Where is he, by the way?'

'Oh, he went out after bringing me home.'

'Where has he gone to?'

'To attend to some business, he said, and begged to be excused lunch.'

Caroline hid her suspicion and displeasure.

# Chapter Seven

A white-capped maidservant came out of the handsome house near Horse Guards Parade, and floated in swaying skirts over the pavement. A gentleman, idly sauntering, stopped and turned abruptly as she came up behind him. He collided with her, although an onlooker might have thought she bumped into him. He showed instant contrition, raising his beaver top hat and expressing profuse apologies. 'Do forgive me.'

'Oh, I don't be hurt, sir,' she said, brown-eyed, pert and with an eye for personable gentlemen.

Captain Burnside smiled, and her lashes flickered coyly. 'You're very tolerant of my clumsiness,' he said. 'Are you sure I didn't bruise you?'

'Oh, no, sir, hardly at all.'

'Well, you're sweetly forgiving,' he said, and smiled again. 'Let me see, have I chanced on you before? Aren't you Felicity, the personal maid of Lady Spooner-Watts of Carlton Terrace?'

'No, sir, I be Betsy Walker, nor never heard of Lady Spooner-Watts, sir.'

'Good grief,' said the Captain. He noted the pertness of her glance, and decided he was in luck. 'I assure you, Betsy, you're so like Felicity you could be her twin. No, perhaps you ain't, for you're prettier.'

Betsy dropped her eyes demurely. She was not an innocent, and if this handsome gentleman was seeking a flirtation, she was very willing. Well set-up gentlemen were exciting, and gave a girl presents for loving kisses and loving squeezes. 'Sir, you be gammoning me,' she murmured.

'Indeed I'm not. You're all of pretty. Who's your mistress?'

'Mistress, sir?' she said, darting an arch glance.

'Your employer?'

'Oh, it be no lady, sir, but a stern and royal gentleman.'

Captain Burnside eyed the handsome house. 'Faith,' he said, 'not His Royal Highness, the Duke of Cumberland?'

'That be him, sir,' said Betsy, 'though I aren't encouraged to throw his name lightly about.'

'Very right and proper,' said the Captain, 'and very interesting.'

'Sir?'

'Are you on an errand, Betsy?'

'No, it be my free hour, sir.' Betsy, in no hurry to detach herself, added, 'I be taking a walk to the Parade.'

'To brighten the eyes of the soldiers, I'll wager.'

'Oh, I don't take up with common soldiers, sir.'

'Good. So come with me, Betsy.'

'But, sir, I doesn't know you,' she said.

'Fortunately, that don't signify in this case,' said Captain Burnside encouragingly. 'The fact is, I'm on Government business, and you are just the young lady who can help me in a confidential matter. I'll walk you to Collins Coffee House.'

'But that be all of a fancy place for a servant girl.'

'A private room there, that's the thing, where we can talk and I can find out how you can help me, and what it will be worth to you. Government business can be pleasantly rewarding.'

'Government business in a private room, sir?' said Betsy, who thought of such places in more exciting terms.

'Well, it can't be done in public, Betsy, any more than kissing should.'

Betsy strove to look shy and reluctant, but failed. A flirtatious smile peeped. 'Sir, you'll treat me right?' she said.

'Have no fears, Betsy,' said the Captain reassuringly. 'The business will be our paramount consideration and, as to anything else, I'll not ask for more than a single kiss, though you're pretty enough to be kissed all day, by heaven you are. Now, let's be on our way.'

Betsy went with him, thinking more about flirtatious dalliance than dull Government business, for he was such a fine gentleman. If it was to be much more of a kissing interlude than a business matter, the prospect did not alarm her. She was twenty-three and an amorous young lady, with hopes that one day a gentleman would set her up in a comfortable apartment and bestow on her the kind of presents she could turn into savings. However, after only a few minutes conversation with this particular gentleman in a private room of the coffee house, she had shed for the moment all thoughts of dalliance.

Brown eyes round with alarm, she gasped, 'Sir, it be prison for me if I really breathe a single word?'

'Alas, I'm afraid so,' said Captain Burnside. 'Having consented to give your help—'

'But I never did, sir.'

'Ah, but you consented to be taken into my confidence, and so became my accomplice.'

'What be an accomplice?' asked the bewildered Betsy.

'A partner, Betsy, a partner.' Captain Burnside nodded in grave agreement with himself. 'We must both avoid blabbing, for we don't either of us wish the Lord Chancellor to clap the darbies on us himself. Although I'm a Government man, I'm under an oath of secrecy, and if I broke it I'd have to take the consequences in the same way you would. However, your help will be rewarded. Did I mention that?'

'How much, sir?' asked Betsy, putting her qualms aside.

'Why, as much as ten guineas,' said the Captain.

'Ten guineas?' Her eyes grew bright. 'That be a year's wages, sir.'

'Then bring me into the house, as I've said, to where I can examine the Duke's official diary, and you'll have earned it. His secretary has charge of the diary, I fancy.'

Flustered, but with the promised ten guineas still a brightness in her eyes, Betsy said, 'Oh, sir, you'd not be

73

false to a poor girl, would you? You'd not be thinking of pocketing His Highness's snuff boxes?'

'Come, come, Betsy, do I look like a flash cove? You may stay while I examine the diary. Remember, as I said in the beginning, it all concerns the safety of His Royal Highness, although it's outside his cognisance. I wager you can do it; I don't doubt you're clever enough.'

'Sir, I be more quaking than clever. His Highness be a terrible stern gentleman.'

Captain Burnside smiled and patted her shoulder. 'An evening, Betsy, when you'll know he won't be there. Now, which evening would be suitable for you?'

Betsy thought and said, 'Thursday be very suitable, sir.'

'Capital!' Again he patted her shoulder. 'Betsy, I'll make no secret of the fact that mine ain't the easiest of commissions at times. It's a pleasure, therefore, on this occasion, to find an assistant who looks to be as adroit and clever as you.'

Certainly, she was too adroit to be disadvantaged by menservants who thought that, as a country girl from Sussex, she was a simpleton whose favours were theirs for the taking. Her preference was for gentlemen, for in some gentleman, some day, lay the possibility of a more pleasurable way of life than that of a maidservant. Of course, there were gentlemen and gentlemen. One could tell the right kind by the way they spoke to a girl, or by the way one's instinct reacted to them.

This gentleman spoke to her as if she had as much standing as a lady. Further, her instinct told her he would not do her down. Additionally, her eyes told her, from the fit of his clothes, that he had a perfect body.

However, she was still cautious. 'You be a strange gentleman, sir, taking me up in such a pleasant way and then saying I must do what you want or be sent to prison. That were the nastiest shock I were ever given.'

'Well, my pretty partridge, you're needlessly fluttering,' said Captain Burnside, 'for you may refuse to do anything you don't wish to. What you may not do is mention our conversation to anyone, anyone at all. On

74

that understanding and promise, I shall be the first to see that no prison gates close behind you.'

'Oh, I won't say a word, not one, sir – on the Bible I won't,' she breathed, and further thoughts of the ten guineas caused sensations of pleasure far above her fears. Such a sum was a little hoard in itself, to be placed with the silver crowns gentlemen had given her just for the pleasure of squeezing her bosom. 'You be sure it's all for the safety of the Duke, sir?'

'Quite sure, Betsy, but not to give him worry, d'you see. So on Thursday evening, then, I'll be waiting near the side entrance at nine o'clock. At any moment between nine and ten, when you're certain the coast is clear, let me in. There, you have an hour to choose the right moment. Could I be more considerate? Yes, perhaps I could. By advancing you one of the guineas now.'

'That be truly considering of me, sir,' said Betsy, and her eyes shone as he placed the golden coin in her hand. 'I'll let you in, even if my knees be knocking something cruel.' She eyed him demurely. He smiled. Quite charmed, she murmured, 'I be fair amazed about the business, sir, and no kissing.'

'Ah, kissing,' said the Captain. 'Well, although the Lord Chancellor ain't inclined to encourage kissing that might confound the serious matter of business, I'll stretch a point on this occasion, for I'd be a very dull fellow not to seal our partnership with a small kiss.'

'Oh, I hardly knows if I should, you being such a flummoxing gentleman,' said Betsy, but lifted her face and pursed her willing lips.

Captain Burnside, a professional, gave her the kiss she was happy to receive. It made her shiver with delight, it made her mouth eager and ardent, and it also made her feel what a very pleasing gentleman he was.

'There,' he said, 'now I'll walk you back.'

On the street again, she tripped along with him. Discreetly, he parted from her at a distance of a hundred yards from the Duke's residence. She understood.

'I be in a rare diddle-daddle of agitation, sir,' she said,

but she did not look so to the shrewd and satisfied eye of the Captain. She looked very pleased with herself.

'Courage, Betsy,' he said, 'it ain't a hanging matter, only a sweet partnership.'

'Oh, it be uncommon sweet, sir,' she said, and floated away, the golden guinea fast in her hand.

Captain Burnside made his way back to Lady Caroline's house, and presented himself to her in her drawing room. Annabelle was up in her bedroom, confiding her hopes and dreams to her diary.

Caroline said aloofly, 'I'm gratified, sir, that you've condescended to return. Where have you been?'

'On a matter of business, marm.'

'What business, pray?'

'Yours, marm.'

'Explain it, sir,' she said. He seated himself. 'You may sit down,' she added, cuttingly.

'Thank you, marm. It's advisable, don't you see, that I make myself at home. Well, marm, this is the way of it.' And he explained that he had taken up a watching brief close to Cumberland's house, with a view to finding an opportunity to subvert a member of the Duke's household.

'Subvert?' said Caroline.

'Ah . . . seduce,' said the Captain.

Caroline stiffened. 'Sir?' she said coldly. Her years with Lord Clarence had given her an utter detestation of all men who dealt in seduction.

'No, not of that significance, marm. I had in mind a maidservant whom I could seduce into using her eyes and ears for us. Should your sweet but gullible sister—'

'Annabelle is not gullible. Impressionable, yes, unfortunately so, but not gullible.'

'Sometimes, marm,' said the Captain gently, 'there's little difference. Now, should Annabelle allow herself to be lured to Cumberland's house, it would advantage us to have an accomplice there, someone who could arrange to send us a message as speedily as possible, for once inside the house Annabelle would be all too close to Cumberland's bed. I fancy, however, he would take his time to get her there. I

76

fancy he would wine her first and cosset her. That would give you the necessary time to descend on him and frustrate his devilish intentions. It's what I'd do myself with so young and lovely a girl as Annabelle, for there'd be a deal of sweetness in wining her and wooing her at leisure—'

'Stop!' she commanded. 'I vow, Captain Burnside, that you have more unlovely traits than Cumberland himself. I shudder at what I'm doing, conspiring with you to bring Annabelle out of Cumberland's arms into yours. How dare you entertain thoughts about what you yourself would do with my innocent sister? Listen to me. Should you accomplish this turnabout in her feelings, it is to be left at that. You are not to lay even a finger on her, do you hear?'

'Quite so, marm,' said Captain Burnside. 'Your concern for her welfare is no less than mine. Under your patronage I am devoting myself to the preservation of her innocence. And we're in luck, d'you see, for by good fortune I chanced upon a maidservant entirely right for our purpose – a pretty and likeable baggage with an eye for gain. She had an hour free of duty, so I took her to Collins Coffee House—'

'Collins? Where you could be seen with her by a score of eyes?'

'I ain't quite as bird-brained as that, marm. We took a private room off the private entrance, and there she came to compliance at gratifying speed.'

'Captain Burnside!' Caroline positively leapt to her feet, gown rustling, bosom arching and green eyes furious. 'Worse than your deliberate seduction of a simple servant girl is your detestable impudence in describing it to me. Have done with you, sir. Leave my house.'

'Gently, marm, gently,' said Captain Burnside. 'It was not, as I've said, a seduction of her body, but of her cupidity. An offer of ten guineas brought her promise of assistance. To be truthful, I don't play the romantic with maidservants. It ain't financially gainful. It's merchants' daughters and bankers' daughters who are profitable.'

'Profitable?' Caroline swished about, feet kicking at her skirts, arousing admiration in Captain Burnside. 'I have never known a more unconscionable rogue. If, sir, you meet

77

your deserved fate – transportation to a convict settlement – I declare I shall be glad to watch you hustled aboard. However, for ten guineas you have enlisted the aid of this servant girl?'

'I have, marm, and you may reimburse me at your convenience. It need not be immediately.'

'It will come to your hand, sir, only after much thought. Why did you not tell me what you were intending to do?'

'You were out when I brought your sister back from our drive,' said the Captain. 'Incidentally, marm, I have made a little progress with her. She has confessed she regards me as a dear and understanding friend.'

'God help my poor sister,' said Caroline, 'and may He forgive me for bringing such a man as you into her life.'

Those first days were not the easiest for Caroline. Enduring Captain Burnside as a guest was bad enough; pretending a liking for him as an old friend was worse. And watching his progress with her sister rattled her beyond anything. She felt no satisfaction at all in seeing how Annabelle began to show animation whenever she was in close company with him. True, he did not play his part in an oily way; rather, his approach was that of a friend entirely at his ease. Perhaps they were at their most intimate whenever they sat down at the piano together and played little duets. Then Caroline found herself gritting her teeth at the physical proximity this entailed. How wretched that this could not be avoided.

However, although Annabelle was taking obvious pleasure in his company, she did not look as if he had become vitally necessary to her happiness – which was a relief to Caroline on the one hand, and a frustration on the other.

'You are still quite comfortable.' It was a statement from the austerely clad Erzburger, not an enquiry.

'Comfortable as I ever was, Your Honour,' said the small, wiry Irishman, 'but could I draw Your Honour's kind attention to my health? Sure, it's meself that's ailing, so it is, and all for want of using my legs.'

'You have been using them, and expressly against our advice,' said Erzburger.

'So I have, Your Honour, in the house . . .'

'Outside the house,' said Erzburger reprovingly.

'Well, so I did, Your Honour, to taste the fresh air.'

'You were seen walking, Mr Maguire.'

'It's cruel hard on a man's legs not to let them go for a walk once in a while.'

'It could prove harder if your legs were discovered and you with them,' said Erzburger. 'The men you described have not yet been apprehended. If they have disappeared, Mr Maguire, it is probably because they were aware they had been overheard. Which means you are in the gravest danger, as His Royal Highness and I suspected. We must impress on you again: do nothing to draw attention to your presence here. Do not show yourself at the windows or venture into the street. If you do, we cannot guarantee your safety. It was fortunate that it was a friend of mine who saw you out this morning, and a credit to your good sense that you allowed him to persuade you to return.'

'Ah, the divil of a persuasive gintleman he was,' said Mr Maguire, and looked uneasy. 'Was it Your Honour's own friend?'

'It was. He lives close by, and while he knows nothing of the real reason why you are in danger, he has promised to keep your welfare close to his heart. I have told him you have enemies, and he will raise the alarm if he suspects they have entered the neighbourhood. I have also told him you are a loyal and worthy subject of His Majesty the King. Accept, therefore, that you have a sympathiser close by and do not give him further worry by showing yourself on the street again.'

'The divil I will,' said Mr Maguire, convinced now that he was indeed in danger. 'The kindly gintleman is three times my size, so he is, Your Honour.'

'Be sure, Mr Maguire, that your safety is our first concern,' said Erzburger, 'and that we shall look to it until the papists are in the hands of the law. The food I have brought you now should be enough for today and tomorrow, when I will see you again, as usual.'

'Thank you, Your Honour, and God keep His Royal Highness.'

# Chapter Eight

On the morning of Thursday, with the river outing arranged, Caroline spoke to Captain Burnside while they waited for Annabelle to come down. 'You are making haste too slowly, Captain Burnside.'

'Oh, we have Cumberland's IOU, marm, and his request for a return game. And we also have eyes in his camp.'

'Yes, we have all that,' said Caroline, 'but although Annabelle is showing interest in you, we do not have any lessening of her feelings for Cumberland. I put a plain question to her ten minutes ago, and was appalled by her answer, for she has now acquired an impossible notion that in order to possess her Cumberland will marry her.'

'Ah,' said Captain Burnside, 'and if he says he will, you suspect she'll believe him – and that in her infatuation she'll then yield?'

'Don't speak of it. Prevent it.'

'Time, marm, that's the thing. Give the sweet girl enough time and she'll come to see Cumberland as a ruination, not a husband, and by then she'll be seeing me as a far worthier candidate for her affections.'

'I could wish she might see what was true, sir, that you are as much of a ruination as Cumberland, but that would not do if she were still blind to his tricks. As for time, I hope you aren't contriving to engage in a marathon, for I vow I should find it all of unendurable to house you here indefinitely.'

'Be in good heart, marm, it won't take as long as that,' said the Captain cheerfully.

'Your deeds, sir, have not yet quite matched your words,' said Caroline, and wondered, not for the first time, if her scheme was a sheer absurdity and Captain Burnside the most ridiculous part of it.

Both sisters were in summery, patterned muslin, and each wore a white bonnet. Annabelle looked young and extremely pretty. Caroline looked superb. The sunny day was an embracing warmth. Captain Burnside, handsome in a dark brown coat and light brown breeches, beaver hat jauntily set on his head, drove the carriage. He handled the pair in the fashion of a man whose main consideration was for his passengers, and the jolts sustained over the rougher roads were of the gentlest.

Arriving at Richmond a little before noon, he hired a cushioned punt, and with the sisters comfortably ensconced and the picnic hamper safely stowed, he doffed his coat and hat, took up the pole and set off up river. His application was smooth and easy, and the punt glided over the smooth waters of the sun-dappled Thames. On either side, the green banks and riverside gardens were a pleasure to the eye, although Annabelle, with her virginal interest in men, found Captain Burnside even more of a pleasure to behold. In his cream-coloured waistcoat, casually-folded cravat and tight breeches, his slenderness was of a sinewy kind, his looks commendably personable.

Reclining beside her sister, their parasols up, she murmured, 'Caroline, I do declare your friend, Captain Burnside, very pleasing and versatile.'

'Captain Burnside, I'm sure, is happy to hear you say so,' said Caroline.

'Flattered, on my honour I am,' said the Captain. 'I confess, of course, to lacking the high majesty of a man like the Duke of Cumberland, but there are few men who can compare with him.'

Caroline frowned.

Annabelle looked as if she would like to hear more. 'One must agree the Duke carries himself like a man born to be a monarch,' she said.

'He won't be monarch of this country, I fervently hope,' said Caroline.

'His four elder brothers stand between him and the throne,' said Captain Burnside, plying the pole lazily. The light rippled over its wet length, and that same light enriched the colours of the sisters' gowns. Caroline's ankles peeped in their white silk hose, and the warm river breeze stirred the hems of her gown and underskirt.

'Since none of his brothers has a son,' she said, 'one must pray he doesn't outlive them, for I could not bear England to have Cumberland for King.'

'You are very hard on him,' said Annabelle, 'and surely he would make a better monarch than the present one, whose obstinacy was the cause of such a bitter quarrel between England and the American colonies.'

'Cumberland would have been no less distant and haughty,' said Caroline, 'but today is really too beautiful for us to examine our differences. Instead, let us enjoy the tranquility of this peaceful Thames, down which Captain Burnside is rowing us.'

'Up,' said the Captain.

'Up?' said Caroline.

'We're proceeding up-river, my dear Caroline, and – ah – we're punting, not boating.'

Caroline's parasol shifted a little to uncover her eyes, which held their cool look. 'A punt is a boat, Captain Burnside,' she said.

'Well, not precisely, d'you see,' he said from high above her, 'and this is a pole, not an oar.'

'A pole or an oar, what an absurd basis on which to build an argument,' said Caroline.

Captain Burnside smiled and took the punt leisurely on. Annabelle, languorous, dreamed of becoming wholly irresistible to the magnetic Cumberland. With riverside mansions and green lawns gliding by, Caroline found herself in unexpected enjoyment of the outing. She had not wanted to come, for there was no pleasure to be had from the artificiality of her relationship with Captain Burnside. Further, without her there, he could have been making unhindered progress with Annabelle. Not that she cared to think too much about what unhindered progress meant, especially as it was not too difficult to picture how an unprincipled rake like her hireling would go about it. They would be moored beneath the shade of an overhanging willow, the profuse green fronds hiding them, Annabelle reclining and the blackguard reclining with her; Annabelle, fresh and eager, too dazzled by London society and its sophisticated men for her own good, her gown far too revealing, her bosom far too defenceless, and Captain Burnside all too despicably accomplished in the art of reducing a young lady to weakness.

Caroline quivered at her imaginings, and her own gown, with its low bodice, seemed far too revealing then. Her breasts tautened sensitively. She had not known a man's caress for years, not since she had refused to be a wife to Clarence and locked him out of her bedroom.

She could have withdrawn from this outing and accepted an invitation to lunch with Lady Wingrove and her son Gerald Wingrove. Mr Wingrove was a man of fine looks and sterling character, the kind of gentleman she favoured. He was lately an admirer, and made no secret of the fact that he would like to become a suitor. She was still wary of all suitors, but Mr Wingrove could not be said to be objectionable in any way. She might have been in pleasant and civilised conversation with him now instead of being in this punt, with Captain Burnside looming above her and Annabelle, eyes sometimes on the river ahead and sometimes on their escort. In her sudden excess of sensitivity, Caroline tilted her parasol so that it hid her from him. His eyes could be very impudent.

Yet, because the day was so lovely, the river so tranquil, she did not feel certain that she would rather have been at Lady Wingrove's. Her temporary dislike of the moment slipped away and she relaxed, listening almost dreamily to Annabelle lightly conversing with the Captain. Annabelle always had a fund of appealing chatter, and the Captain had the facile tongue of his kind. She heard Annabelle laugh. Did she find him amusing?

What had he said? It did not matter. He was playing his part in making himself appealing to her sister.

Captain Burnside brought the punt into an inlet, where huge willows hung over the water and a grassy bank beckoned. A protruding notice board advised that the land beyond the bank was private property.

'Should we picnic here?' asked Caroline.

'A capital suggestion,' said Captain Burnside.

'It's private property,' she said.

'A guarantee that we shan't be disturbed by Tom, Dick and Harry,' said the Captain. He edged the punt gently against a little timber landing stage and moored it.

Caroline saw an inviting expanse of grass that was patterned by sunlight and shade. 'How charming,' she said.

'How romantic,' said Annabelle.

'It seems uncrowded,' said Captain Burnside.

'We shall trespass only lightly,' said Annabelle.

'Should we trespass at all?' said Caroline, who sometimes suffered a small army of poachers on her Sussex estate.

'Perhaps not,' said Captain Burnside, wishful to play a faultless role as a gentleman.

'But it is so perfect for a picnic,' said Annabelle.

'Well, we shall do no harm,' said Caroline.

Captain Burnside gave each lady a hand on to the landing stage. Caroline's clasp was very light, and she freed her fingers the moment her feet were secure. Annabelle's hand lingered a little in his, and her smile let him know she was delighted with his choice of a picnic spot. Caroline did not miss the lingering of the handclasp. She was not displeased, but neither was she glad. She was suffering paradoxical reactions, probably because she suspected that if Captain Burnside did win her sister's affections, he was quite capable of pleasuring himself. Annabelle, wilful though she was, was also very sweet.

Captain Burnside lifted out the large hamper.

Caroline, deciding she must put aside her qualms and give the rogue every opportunity to exercise his talents, said, 'If Annabelle will help you set out the picnic, I shall take a little stroll, for I declare we have found ourselves a meadow of buttercups.'

'Oh, I'm sure Charles and I will set it out to perfection,' said Annabelle. 'He is so capable, and I am not actually helpless without servants around. Together, we shall lay a very inviting picnic cloth, shall we not, Charles?'

'Heaven help my part in it if we don't,' said Captain Burnside, 'for I recollect your sister can be very exacting.'

'In some matters, yes, Captain Burnside,' said Caroline. 'In other matters, I am an angel in my tolerance.' And she strolled away under her parasol, her summery gown a fluttering lightness that made her look as if she were floating into the embrace of the warm, amorous sun.

Annabelle opened the hamper and extracted the large, white picnic tablecloth with lead weights sown into its hem to prevent summer breezes lifting it. Captain Burnside spread it out over the grass. Annabelle, unloading neatly packed items, returned compulsively to the subject of the Duke of Cumberland, insisting that although he could be very audacious he was really very much maligned. Naturally, as a royal Duke, he was formidably aristocratic, but that gave him a majesty which suited him. Alas, however, such majesty was apt to make her feel weak when she needed to be strong.

'So you have said before, young lady,' said Captain Burnside.

'It surely is a sweet blessing to have your sympathy and support,' said Annabelle, 'and to confide my weakness to you.'

'Ah,' said the Captain, receiving plates from her, 'we all suffer far more from our weaknesses than our strengths. Young ladies can suffer excessively. However, miserable consequences can be avoided when a young lady is as determined as you are not to yield. And, of course, as a young lady adorably American, you'd never yield unconditionally to a son of King George, who made himself so unpopular with all of you.'

'Oh, not to *all* of us,' said Annabelle, liking the fact that Captain Burnside was a pleasure to talk to. 'My parents will tell you that many colonists did not want the war, but were forced into supporting it, on pain of being brutalised. My family and many relatives are proud of our kinship with you, and I vow I am acquiring much affection for England.'

'Well, I'm sure Cumberland ain't the only one acquiring much affection for *you*,' smiled the Captain, and Annabelle, on her knees beside the picnic cloth, raised delighted blue eyes to him.

'I do declare you the sweetest man,' she said.

'Oh, there's a deal of water to flow under the bridge yet,' he said, and returned to the punt to fetch the cushions.

Annabelle finished setting out the picnic. Caroline came back at a graceful, leisurely saunter, looking not unlike a Georgian Diana in her lightly gowned magnificence. Captain Burnside set the cushions down, and with a murmur of thanks Caroline closed her parasol and sank billowingly on to one.

Beneath the shade of a tree, Annabelle regarded her sister with a smile. 'Caroline is very queenly, don't you think so, Charles?' she said, her round eyes a perfectly innocent blue.

'An acquired queenliness,' said the Captain, accepting a chicken leg from Annabelle, 'for I recollect that when she was younger—'

'You recollect nothing of the kind,' said Caroline, examining lamb's tongue in aspic.

'Nothing of what kind?' asked Annabelle, glancing from one to the other of them.

'Of whatever kind Captain Burnside was going to say,' murmured Caroline, deciding the tongue was irresistible.

'And what were you going to say, Charles?' asked Annabelle.

'The subject is closed,' said Caroline.

'But, sister dear,' said Annabelle, 'it has hardly begun.'

'I was going to say,' murmured Captain Burnside, 'that

when Caroline first came to my eyes as the young fancy of Lord Percival—'

'Fiddle-faddle,' said Caroline.

'Caroline, do let him speak,' said Annabelle, spooning creamed mussels from a jar. 'I'm all agog to hear what were his first impressions of you.'

'It's so long ago, of course,' said the Captain, 'that those first impressions are hazy.'

'Wretched man,' said Caroline, green eyes glinting and her fixed smile false, 'it's only a few years.'

'I can, however, recollect a shy smile, a faint blush and a gown of pink organdie,' said Captain Burnside, and began to enjoy his chicken leg.

Annabelle shrieked with laughter.

Caroline's smile became even more fixed. 'Your recollection is more imaginative than true,' she said.

'Well, perhaps the organdie may have been blue,' observed the Captain, credibly reminiscent.

'But, Charles, a shy smile and a faint blush?' laughed Annabelle. 'Had you caught her tying a garter, then?'

'Alas, no,' said the Captain, 'Lady Caroline was ever the most modest of ladies. Ah, shall I pour the wine?' He took the bottle from its chilled container, removed the cork and filled the crystal glasses. Caroline received hers with a glitter in her eyes, and a look that told him to expect the more cutting edge of her tongue before the day was out.

They picnicked on a variety of good things, and the dry white wine was a perfect accompaniment. Captain Burnside favoured Annabelle as far as his pleasantries were concerned, but his attentiveness was by no means too unctuous or too obvious. That Annabelle enjoyed his conversation was plain to see.

The warm air caressed the sisters and the sunlight that came shafting through the branches of the tree dappled their summer gowns. Caroline looked handsomely beautiful, Annabelle young and fresh and pretty. Captain Burnside, his hat and coat cast off, seemed informally at ease.

The picnic over, they tidied up, and Caroline remarked how refreshing it was not to have servants fussing around.

'Oh, we have Charles,' said Annabelle, 'and he is very refreshing.'

When the hamper had been re-packed, Captain Burnside placed it back in the moored punt, then sat on the edge of the bank, legs dangling, eyes musing on the water. Annabelle joined him.

After a moment's hesitation, Caroline walked over to them, and she too lowered herself to sit on the bank. 'How peaceful,' she said.

'Hello, hello, what's all this 'ere, then? Trespassers, is it?'

They turned their heads at the sound of the rasping voice. Behind them stood three men. They were all dressed in brown coats, brown breeches and hard brown hats. The middle man was tall and burly, a stick of thick ash in his hand. The other two men were thin and wiry. They all looked aggressive, and each had the slightly bloodshot eyes of men slightly the worse for their midday drink.

'Who are you?' asked Captain Burnside mildly.

'Never you mind.' The burly man was patently offended by their presence. 'Who are you, that's more like, and who's yer wenches?' He poked his stick first at Annabelle, then at Caroline. 'There's a notice, plumb out there for reading, hobserving and digesting. No landing nor fishing, no loitering nor sitting.'

'Unfortunately,' said Captain Burnside, 'we passed it by.'

'Oh, yer did, did yer?' said the burly one. 'Well, up yer get and off yer go, and lively, or yer'll get pitched into that there river and yer wenches'll come tumbling after.'

'Upon my soul,' said Captain Burnside, 'have you no manners?'

'Eh, what's that?' demanded the offended gentleman.

'Stow yer gab, mister,' said one of the other men, his voice thick, 'or Jonas'll top yer with his nob-smasher.'

'That he will,' said the third man. 'Did yer hear him, Jonas, did yer hear him ask about yer manners?'

'I heard him,' said Jonas, the burly one, 'which don't himprove his prospects nohow. So, me fancy cove, up yer get, like I said afore but ain't a-saying again, and off yer go.'

'Kindly remove yourself,' said Caroline icily, 'and take your drunken friends with you.'

'Well,' gasped the second man, 'if that don't beat all the king's 'orses and all his other capers too. What imperence. Did yer hear her, Jonas?'

'I heard,' growled Jonas. 'You take her, Willum, and you take t'other 'un, Jake, while I sees to 'is lordship 'ere. Yes, you.' He prodded Captain Burnside with his stick. 'Up yer get, and smart. I'm going to chuck yer in, then pull yer out, then take yer, with yer wenches, to Mr Meredith, what's a gent who'll clap yer in his stocks for yer trespass. Now then, me cove.' He rapped Captain Burnside heavily on the shoulder. The other men, darting, seized the sisters. One took Caroline by her left wrist and pulled her to her feet. Caroline flashed her right hand and smacked his face, hard. Annabelle, hauled bruisingly to her feet by the other man, gave a little outraged shriek and kicked him.

Captain Burnside, on his feet, took the man by the shoulder and wrenched him round. The burly Jonas intervened and smote with his stick. It caught Captain Burnside a glancing blow on the side of his head. He fell. Caroline's assailant, incensed by her slapping of his face, threw her unceremoniously to the ground. Annabelle, treated no less brutally, staggered and fell over her sister. She screamed. Captain Burnside, hurt by the blow from the stick, but by no means incapacitated, rolled aside as Jonas struck again. The stick bruised the turf. Again it was raised to strike. Again it descended. Too late. Arms like steel wrapped themselves around the burly man's legs and heaved. Upended, he crashed like a falling caber, big and heavy. His bellow of rage was cut short as the fall took his breath from him.

Captain Burnside, upright, saw Annabelle and Caroline on the ground, struggling and kicking, the louts trying to pin them. Gowns and underskirts were billowing, lacy pantaloons gossamer-like in the sun, bonnets off and hair dishevelled. Annabelle was yelling, but Caroline was in a silent fury, her teeth clenched and her nails scratching.

The Captain wrenched the stick from the dazed Jonas. He used it mercilessly, striking off the hard hats of the bruising louts and then smiting their unprotected heads. The blows brought gasps and shudders. The two men rolled over. The metal-capped end of the stick thrust hard into one man's stomach. He emitted a gasping yell. A hand seized his collar, jerked him to his feet and sent him whirling. He fell, sprawling over the still winded Jonas. Captain Burnside dealt with the other oaf as the man came to his feet. His left fist shot straight out and took the man in his eye. He plummeted backwards. Annabelle and Caroline watched, eyes wide open, bosoms heaving.

Captain Burnside used his foot to shift aside the man who had fallen on Jonas. And Jonas gazed up into a face fierce and cold. His colleague rolled over, came up on his knees and shot to his feet, expression livid. He threw himself at Captain Burnside. The Captain sidestepped, thrust out a foot, tripped the man and accelerated his further fall with a blow to the back of his neck.

Jonas scrambled, came up, flexed his muscles and advanced. 'Yer'll get yer liver cut out for this, yer'll get transportation,' he wheezed, 'but first yer'll get this.'

He swung his fist at the Captain's jaw in a tremendous round-arm blow. Annabelle gasped, the Captain ducked, the fist travelled over his head, and he delivered a blow on his own account, an uppercut that took Jonas clean under his chin. His head snapped back and the turf shuddered as he hit it.

He looked at the blue sky, and the blue sky seemed red. A face appeared, a cold face. The stick prodded his chest.

'Get up,' said Captain Burnside, 'and get your ruffians on their feet.'

'Oh, yer've got a bad time coming,' wheezed Jonas, 'you and yer wenches, that you 'ave.'

Captain Burnside applied the toe of his boot to the man's ribs. 'Get up,' he said again, and Caroline could not believe that her smooth-tongued hireling could look so icy and menacing. He was rigid with controlled fury.

Jonas shook his dizzy head and climbed ponderously to his feet. His colleagues came totteringly upright, one man with a hand clasped over his damaged eye and emitting groans.

'You, and you.' Captain Burnside gestured with the stick. 'Line up, all of you.'

They lined up, Jonas drawing in air and watching the stick.

'Blinded me, that's what he's done, blinded me,' said the damaged man.

Captain Burnside cast a glance at the sisters. They were dishevelled, but on their feet.

Jonas made a rush, and his arms lunged. The stick struck his left arm. He roared with pain.

'Oh, yer son of Satan, yer've nigh on broke it,' he bellowed.

'Turn round, all of you,' said Captain Burnside.

They turned, presenting their backs to him. He used the stick again. He struck the buttocks of each man. The man called Jake whipped round in fury, and aimed a savage kick at the Captain's middle. It struck only empty air. A hand took him by the collar, and he was literally run over the grass and pitched into the water. He hit it with a frightened scream and disappeared. He came up choking and panic-stricken.

'Oh, yer lordship – for God's sake – I can't swim . . .'

Captain Burnside, from the bank, watched the miserable fellow kicking, struggling and splashing. Jonas and his companion stared numbly. The frightened man sank again amid a frenzy of thrashing limbs.

'Captain Burnside!' Caroline, gown hitched, came running. 'Captain Burnside, you can't! I implore you, bring him out!'

The man's head reappeared, and he spat out choking water. Captain Burnside leapt on to the landing stage, leaned and held out the stick. The drowning man took desperate hold of it, and the Captain drew him to safety.

91

He scrambled up, his soaked garments plastering his body.

'Go,' said Captain Burnside. 'Go. All of you.'

They went, all of them, mouthing in fury. Caroline and Annabelle watched their figures stumping angrily over the meadow. Annabelle, white and shaken, flung her arms around the Captain. Caroline stared at her sister, and bit her lip.

'Captain Burnside,' gasped Annabelle, 'oh, mercy me, those dreadful men!'

He patted her shoulder. 'Not the friendliest people one expects to meet in so idyllic a spot,' he said.

'Oh, I surely thought that together they would batter you senseless.'

'Ah, well, we divided them and so they fell, and I fancy they're more bruised than we are.' He patted her shoulder again. Annabelle, distressed, clung tighter, liking the feel of his body, reassuringly firm and strong, his warm chest a comfort to her bosom.

Caroline regarded the embrace uncertainly. She supposed nothing could have impressed Annabelle more than Captain Burnside's rout of the tipsy oafs. But she was not sure she liked the way her sister was clinging to him. And she certainly did not like the way he was caressingly comforting Annabelle.

'Captain Burnside,' she said, 'is my sister in a swoon?'

'Faith, I hope not,' he said, 'for I don't precisely shine when it comes to doctoring swooning ladies.'

Annabelle detached herself. Reluctantly, thought Caroline. And, heavens, her bodice. The visibility of her bosom. Catching her sister's eye, Annabelle pinked, turned aside and made the necessary adjustment. The accident of exposure had, of course, been facilitated by the lowness of the bodice. For months now, Caroline had recognised in her sister all the symptoms of a girl dangerously infatuated, buying gowns far too revealing in her desire to bring her figure to the attention of Cumberland. Caroline knew herself to have been similarly disposed during those days when her own infatuation made her crave Clarence's attention.

She bit her lip. Captain Burnside, retrieving fallen bonnets, expressed the hope that she had escaped serious hurt.

'I am not hurt at all, thank you. But did you intend to let that man drown?'

'Oh, the well-being of men who brutalise women don't concern me too much,' he said.

'Heavens,' breathed Caroline, 'you would have watched him drown?'

'Not with ladies present. Far too harrowing for them. I felt it was enough to scare him to death before fishing him out.'

For his ears alone, as she accepted her bonnet from him, Caroline murmured, 'You feel, sir, that brutalising ladies is less forgivable than deceiving them?'

Before he could answer, Annabelle called, 'Do you think that is Mr Meredith himself?'

They turned. In the middle of the meadow the three men were talking to a large, heavy-looking gentleman, and gesticulating as if very angry and offended. The large gentleman suddenly exploded. Brandishing a stick, he strode towards the river bank like a man bent on furious confrontation.

'That, I fancy, is almost certainly Mr Meredith,' said the Captain, 'and he don't look too sociable. To the punt, ladies.' He escorted them in wise haste to the landing stage. He stepped aboard the punt, and brought the sisters carefully into it. He untied the rope, took up the pole and pushed off. The punt began to drift. 'A most enjoyable picnic, but I don't think we should stay to see what Mr Meredith means to offer us in the way of post-prandial pastimes.'

Annabelle, recovered, gurgled with laughter. Caroline smiled. The pole dipped, found purchase, and the punt surged forward as the large gentleman, in a brown coat, buckskin breeches and beaver hat, arrived on the river bank.

He shook his stick furiously at them. 'Damn your eyes, sir, come back!' he shouted. 'I'll have your damned head for battery, assault and trespass! Come back, y'scoundrel, d'you hear?'

'Gently, sir,' said Captain Burnside, 'there are ladies present.'

'Be damned to their petticoats, and be damned to you too for hiding behind 'em!' roared the red-faced landowner. His stick executed a violent dance in the air. The punt surged on. 'Come back, you fly-blown blackguard, and take a flogging.'

'Mercy me,' cried Annabelle indignantly, 'our gentleman friend will do no such thing, sir. It is your men who should be flogged, not he.'

'Hold your tongue, damned wench! Come back, you gipsy scoundrel!'

'Must point out, sir,' called the Captain, 'that though you're better dressed than your servants, up to a point, you've no more manners than they have. Beg to give you good day, sir.' And he sent the punt skimming out of earshot, ensuring livid curses went unheard by the ladies.

'Oh, how cool and capable you are, Charles,' said Annabelle, settling back on the cushions beside her sister. 'Caroline, I vow we might have been murdered if Charles had not been so sternly brave on our behalf.'

'Or if he had not landed us on forbidden ground in the first place,' said Caroline.

'True,' said the Captain, poling fluently. 'Beg you'll overlook it.'

'But, Caroline,' protested Annabelle, 'how can you rebuke him when he has just saved us from those dreadful bullies? You all are very unkind to an old friend.'

'Oh, Captain Burnside and I understand each other, I think,' said Caroline, a sun-splashed figure in graceful repose, 'but I declare myself very happy that he was able to prove himself an officer and a gentleman.'

'Who would ask him to prove that?' said Annabelle. 'Not I.'

'Upon my soul, such faith in a man is decidedly uplifting,' said Captain Burnside cheerfully, and the punt glided smoothly on its way back to Richmond.

# Chapter Nine

Arriving back home with Annabelle and the Captain, Caroline declared herself in need of some refreshing tea. Annabelle declared a similar need, and the Captain declared himself willing to join them.

They partook of it in the drawing room, Captain Burnside so much at his ease that Caroline thought him far more at home with its graciousness than he had any right to be. She was beginning to despise herself for what she was doing, and could not put aside the feeling that she should pay her hireling off and have done with him. But no, she could not do that. She must at least retain his services in respect of the acquisition of the letter that was driving her dear friend, Lady Hester Russell, to despair and distraction. He must procure it from Cumberland. Concerning Annabelle, there was still a strong aversion to seeing her in Captain Burnside's deceitful arms. She could not bear to think of further embraces, all contrived by the blackguard. It was an unlovely thing to have hired him for the purpose of being falsely sweet to her sister. If Annabelle did not deserve to become a mere plaything to Cumberland, no more did she deserve to become a victim of deception. Yet if she were left to the mercy of Cumberland, the consequences could be disastrous. Captain Burnside still represented the better alternative, providing he kept his word to disappear from Annabelle's life the moment she transferred her affections to him. And from the glances and the smiles she gave him, her interest did seem to have taken a positive turn.

Caroline's secretary, William Anders, knocked and

entered when the teapot was empty. Quietly, he advised her that Lady Hester Russell had called and wished to see her. Privately.

'Oh, yes. Very well, William.' Caroline excused herself and received Hester upstairs, in her suite.

Lady Hester Russell, in her early twenties, was a vivid brunette, richly favoured in her looks and figure. And since she was also a warm and affectionate person, she was a sweet wifely pleasure to her husband, Sir George Russell. At this moment, however, she was a woman in distress. Her yellow satin day gown itself seemed beset by quivers. Not long since it had been forced to desert her body. Cumberland had been responsible, and she had come shame-faced from her rendezvous with him to seek comfort and hope from Caroline.

She had received the usual kind of command from him two days earlier, and this afternoon had reluctantly and despairingly presented her veiled self to him. In his bedroom, spacious but austere, as befitted a man who despised decorative fripperies, she showed an unhappy face and pleading eyes as he removed the veil that had given her anonymity. She was a reluctant mistress to him, and so she had an appeal that compliant mistresses did not.

'Cumberland, I cannot continue like this,' she whispered. She was the victim of a brief period of madness. Ravished in a country house while her husband lay with his senses and the pain of his broken leg dulled by laudunum, she had incredibly conceived infatuation of a shamelessly physical kind for the Duke. It did not last long, but at its height she had written him a love letter insanely foolish in its passion. It was that letter he used to keep command of her favours. Whenever he called, she had to go to him. 'Cumberland, today must be the last time, for my dearest George will surely find me out if you do not show me mercy.'

Cumberland's eye quizzed her flushed face, her pleading look. 'Come,' he said, 'nobler and prouder husbands than George have found out wives just as sweet as ye without ruining the marriage. It ain't civilised to raise a roof when it's only a matter of a little indiscretion.'

'But it will ruin his love for me,' she breathed.

'Will it so? Ye're overlooking the other consideration, my rosebud. When a man discovers his wife has the love of royalty, he also discovers she is thereby newly desirable.'

'No, George will never be a complaisant cuckold, never. Cumberland, I beg you, give me the letter.'

'It's a sweet letter,' said Cumberland reflectively, 'a treasure of its kind. Am I to part with it, and with ye too? However, ye've been a delicious pleasure, and I'll concede I should at least think about it.'

'You have said that before, and nothing has come of it,' cried Hester.

'Well, I'm uncommonly attached to ye,' said Cumberland. 'Come, waste no more time, for ye have me in impatience. I don't suffer my own impatience too gladly, ye know that.'

She did know it. He was capable, in a moment of temper, of doing that which would devastate George and the marriage. She shivered and clenched her teeth as he turned her and unbuttoned her gown. It slid whisperingly to her feet, and her short silk shift dropped to her waist. His arms came around her from behind, and his hands gently, devilishly, caressed her. Once she had been responsive to his touch. Now it only shamed her.

In bed with him a little later, she burned and shivered, and afterwards the tears spilled. He regarded them mockingly.

'How so, when ye were sweetly passionate?' he said.

'That is what shames me so,' she gasped.

Because of this she rushed to confide in Caroline, to entreat again her help. And Caroline, coldly furious with Cumberland and his carnality, assured Hester that she had taken steps to give the necessary help, that she would accelerate progress.

'I vow I shall, Hester, although I cannot tell you the details. There, dry your eyes, or George will discover every mark of your tears.'

'It is so much worse than you can imagine,' wept Hester, 'for though I swear I hate Cumberland and his bed, he contrives to arouse in me the shamelessness of the bawdiest doxy.'

'The weakness of our flesh is very traitorous,' sighed Caroline, but could not imagine herself anything but fiercely resistant in the arms of any man whom she despised. Which brought her to think of Captain Burnside and the disgust she would feel if she were subjected by him to mere kisses alone.

'Caroline,' whispered Hester, 'if the letter is not soon retrieved, I will kill either Cumberland or myself.'

'Don't say such things, dearest Hester. Cumberland will give it up soon enough, I promise.'

Downstairs, Annabelle was being sweet to Captain Burnside before going up to her room to take a bath. 'Such an exciting day,' she said, 'and although Caroline has been quite cool about your bravery, I cannot myself be less than grateful.' She laughed. 'I am more human than a goddess, and must show you.' She came up on tiptoe, lifted her face and kissed him on the mouth. There was unreserved warmth in the kiss she bestowed, and he realised then that her sister was right to be in concern for her. She was in danger as much from her own self as from Cumberland. She was brimming with health and headiness, her body perceptibly excited. He guessed she had recently discovered the pleasure of kissing a man not modestly, but with sweet ardour. 'There,' she murmured, 'that is to thank you for saving us from brutality. Will you scold me for being as grateful as that?'

'Oh, a grateful kiss is very allowable, young lady,' he said. 'But be careful of kisses of another kind.'

'Another kind?' The telltale pink coloured her cheeks. 'Do you mean kisses from Cumberland?'

'I mean that before she's kissed by a would-be lover, a resolute girl should determine his intentions, whether they embrace marriage or merely pleasure.'

'To be sure, intentions are everything,' said Annabelle, 'but Cumberland is an exciting man, is he not?'

'To you, yes,' said the Captain.

'However, because of your support and advice, I am of all things resolute,' declared Annabelle, 'and shall stand up to the Duke very resolutely tomorrow. And how inspiring it is to know you can stand up to Caroline. Of course—' Annabelle became demure. 'Of course, she will never think anything of a man who can't.'

'Is it important she should?'

Annabelle became more demure. 'It is to you, Charles, isn't it?' she said. 'You are in love with her, aren't you? When you returned to England with your regiment and heard she was a widow, you could not resist coming to see her, could you?'

'Those questions are all rhetorical?' said the Captain.

'Oh, I vow you are just the man to sweeten my grand sister,' smiled Annabelle. 'Caroline used not to be at all grand. At least, never as much as she is now. But she did not enjoy a very happy marriage, and put on a proud face to hide its failure. That is what her friends have whispered to me. Sometimes she's as haughty as a duchess, don't you think so?'

'I try, young lady, only to think of her with respect.'

'Oh, fiddle-de-dee, you don't,' laughed Annabelle. 'How exciting you were when you were dealing with those brutes by the river. Yes, you are just the man for Caroline, and will make up for all her unhappiness.'

'Your sister, I fancy, will declare herself roundly opposed to that,' said the Captain.

'Captain Burnside.' Caroline made a statement of his name as she entered the drawing room prior to supper. He had just come down himself, as well-dressed as ever, his cream cravat a model of unostentatious comfort. Some men wore cravats so high and in such complicated folds that they were compelled to keep their chins permanently elevated for fear of disturbing the careful arrangement.

Caroline, in a satin gown of deep, shimmering crimson, looked bewitchingly splendid.

'Marm?' said Captain Burnside, deferential to his patron.

'I must ask you – no, I must beg you – to procure that letter from Cumberland immediately.'

'Immediately?'

'By the weekend,' said Caroline firmly. 'On Friday evening, therefore, when you will be contesting with him at the card table, please use every trick of skill and deception to burden him so with debt that he will be only too glad to give up the letter in return for the IOUs. Otherwise, the matter in question may take a tragic turn. I may count on you to achieve what is necessary?'

'You may, marm, if luck is with us.'

'No, I cannot afford to rely on luck, sir.'

'Very well, marm, I'll ensure Cumberland is tricked into losing a fortune.'

'I believe you, Captain Burnside,' she said. 'I have great faith in your talents as a trickster, which I am sure you will be able to apply as skilfully as you are at present applying yourself to the affections of my sister. One could positively admire your gifts, if they were commendable, which they aren't. I cannot dispute Annabelle is showing more interest in you than she has in other men, except Cumberland, and if you do save her from him I shall not be ungrateful, although I must tell you, sir, it gave me no pleasure to see her in your arms today.'

'Quite understood, marm, pray don't distress yourself.'

'I am not distressed, sir. I have qualms. However, if you can procure that letter by the weekend, then I shall try not to speak as many hard words to you as I do. And I must at least thank you for sending those brutes packing today.'

'A small service, marm. And I shall always recollect with admiration the fearsome right-hander you delivered to one of them.'

Just for a brief moment, there was a reminiscent gleam in her green eyes, much as if the memory of the blow she had struck was very self-satisfying. Then she said, 'It is not something I wish to remember myself.'

Annabelle entered, gowned in pale blue, her pearly bosom lightly powdered, her hair a crown of fair ringlets. 'Charles, why, how handsome you look,' she said.

The Captain took her extended hand and raised it to his lips. 'I fancy I ain't as pretty as you, Annabelle,' he said, and she laughed and fluttered her fan at him, giving Caroline the impression that her affections were positively engaged. The supper gong sounded.

Conscious of no real satisfaction, Caroline said, 'Shall we go in? And perhaps after supper we might play whist, for Mr Gerald Wingrove will be joining us to make four.'

'Alas, do forive me,' said Captain Burnside, 'but I have to go out this evening. Ah, on business. Concerning a suitable apartment, d'you see.'

'A suitable apartment?' said Caroline, having forgotten he was supposed to be looking for one.

'I've an appointment with the owner.'

'Oh, dear,' said Annabelle, sighing, 'how mortifying, Caroline, that you and I don't own as much appeal as a whiskery landlord.'

Caroline, recollecting, said, 'Naturally, Captain Burnside, Annabelle and I would not want whist to stand in your way.'

Mercy me, thought Annabelle, my dear sister seems oddly prickly at times in the way she reacts to her old friend. Perhaps he is more than an old friend; perhaps he was once her ardent admirer, and perhaps she dislikes him conducting business when he might be partnering her at whist.


Mr Gerald Wingrove proved a most agreeable after-supper guest, as Caroline had known he would. He was knowledgeable and informative on a variety of subjects, including the health of the King, which he described as erratic, but not so erratic at the moment as to require the Prince of Wales to act as Regent again. Mr Wingrove informed Annabelle that the Prince had served as Regent for a short time several years ago. Annabelle could not resist suggesting that the King, having lost his American colonies, had subsequently lost his mind as well, and that it was not surprising. Mr Wingrove replied gravely that he did not think that was the case.

Annabelle began to feel Mr Wingrove was rather boring, although he seemed to appeal to Caroline – perhaps because he had an air of sobriety and respectability. Lord Clarence had lacked both these virtues.

In truth, Mr Wingrove was not holding Caroline's interest as much as he appeared to be. Certainly, she smiled and nodded, and occasionally responded, but much of what he said did not register too precisely, for she was pestered by thoughts of what her wretched hireling was up to. It was vexing that his absence should distract her attention, that he should be all too often on her mind. She supposed she had a guilty conscience about what his presence in her house stood for. But there it was, she was committed and so was he; and he should have been here, partnering Annabelle and fascinating her, for that was what he was to be paid for. How dared he go out, and on what business, pray? He knew, and she knew, that it was not to see the owner of an apartment.

She concluded he was spending the evening in deceitful pursuit of some innocent young lady who owned a few jewels. Wretched, wretched man.

# Chapter Ten

The evening twilight was warmly caressing as Captain Burnside took up his station at a spot close to the residence of the Duke of Cumberland. He chose a convenient recess, from where he had a view of the side door. He waited patiently. The occasional carriage passed, and the occasional strollers appeared. Captain Burnside remained unobserved, but observing. At twenty past nine the side door opened and a passage light glimmered. It outlined the head and shoulders of the maidservant Betsy. She stood at the open door, nervously peering. Captain Burnside moved, looked up and down the street, saw that it was clear, and advanced quickly and silently.

'Oh, be that you, sir?' whispered Betsy anxiously.

'I am me, Betsy, and all is clear, my pretty one,' he murmured.

'It be all clear inside too, sir, and I'm glad I be pretty. Come in, but very quiet, like, for I be trembling all over in fear someone might hear. His Highness be out, and Mr Erzburger, his secretary, and the servants all be downstairs. Follow me, sir.'

He stepped in. She closed the door soundlessly, and tiptoed along the passage. She turned into a lamplit corridor. He followed, and she turned again to ascend the back stairs of the house. Their feet were cautious and quiet, their tongues still. She traversed another corridor, stopped outside a door and opened it very carefully. She took him into a room where the curtains were drawn, and illumination came from a wall lamp burning a candle. Betsy whispered she had lighted it minutes ago, so that he would not be blind or have need to open the curtains.

'Splendid girl,' he murmured, and she pushed herself close to let her warm body brush against his for a friendly moment. In her nervous excitement she was in need of reassuring contact.

'I be fair gone on you, sir, that I be,' she whispered.

'Well, that shows sound judgement, Betsy, for I'm a fine fellow and a credit to my Lord Chancellor. Now, let me see.' He eyed the furniture. In the light of the candle flame, it seemed solid and business-like. A huge desk interested him. He opened the central drawer, and saw at once what he was looking for, a leather-bound diary. He took it out, placed it on the desk and sat down. Betsy breathed a little noisily at his unhurried coolness.

'Be you staying long, sir? I be in tremors if you are.'

'A few minutes, Betsy.' He thought. 'Say ten or fifteen.'

'Fifteen?' Betsy swallowed. 'Oh, I daresn't think who might be wanting me and calling for me.'

'Then leave me to it, Betsy. Trust me. A thousand honest men will vouch that I'd never let a partner down. Take yourself off, and I'll make my own way out.'

'Sir, I aren't sure—'

'Oh, you can be very sure, Betsy.'

'Well, I'll go down, sir, and come up again in ten minutes. It'll take care of some of my tremblings, going down and showing myself.'

'Good girl,' he murmured, and she flitted away. He opened the diary, and scanned it, remarking Erzburger's neatly inscribed entries relating to appointments, official and private. He was not sure he would find a plain pointer, or any kind of pointer at all. He got up, went to the door, closed by Betsy, and he opened it and listened. The house was quiet. He closed the door again, and moved to an inner door. It opened on to Cumberland's large study. Quickly, he crossed it, opened another door and entered Cumberland's private suite. He made a

104

speedy survey of the rooms, then returned to the study. The twilight was turning to dusk, but the open curtains saved the room from darkness. A large, inlaid satinwood escritoire caught his eye. He took a bunch of keys from his coat pocket. Choosing the smaller ones for his purpose, he attempted to unlock the desk. Unsuccessful, he made use of a thin metal rod, finely corrugated. The delicate lock clicked, and he opened the desk.

The faintest smile touched his lips. Before him was Cumberland's treasure trove of separate little bundles of letters, all neatly stowed. He did not disturb them. He looked for a single letter. The unfortunate lady in question had written only the one. And there it was, of pale blue parchment, visible between two tied bundles. Carefully he extracted it, opened it, glanced at the signature. The signature was confined to a solitary 'H'.

He put the letter in his pocket, closed the desk and used the thin steel rod to lock it. Swiftly, he returned to Erzburger's office. He seated himself at the desk again, and began a new examination of the diary. Some six or seven minutes had passed. He was looking for the date of a certain appointment, if that appointment had been set down. He thought it would be, for Cumberland, through his secretary, was a meticulous and methodical man, given to ensuring that everything of consequence was recorded in one way or another, as was every royal personage.

The Captain ran his eye quickly over one page after another, concentrating on the immediate future. He noted the entry for 29th July: '*3 pm. Geo. Pn. from Lady K.*'

He construed that as 'George, Prince of Wales. Petition from Lady K.' Cumberland, no doubt, had received a cry for help from one of the many foolish ladies who had allowed herself to be bedded by the Prince. Distraught by the consequences, and finding the Prince typically out of sympathy with her, she had probably turned to Cumberland for help, perhaps because she had once been his own fancy. Ladies were foolishly eager to bed with royalty.

The Captain did not think this one would receive too much help from Cumberland. It was very unlike him to intercede with Wales on behalf of any lady.

Betsy returned with a hastening whisper of garments. 'Oh, be you still looking, sir?' she breathed.

He nodded. He was examining a further entry for 29th July. Betsy regarded his bent head and his profile. Oh, he were such a pleasing gentleman in his looks and manner, just the kind she would like to set her up. He had promised her nine more guineas. Perhaps he would give her kisses too. Her fingers stole to her laced-up bodice and loosened it.

The Captain was absorbed by that further entry, in Cumberland's own hand: '*3.30 pm. Fd, Wm & Ed also. Concerning poss. marriage to Lady CP. Bty and riches.*'

Lady CP. Lady Clarence Percival, of course. Caroline. Beauty and riches both. Very true. So, hereby hangs a tale that would make the telling painful to Annabelle. But what man of Cumberland's ilk would not prefer the magnificent elder sister to the pretty younger? What was Cumberland's interest in the younger? Her virginity, probably, and the challenge this represented to a man who would find it an amusing pleasure to be the first to bed her. Or was his leisurely pursuit of her motivated by another reason? It was Caroline he wanted. Perhaps he thought he could win her if he promised to leave her sister with her virginity intact. Would a woman sacrifice herself for her sister to that extent? Lady Caroline had expressed utter dislike and contempt for Cumberland. But were they her true feelings? Cumberland had a strangely magnetic effect on all kinds of women. Yet if Lady Caroline did have a weakness for him, she would have found it easy to outshine her sister and so save her. If not, Captain Burnside doubted she would sacrifice herself for Annabelle. Some women did not consider virginity as sacred as most men thought they did. What concerned them primarily was not preservation, but the attendant risk. Did Lady Caroline know Cumberland was to discuss marriage to her with his elder brothers, Wales, Frederick, William and Edward? Was her dislike simulated?

Something was not quite right; something did not make sense. Unless Lady Caroline had said she would favourably consider a proposal, Cumberland would not make a fool of himself by asking for his brothers' approval of a marriage that was only a hope in his mind. He was not a man to make himself look a fool. And he would still require the King's sovereign approval. The King, of course, would refuse, and ragefully. Under no circumstances would Cumberland be allowed to marry a commoner, an American commoner at that. Cumberland must know that. His discussion of the proposed marriage with his brothers was an absurd and empty gesture.

There was another curious aspect. Why was Cumberland arranging to receive only his elder brothers? Why had he excluded his younger brother, the Duke of Cambridge? Cumberland could insult people by being casually indifferent, and not spare members of his family, but it made no sense for him to be as indifferent as this to Cambridge.

The pointer, thought Captain Burnside was here, at 3.30 pm on 29th July. But what was it pointing at?

'Sir?' It was a worried whisper from Betsy. The Captain closed the diary, restored it to the drawer, and stood up. 'Oh, you be done, sir?' Betsy breathed in relief.

'Done and finished, Betsy.'

'Then come down quick, sir, I be quaking in my everythings.'

'Your everythings?'

Betsy stifled a sweet giggle. 'All of 'em, sir,' she said, and led the way cautiously. He followed her down. He heard murmurs from below stairs, murmurs from the servants' quarters, but no one came to question Betsy during her careful journey to the side door. In the passage she faced him, the candlelight revealing the faint flush on her face, and the limpid look of melting eyes. 'Sir, you be giving me the dibs now?'

'What I promised, you shall have, Betsy. And if I need to come again?'

'Oh, you're a sly one, sir, that you are, with them

107

guineas still in your pocket and poor me not knowing how to say no to you in case you diddle me.'

'Come, come, pretty buttercup, would any fine, honest fellow diddle a girl as obliging as you?'

'Oh, you be a straight-up, loving-speaking gentleman, sir. There be no Flash Harry about you. You'll give me what you said, you'll play fair with me?'

'As fair as fair comes, Betsy,' he whispered, and placed nine guineas in her eager hand. She peered at them in delight, then lifted her dark blue servant's gown and stowed the gold coins. There were faint little chinks of sound as the coins dropped into the pocket of an under-garment. Her breathing was quick and excited, for she had received ten guineas in all, a sum that was a regular, palpitating windfall. Her face beamed blissfully.

'I be fair knocked out, sir. Ten guineas be rapture to a girl. It won't matter now if anyone comes and finds us, I can say you're a gentleman friend who's stepped in to buss me. You be wishful of bussing me, sir, and kissing? I be willing.'

'Sweet puss, never think I wish to ask more than help from you. Tell me, do you know which visitors come and go each day?'

'I see some, I don't see all, sir.' Betsy pushed herself to him. 'It be Mr Pringle's job to receive visitors and to take 'em to Captain Heywood, who takes 'em up to Mr Erzburger, who takes 'em to the Duke if they be on the reception list, sir.' Betsy paused for thought. She was always a thinking girl. 'Mostly visitors be high and haughty people, sir.'

'So anyone not high and haughty would stand out as unusual? Have you noticed anyone unusual lately?'

'No, sir, I ain't.' Betsy wriggled amorously. 'But I noticed Mr Erzburger's been unusual, going out regular every day and carrying a bag.'

'That's unusual, sweet puss?' They were conversing in murmurs.

'It be unusual for him, sir, him being haughtier sometimes than His Highness.'

'Does he go out at the same time every day?'

'Thereabouts, sir. Say near to four o'clock.'

'Four o'clock. I fancy our Lord Chancellor would commend you for being an observant young beauty.'

'Oh, I be a young beauty to you, sir?'

'And observant. Thank you, Betsy.'

'You be off now, sir? Without no kissing? You be a confusion to a girl, loving her with words but not kissing her, and I hardly mind you kissing me at all.'

Business being his first consideration, Captain Burnside said, 'If I need to see you again, how shall I let you know?'

'Oh, push a note under this door when the evening's dark, sir, and I'll look each night to see if it's there. Just put day and time, sir, evening time, like tonight.'

'You can read and write, pretty puss?'

Betsy pushed herself against him and murmured, 'That I can, sir, or I wouldn't be working in His Highness's household, would I? Mr Erzburger be very particular about them kind of things. Best you buss me now, sir, before I die blushing.'

There were no blushes that Captain Burnside could see, but there was a lifted, pouting mouth, and a bosom that pushed. Since she was invaluable as a thinking young accomplice, when she might have been a muddleheaded one, he kissed her pursed lips, several times. Betsy sighed like a girl gently languishing, and her warm breath left moisture on his lips.

'That wasn't too confusing, I hope?' he said.

'It were terrible weakening on my knees, sir, being so pleasuring. I don't know how I could say no if you asked me to visit you in your lodgings, but I daresay you'd treat me fair with the presents you'd give me.'

He murmured with laughter and kissed her again. Betsy shivered with delight.

'There, saucy puss, take that to bed with you.'

'Oh, you be a rare pleasuring gentleman, sir, with the way you kiss, and if you wanted to set me up and be my regular gentleman, I can't think how I could bring myself to say no.'

'Egad, that's an enchanting proposition, Betsy, but an honest fellow must consider the feelings of his wife.'

'Oh, you needn't tell her, sir,' whispered Betsy eagerly, 'for I won't, nor ever would.'

'Not a word to anyone, Betsy, about anything, or the Lord Chancellor would lay the axe on our necks himself.'

'I be able to hold my tongue, sir, for I couldn't abide having my head chopped off, nor being hanged till I'm dead.'

'Well, it's unpleasant, being dead when one is so young. So?'

'Yes, sir, I know. Not a word to no one.'

'Splendid puss. Goodnight.'

Captain Burnside slipped quietly away, knowing the golden guineas ensured her discretion, since she would be hoping for more. And why not? The labourer was worthy of his hire. He was worthy himself.

Betsy was left sighing. She had never known a gentleman more pleasuring.

Arriving back at Lady Caroline's house, Captain Burnside found her still up. Mr Wingrove had departed, and Annabelle, who had found the evening lacking sparkle, retired to dream of how determined she would be with the Duke of Cumberland tomorrow. Captain Burnside had given her so much confidence in herself that she imagined the impossible. She imagined she could be Cumberland's equal in sophistication.

Caroline, reclining in languorous comfort on a long, gilt Louis XIV sofa, upholstered in Cambridge blue, looked up from the book she was reading. Her gown was a vivid crimson against the blue of the sofa, its hem hitched. Around her silken-hosed calves, a froth of snowy white petticoats peeped. The lacy flounces of her pantaloons flirted with the froth of the petticoats.

Captain Burnside coughed and lifted his eyes to the ornamental ceiling.

Caroline regarded him coolly. 'You have condescended to return?' she said.

'I have returned, marm. I ain't given to condescension, except if it's a professional requirement.'

'You, sir, in your impudence, can be more condescending than any man I know. Is something wrong with my ceiling?'

'Nothing at all, marm. It's an embellishment of gracious splendour.'

'Really?' Caroline, after an evening that had been annoyingly unsatisfactory, found herself quickening to the challenge of confrontation with her wretched hireling. 'Is that why you are staring at it?'

'It's a work of art, marm. Yet there are prettier spectacles.'

'Such as, sir?'

'Ah,' said Captain Burnside obliquely.

'Speak, sir. Your tongue is usually facile enough to keep you from mumbling.'

'Perhaps, marm, you'll give me leave to retire?'

'No, Captain Burnside, I will not,' said Caroline in the firm manner she adopted whenever it was necessary to let him know hers was the right to command. 'I require from you an explanation for your absence. Heavens, do stop looking at the ceiling. Show me your face, sir, for I suspect a shiftiness in you at this moment.'

Captain Burnside looked at her. It was impossible not to notice how her garments softly traced the lines of her body and the long length of her legs. And her silk-stockinged calves and lacy flounces were indeed the prettiest of spectacles. He coughed again.

'Faith,' he said, 'at this moment, marm, shiftiness apart, I can see that a ceiling is only a ceiling.'

'Are you drunk, sir?' she asked.

'Slightly intoxicated, I confess, but not from London gin or French wine,' said the Captain, and coughed yet again.

'Fiddlesticks,' said Caroline, surprising herself in her enjoyment of the dialogue. She sat up, and noticed her hitched gown and her peeping petticoats. She did not blush. She gave Captain Burnside the coolest of looks. He raised his eyes to the ceiling again.

'Ridiculous wretch,' she said, 'are you trying to make me believe you have never seen a petticoat before?'

111

'Oh, I've seen a hundred, marm, and quite a few pretty pantaloons, but . . .' He coughed a fourth time.

'But, sir, but?'

'I ain't ever clapped my eyes on the petticoats and pantaloons of a lady patron before. You'll forgive me, marm?'

'So, you have another talent, have you, Captain Burnside? A talent for pretending coyness? That is hardly much of a talent in a man.' Caroline slipped her feet to the floor. A little smile showed itself. Now why should that happen, why should she smile? She frowned. 'We will dispense with the absurd, sir. Where have you been, and what was the business that took you out? I am entitled to know, I think, since I believe I have exclusive use of your services and your time at present.'

Captain Burnside observed the chandelier that cast light over her dark auburn hair and tinted it with fire. Her magnificence was unquestionable. Cumberland would never find a German duchess to equal Lady Clarence Percival, eligible widow.

'Oh, an appointment with Betsy, our pretty go-between at Cumberland's town house—'

'I thought so!' Her interruption was fierce. If she could not understand why she had smiled at his ridiculous behaviour over her petticoats, even less could she understand why she felt so angry over his meeting with some flighty maidservant called Betsy. 'How dare you conduct one of your disgraceful intrigues when you are wholly committed to my employ?'

'Gently, marm . . .'

'Gently, sir, gently? How dare you!' Flushed, she was more magnificent.

'The point, marm, is that servants gossip. One never knows just how much useful information one can extract from a sweet creature eager to see the glint of a golden guinea—'

'And to be kissed, no doubt, and fondled!' Again her interruption was fierce. 'You are disgusting, Captain Burnside, disgusting.'

'Only in a professional way, marm,' he said placatingly, and her green eyes burned. 'Servants can put one in touch with appointments, and you'll agree, I'm sure, that it would be useful indeed to know in advance any appointments Annabelle might have arranged with Cumberland.'

'Very well, I will concede that,' said Caroline, but was still flushed, still angry, and perplexingly so to herself. 'But Annabelle, infatuated though she is, would never arrange a clandestine appointment with Cumberland, not while she is hoping he'll marry her.'

'My own feeling, marm, is that one can never be sure what infatuated ladies will get up to.'

'My sister does not get up to anything.'

'I thought, marm, that the reason you hired me was because you were afraid she would.'

'I am afraid of what might eventually happen because of Cumberland's lack of all decency.'

'Well, sweet Betsy—'

'Must you, sir? She reads like a flirtatious baggage to me.'

'Quite so, marm. However, she had no knowledge of anything relating to Annabelle. I thought it worth a question or two, without, of course, naming your sister. With all respect, marm, may I ask how you yourself truly see the Duke of Cumberland?'

'See him?'

'He has a devilish fascination for many ladies,' said the Captain.

'He has none for me, sir. I consider him close to a reincarnation of Caligula.'

'You'd not, then, favourably regard a proposal of marriage from him?'

'That royal rake? How dare you! You are surpassing yourself tonight, and coming close to a slap on your face. Dismiss from your mind, sir, any thought that I would marry Cumberland for any reason at all. I despise rakes, philanderers and all other men who are dissolute and promiscuous. I despise you, sir.'

113

'Well, so you do, marm, and not without cause, but it ain't likely you'll require to marry me any more than—'

Caroline delivered the threatened slap, and stingingly. Captain Burnside received it manfully, rubbed his cheek and eyed her in rueful fashion.

'Leave my house, sir,' she said stormily, 'your commission is at an end. If my secretary is still up, ask him to bestow a shilling on you. That shall be your quittance money.'

'Very well, marm, but before I go, allow me to give you this.' He extracted the letter he had come by with professional ease, and handed it to her.

'What is this?' she asked.

'The letter,' said Captain Burnside.

'The letter?' She gazed at the folded sheet of crisp paper as if it were an irrelevance. She was still too furious to comprehend, her gown still rustling from the angry vibrations of her body. It took long seconds for her mind to clear and for the impossible to dawn. 'Captain Burnside?' she breathed throatily.

'I fancy you'll find it's the one Lady Russell has been so anxious about, though I assure you I ain't read it.'

Incredulous, she opened up the letter. She glanced at the handwriting, with which she was familiar, and at the signature, the single letter 'H'. Just as incredulous, she looked at Captain Burnside. He gave a nod that was both confirmatory and reassuring.

'Am I to believe. . . ?' For once she faltered. Her bosom surged as extreme emotion engulfed her.

'You may believe, marm, in a venture accomplished,' said the Captain. 'That is, one half of it.'

In her emotion, born of the breathless wonder of knowing he had secured for her the means to deliver Hester from her anguish, moisture rushed to her eyes. Agitatedly, she turned her back on him, hiding her weakness.

'Captain Burnside, I . . .' Again she faltered.

'Quite so, marm. I'll go up to my room and pack.'

'No, you will not,' she breathed, 'you will stay, I beg.

114

Captain Burnside, how can I ever thank you? I declare myself in shame to have been so angry with you. Forgive me, please.'

'The slap? Deserved, marm, deserved.'

'No – oh, perhaps it was. But if you're an unconscionable rogue, you have redeemed yourself in a way I cannot put words to. You have no idea what the return of this letter to Lady Russell will mean to her. She will be overjoyed. Captain Burnside?' She turned and faced him, and he saw the glitter of wetness in her green eyes. She extended her hand. He lifted it to his lips. 'Thank you, sir,' she said, striving to regain control of herself. It was not to be. She was too overwhelmed, too sensitively conscious that he had returned her furious slap with a gesture entirely breathtaking. Unable to say more, she picked up her skirts and made blindly for the door. Interceding, he opened it for her and she rushed out.

'H'm,' said Captain Burnside thoughtfully. She had omitted to ask him how he had procured the letter. Perhaps that was just as well. He would have had to mention the sweet puss Betsy again, and she had taken a fierce dislike to Betsy.

Caroline, her mind clamorous with the glad tidings she was going to bring to Hester, did not get to sleep for hours. Consequently, she awoke late and took a late breakfast in bed. Afterwards, her toilet finished, she dressed herself in radiant primrose and descended to the drawing room in search of her hireling. Annabelle, about to go shopping, informed her that Charles had gone to keep an appointment.

'What appointment, pray?' asked Caroline, feeling she was suffering a setback. She had intended to take the Captain aside, speak graciously to him and ask questions of him.

'He did not say,' smiled Annabelle, aware that her sister had clothed herself in radiance. 'But perhaps it's to do with regimental matters, for I daresay we cannot expect him to be permanently on leave, can we? I shall be quite put out when he's recalled. He is of all things a sweetly entertaining man.'

'I'm happy to hear you say so,' said Caroline.

'Alas, dear sister, that he's not here to see you looking like a morning goddess.'

'Ridiculous child,' said Caroline. 'I am lunching with Lady Wingrove and Mr Wingrove.'

'How enchanting for Mr Wingrove,' murmured Annabelle, drawing on her gloves. 'How boring for you.'

'Boring? Mr Wingrove is the most agreeable gentleman in London.'

'Mercy me,' said Annabelle, 'is he to be my new brother-in-law?' She floated out, laughing.

'That, Your Grace, is as much as I know at present,' said Captain Burnside to the imposing, dignified-looking gentleman who stood with his back to an empty fireplace, hands behind him.

'Well, the devil, but it's as much as I can expect. However, the word from Ireland being as definite as it is, we can't afford to be merely hopeful. Something very unpleasant is afoot. Wales is being watched, but it ain't to his liking to have a guard pussyfooting around him. And Cumberland?'

'Cumberland can look after himself,' said the Captain, 'and will.'

'I take your meaning. But what makes you think his meeting with his elder brothers has a significance?'

'It's unnecessary, Your Grace, if the subject to be discussed is as set down.'

'And why did Cumberland set it down in such a way?'

'It occurs to me,' said Captain Burnside, 'that a diary entry is an official notification. It can always be conveniently pointed to.'

'Cumberland's up to something?'

'I fancy I can't say yes, but I ain't prepared to say no.'

'And what of Lady Clarence?'

'Entirely magnificent, Your Grace, in appearance, character, intellect and sensibilities. She'll not marry Cumberland.'

'God's life,' said the dignified gentleman, 'I hope not. She

116

don't deserve another impossible husband. But women are strange creatures, Burnside. They're apt to be drawn more passionately to the wicked than the good. Cumberland has dined with Lady Clarence, frequently, yet she says she hates him.'

'Faith, some women find a deal of pleasure in hating a man,' said the Captain.

'Well, I'm relying on you to find every loose end and to tie 'em neatly together.'

Caroline left her house at eleven and called first on Lady Hester Russell, who received her with an emotional kiss on the cheek, and rushing words.

'Caroline, how good to see you, and how ravishing you look. George will be sorry to have missed you, for he declares you the grandest sight in London. But he is out, walking again, would you believe. He is still determined to exercise his leg and cure his limp, which he says he will and despite the contrary advice of Doctor Purvis, whom he says is becoming an old goat and too fond of keeping patients in bed. Oh, am I going on a little foolishly? But everything is more and more unbearable, and it's even a terrible effort to show my face to George . . .'

'Hester, it need no longer be unbearable,' said Caroline, 'for I've called to give you this.' She handed Hester the letter, tactfully and securely wrapped. She had not read it. 'There, that is it, dearest. But don't ask me how I came by it.'

'Caroline?' Hester was as incredulous as Caroline had been. Feverishly she undid the wrapping, opened the letter and scanned it. There was pain in her eyes to see what she had written in her excessive infatuation. Then tears welled. 'Oh, darling Caroline, thank you, thank you. You have saved my life, and I hope too you have saved my marriage.' She embraced Caroline, then sank into an armchair and wept tears that were bitter as well as joyful.

'I cannot stay,' said Caroline gently, 'I am on my way to lunch with Mr Wingrove and his mother.'

117

'Yes. Yes. I shan't detain you.' Hester brushed away her tears and smiled mistily. 'Mr Wingrove is so exceptionally pleasant, and such an upright gentleman. He'll be delighted to see you looking so ravishing. We must value gentlemen like him, and fight the weaknesses we have for the other kind. Oh, Caroline, how very, very grateful I am to you.'

# Chapter Eleven

Lunch with Mr Wingrove and his mother, Lady Wingrove, was, as usual, an agreeable occasion for Caroline. Lady Wingrove personified the cheerful kindness of her sex; she had been among those friends who had given Caroline tactful and sympathetic support during her years of marital disillusionment. On the death of Lord Clarence, she had remarked that the deceased gentleman, having earned his place in hell, would give the devil himself a run for his money, as would Cumberland when his turn came. Mr Wingrove never spoke of Caroline's late husband, for he could not bring himself to speak ill of the dead. In his honesty, he could have said nothing that was complimentary.

Lady Wingrove had an endearing charm, and the personable Mr Wingrove an easy flow of conversation. So, since the lunch was excellent and the atmosphere so agreeable, Caroline could not think why she kept losing her way in the table talk. Naturally, she did have Hester's letter on her mind, and just as naturally she was curious about how Captain Burnside had laid his hands on it. Even so, it was ridiculous that Mr Wingrove frequently had to repeat himself to get a response from her. It was also discourteous. She was compelled to excuse herself on the grounds that she had something on her mind.

'Ah, the mind,' smiled Mr Wingrove, 'how it can run away with us when we would prefer it to remain close by. But who can define the mind in all its complexities? It is the voice of the soul, of course, and I daresay nothing is more abstract than the soul.'

'La,' said Lady Wingrove, 'to concern oneself with one's soul is a hopeless essay. I am much more addicted to people, who are fascinating in their variability.'

'We are, of course, all individuals,' said Mr Wingrove. 'How say you, Caroline?'

'Pardon?' said Caroline, wondering if Captain Burnside was yet back from his appointment. What appointment? Was it with his present fancy, that covetous serving wench, Betsy, who worked in Cumberland's household? 'Oh, I do beg your pardon, Mr Wingrove, what was it you said? I have my sister on my mind. She is delaying her return to South Carolina and my parents write me in concern about this.'

'From my observations of Annabelle,' said Mr Wingrove, 'I doubt if she means to return. She has taken London's Corinthian scene to her young and impressionable heart, and one can only sympathise with your parents. I fear too that she is developing a fondness for your friend, Captain Burnside, whom I've not yet had the pleasure of meeting.'

'Do you fear for Annabelle, Gerald, because you haven't met the Captain?' asked Lady Wingrove. 'But I am sure Caroline can vouch for him as a wholesome gentleman.'

'Annabelle is friendly with him, that's all,' said Caroline, and felt a perplexing restlessness, as if this entirely sociable lunch was becoming too drawn-out in the face of a wish to return home and examine her hireling. But it was not until well after they had risen from the table that the arrival of her chaise was announced. By then she was all too ready to depart. Mr Wingrove said a lengthy and fluent goodbye, having accepted her invitation to meet Captain Burnside on Friday evening and to join him at the card table with the Duke of Cumberland and Mr Robert Humphreys.

Stepping into her chaise, she said, 'Off you go, Sammy, at a spanking trot,' to her young coachman.

'Yes'm,' said seventeen-year-old Sammy, son of her previous coachman, retired on account of crippling rheumatism.

Caroline would have liked to drive herself, but in town it was simply not the thing for a lady to take up reins. In Sussex, life was less conventional, and there she drove every kind of vehicle with dash and elan. She had learned to handle a pair in South Carolina, even though conventions there could be stricter than in London.

As Sammy took the chaise through the streets at a smart trot, she thought of Sussex. Why should she not take Annabelle there for a while? It would remove her from such easy contact with Cumberland. Captain Burnside could accompany them. He could conduct his own devious pursuit of Annabelle in the quiet countryside. Indeed, Annabelle would probably refuse to go unless she had the company of a man she liked.

Captain Burnside had achieved wonders in laying his hands on that letter. She could not now doubt he would be entirely successful in winning Annabelle's affections.

Caroline frowned.

On arriving home, she looked for her hireling. Neither he nor Annabelle were in the house. Her secretary informed her that Captain Burnside and Miss Annabelle were out on an afternoon drive.

That left Caroline definitely restless. She was burning to know exactly how he had procured the letter. Had Cumberland given it up in exchange for the standing IOU? It was, after all, for a considerable amount of money. Yet she did not think that likely, for Cumberland was bent on cancelling it out on the return game. Wait. His house, and that baggage called Betsy, one of his servants . . .

A thought seized her and shocked her. Captain Burnside had been inside Cumberland's residence, yes, through the agency of the maidservant. Had he committed an act of burglary? He was quite capable. He was a smooth, polished professional, and probably accounted thievery as useful to his ends as trickery.

For some reason, her heart sank.

Captain Burnside, at the reins of Caroline's handsome carriage, drove at a leisurely pace to Cumberland's residence. Annabelle, beset by quivers, hid them under light observations of the London scenes. The traffic itself was colourful, a slow-moving procession both ways in the vicinity of Horse Guards Parade. Spanking traps and other two-wheelers vied with stately carriages for possession of the thoroughfares. Kitchen boys darted in and out on domestic errands.

'I'll deliver you at the door of your majestic swain, Annabelle,' said the Captain, 'though I'll be reluctant to part with you. You're a picture, young lady, a delicious picture.'

'Oh, you surely do your best to convince a lady she's irresistible,' said Annabelle. Her parasol was up lest the humid sun laid its spoiling light and heat on her complexion. In a blue and white bonnet, and a turquoise blue day gown, she looked very pretty, very charming and very innocent. Bucks on horseback on their way to parks paused in their cantering to raise their hats to her, thus suggesting they had met her somewhere and would not say no if she invited them to renew the acquaintance. But it was not done, of course, for any young lady to fall for such a ploy. 'It's flattering to be looked at,' she said.

'Annabelle, the strength of young ladies, don't you see, is that each is irresistible in some way, which is a fact of life and a principle of nature.'

'But, Charles, I never feel irresistible, only unsure. Are my eyes the right colour? Is my face in fashion? Is my hair style a triumph or a disaster? Is my nose a little too retroussé? Oh, how can one's self-confidence be assured when one's self-doubts are so profuse?'

'Your nose is faultless, your eyes are finely blue, your hair style is delightful, and your face will always earn you kisses,' said Captain Burnside.

'I vow you a dear man. But I am not the magnificent beauty that Caroline is.'

'You are young and delicious.'

'And you are cutting a superb dash,' sighed Annabelle. Captain Burnside had donned his uniform. His red jacket, high blue collar, thigh-hugging white breeches, shining

122

black boots and cavalry officer's cap, made her eyes linger. Of all things military, she adored a redcoated soldier, for no other colour gave a man more dash. And a redcoated cavalryman, could any soldier come more bravely to the eye? 'Charles, I declare, you have the eye of every lady we pass. Even Caroline will sigh when she sees you.'

'Will she?' Captain Burnside avoided a collision with a badly-handled cabriolet by drawing up his pair into a sudden halt. 'Tut, tut, sir, you should learn to walk before you ride,' he called.

The driver of the cabriolet, a fop of frills and flounces, smiled at him with sweet malice. 'Damned, sir, if your head ain't remarkably like a cannon-ball,' he said, and drove on, heedless of his lack of skill.

'The pretty sprigs of London are very petty,' said Annabelle.

'H'm,' said Captain Burnside. 'Now, young lady, in a few moments we shall arrive. I enjoin you to take care. Your sister won't think too kindly of me for delivering you to Cumberland, nor will she like the thought of your being alone with him in his house – for if he seizes you, I fancy you'll not be able to count on help from his servants.'

Annabelle's laugh was a little nervous, a little excited. 'Seizes me? Charles, how melodramatic.'

'Very,' said the Captain drily. 'But a prince so dark of brow and so enamoured ain't averse to seizing enchantment and making off with her.'

'Making off?' Her laughter bubbled. 'Dear Charles, how amusing you are, and not at all boring, like Mr Wingrove, who is so constantly agreeable that he comes close to sounding like a single note of a flute. Whatever else is said about the Duke of Cumberland, no one could accuse him of being boring.' Annabelle laughed again. Thoughts of Cumberland always excited her, and London never failed to exhilarate her. Before her and around her, all was a colourful panorama of carriages and people, handsome brownstone buildings and uniformed soldiers.

A troop of Horse Guards rode by in jingling panoply, every horse a sleek, shining black. 'Please do not forget the Duke and I are meeting only to converse.'

'About his intentions or your irresistibility? To be sure, Annabelle, it's plainly time you determined whether you are being lovingly courted or passionately pursued.'

'Passionately pursued?' Annabelle blushed, thought of the pleasure the Duke took in caressing her bosom, and blushed again.

'Quite so,' said Captain Burnside, fully aware that this sweet but naive young lady was going to stand or fall according to the amount of instinctive feminine caution and commonsense she could bring to bear. 'Cumberland don't lack passion, nor purpose. So be strong, dear girl. Ask him quite plainly if he has marriage in mind. If not to you, then whom.'

'But it's so difficult to be strong when he's so formidable.'

'The first thing you must do is forbid him your lips.'

Annabelle hid herself under her parasol. 'Charles, I beg you not to embarrass me so.'

'Cumberland has stolen some sweetnesses from you, I'll wager.'

'Oh, land sakes, must I discuss such intimacies?'

'What you must do is remember that gentlemen who deny a lady honest answers to honest questions must be denied favours in return. Point out to Cumberland that you're a guest of his country, and that he, as a royal Duke, should at least be truthful with you. Tell him some men have been assassinated for playing false with young ladies.'

'Assassinated?' gasped Annabelle.

'Yes, mention assassination by all means. You've hit on a powerful argument there, Annabelle. Point out that his brother, the Prince of Wales, has wronged so many ladies that he may yet be assassinated before he inherits the Crown. See how Cumberland reacts.'

'Charles, you are making me quake and quiver,' breathed Annabelle. 'I am to imply I might assassinate the Duke unless his intentions are honourable? I vow he will burst out laughing.'

'I fancy, if you speak firmly enough, you won't hear him laugh. I fancy he might look as if he's in serious admiration of you.'

'It's true he contempts weak people. Oh, dear, I pray I shan't be miserably weak.'

'You're a sweet gift from America, dear girl, and not to be trifled with. I ain't intending to let anyone trifle with you, not even Cumberland. Well, here we are. I'll wait not far away, and will give you thirty minutes. Out of respect for Lady Caroline, your sister, I can't give you more. It won't do to let you linger with His Magnificent Highness.'

Annabelle, escorted upstairs by the senior flunkey, a Mr Pringle, was shown into the drawing room of Cumberland's private suite. It was a room of spacious, high-ceilinged splendour. Patterned carpets proliferated, and the walls were hung with gilt-framed paintings, some depicting scenes of peaceful nature, others scenes of battle and strife. The furniture was large and opulent. Cumberland was not present, and the flunkey left her to await the Duke's arrival. Annabelle, her excitement a distinct nervousness, seated herself. Her fan fluttered.

A door opened a little, and through it she heard Cumberland's deep voice, 'Comfortable he may be, but is he still secure?'

'As secure as you could wish, Your Royal Highness, and, in his own mind, for his own sake.'

'And ye're sure ye alone among my staff know he's where he is?'

'Only you and I—'

'Myself, I know nothing, ye hear?' Cumberland's voice was swift and harsh.

'Indeed I know. My apologies, Your Highness.'

'There's still a watch on him?'

'There is, Your Highness. I shall be going later to look things over, as usual. I suggest, sir, we must consider the importance of silence.'

125

'Well, ye have the responsibility, not I.'

Annabelle experienced a little uneasiness, for the conversation had unappealing nuances, and she knew there were people, unkind people, who spoke in whispers of the dark soul of the Duke of Cumberland. She shook herself free of the uncomfortable thoughts as the partly opened door was pulled wide and the Duke entered. He came to an abrupt halt as he saw her, his brows drew together and his muscular body seemed to tighten. He loomed, silent, dark-faced and intimidating. Then a smile came, creasing his scarred face.

'I am mortified,' said Annabelle, 'you have forgotten this arrangement.'

'Indeed not,' said Cumberland, 'but devil take whatever servant of mine left ye waiting and unannounced.' He refrained from saying that various ladies who called were merely brought quietly up to his drawing room and never announced. Some ladies preferred not to hear their names spoken.

'Oh, I've only this minute arrived,' said Annabelle, and came to her feet, lashes nervously flickering. In his presence, she was invariably afflicted with palpitations.

'I naturally wish I'd been able to greet ye, but I needed to speak to my private secretary,' said Cumberland, his sound eye searching.

'Oh, I surely know you to be a man who never has time to sit and wait,' said Annabelle, defensively ambiguous. 'I managed to come, as you see, Your Highness, but should not have wanted to interrupt you.'

'Oh, a small formal matter. Yes, formal, but not important. And by no means as important as ye, my sweet.'

Cumberland advanced then. His brown suede knee-breeches moulded his powerful thighs and shaped his loins. His tailed black coat was buttoned tightly over his broad chest. His movements reminded Annabelle of a pantherlike creature about to spring. His face twisted itself into another smile.

'We are to talk?' she said breathlessly.

'Talk?' His eye was still searching, his smile a teeth-gleaming facade. 'Does one talk to roses, or does one cosset them? Well, one at least acknowledges the tenderest of them.'

If Annabelle had arrived full of resolution, most of it began to run from her as he lifted her hand to his lips. He took her parasol from her, and gently freed her bonnet, placing it, with the parasol, on a table. For a man whose uncompromising maleness was legendary, he could be surprisingly gentle and frequently was. Like a woman mesmerised, Annabelle watched his every movement, his aura of arrogant, infallible masculinity holding her in thrall.

'Sir,' she said as bravely as she could, 'as a rose, am I to be placed in a vase among others, to become merely one of many, and all of us discarded when we fade and our petals drop?'

'Ye gods,' said Cumberland, voice guttural with Germanic undertones, 'one of many? D'ye think I collect young ladies to make a bouquet of them? I'm content with one rose, fresh and sweet and unblemished. Come, we're to talk, I believe, and I swear ye'll be far more entertaining than Erzburger, my secretary, who has only just finished plaguing me with his dullness.' His low laugh vibrated, but the searching glint in his eye did not relate to amusement.

Annabelle sensed he was inviting her to disclose what he suspected, that she had overheard his conversation with Erzburger. Uneasy again, she simulated a light, inconsequential smile. 'Oh, I've no knowledge of your secretary or his dullness,' she said. 'I am only concerned with how you regard me.'

'Ye're not aware it's a warm and loving regard?' said Cumberland. 'How could it not be when ye show fresher than September's morning dew? How d'ye sustain such an unspoiled look in a city that nurtures pretty men and enamelled women?'

'Your Highness, I sustain myself as I am by my belief in God and the honourable conduct of gentlemen.'

His smile was brief and mocking. 'D'ye say so?' he said.

127

'I do, sir.' Annabelle thought of Captain Burnside and his support and advice. 'I am not to be trifled with.'

'Good God,' said Cumberland, vastly amused.

'I have a proud family, Your Highness, and proud blood. My sister has a temper, and so have I.' Annabelle drew on her courage, all for the purpose of making him declare himself, one way or the other, as Captain Burnside had advised. 'I have heard, sir, that even the sons of a monarch can stand in fear of assassination when the circumstances concern dishonour.'

Cumberland's face darkened, and his powerful frame stiffened. His mouth broke apart and his teeth gleamed. His look frightened her for a moment. 'Ah, is innocence not so innocent?' he said. 'Who has been talking to ye?'

'Oh, it is read in books, or comes from hearsay, that is all.'

'Books?' Cumberland laughed. 'Food for butterflies. Hearsay? Meat and drink for old women. Come, let's discard the trivial and take up kissing.'

'No, Your Highness.' Annabelle fought weakness as he moved closer. 'If that is all I mean to you, a kiss or two, then I have no future with you.'

'Your future with me, sweet one, is under consideration.'

'Sir?' she said, her breath catching.

'Serious consideration.'

'Am I to believe – Your Highness, no—' But there she was, in his arms, swept close by his truly pantherlike action, and her intention to avoid all embraces was defeated. His mouth smothered hers, and the kiss took her breath and bemused her mind. Prolonged, it made a trembling thing of her resolution. However, the moment he released her lips she placed her hands on his chest and pushed. She broke free. 'Sir,' she gasped, face flushed, 'I beg you to be in nobler understanding of my true self than this.'

Cumberland quizzed her. She was, in essence, merely one more pretty face. Did she own anything of note other than pretty looks and a plump bosom? She was easily aroused, and he might have bedded her months ago had it not been for his designs on her sister.

'Well, what is your true self?' he asked, as if her true self found him suspect.

'Virtuous, Your Highness, and accordingly I must ask if I may expect more from you than ardour.'

Cumberland laughed. 'What more is there than ardour sincere and profound?' he said.

'Serious consideration of my future, as you said, sir. Surely a son of the King must be concerned with honour.'

Cumberland laughed again. 'The King himself ain't above compromising with honour for the sake of the outcome,' he said.

'I cannot compromise, sir,' said Annabelle, and blushed as he eyed her bosom. 'I cannot,' she breathed, and put herself at a distance from him by moving to a window. Her eyes took in nothing at first of the scene below. Then she made out her sister's carriage waiting a little way down the street. Captain Burnside was there too, seated, the reins relaxed, his posture one of unimpatience.

Cumberland, watching her, saw her fixed, thoughtful gaze. He came up beside her. He saw the waiting carriage and the man in a cavalry uniform. His brows drew together.

But he said quite lightly, 'Ye'll not be asked to forgo honour, only to be sweet, for sweet I know you could be.'

'Your Highness!' Annabelle gasped as he swept her into his arms again and even lifted her off her feet. He placed her on a couch and seated himself beside her. He cupped her chin. She stared at him, her body quivering, her heart beating riotously. He kissed her, quite gently, but lingeringly, and she experienced an alarming sense of vulnerability.

'God's heaven,' he murmured, when he had reduced her to her weakest, 'ye're a warm and shapely piece, and I'll not deny it. Ye'll allow me to remove my coat and so come cooler to the tender business of loving ye?'

He stood up to unbutton his coat. Annabelle, crimson

and trembling, adjusted her bodice with shaking fingers. The sense of alarm rushed at her, clearing her head. It was terrible to be in love with a man who dissimulated so much, a man who would not marry her, either because, as a royal Duke, he could not, or simply because he would not.

She was close to yielding, her weakness alarming. However, Captain Burnside's words of warning entered her mind, and there was present too a sense of uneasiness that would not go away. As Cumberland began to peel off his coat, she rose swiftly, snatched up her bonnet and sped to the door. Cumberland turned. She feared for a moment that the door might be locked, that he would have her trapped. But the door opened as she turned the handle. She heard Cumberland laugh as she fled, nor did he make the slightest effort to detain her.

Cumberland, indeed, only moved to the window.

Captain Burnside saw her come out of the house and hurry towards him, crossing the wide street in floating haste. Cumberland, at the window, missed nothing.

'Upon my soul,' said Captain Burnside, out of the carriage and giving her a hand, 'is it love that brings you in such flushed haste, Annabelle?'

Annabelle, emotions confused, yet in some relief to be with him, said, 'Sir, I declare! You are laughing.'

'That I ain't,' said the Captain, 'I'm shocked. Young lady, you ain't even dressed.'

Annabelle realised her bonnet was still in her hand. She put it on and tied the ribbons. But even beneath the shade of the bonnet, she could not hide her high colour. Captain Burnside took his seat, thinking that Miss Annabelle Howard of South Carolina had a dangerously appealing sweetness, and a dangerous weakness for Cumberland. Only the unpalatable would shock her into plain, sober thought. It had been necessary to assist her to come face-to-face with the unpalatable. He had a feeling that this had just happened. He did not think Cumberland would forcibly seduce her in his own residence, but he was always more than likely to show his dark, frightening side. The pretty young American girl was patently shaken.

130

'You may proceed, Charles,' she said, 'instead of looking me up and down.'

Captain Burnside took up the reins and gentled the pair into life. The carriage began to move. 'May I hazard a guess, dear girl, that you did not take formal leave of Cumberland, but escaped him at a rush?'

Annabelle, looking about her, said ruefully, 'I do confess, he was alarmingly pressing. His affection is very ardent. Mercy me, it surely is upsetting to be loved but not to be properly courted.'

'Are you sure he loves you?' asked the Captain, entering traffic.

'Oh, his declarations, his manifestations—'

'Manifestations?'

'So ardent,' said Annabelle.

'Ah, his kisses, his caresses?'

'Must I confess them?'

'Not to me, dear girl, but certainly to your sister, your caring guardian while you're in her charge.'

Annabelle, alarm and fright receding to leave only the sweet, tingling confusions that had come from being extravagantly kissed and caressed, made a little gesture of protest. 'Truly, I vow no one could love a sister more than I love mine,' she said, 'but I could not confess to her anything concerning the Duke and myself. She would fly at me and allow me to go nowhere except in her own company. Not that the Duke was ungentle; he was merely demonstrative in assuring me of his love.'

'Demonstrative, h'm,' said the Captain.

'And I was firm with him, of course, as you advised.'

'He was demonstrative and you were firm.'

'Yes. It was a question, you see, of his ardour and my honour.'

'Well, I should tell you, young lady, you come from his house looking as if you had either been kissed to distraction or shocked into flight, and there ain't too much difference between one and the other.'

'Oh, mercy me,' gasped Annabelle, 'how disconcerting you are.' She needed her parasol to hide her blushes.

131

There was no parasol. There were only more confusions, all to do with the Duke's masculine strength and her feminine weakness. 'No, no, Charles, you must not think he was shocking.'

'But your flight from his ardour was desperate?'

'I simply insisted on leaving,' said Annabelle.

'Without your parasol?'

'Oh, dear,' she sighed, 'you are quizzing me unmercifully.'

'Well, I repeat, I ain't having you trifled with,' said the Captain. 'It's certain that in your sweetness you're bound to be kissed, but I ain't being party to anything that will encourage him to bed you.'

'Oh, land sakes, I beg you to spare my blushes,' breathed Annabelle. 'See, you are catching the eye of promenading ladies, and I am sure they are wondering what you are saying to turn me crimson.'

'Oh, a blush or two sits sweetly on young ladies. What came out of your talk with Cumberland, apart from your distracted escape?'

'I confess he has a way of dissembling that is very frustrating. But I did point out that if they were too dishonourable, even sons of the King might walk in fear of assassination.'

'Ah, you did make that point, did you?' said Captain Burnside, allowing the pair to amble lazily.

'I don't think he liked it. He looked shocked for a moment.'

'Did he question you?'

'No.' Annabelle wondered then if she should tell Captain Burnside about the strange conversation she had overheard. No, she could not. One should not talk about something one was not supposed to listen to. Also, it would be disloyal to the Duke. 'He laughed it off, Charles.'

'So he would. And although you were firm, he made no marriage proposal?'

'He said I was under his serious consideration.'

'Well, I don't doubt he's seriously considering bedding you . . .'

132

'Charles, oh, you dreadful man, must you say such things?' Annabelle gasped.

'To you, dear girl, yes, for you've a sweet nature and a delicious sense of humour, and enjoy laughing far more than sulks.'

'But I am not laughing.'

'Somewhere I fancy you are,' said the Captain. 'Do you want to go back for your parasol?'

'I surely do not,' she said, and added unthinkingly, 'I vow that would return me to the lion's den.'

'So he sprang, did he? Has it made you doubt him?'

'Oh,' said Annabelle, liking her sister's friend very much, 'I confess he fascinates me, but I know I must think more sensibly about my weaknesses and his intentions, and not be alone with him so much. I am very happy to have you as my caring friend, and beg you will not tell Caroline I visited the Duke, but spent the afternoon driving with you, which is almost true.'

'Almost,' said the Captain.

## Chapter Twelve

'Annabelle?' Caroline intercepted her sister as Annabelle glided through the hall towards the staircase. The hall, its floor laid with black and white tiles, its walls painted white and hung with landscape paintings, offered a bright introduction to the handsome house. 'You're back from your drive? But where is Captain Burnside?'

'Already in his room, I daresay,' said Annabelle. 'He was in a hurry to change and to go out again.'

'He has another appointment? Another?' Caroline repressed indignation. She could not be angry, not after his achievement in securing the letter.

'I really don't know,' said Annabelle. In the bright hall, she was a summery prettiness in her blue finery, Caroline spectacular in her silken primrose. 'He could perhaps be thinking of cutting a dash with strolling ladies. He wore his uniform for our outing as a compliment to me, and I swear he caught the eye of every lady we passed. I vow he looked so exciting that I could not count the many who glanced at him, and I should not be surprised to find he has arranged to meet those whose eyes were boldest.'

'Tush and nonsense,' said Caroline, suspecting the Captain had worn his uniform further to impress Annabelle. She tried to be convincing as she added, 'He is a gentleman. He would not take you out for a drive if his intention were to attract the eyes of other young ladies. I shall send word up to him to join us for tea. Do you wish tea?'

'Oh, yes, but not for twenty minutes,' said Annabelle. 'I must freshen up and change first.'

'Twenty minutes, then,' said Caroline.

Captain Burnside appeared in the drawing room five minutes later, clad in quiet grey, with a neat white cravat. 'Marm? You sent word for me to join you. Do excuse me, for—'

'No, I am not going to excuse you,' said Caroline, seated on the chaise-longue. 'I have not seen you all day. We shall take tea together in fifteen minutes, when Annabelle will join us.'

'Frankly, marm, I'm pressed for time,' said the Captain, conscious of the soft ripple of primrose as she gestured for him to seat himself. 'I assure you, I'll be back for supper.'

'No, it won't do, sir.' Caroline braced herself for a new battle of words. The challenge was there, in his presence and his assumption that he could go against her. 'It was agreed at the outset that you would do as I directed. I direct you now to seat yourself and answer some questions.'

'I'll answer a hundred later, marm.'

'No, *now*, sir.'

'Oh, egad,' muttered the Captain.

'I am afraid I did not catch that,' said Caroline.

'A frog in my throat, marm.'

'Please sit down, Captain Burnside. I really do not think the business that seems to be calling you can take priority over your agreed commitment to me.'

Resignedly, he seated himself in a gilt and blue tub chair. 'Your servant, marm.'

Excessively poised and grand, and also uncommonly ravishing, Caroline bestowed a kind smile on him. 'Well, that is not incorrect, is it?' she said. 'But come, I am determined to be gracious, not quarrelsome, for I cannot forget the wonder of your accomplishment last night. I am greatly in your debt, as is my friend, Lady Russell, although you are an unknown figure to her.'

'Oh, a remittance for half the agreed fee will make us quits, marm, and no more need be said about it. However, should Lady Russell, or her husband, ever require my services directly, I trust you'd recommend me. Ah, you are sure I must stay for tea?'

'I am sure you must continue striving to bring about the required change in the feelings of my sister,' she said, although she was coming to favour this less and less each day. 'You dazzled her by wearing your uniform this afternoon, and she has stopped sighing over her infatuation with Cumberland. She is no longer mooning and languishing. However, please tell me how you managed to obtain the letter from Cumberland.'

'Ah, yes,' he said, and fully resigned himself to his patron's refusal to allow him to depart.

'Well?'

'You'll recall my suggestion that it would be useful to have a friend in the camp of the enemy? I'm happy to inform you the sweet puss proved an invaluable help.'

'Spare me, please, the endearments you bestow on the wench,' said Caroline, disliking intensely the thought of what went on between him and Cumberland's trollop of a maidservant.

'In short, marm, with Betsy's assistance, the letter came to my hand.'

'How, sir, how?'

'I opened Cumberland's private writing-desk, marm, and filched it.'

Caroline winced. 'Captain Burnside, you entered his suite, broke open his writing-desk and stole the letter?'

'Tricky, marm, I agree, and there was also the risk of being nabbed and topped.'

'Nabbed and topped?'

'Well, it was Cumberland's house, d'you see, and his private correspondence, and he's fifth in line to the throne. He'd have had me dangling from Tyburn Tree if—'

'Oh, dear God,' gasped Caroline, shocked, 'I did not ask you to commit yourself to the crime of burglary in the house of a royal Duke, nor would I.'

'Well, I'm a professional, marm, and as such I'm as nimble-fingered as the best. All in a day's work for a patron, I assure you.'

136

Caroline rose in agitation and swept about, silken gown and underskirt rushing and rustling. 'Captain Burnside, I don't wish to be assured that such actions are all in your day's work for me. I don't wish to hear you are a common thief as well as an adventurer.'

'Oh, I don't count myself a common thief, marm. I can simply claim to being versatile.'

'Have you no shame, sir, none at all? Are you also a footpad and a highwayman?'

'A footpad?' Captain Burnside looked askance at her. 'A dark alley, an unsuspecting victim, and a blow from a cudgel? That's a wounding question, marm. But I won't say I couldn't turn highwayman if a patron's fee were encouraging enough. It's a risky business, d'you see, with some coach drivers quick to try blowing your head off with a blunderbuss. Regarding Cumberland's writing-desk, marm: rest assured there was no damage. I merely picked the lock.'

Caroline stopped sweeping about and drew needed breath. 'I shall pray for you, Captain Burnside. I shall pray for you to come to an honest turn in life, to use your many talents for the good of society and your own self. I beg you to change your ways, for the sake of your gentle mother and out of respect for the memory of your late, devout father.'

'A kind thought, marm, and a shipping clerk's work could well be for the good of society, but I ain't too set on boring myself to death.'

Caroline confronted him. He sat at his ease, the scoundrel, his expression that of a man in deferential respect, but she thought she caught a glimmer of amusement in his grey eyes.

'Sir,' she said, the warmth of South Carolina in her voice, 'I vow you a monster of prevarication. I do not believe you filched the letter, that you broke into Cumberland's private rooms and opened his writing-desk. You are amusing yourself at my expense. I won't have it. The truth, I declare, is that you prevailed on Cumberland to exchange the letter for the IOU. Come, confess it.'

'The truth, marm, is exactly as I presented it to you,' said the Captain affably.

Caroline vibrated. 'Then I must pray for you,' she breathed, 'for, conscienceless reprobate though you are, I cannot forget you brought blissful relief to Lady Russell, and I am unable to bear the thought that one day you will end up being hanged.'

'It don't make me feel too comfortable myself, marm.'

'Oh, you are a clown, sir, an idiot, senselessly wasting your talents,' she cried, out of all patience with him. Captain Burnside silently remarked the splendour of her renowned beauty, her figure a tribute to the fertile nature of the American South, which bestowed lush ripeness on its lovelier female blooms. Caroline, fiery, was seized with a desire to slap his face again, not because of his impudent eyes, but because she wished to shock him into an awareness of his idiocy. But she controlled herself. A little shakily she said, 'Captain Burnside, see, I will lend you sufficient money to set yourself up in a business of your own choice, a business that will not be boring to you. No, do not dismiss the offer out of hand, but give it sensible consideration, I beg.'

'Very well, marm. I should be churlish beyond anything not to consider such generosity.'

'There, I shall regard that as a promise from you, and perhaps from now on we might do away with a pretence of friendship, and strive to make it sincere.'

'Well said, marm,' murmured the Captain, 'although it's a strict principle of mine, in my relationship with a patron, to—'

'Oh, a pest on your silly principles, sir! Your talents are proven, yes, but your principles are tush and taradiddle. I wish our relationship to be more friendly, and shall constantly press you, as a friend would, to turn over a new leaf and become an honest and worthy person, with aspirations even to become a gentleman. Do not look down your nose, sir, there is much to be said these days for becoming a gentleman. England, I know, has never lacked its sturdy yeomen and brave soldiers, but there is presently a regrettable lack of true gentlemen. You, sir, as an adventurer, are no worse than many persons of the Quality in your pursuit and deception of innocent young ladies, or in the company you keep with baggages and trollops. I declare, sir, because of what you have done for Lady Russell, that I shall not only pray for your redemption, but do my utmost to discourage you from further promiscuity and even cure you of it.'

'Faith,' said Captain Burnside in honest admiration, 'you've a deal of determined Christian goodness in you, marm, and I ain't too sure I'll be able to resist being saved. You, marm, are—' He checked as the door opened and Annabelle came in, looking very refreshed. She had changed into a light muslin gown of cream ivory shade, and there was a peaceful smile on her face, as if she had collected her thoughts and analysed her confusions to her satisfaction, at least for the moment.

Seeing Caroline standing before Captain Burnside, she said demurely, 'Caroline is giving you a lecture, Charles?'

Captain Burnside, acknowledging her arrival by coming to his feet, smiled. 'A lecture, Annabelle? Not by any means. We've been enjoying a delightful conversation concerning friendship, and the pleasant obligations of one friend to another.'

'Obligations?' said Annabelle. 'How dull.' Reaching the Captain, she tapped him lightly on the shoulder with her fan. 'Charles, I would much rather have you wicked than dull. Why, I cannot conceive how you managed to be dull at all, for of all things you are the most entertaining of men.'

'I ain't remarked too much dullness in you, either,' said Captain Burnside.

Annabelle laughed. Abruptly, Caroline turned away and pulled on the bell sash to signal her servants that tea could now be brought in. In the kitchen, the bell rang loudly and demandingly, jerking angrily on its spring.

Turning again, Caroline saw that her sister and the Captain had seated themselves on the sofa, a light, delicate Hepplewhite original that was not outshone by the rest of the furniture, all French. Annabelle was close to the Captain, turned to him, her smile signifying the pleasure she found in his company. Caroline felt her own company was now unrequired. She also felt that Captain Burnside was not far from accomplishing the remaining part of his venture. All too visibly, Annabelle was as responsive to him as she could be at this stage. Their conversation was a lightness, she slightly teasing, he proof against all teasing in his imperturbability, and therefore that much more of a challenge. He really seemed to make no effort with Annabelle. He neither flattered her with his tongue, nor caressed her with his eyes. He returned her teasing remarks with the driest of comments, arousing gurgles of laughter in her.

The silver tea tray arrived and was set down.

'Your Ladyship?' said Helene, Caroline's senior maidservant.

'You may go, Helene. I will pour.'

'Yes, milady.'

A few moments later, acknowledging herself *de trop*, Caroline said in her cool voice, 'I have letters to write, and will take my tea into the library. You may serve Captain Burnside and yourself, Annabelle.'

Captain Burnside was up at once, to open the door for her. He also accompanied her to the library door, and opened that for her.

'The bird's coming to hand, marm,' he said.

'Pardon?'

'Well, she ain't quite so set on yielding unconditionally to Cumberland, I'll wager that.'

'If you are referring to my sister, Captain Burnside, kindly do so in civilised language.'

'Well, there it is, Caroline, I'll swear she could have yielded unconditionally, and I ain't sure I could have put it in more civilised language than that.'

'I meant, sir, that my sister is not a bird. Nor have I given you leave to call me Caroline.'

'Ah, our new relationship of friendliness is yet to begin, marm?'

Caroline hesitated momentarily before replying. 'You are making such a close and intimate friend of my sister, Captain Burnside, that I hardly feel you need my own friendship, after all.'

'Quite so, marm, and allow me to carry your tea in for you,' he said. He took the delicate cup and saucer from her, entered the library, and placed the tea on the desk. Following on in her coolest and most aloof manner, she seated herself at the desk.

'You may return to Annabelle now,' she said. 'I will see you later, at supper, unless you have an assignation with some unfortunate innocent.'

'Ah, yes,' he said. 'That is, no. I'm considering the advisability of leaving innocents to their innocence. I thought, for this evening, a three-handed game of cribbage, if you'd care to, and if you and Annabelle have no ball to attend.'

'Cribbage?' she said, and her aloofness slipped away and her eyes sparkled. She adored cribbage, and was quick and decisive in her play. Annabelle was also an enthusiast. 'Very well,' she said, and began to sip her tea.

'A guinea a game, shall we say?' murmured the Captain. 'And half a guinea for each hand of double figures?'

'Certainly not,' said Caroline, 'you will cheat, and Annabelle and I will lose a small fortune each.'

'Give you my word, marm.'

'As a gentleman?' she said drily.

'As a friend,' he said.

Caroline, having mellowed, smiled. 'You must first receive Annabelle's agreement,' she said. 'We are both free to play. The only ball we have to attend this week is Lady Chesterfield's, on Saturday evening.'

'You will grace it, marm, grace it,' said the Captain, and returned to Annabelle.

Two coiffured heads were bent over their cards. Annabelle's fair hair shone softly golden in the light of the evening sun that streamed through the windows of the card room. Caroline's auburn curls showed tints of dark, fiery red. Her lips were pursed, her eyes animated.

Captain Burnside, leaning back in his chair, viewed her from over the top of his hand. Magnificent. Her bosom, powdered, rose and fell gently to her even intake of air. She held her four cards fanwise in her left hand, having made her discard, as usual, with no obvious self-doubts. One might have thought her pursed lips an indication that she had not left herself with anything but an average hand. But the light in her eyes belied this.

Annabelle, not yet having made her discard, rearranged her cards and studied them again. Her blue eyes were roundly contemplative. It was their roundness that contributed so much to her young look. She too pursed her lips, and at once looked prettily kissable.

Captain Burnside waited patiently, but Caroline murmured, 'Why not shut your eyes, Annabelle, and make a blind discard?'

'I am considering tactics, not a score,' said Annabelle. They were into their third game. Caroline had won the first, and might have won the second too if Annabelle had not pipped her with a resounding final hand of twenty-four. All three of them were close to home in this third game. Caroline was on her mettle, frankly hoping to do Captain Burnside in the eye, and Annabelle was no less ambitious to pip her sister again. Annabelle was five guineas up on the Captain and two guineas up on Caroline. Caroline was three guineas up on the Captain.

Annabelle made her discard, and cut the pack for Caroline, who turned up a two. Captain Burnside led.

'Nine.'

'Nineteen,' said Annabelle, placing a king down.

'Twenty-nine, and a pair,' said Caroline, also showing a king.

'Thirty-one,' said Captain Burnside, coming up with a two. He and Caroline advanced their pegs. They each had a cribbage board of black ivory, with white ivory pegs. The Captain needed nine for game, Caroline five and Annabelle seven.

'Four,' said Annabelle.

'Two for a pair,' said Caroline, matching her sister again.

'Bother,' said Annabelle.

'Six for three pairs,' said the Captain, putting down a third four.

'Oh, you sweet man,' laughed Annabelle, and put down the fourth four, which scored her twelve and gave her the game. It also credited her with half a guinea, on top of a guinea for the game. 'You are lagging, Charles.'

'Early days, dear girl,' said the Captain, 'and my blood ain't up yet.'

'The decanter is at your elbow, Captain, if that is any help,' observed Caroline, graciously the hostess.

'I'm obliged, Caroline, much obliged,' he said, and poured a measure of brandy into his glass.

He had one virtue at least, she thought. He was never in his cups. He drank modestly. He had an acceptable liking for red wine, and a reasonable partiality for good brandy. She did not like men who were primly teetotal. It made them lack a zest for living. But she liked even less those who drank to excess, for in their cups they lost all manliness.

The fourth game began. Caroline ran away with it. Annabelle had not seen her sister so animated. She rarely spoke about her marriage, but Annabelle knew it had robbed her of sparkle. It was surprising that a mere game of cribbage could bring that sparkle back. The light in her expressive green eyes was almost as brilliant as her jewelled hair clasp.

'Damn me,' said Captain Burnside mildly, as she ran out with a hand of twenty, a combination of sevens, eights and a nine, 'are you sure one of those eights ain't been up your sleeve? I'm holding three myself.'

'What?' Caroline pounced and scattered his cards. 'Oh, you are not, sir! There, you have two eights and two sixes.'

'Egad, so I have. I own to sweet relief, dear lady, that there's been no sharping.'

'Idiot!' cried Caroline, and burst into laughter.

'Temporary myopia on my part,' murmured the Captain, 'so sorry.'

Annabelle's eyes danced.

The play continued. The sisters were at one in their desire to get the better of Captain Burnside, Annabelle because it was fun, Caroline because it was a challenge. Annabelle played her cards either with gurgles of triumph or moans of despair. Caroline played hers with an animated flourish. The Captain played his affably, and with a sporting acceptance of all the knocks he took. Fortunes fluctuated, then took a decided turn in his favour. Caroline's butler came in to light the candelabrum above the table, and Helene brought glasses of fresh lemonade sweetened with honey for the sisters.

The Captain laid down a hand of sixteen to win his fifth consecutive game, and to put the sisters in debt to him.

'Oh, you wretch,' said Annabelle.

Caroline, catching his eye, said, 'Your hands are becoming almost unbelievable, Captain.'

'I can't dispute it,' he said. 'Shall we cry quits?'

'Certainly not,' said Caroline spiritedly.

'I shall play one more game, then retire,' said Annabelle. 'I am feeling sleepy.'

They played the game, which Caroline won. Annabelle stifled a yawn and rose from the table.

'You are owing me two and a half guineas, dearest,' said Caroline.

'Am I, dearest?' Annabelle smiled. 'Well, you would not take money from a sister who has so little, would you? There, I'll settle with a kiss.' She leaned and kissed Caroline on the cheek. 'And what do I owe you, Charles?'

'A trifle, a mere trifle, dear girl,' said the Captain benevolently. 'Ah, nine guineas. And a half.'

'So much?' said Annabelle. 'Oh, dear. You would not accept a kiss too, I suppose?'

'Willingly,' said Captain Burnside.

'There, you are the sweetest man,' said Annabelle. A little dreamy, a little melting from the fun of the evening, she dipped her head and kissed him. On the mouth. Caroline stiffened, for her sister's kiss was warm, generous and quite against acceptable behaviour. 'Goodnight,' said Annabelle, now a little flushed, 'I'll leave you two to play on until the candles gutter, if you wish.'

When she had gone, Captain Burnside said, 'Shall you retire too, marm?'

'Shall you?' asked Caroline coldly. 'Or shall you sit and dream of more kisses? Oh, how I despise myself for placing Annabelle in your path, for I cannot help feeling you will take advantage of her in the end.'

'You have my word I won't, marm. If I read her correctly, she has no money.'

'Oh, you are an out-and-out blackguard, sir. I vow myself feeble for being concerned at your probable fate, for you deserve the most miserable one. As for Annabelle's lack of money, there are always her trinkets.'

'True, her jewellery has its appeal,' murmured the Captain, idly shuffling the pack, 'but I ain't diposed to lift 'em from so sweet a girl. No, she shall be safe from me, marm. Be assured. Well, shall it be two-handed cribbage, patron, or bed? It's almost midnight.'

'We shall cut for deal, Captain Burnside, and play for five guineas a game, not one, and I will give you a hiding, sir, and collect from you every last shilling of what you will owe me.'

'It's to be war, then, marm, with no talk of kisses?'

Flushed, her eyes glittering, she said fiercely, 'I would rather kiss the hangman.'

'Quite so, marm. Ah, at the moment, you are owing me several guineas from the three-handed game.'

'You may take them into account at the end of this game.'

She played then in a spirit of fierce determination, while knowing determination needed luck as an ally. Her mouth was set, her eyes gleaming, her concentration prevailing over whatever tiredness she felt. She sent her servants to bed at Captain Burnside's solicitous suggestion. She and he alone remained awake, he retaining his smooth, affable approach, and she sustaining her spirited challenge. If he wondered what had upset her so much, he did not ask.

She seemed reckless in her discarding, so quickly did she place each pair on the table, but the turn-up cards consistently went her way. She pegged advantageously, and her hands scored generously. She outran him by four games out of the first five. A candle spluttered. Her eyelids began to feel heavy. Her lashes began to droop. The quietness of the house, the silence of the street outside, and the lateness of the hour all induced a soporific effect. But she played on.

'You are ready now to cry quits, marm?' The Captain had won three in a row.

'No, sir. I shall not be the first to yield. I am a Howard of South Carolina, and my ancestors were pioneering the first settlement of Charleston while yours were no doubt running errands for Sir Walter Raleigh. Deal, sir, you are not yet owing me half enough.'

'I ain't quite owing you anything yet, d'you see—'

'Deal, sir, I like you better when your tongue is silent, though in truth I like you not at all.'

Captain Burnside smiled. She eyed him simmeringly from under languid lids, thinking of his cool, outrageous acceptance of the kind of kiss Annabelle should not have given. How dare he, a man so undeserving and unprincipled, allow himself such intimacy with her impulsively indiscreet sister?

They played on. She fought her creeping tiredness. Her head sank, her jewelled hair clasp glittered as it nodded. She jerked herself awake. She laid a card, a jack. 'Ten,' she said.

Captain Burnside, laying down a jack himself, said, 'Twenty, and two for a pair.'

'Thirty,' she breathed in sleepy triumph, and showed a third jack. 'Which scores me six.'

'Fiendish,' murmured the Captain. 'Pass,' he added.

'Thirty-one,' she said, placing an ace down to score another two.

'Faith,' he said, smiling, 'you're a tigress.' But his patron did not respond. Her head was down, heavy eyes closed. A slumbrous little murmur escaped her. 'Damn me, here's a pretty kettle of fish, our magnificent magnolia has closed her petals for the night.'

He came to his feet and touched her lightly on the shoulder. She did not stir. She was in sound, healthy sleep. He stooped and lifted her from her chair. She was full-bodied, but he made light of her. She murmured, put her arms sleepily around his neck, turned herself in on him and warmed her bosom against his chest. Her head sank on to his shoulder. He carried her up the stairs, and at her door he set her gently on her feet. She swayed against him. With one arm around her, he opened the door and carried her into her dressing-room. There he placed her in an armchair. Her head fell forward, causing her bodice to sigh and gently gape. Curving splendour softly gleamed in the light of a night candle, and tender nipples lay within the shadows of lined, protective silk. Carefully, the Captain set her head back, and the bodice corrected itself. Curving splendour for the most part disappeared into the shadows. He went to his own room, smiling. There was nothing about feminine magnificence to cause any man to frown.

147

# Chapter Thirteen

'Your Ladyship?'

Caroline, awakening very late, looked up at Helene, efficient, devoted and still single at thirty, although Mr Harris, the forty-year-old butler, had a firm and affectionate eye turned her way.

'Helene? What is the time, pray?'

'Gone ten-thirty, milady. Shall I bring—'

'No breakfast, please. Just coffee. And have my bath filled.'

She sat back in the large hip bath that had been carried into her dressing-room and filled from pots of hot water. The pink soap flakes, melting, created a foam that danced around her floating breasts, for the bath was deep. She relaxed, but she frowned. She had fallen asleep at the card table and woken up in her dressing-room. Even then she had been almost too sleepy to undress herself, and had finally left her clothes in the most untidy heap.

Captain Burnside. Such an idiotic man in his preference for the dubious when he could have established himself in good, honest work. If he applied himself industriously, he would make an excellent steward for someone's country estate, and be remote from the temptations of town.

She must, she supposed, allow him to continue his role with Annabelle, for Annabelle must be turned aside from Cumberland. The unacceptable factor, of course, was that which might bring Annabelle amorously into the arms of the Captain, whose morals were as casual as they could be. He might not extract money from Annabelle, or lay his hands on any of her jewellery, but he might take his pleasure of her.

She discovered him in the library later. He was seated on the little step-ladder, reading a volume he had taken from a shelf. He looked as if the book was earnestly engaging him. It was a history of Ireland.

'Captain Burnside?'

He glanced up. 'Good morning, marm.'

'I must apologise for falling asleep last night.'

'Not at all,' he said pleasantly, 'you were game to the end, and it was no effort to deposit you safely in your suite.'

'Deposit me?'

'Ah,' he said, and put the book away and studied the ceiling.

'What do you mean, sir, *deposit* me?'

'Well, there you were, marm, claimed by the rosy goddess of slumber and fast in her arms. Since I had to climb the stairs to my own room, I – ah – took you with me.'

'Took me?'

'Carried you, marm. You were sweetly dreaming, d'you see, and it seemed a pity to wake you.'

'I am incredulous, Captain Burnside,' said Caroline, although she had wondered how she arrived in her suite. 'Do you seriously say you carried me?'

'I ain't given to the crime of dragging a lady up a staircase, marm. If I'm going to be hanged, it don't signify I'll risk being hanged for that.'

Caroline stared at him. He asked her indulgence with a smile. She shook her head at him.

She laughed. 'Captain Burnside, you are lamentable, sir. You carried me up and placed me in the chair?'

'I did, marm, and as gently as I could.'

'You did not find me too heavy?'

'Lord, marm, you were as light as a feather.'

She laughed again. 'Light as a feather?' she said. 'I think not. Am I to thank you for your gallantry? I am not sure. However, to another matter. I have just despatched my young coachman to Lady Chesterfield's house with a note, requesting she will permit you to accompany Annabelle to her ball on Wednesday evening. I shall be accompanied myself by Mr Gerald Wingrove. Cumberland will be there

149

and, if you are there too, I will rely on you to prevent him bestowing his attentions on Annabelle. My sister is bound to take on a giddy mood, for a London ball is of all things exhilarating to her. In such a mood she is likely to disappear with Cumberland.'

'Well, he has a way with him,' said the Captain, 'but you have my word that if she should disappear, it'll be with me.'

'No, I won't have that,' said Caroline, 'for I can no more trust your inclinations than Annabelle's dangerous giddiness. You understand my frankness, I think.'

'It's true she's sweetly tempting . . .'

'Sir?'

'Assure you, marm, I'd not take advantage.'

'You are not to disappear with her, Captain Burnside. You are to be a model of chivalry.'

'Chivalry,' he murmured, 'ah, yes.'

'Now, sir, the cribbage,' she said. 'Do I owe you, or do you owe me?'

'You owe me five and a half guineas, marm. And – um – I'm a little short of funds. Expenses, d'you see. There's little left of the advance. I paid the girl Betsy ten guineas for her help—'

'A small amount of silver would have been enough for any other trollop.'

'So it might, marm, so it might. But not for a wholehearted commitment and a tight mouth. Most trollops gab—'

'Gab?'

'Talk, marm. Chatter. You must pick one you can be certain of.'

'Oh, never mind,' said Caroline. She went to the desk, unlocked the central drawer and took out some money. 'What did you say my cribbage losses were?'

'Oh, say ten guineas, marm.'

'I shall say nothing of the kind, since it was, yes, five and a half, I think. Well, I shall give you fifteen, the balance being to augment your expenses fund.' And she gave him that amount.

'H'm,' he said, but nodded and smiled.

'There,' she said, 'now perhaps we can contrive our more friendly relationship.'

'With pleasure, my dear Caroline,' he said, at which she gave him a firm look.

'It means, Captain Burnside, that I wish to encourage you to turn over a new leaf. It does not mean you may indulge in familiarities. What is your programme for today?'

'I'm driving Annabelle to Vauxhall Gardens, which you'll know are greatly favoured by romantic couples. There we shall stroll and promenade, and take lunch, and I shall have the sweet girl sighing and languishing in the seclusion of arbours and shrubberies.'

'Your conceits take my breath,' said Caroline. She thought of the secluded arbours and shrubberies of Vauxhall Gardens, and of Annabelle's obvious liking for Captain Burnside, and it gave her no happiness at all. 'I shall come with you,' she said.

'How very friendly of you, marm.'

'I do not wish to discourage you in the part you are playing, but I do wish to protect my sister to some extent.'

'Very right and proper,' said Captain Burnside, 'for I own I can be carried away by an excess of enthusiasm on behalf of a patron.'

'Captain Burnside, you are a wretch,' said Caroline. 'I wonder, do you think Cumberland might have discovered the letter is missing?'

'Not unless he makes a daily check, dear lady, which I doubt.'

'Move him,' said Cumberland through grating teeth.

'Yes, Your Royal Highness, I think that advisable now,' said Erzburger. 'And in the long term, silence is also advisable.'

'On more than one tongue,' said Cumberland. 'I fancy I must talk to Captain Heywood.' Captain Heywood was the Duke's dedicated familiar, the medium through whom he achieved his darkest objectives. 'Advise him to be available this afternoon. I'll take no chances that ears didn't hear and a tongue didn't wag in curiosity.'

151

'We spoke only in a guarded way, Your Highness, so that whatever she overheard had no great substance. Yet it would have aroused her curiosity. So although commoners might take chances, princes cannot.'

'This prince don't intend to,' said Cumberland.

Vauxhall Gardens, patronised by the elite, boasted a summer blaze of colour. Although the most spectacular of the shrubs, such as the azaleas and the rhododendrons, had shed their blooms, magnificent flower beds were a sunlit radiance. Shady walks and leafy promenades drew the strollers, and the elegant refreshments pavilion was an irresistible temptation to those desiring to quench their thirst or pleasure their palates.

Annabelle and Caroline glided arm-in-arm with Captain Burnside. Ladies needed to demonstrate they were under the guardianship of an escort, for the Gardens were among the more favoured haunts of young and dashing Corinthian bucks, ever ready to catch the eye of sweet things seemingly unattached and to pick up a handkerchief apparently dropped. 'No, no, sir, it is not mine.' 'Egad, then, whose can it be?' 'Perhaps, sir, it's your sister's.' It was all done in the politest and most civilised way, for the Gardens clung jealously to their reputation for respectability, and patrons who breached the conventions were requested to leave. Nevertheless, the young bucks were a ubiquitous element, and sweet things knew it and played the game in their own demure way, under the eyes of their chaperones or their parents.

Caroline, right hand on Captain Burnside's left arm, parasol executing animated little twirls on her left shoulder, was clad in white muslin delicately patterned with green and pink. Its long skirt swayed lightly around her limbs. Annabelle, on the Captain's other arm, a new parasol shading her, was in pale blue silk. It was her first visit to the Gardens, and she was enchanted. She felt herself in romantic Arcadia. The ladies were so elegant in their summer finery, the young men had so much *ton*. And Captain Burnside was all of debonair. Why Caroline did not set her cap at him she could not think. But perhaps it was Mr Wingrove who had recently brought her to life. She was almost vivacious in her enjoyment of this outing. If Mr Wingrove was a little dull in his conversation, one could not say he was disagreeable, and had he been here he would have supplied a most informative dissertation on every plant, flower, shrub and tree. Caroline, perhaps, had come to favour informative dissertations. Annabelle herself much preferred Captain Burnside's whimsical qualities.

Caroline detached herself to gaze in admiration at a huge bed of geraniums. After only a few seconds, a voice murmured in her ear.

'Why, it's Charmian Merryweather. How very delightful.'

Caroline, turning, found a gentleman in an exquisite, silver-blue coat, smiling at her with a great deal of pleasure. Courteously, he lifted his top hat.

At her coolest, she said, 'I regret having to disappoint you, sir, but I am not the lady in question.'

The gentleman looked convincingly startled, surprised and taken aback. 'But we met, did we not, at Marlborough's place no less than a month ago?' he said, remarking beauty richly healthy.

Caroline knew precisely what he was about. A week or so ago she would have dealt with him by giving him an icy look and turning her back on him. Now, for some reason, the sweeter aspects of life had been rediscovered, and to have a Corinthian of impeccable dress and appearance attempt to win her favour aroused an impulse to make a different kind of play. 'Do you mean Blenheim, sir?' she said.

'There, I knew it, b'gad I did.' The gentleman's smile returned. 'Blenheim, of course. I'm not making a mistake, am I?'

'No, you are not making a mistake,' said Caroline, suspecting Captain Burnside and Annabelle had stopped to turn and look back. 'You are proceeding correctly to plan.'

153

'Dashed if I've any plans at the moment, except to suggest a walk to the pavilion for some refreshing sherbert.' The gentleman executed a light, inviting bow. 'You're from Devon?' he enquired, attempting to place her accent.

'I am not, sir.'

'Ah, I've got your home and name wrong?'

'I am sure you have everything quite right,' said Caroline, 'except that in meeting a lady called Charmian Merryweather at Blenheim a month ago, you did not meet me. It is three years since I was at Blenheim in company with my husband.'

'Then I was out of luck a month ago,' said the gentleman, not at all put out at the mention of a husband.

'You are also out of luck now, sir,' said Caroline. She turned and went on her way, leaving the gentleman sighing that so rare a beauty should have shown so little interest in him.

Annabelle and Captain Burnside were not in sight. They had strolled unconcernedly on, it seemed. Caroline was at once offended. For a gentleman to leave a lady unescorted was a social sin in the Gardens. It was not even permissible. But the Captain, of course, was no gentleman. She quickened her steps, glancing left and right. Other paths and leafy walks intersected this path. Really, what was Annabelle thinking about to go off like this with the Captain?

She searched the walks without success. She turned to retrace her steps. Before her, a path between verdant shrubs was bright with sunlight. The chatter of visitors was fading. In their twos and threes, they were stepping aside to the very edges of the path, nervously leaving it clear for a man approaching at a leisurely stride. Tall, powerful-looking, the sun at his back, he brought a darkness with his advance. His coat was dark, his boots were black, his top hat the colour of charcoal. Only his tight, light grey knee breeches were a concession to the bright day. His massive, muscular shoulders cleaved the air unhurriedly. He carried a walking-stick of black ebony with a silver handle, and in his natural arrogance he was entirely indifferent to the people stepping aside for him. He neither looked at them nor acknowledged them.

A whisper broke the silence. 'Yes, it's Cumberland.'

Behind him two men followed, one in a military uniform, the other in sober dress. Caroline, standing in the middle of the path, and with the sun on her, was a vision. Cumberland, seeing her, did not quicken his pace. His advance remained slow and deliberate. Reaching her, his blind eye peered unseeingly, and his sound eye gleamed. Erzburger and Captain Heywood came to a halt at a discreet distance from him. Erzburger had a parasol tucked under his arm.

Cumberland bowed to Caroline, and his strong mouth twitched in a faint smile. 'So, there ye are,' he said, 'but have ye no companions?'

Out of the rules of etiquette, Caroline curtseyed. 'Yes, I have companions, Your Royal Highness.'

'I'll take ye up if ye ain't,' he said.

'They will appear any moment, sir,' said Caroline, straight of back and politely proud, though very vexed indeed with Captain Burnside for so discomfiting her.

'Your sister Annabelle and your friend Captain – ah – something or other?' enquired Cumberland. 'I dropped in on your house, y'see, and was informed the three of ye were here. A pretty place for canaries, parrots and peacocks. Ye're worthy of grandeur, and a few shrubs and flowers don't do ye justice.'

'I am happy, Your Highness, in so pretty a place, and don't demand a vista of mountains,' said Caroline, aware that the people who had made way for Cumberland had halted in their promenading. Every eye was on herself and the Duke. If she was sensitive to this, he was not. He cared not a fig for what people said or what people thought. The Prince of Wales courted popularity. Cumberland had no use for such nonsense. 'Have you come from my house, sir, in pursuit of me here?' asked Caroline.

'God's life, would ye make such pursuit worthwhile, Caroline?' he said, his henchmen standing off in impassive silence. 'Have ye more liking for me?'

'My feelings for you are as they have always been,' she said.

The cloudy eye expressed nothing. The sound eye mocked her. 'Ye discovered a faultiness in Percival,' he said, 'ye'll discover a man in me. However, since I was coming this way I thought to look for ye.'

'To advise me you'll not be coming tomorrow evening for the card game?' she said in swift impulse, for she immediately thought Captain Burnside had amused himself by spinning a fairy tale, and that he had indeed surrendered the IOU for the letter.

Cumberland laughed. 'I don't intend to forgo my revenge, my sweet beauty,' he said, 'for I've a keen desire to reduce Annabelle's pretty Captain to tatters.'

'I would not call him pretty, sir, nor would I say he is Annabelle's.'

'Come, I've heard they're seen together everywhere, and that her smiles for him ain't less loving than they are for me.'

'I cannot enjoy this kind of conversation, Your Highness. May I know why you've come looking for me?'

'To ask if I'll be seeing ye at Lady Chesterfield's ball tomorrow, for I swear it'll have no spice for me if ye ain't there.'

'I shall be there, sir.'

'And your sister and the pretty Captain?'

'Lady Chesterfield has invited them both.' Caroline had received an immediate affirmative from Lady Chesterfield.

'Ah.' Cumberland looked satisfied. 'Ye're sure I can't favour ye?'

'How favour me, sir?'

'By escorting ye to a flowery alcove and convincing ye of my unchanging affections, for I see no sign of your companions, whom I fancy have found their own alcove.'

'You will allow me to decline, Your Highness?'

'Not without a sigh for your own lack of affection,' said Cumberland. 'But I ain't impatient where you're concerned, and though ye may see some imperfections ye'll

156

come to admire in me that which will tell ye I'm a man above all else.' And his dark eye searched her, as if looking for a revealing flash of distrust. But he saw only her inveterate coolness.

'I cannot respond to that,' she said.

'Ye might, ye might in time. Ah, yes, something else.' His smile was that of the devil in jest. He made a gesture, and Erzburger came forward. He handed the parasol to the Duke, and retreated. The Duke proffered the parasol to Caroline. 'Your sister's,' he said. 'She forgot to take it with her when she left my house yesterday afternoon. Good day to ye, Lady Clarence.' He lifted his top hat and walked leisurely away. His henchmen followed. Caroline, the folded parasol in her hand, quivered, and her mouth set in an angry line.

Swiftly, she made her way towards the pavilion, for there she and Annabelle were to have lunch with Captain Burnside. Turning into another walk, she saw them. They had come to a halt on their approach to the pavilion, and were facing each other. Annabelle was laughing up at him, and her closeness to him was positively unseemly. Caroline swept up to them.

'You have had an excessively long tête-à-tête,' smiled Annabelle.

'Go aside,' said Caroline.

'Caroline?' Annabelle looked perplexed.

'Go aside. I wish to speak to Captain Burnside before I speak to you. And take this. It is yours.'

Annabelle flushed as Caroline thrust the parasol at her. Captain Burnside looked rueful.

'But, Caroline,' said Annabelle, taking the parasol, 'it is so unfair to treat me as if I were a child—'

'You are a child. Go aside, do you hear?'

Annabelle flushed again, but found the spirit to draw herself up and walk until she was out of earshot, when she stopped and began her enforced wait.

Caroline confronted Captain Burnside, her green eyes on fire. 'Trickster, villain, deceiver, I vow you wholly contemptible,' she hissed.

157

'H'm,' said Captain Burnside, and allowed a lady and gentleman to pass before he said more. 'Cumberland has scored a paltry victory at the expense of sweetness.'

'He is in the Gardens, sir. He spoke to me, returned the parasol to me and scored his victory at my expense too.' Caroline was so angry that she could have struck her traitorous hireling. His utter lack of principles and his unholy deception created within her the kind of emotional turmoil worse than any she had suffered during the years of her disastrous marriage. 'I cannot believe such treachery. You swore, sir, to keep Annabelle apart from Cumberland, to do all you could to turn her aside from him. But yesterday you drove her to his house, you contrived behind my back to help her keep an assignation with him! Do you deny it?'

'Faith, I might to another patron, marm, but not to one as magnificent as you—'

'Speak me no honey, sir. If there is any kind of a man in you at all, confess your betrayal!' There was the fury of almost uncontrollable anger in her expression, and fiery contempt in her eyes. 'Oh, in South Carolina, sir, make no mistake, I would have you whipped for such unforgivable duplicity.'

'Understandable, I fancy,' said the rueful Captain, 'and you'll not believe, I dare say, that it was all to do with policy.'

'Policy? *Policy*?'

'If one brings the lamb to look into the face of the wolf often enough, the lamb will begin to question the sharpness of the wolf's teeth.'

'But once too often, sir, and the lamb will be devoured. You have driven out with Annabelle several times. Have there been other betrayals?'

'Only in pursuance of the policy, marm. Be assured Annabelle is coming to suspect Cumberland is interested only in her appeal as a virgin, and I fancy she ain't now as disposed as she might have been to surrender herself on account of excitement and pleasure alone.'

'I declare, sir,' she breathed, her parasol itself quivering, 'that the familiarity and indelicacy with which you speak of my sister and her virginity make you no more endearing to me than your general infamy.'

'Well, marm,' said Captain Burnside placatingly, 'I spoke in the frankest terms, d'you see, to Annabelle herself concerning the possibility that it was her sweet innocence that makes Cumberland keen to bed her. Perceptibly, marm, it raised her guard.'

Caroline felt the frustration of a woman who knew there were a thousand fiery words she could fling at him, but could not lay her tongue to any of them. For all his air of apology, there was not the slightest sign that he was truly perturbed or truly ashamed. He even smiled at her.

'Oh,' she said, 'were it not for your acquisition of the letter, I would send you packing here and now. I trusted you. You assured me that as your patron, I could rely on you to act only as I wished you to. Why did you not confide your tactics to me?'

'A reasonable question, marm, very reasonable,' he said, while Annabelle waited and watched. 'The fact is, I've a lamentable tendency to do things my own way, and it don't always make for harmony to let a patron know precisely what I'm about. Moreover, most patrons are only concerned with results. Beg to point out, marm, that poor Annabelle don't look too blissful at being out in the cold, as it were. Beg to suggest, marm, you forgive us both and bring her back to the comfort of your merciful bosom.'

Caroline could hardly believe her ears at such speciousness and such high-falutin' tush. Her merciful bosom indeed! She eyed him warningly. He coughed and lifted his gaze to the little galaxy of fluffy white clouds sailing through the blue sky. A quiver took hold of her. It travelled, it reached her mouth. She could not control it. Her lips broke apart. She laughed, almost helplessly. Annabelle heard it, richly ringing.

Her sister looked at her and beckoned. 'Come, Annabelle, take this impossible man off my hands.'

Annabelle rejoined them, though she looked a little hesitant. 'Caroline?'

'Oh, yes, you surely need to cast your eyes down, sister.'

'But I am not,' protested Annabelle.

'More shame on you, then,' said Caroline. 'Oh, how difficult it is to protect a sister when she won't obey London's first rules, which are that no young lady should place herself alone with a man, that a chaperone must always be present. Nor can I rely on Captain Burnside, despite our friendship, to help me, it seems.'

'Oh, but Charles has been a dear friend to me,' said Annabelle, 'and given me such good advice, oh, he surely has. I cannot help my feelings for the Duke of Cumberland, but I know Charles will let me do nothing that will put you in a truly rageful pet.' And she slipped her arm through the Captain's to show the affectionate confidence she had in him.

If this signified she was becoming very attached to him, and if this meant the desired result was in the offing, it was not something that seemed to please Caroline. She bit her lip. 'I do not get into rageful pets,' she said, 'but I own myself sensitive enough to feel discomfited when I am left to be accosted by the Corinthian element.'

'Accosted?' murmured the Captain, looking a stylish Corinthian himself in his dark brown coat and light brown pantaloons. 'Here, in Vauxhall Gardens?'

'Yes, here, sir, and I'm sure you saw the person in question.'

'But we thought him a most elegant and aristocratic gentleman, not a person,' said Annabelle, 'and we also thought that perhaps you knew him.'

'It won't do,' said Caroline, remembering the embarrassment of being alone when Cumberland saw her. 'Captain Burnside, I'm sure, is well aware of the subtle importunities unescorted ladies can suffer here, and I was mortified to find myself deserted by you and by him.'

She did not look mortified, thought Annabelle; she looked full of challenging life.

'It's true the atmosphere of the Gardens invites shy glances from unattached ladies,' said Captain Burnside, 'and shy glances provoke subtle advances . . .'

'Fiddle-de-dee, sir, and tush,' said Caroline. 'I am not given to glancing shyly or otherwise at persons I do not know.'

'True, true,' said the Captain, 'but then you don't need to, my dear Caroline. Your beauty alone is enough to provoke a hopeful advance, and I daresay even a blind man might be smitten.'

Again Caroline's mouth quivered, but she said, straight-faced, 'Sir, you are above yourself.'

Heavens, this is delicious, thought Annabelle. There is something between these two that has nothing to do with mere friendship.

'Well, I apologise sincerely, Caroline, for mistaking the situation,' said Captain Burnside, 'but we did indeed think you knew the – ah – person. Might I now recommend we go on our way to the pavilion and see what is on offer for lunch? Yes, capital. Now, your hand on my arm, Caroline, and don't detach it, for there in the distance are two more persons, both already quizzing you, and capable, I don't doubt, of running off with you given only half a chance.'

Annabelle laughed in delight. Caroline gazed at her impossible hireling. He smiled and offered his arm. She took it, worryingly aware of feeling indefinably susceptible. There was no denying he was a thief, an adventurer, a deceiver. He had done with Annabelle what he should not have done. He deserved to be dismissed and sent on his way. He deserved a thousand fiery words, and each should have left the scar of a burning arrow.

Instead, she and Annabelle were walking to have lunch with the unconscionable rogue in the bright pavilion, and both were arm-in-arm with him.

# Chapter Fourteen

At a quarter to four, Annabelle, having been persuaded to do so by her sister, was writing a letter to her parents, a letter detailing many of the current excitements of the London season and into which a host of aristocratic names were being dropped. But, with the letter almost finished, she had made no mention of plans to return home.

In the drawing room, rested and refreshed from the outing to Vauxhall Gardens, Caroline asked Helene to serve tea. 'Let Miss Annabelle know,' she said, 'and let Captain Burnside know too. I think he is in his room.'

'No, milady, he is out,' said Helene. 'He left the house ten minutes ago, and took the curricle.'

'I see.' Caroline appeared to receive the news calmly. 'Then tea just for Miss Annabelle and myself, please.'

'Yes, Your Ladyship,' said Helene and made her way to the kitchen.

Caroline simmered. The man was an atrocious wretch. He had sneaked himself out of the house and taken the curricle. Positively, his objective was either to fleece some trusting, innocent girl or to meet a trollop. His time was not his own: it belonged to her. But she supposed he was so addicted to fleecing innocents or pleasuring himself with trollops that either pursuit was compulsive.

Fleecing innocents was bad enough, pleasuring himself with trollops was worse, far worse. The thought actually pained her, dreadfully.

Captain Burnside sat in the curricle, its hood up. Sammy, the young coachman, had harnessed the two sleek horses for him. He liked the Captain, and not just for the tips he gave him.

Mr Franz Erzburger left the Duke's residence at five minutes after four. Outside, a diminutive groom had the smartest kind of curricle ready. Erzburger climbed into the seat, nodded curtly, and the groom stepped aside. The pair went off at a fast trot. Captain Burnside followed at a discreet distance. Erzburger took himself neatly through the town traffic and headed north-west. The traffic lightened outside the city environs, and he made brisk progress all the way to the pretty village of Islington, where recent development had taken place to provide city merchants with attractive houses. Older and smaller houses offered modest comfort to clerks and civil servants.

Erzburger pulled up outside a small, cottage-style house on the eastern outskirts. Well behind him, Captain Burnside turned off the dry, rutted road into a lane. He tethered his pair and walked back to the road, from where he saw Erzburger entering the house. The Captain waited. It was fifteen minutes before the Duke's secretary came out of the house, in company with a slight, wiry man, a bundle under his arm. They both boarded the curricle, and Erzburger began a turning manoeuvre. Captain Burnside retreated to his own vehicle, positioned himself out of sight in front of his pair and waited again. Erzburger drove past the lane. The Captain jumped back into Caroline's racy curricle, turned it quickly with the intelligent aid of the horses, and went once more in pursuit of Erzburger, but always at a distance.

Erzburger drove to Aldgate and to the district a little south of it, into an area somewhat less salubrious than Islington. The evening was fine, fine enough to reveal shabbiness and poverty. Men, rough-hewn and weary from work at the docks, sat outside their doors. A few women stood on doorsteps. Erzburger passed them and turned into a cobbled street where the dwellings showed cleaner windows and the refuse on the cobbles was not an especial eyesore. He stopped. A small urchin darted to offer his services in holding the bridle.

Captain Burnside went past the cobbled street without halting. He cast only a quick glance. He noted the door outside which the Duke's secretary had stopped. He drove out of the area. He was within seeing distance, however, a minute or two later, and remained there, keeping himself inconspicuous. This time he had to wait almost half an hour before he saw the smart curricle re-emerge from the cobbled street and turn back the way it had come. In the curricle was Erzburger alone.

'H'm,' murmured the Captain to himself, 'so this is what sweet Betsy said was unusual. Erzburger has a small, wiry friend latterly residing in Islington and now domiciled in Aldgate South. H'm.'

'Your Grace,' said Captain Burnside a little later that evening, 'I'll speak to Jonathan. I fancy he's our man.'

'That irreverent rascal?' said the gentleman of impressive dignity.

'Oh, he's Christian enough at heart, and ain't ever likely to consort with the devil. Put him unshaven into coarse cloth, and I'll wager he'll worm himself inside the house and become the new lodger's best friend inside an hour.'

'Proceed, then, for I've a feeling the plot's thickening. But who precisely it's aimed at, God knows. The King, the Prime Minister, the Prince of Wales, which of them, if any of them? You've a feeling about Erzburger's man. Damned if I can deduce a connection myself. But very well, put Jonathan Carter on to him. You're still in touch with Cumberland?'

'As much as I can be with the assistance of Lady Caroline and her sister, sir.'

'She's easier in her mind?'

'Concerning her foolish friend, Your Grace? Yes, I fancy so. Concerning her sister? She has high hopes I'll wean Annabelle off Cumberland, though she's in a fret at the distasteful thought of Annabelle in my arms.'

'So will I be if you play the blackguard, sir,' said the gentleman, frowning at the Captain.

'Oh, Annabelle will be saved by her own instincts.

Cumberland fascinates her, but I'll wager in the end she'll sense he'll do her no good, and will back off, for it's my belief she don't hold her virginity as lightly as that. Otherwise, she'd have lost it to Cumberland long since. It's a fact she ain't going to fall in love with me. There's affection there – faith, she's an affectionate girl – but it's no more than the affection of a sister for a supportive brother. I hope to God, Your Grace, that Lady Caroline never discovers my true part.'

'She'll have your head, sir, I don't doubt.'

'She will. She'll see me into my coffin.'

The distinguished-looking gentleman permitted himself a smile. 'She has American blood, Burnside, blood rich and vigorous.'

'And ain't to be trifled with on any account,' said the Captain. 'Cumberland comes tomorrow for the return game. If there's something afoot and he's discovered it concerns him, because of his connection with the Orange Order, he'll be edgy for all his royal complacency.'

'And if he has discovered it so, why hasn't he set up a hue and cry about it?'

'That, Your Grace, is a very interesting question. I'll drop in on Jonathan now.'

He did so, and he also slipped a note for Betsy under the side door of Cumberland's residence. It was past nine-thirty when he finally arrived back at Caroline's house, where coachman Sammy took charge of the curricle and the tired horses.

The Captain sought out his hostess. She was in the drawing room, reading. Annabelle was at an evening reception for young ladies, the reception arranged by Lady Hester Russell. Sammy was due to collect her at ten-fifteen.

Caroline, who had spent the evening alone, acknowledged the belated return of her hireling with a few biting words. 'Your absence, sir, I found agreeable. You could have spared me your reappearance.'

Captain Burnside crossed the room in such penitent haste that his coat tails fluttered. Reaching the chaise-longue, on which she reclined in shapely grace, he detached her right hand from her book and clasped it fervently between his own.

'Marm – Lady Caroline – I beg your sweet forgiveness,' he said in earnest contrition. 'Not for the world would I consciously offend so estimable a patron as you.' His grey eyes held her green, and her green swam with the warning light of a woman who found him suspect. 'Your generosity and hospitality have passed all expectations, your trust in me has warmed my heart . . .'

'My trust in you, sir, scarcely exists,' she said, 'and the hand you are holding is my own property, not yours.'

Captain Burnside clasped it even more fervently. 'Undoubtedly, marm, I have offended you, despite my devotion to you, and I count myself an ungracious and ungrateful gentleman to have done so. I—'

'I have never made the mistake, sir, of looking upon you as a gentleman.'

'True, dear lady, true; you have always been commendably frank, but I have endeavoured to be as much of a gentleman as possible to you.'

'You have not, sir, and please release my hand.'

He released it. Freed from his warm, firm clasp, it felt strangely deserted. It hung for a moment, then dropped to her lap. His eyes, darkly grey in their penitence, still held hers, and she suffered a moment of perplexing weakness.

'The fact is, marm—'

'The fact is, Captain Burnside, that you sneaked your devious self away without a word to me. You did not advise me you would be absent for supper and for the rest of the evening, but of course such discourtesy is to be expected of you.'

Captain Burnside ran a hand over his hair in a rueful gesture. Caroline, her shimmering evening gown revealing of the sumptuous lines of her body, gazed up at him in a self-questioning way, as if her feelings were not as they should be.

'Well, marm, it's a singular consequence of my professional talents that when I'm using 'em on behalf of one

166

patron, they come to the notice of another, and I ain't in a position to ignore an approach. You have my word I had no idea that my contact with a possible new patron this afternoon would mean such a prolonged absence from your sweet and gracious company—'

'Familiar taradiddle, sir,' said Caroline, but there was laughter being born at his facile speciousness and his absurd notion that she could take him seriously.

'I assure you, marm, that as time went on I thought only of the vexation my absence must be causing you. Yet you'll understand in your Christian tolerance that continuity of commissions is important to me. There are my tailor's bills, d'you see, and the price of bread and meat and other sustenance. I pride myself on owning an extensive and variable wardrobe, dear lady, and can fit myself out as an unquestionable gentleman for patrons whose requirements match yours, or as a thieving gipsy for others. I'm to take on the guise of a Bow Street Runner for my next patron. Marm?' He came to a halt, for Caroline's laughter arrived in a rush. It sang and echoed. 'Marm, my struggle to maintain a civilised existence ain't as amusing as that, is it?'

'I am hysterical,' gasped Caroline. 'Oh, Captain Burnside, what am I to do with such an impossible man as you? I vow it would be all of commonsense to throw you out, but there it is, in my devotion to Christian charity I am beset by a wish to see you reformed and respectable.'

'Respectable?' said Captain Burnside. 'Oh, egad, that ain't charitable of you, marm, that's unkind.'

'I declare it the best thing that could happen to you. Then, perhaps, you could show an honest face to the world instead of a shifty one, and even find a young lady willing to be a sweet wife to you.'

'Marriage, marm, *marriage*?' he said in alarm.

'Do you know any young lady you might like to embrace as a wife?' asked Caroline, eyes dropping to her book.

'Good God,' said the Captain.

'You may sit down, Captain Burnside, while we discuss your possible reformation and the advantages of seeing you married,' she said, and there was the light of life and the animation of new dialogue gleaming in her hidden eyes.

'You ain't serious, marm?' he said, seating himself.

'It is absurd, sir, your wasteful addiction to dubious adventurism, to the unkind fleecing of trusting young ladies and to consorting with trollops when you have the gifts to become a useful, hardworking husband and a respectable citizen of this beautiful country. Have you no idea, sir, of just how beautiful your country is, and how very satisfying it would be to become worthy of it?'

'Faith, marm, I'm speechless.'

She lifted her eyes. They were bright with laughter. 'You are not speechless, Captain Burnside, you are wriggling. I vow it clearly visible. I have offered to lend you money so that you might go into a business of your own choosing. Since you've shown little enthusiasm for that, I shall offer you honest work on my Sussex estate, on your promise, of course, that you will sincerely embrace both the honesty and the work.'

'God help me, marm, would you ask me to plough your fields?'

'That, sir, would be very honest and healthy work. But no, I should ask you to be assistant to my steward, to look after the books.'

'Books, marm? Clerking books?' Captain Burnside looked aghast.

'And to collect rents from my tenants,' said Caroline, utterly enraptured by the state she was putting him in. Never had she seen him show such consternation.

'I thought, marm, our relationship was to be friendly,' he said, 'but damned if you ain't plotting my downfall.'

'Sir?'

'Beg your forgiveness for my language, marm, but you've struck cruel blows,' he said, shaking his head. 'I dare swear that if I drop my guard again, you'll turn me into a country bumpkin.'

'Bumpkin?' said Caroline, and her drawn-out American vowels became energised, so that they took on a hint of

English crispness. 'Bumpkin? Yes, I've heard that is what you English call folk who live and work on the land. Well, sir, let me tell you such people are the backbone of our United States and the salt of the English earth. If, by a miracle of reformation, you became part of that salt, then you would be among England's worthiest citizens and deserving of a rosy-cheeked Sussex wife. There are no country girls more rosy-cheeked than those of Sussex. They are homespun jewels in their many virtues, Captain Burnside; they shine with true, healthy brightness, and own far more lovable qualities than your town trollops.'

Captain Burnside looked as if he had been dealt a mortal blow. 'God's life,' he said faintly, 'you'd turn me into a country rent collector, marm? A bumpkin? With a rosy-cheeked pudding of a wife?'

'And rosy-cheeked children, who would make you a happy father and give you a sense of caring responsibility,' said Caroline, vastly entertained by the fascinating dialogue.

'Heaven forgive you, marm, for your unsparing tongue,' said the Captain, visibly alarmed. 'If you'll give me leave to retire, I'll totter up to my room and my bed, though I doubt I'll catch a wink of sleep.'

'Why, Captain Burnside, how ridiculous you are,' said Caroline, containing her laughter only with an effort. 'Not a wink of sleep indeed, when you are being offered a chance to become an honest man, a contented husband and a happy father. I declare, sir, I surely do, your alarm is an absurdity.'

'I ain't precisely my best self at the moment, I agree,' said the Captain, 'but there it is, d'you see, never did I think a woman of such warm beauty could be so merciless.'

'Merciless? Why, sir, am I not doing all I can to save you from Tyburn Tree? Even though you have deceived me outrageously? No, I shall not give you leave to retire, but insist you wait for Annabelle to return. She will be disappointed if you aren't here to greet her.' Caroline cast him an enquiring look.

'Well, though I'm playing my part with Annabelle,' he

said, 'I can't deny she's sweet enough to make it enjoyable. Ah, if only she were an heiress, I'd make no pretence of my affections and set about winning her.'

Caroline felt shock. 'You have come to care for her?' she said.

'I feel an affection that prompts me to—'

'Do you, sir? Do you indeed? My sister is not for your devious arms. Don't you dare attempt in any way to lay your hands on her, do you hear?'

'But when I'm reformed, marm, you'll not mind then, if the notion took me?'

Caroline rushed to her feet and pointed to the door. 'You may retire, after all, Captain Burnside. Yes, you may totter up to your room and your bed.'

'If I've—'

'Go, please.'

'Very well. Goodnight, marm.' He walked to the door, strangely quiet in his manner, and she experienced an impulse to call him back. But her pride would not let her. The door closed behind him, and the elegant drawing room suddenly seemed an empty and cheerless place.

What was happening to her that she intensely disliked the possibility he had come to care for her sister?

## Chapter Fifteen

Betsy, sprightly, bobbed in her dancing, hurrying walk. It was her free hour, the only time she was free in each long day. She was always up before six and not off duty until she retired to bed, which was never before ten each night. But she had one Sunday off a month, and the precious hour each day.

Outside Collins Coffee House, her generous and personable gentleman was waiting for her, looking a regular, bang-up nob in his fine clothes.

'Ah, there you are, pretty puss,' he said.

'Oh, I be in pleasure to see you, sir,' she said. 'I got your note last night. But I be shaking as well as pleased, in case I'm to do what makes me quake terrible.'

'I ain't inclined to make you do that, Betsy. Come along now.'

A minute later they were comfortably ensconsed in the cosiness of a private room. There was coffee for Betsy, and confectionery, and she began to consume the latter blissfully.

'Make me do what, sir? You didn't say.'

'Whatever it is that makes you quake terribly.'

'Oh, I don't mind kissing, sir. Kissing be fair after all them golden guineas. And fondling, though I be given to embarrassing blushing, sir.'

'Come, come, business first, Betsy, embarrassment later.'

'Oh, lord,' said Betsy, bosom quivering, bodice straining, 'my sweet ones is going to be that shy they won't hardly know where to look. What business, sir?'

'Be in cheerful heart, Betsy. The Lord Chancellor has faith in you, and so have I. We require only a small service of you. Which is to have you let me into the house on the day of 29th July.'

'During the day, sir?' Betsy gulped and swallowed half-chewed confectionery. 'Oh, I can't, sir, I daresn't, not during the day.'

'Alas, you must, rosy cheeks. The Lord Chancellor insists. Faith, it'll be tricky for both of us, I'll not deny, but we don't want to end up losing our heads and having 'em spiked on the city gates.'

Betsy gulped again. Hot coffee swam untidily into her throat and she gasped, gurgled and choked. In kindly fashion, Captain Burnside patted her back.

Her shaking hand set down the large mug. 'Don't talk like that, sir,' she begged, 'it fair gives me the shivers.'

'Upon my soul,' said the Captain. He put his hand under her chin and lifted her face, looking into luminous eyes. 'Is this the brave Betsy who has shared perils with me as my confederate? Quakings and shiverings before we've scarcely begun to discuss our next endeavour?'

'But, sir,' said Betsy through trembling lips, 'you be so flummoxing with your talk of embarrassments and heads on spikes, and saying I must let you in by day.'

'Oh, I'm as much flummoxed as you are by all we're required to do for the sake of the Duke, but it ain't for us to question it, pretty puss. There.' He gave her a comforting kiss. Her trembling lips sprang into eager life. With so fascinating and exciting a gentleman, kissing was delicious. 'Now, courage, Betsy,' he said, and caressed her soft chin.

'Oh, some kisses be almost better than guineas, sir,' she said.

'You shall have a guinea or two more, and a kiss or two more. Yes, why not, since you own such warm lips?'

'Nor I won't say no to being fondled, sir, only can't I let you in at night and not day? By day, sir, the house be full of comings and goings.'

'The side door is always locked, Betsy?'

'Bolted, sir, and opened only for people coming with goods and eatables and suchlike.'

'Well, Betsy, contrive to draw the bolts as near to noon on the 29th July as you can. You need not wait. Merely slip the bolts, then make yourself scarce, though with such a sweet shape as you have your noticeability ain't ever going to reduce you to invisibility. A small point, but a delicious one.'

'Oh, maybe I could do that, sir. Maybe I could draw the bolts as quiet as a mouse. Just that, sir. I daresn't linger, I always be so busy. It be different of an evening, when I'm not so busy and can say there's a gentleman friend coming to see me.'

'There, that's capital. I'll be delivering a cheese, Betsy.'

'A cheese?' Betsy looked visibly flummoxed.

'Or a small cask of wine. So that if I'm seen I've an excuse, d'you see, and also an apology ready for being at the wrong address.'

'Oh, you be a rare thinking gentleman, sir. And all for the good of His Highness, who be a stern and fearful Duke and not afraid of the devil hisself. Sir, what will you be up to in the house?'

'Looking out for the devil, puss. As our Lord Chancellor says, the devil appears in various guises. Have no fears, my quaking partridge, you have no more to do than draw the bolts. You shall meet with no unhappy fate on the gibbet or the block. Unless you blow the gaff. So, not a word, as before.'

'Lord, no, sir, not a whisper. Oh, you be a kind and caring gentleman, looking after me not being hanged and pleasuring me with guineas. There be one or two coming to me now?'

'For now, some silver shillings, puss.' Captain Burnside slipped several into her receptive hand. She glowed, swivelled in her chair, drew up her servant's gown and slipped the coins into a pocket of her white linen pantaloons. 'H'm,' said the Captain, 'I ain't sure the Lord Chancellor would approve that. He ain't a gentleman given to allowing sauciness in young ladies.'

'Oh, I be in shameful forgetfulness of where I be,' said Betsy, trying to blush. She regarded her pantaloons accusingly. She glanced to see if her gentleman was looking. Her gentleman gave her a kind and forgiving smile. 'Well, 'tisn't as if I be wearing them I keep for my Sundays off, sir. They be rare pretty things, not the kind to be forgetful about.'

'Very well. We'll excuse these. Now, finish your coffee, saucy kitten, and then you and I will go.'

'But there's been no kissing,' protested Betsy, 'and it aren't right I shouldn't let you, though it always puts me in a rare tizzy. Still, seeing you're such a kind and giving gentleman, sir, kissing's only fair, and I won't scream the place down.'

'I'm relieved to hear it,' said Captain Burnside, and gave her a kind kiss. Betsy closed her eyes and parted her lips. Her pink tongue flicked and foraged. She took his hands and placed them on her bodice. Kindly, in his professionalism, he caressed her. Betsy gave a sighing moan and buried her face in his shoulder. 'Come, come, minx, you'll not be feeling this is a fate worse than death, will you?' he suggested.

'Oh, I be feeling terrible shy and embarrassed, sir.'

'Then I shan't press my attentions, Betsy, for it won't do to have you shy and embarrassed. That's a poor reward for the brave service you've given me.'

'Oh, I aren't saying this kind of embarrassment aren't bearable, sir, nor that I won't let you unlace me . . .'

'Unlace you? Heavens, puss, unlacing a loyal accomplice is most strictly forbidden.'

'Oh, I wouldn't breathe a word, that I wouldn't,' said Betsy.

'No, no, there are the rules, Betsy, as well as your blushes. Come, it's time we left.'

Betsy sighed. On the way back to her duties, her gentleman escorting her part of the way, she suggested he might be wishful to set her up. At which he drew her hastily into the shelter of a columned portico.

'Damn me,' he whispered, 'if that ain't my dearly

174

beloved wife.' Betsy saw a lady daintily tripping along on the other side of the street. 'There, d'you see how the quirks of fate can catch one out? If I hadn't clapped my peepers on her first, she'd have spotted us. Dear as she is to me, one look at you and your prettiness, and I'd have been hard put to explain you away. Praise the Lord, she's gone now, out of sight, but no more talk of setting you up, my tempting puss.'

'Oh, I be downright disappointed,' sighed Betsy, 'for I'm gone on you something cruel. Yet it's sweet knowing you're wishful to be true to her. That be nice. Still,' she added hopefully, 'there's always kissing, which aren't as unfaithful as setting me up. Sir, if something happens and I be unable to draw them bolts that day, for I'm sometimes sent out on errands and suchlike, where can I send a message to you?'

He mused. Betsy had perception. She had seen ahead, in a thinking way.

'Well, let's pray something like that won't happen, but if it does, you can send the message. You've a boy in the household you can trust?'

'Yes, there be Isaac the boot boy, sir. I be a favourite with Isaac.'

'Good.' He gave her Lady Caroline's address, without mentioning his hostess, and he merely gave his own name as Mr Burnside.

He took tea later that afternoon with Caroline and Annabelle. Caroline had paid him out a little during the morning. She had insisted he go shopping with her and Annabelle, and in the coolest and most audacious fashion had made him carry all the parcels. Annabelle had had fits of giggles, for of all joyous things Caroline had purchased silk stockings and garters under his waiting eyes, and then planted the daintily-wrapped box in his arms, where rested other packages. The Captain had gazed fixedly at the shop ceiling. And then Caroline had said, 'Come, there are other things, Captain, so please don't dawdle.'

How, Annabelle wondered, could her sister be so deliciously wicked to him?

Over tea, Caroline was a little more mellow. And the

Captain's conversation was engaging. He had been out to call on a friend, he had said, and his outing seemed to have left him pleased with himself. Caroline, when asked if she would permit him to make his call, replied out of earshot of her sister that it was wholly gratifying to be asked, and that he could go providing the friend in question was not one of his more dubious acquaintances. He assured her his friend was a worthy citizen.

Watching him now, as he exchanged quips with her sister, Caroline thought the two of them extraordinarily compatible. Annabelle was entirely alive, her laughter quick to come, her blue eyes dancing. Was she falling in love with him? Or, wait, was her vivacious mood due to the fact that Cumberland would be present this evening? She had confessed it was indeed true that Captain Burnside drove her to the Duke's residence on Friday, but that she went only to talk to him, to try to discover if his intentions were serious. She frankly confessed that she left in a distressed state because she felt it so unfair that he should be in love with her, yet give her only upsetting and unsatisfactory answers. In her distress she left her parasol behind. Caroline told her she was making a grievous mistake if she thought Cumberland was actually in love with her. He was in love with no one. He was capable of only loving himself. Annabelle said that was being very hard on him.

Either she was still infatuated with him and in animated anticipation of seeing him this evening, or she was falling in love with Captain Burnside, which was what had been planned and which the Captain had said would be accomplished. Dear heaven, thought Caroline, how could I have considered this ploy acceptable? It was an outrageous thing from the beginning, a desperately amoral alternative to Annabelle's dangerous relationship with Cumberland. In pushing her sister into the arms of a professional blackguard, she was no less reprehensible than he was.

Annabelle laughed and leaned, and Caroline saw her lay a light, playful hand on the Captain's knee.

'Fie, Charles,' she said, 'I declare that remark out of all order.'

'I remarked only, in so many words, that eventually the gentleman of your romantic choice would find a tease on his hands,' smiled the Captain.

'To the eventual gentleman of my choice, I shall be as sweet as he could wish,' said Annabelle. 'That is, as long as he is sweet to me.'

'Such a gentleman will be a fellow countryman, young lady?'

Annabelle fluttered her lashes and looked at him demurely. 'But, Charles,' she said, 'like Caroline, I have become devoted to the gentlemen of England.'

'I am alarmed,' said Captain Burnside, 'for I see in that the dire prospect of you and Caroline becoming a tease to all of us, and we will be wrecked.'

'I am sure, Captain Burnside, that in knowing me for as long as you have, you are aware I do not indulge in teasing men,' said Caroline.

'Ah, but your warm beauty, that is teasing enough,' said the Captain with a smile, 'and in your younger days, as a newly arrived magnolia bloom, your eyes held the most bewitching tease. Along with other gentlemen, I groaned in acute suffering when you chose Lord Percival for husband.'

Delightedly, Annabelle clapped her hands. 'Caroline, there, Charles has declared he had a passion for you,' she cried.

Caroline vibrated. What a specious serpent he was, with his devious tongue and his smiling familiarities, and the advantage he took of their contrived relationship.

'I do not remember hearing his groans,' she said, 'I only remember his single passion was for cards. Let us see where that will lead him with Cumberland this evening.'

Both chandeliers shed light over the card room. Every candle burned with a tall, steady flame, and every flame was variously reflected by the facets of the crystal glass. Around the card table sat Cumberland, Mr Robert

Humphreys, the Duke's most cordial and obliging friend, Captain Burnside and Mr Gerald Wingrove, currently closest, so it was said, to Caroline's reserved affections.

Very obligingly, Robert had agreed to a suggestion made by Cumberland before they reached Lady Caroline's residence. That to down the Burnside fellow he should stand on all hands when the drawing of another card would risk running him over the top. He should stand, therefore, on any score from twelve to twenty-one. The Burnside fellow was patently an egoistic show-off who, when holding the bank, would always elect for a risky draw. That was when to stand consistently, when Burnside had the bank.

The ploy was working. Robert was collecting steadily each time the Captain held the bank. Cumberland's play was of his usual impassive kind, but his stakes were heavier when he was confronted by the Captain. He had much to make up if he were to reduce the burden of the IOU.

On the other side of the room, Caroline was playing backgammon with Annabelle and Cecilia Humphreys. Cecilia was in placid concentration, but neither Caroline nor Annabelle showed total interest. Annabelle was sensitive to the presence of Cumberland and his muscular magnificence. Caroline, with many a casual gesture – a touch to her curling ringlets, a fingertip caress of an eyebrow, a light change of posture or a hand at her throat – cast brief glances at Captain Burnside. It was of all things the most vexing to find her eye-wandering so compulsive. Naturally, there was the money factor to be concerned about. Her money. She had spoken to him about it before Cumberland arrived.

'It is purely Cumberland's pocket now that you have secured the letter,' she said.

'Well, it's a ravaged pocket at the moment, Caroline, to the extent of nine hundred and eighty guineas.'

She passed over his use of her name, which she only permitted normally when Annabelle was present.

'He'll not pay such a sum,' she said. 'He won't precisely disown the debt, for he can't, not a card debt, as you know. He'll declare, should you press him, that a remittance will be forthcoming. They are all forever in debt, the King's sons, and it would never do to sue Cumberland, for if you do you'll be arrested on a trumped-up charge and you'll be convicted and transported. He'll do his best tonight to win back the better part of the IOU, and he may, perhaps, put you in debt to him. I have agreed with you that I shall discharge such a debt. By the same reckoning, you shall hand to me such winnings that he does settle. He will settle, I think, if he can reduce the IOU to, say, two hundred guineas.'

'Ah,' said the Captain wryly, 'that's a wounding blow, marm. I thought perhaps you'd allow me to line my threadbare pockets.'

'Sir, you have earned yourself half your fee so far, and that should line them richly.'

'I ain't quite able to recall if I've had the remittance from you, marm.'

'You will receive it, sir, when the whole venture is over. I am sure that if you were to receive it now, you would vanish.'

'It don't do, marm, to upset a patron, for if I did I'd earn a reputation for dishonesty, and no patron would recommend me to another.'

She could not help herself. The coolness she had shown him since last night slipped away and the compulsive laughter danced in her eyes. 'Captain Burnside, you take my breath. A reputation for dishonesty? But the principles of dishonesty are what makes you what you are, do they not? A professional scoundrel?'

'Not between myself and a patron, marm. Between myself and a patron exists treasured integrity.'

'Treasured integrity?' She laughed aloud. 'Oh, I shall never make head nor tail of such absurdity.'

'A logical sentiment,' observed the Captain, 'and can I take it that it implies you ain't now set on making an honest country fellow of me?'

Caroline faced squarely up to him. 'I vow, sir, that despite my annoyances I am determined to help you turn aside from a life of crime.'

179

'Crime?' Captain Burnside clapped a hand to his brow. '*Crime*?'

'That is what I said, sir, for what else is it?'

'I ain't ever thought of it as anything else but a pleasing way of settling my tailor's bills.'

'Heaven help you,' said Caroline. She became serious. 'Captain Burnside, be careful this evening. I would even recommend that now it is only Cumberland's pocket or yours – that is, mine – you contrive to let him win. Should you considerably increase his debt, and even though he won't pay, he may contrive your downfall simply because he'll be furious that you've twice bested him. So take care, I beg.' She put an impulsive hand on his arm. 'Cumberland is truly a dangerous man.'

'Well, I ain't disposed to provoke him,' said the Captain affably.

Caroline, however, was not so sure that in his airy self-assurance he would take her advice. At the table, he seemed in no concern about the run of the play, and his voice was as much of an indistinct murmur as the others. He sat at ease, his hands dexterous whenever he was dealing, his quill pen moving swiftly whenever he made a note of credits or debits. Cumberland sat in his own way, dark, lowering and inscrutable. Robert seemed his usual easy-going self, and her friend, Mr Wingrove, quite impressed at being at a card table with the Duke, was in murmurous, conversational fluency, it appeared. She stiffened as she heard Cumberland suddenly speak in a chilling way.

'Sir, whoever ye are, for I ain't taken a note of your name, if I had come for the purpose of listening to your opinions on potted plants and cabbages, I'd not be sitting here with cards in my hand. Ye take me, I hope?'

'Your Highness,' said Mr Wingrove in protest, 'I made no mention of cabbages, I was merely pointing out that a fig tree can be grown in a tub.'

'So can cabbages, I don't doubt,' said Cumberland, 'so are ye for cards or cabbages, sir?'

'Oh, dear,' murmured Annabelle.

Mr Wingrove gathered up the cards and shuffled them, frowningly. Captain Burnside regarded the ceiling. Robert cast an eye at Cumberland. The Duke was down, mainly to Captain Burnside.

Cumberland acquired the bank. Captain Burnside began to plunge, heavily. Cumberland flipped cards at him, his dark eye measuring his man, reading him, analysing him. The Captain lost two successive hands to the tune of seventy guineas and sixty guineas.

The Duke, about to deal again, said, 'I don't think I know your regiment, sir.'

'9th Dragoons, sir,' said the Captain.

'The 9th? Colonel Masterton, ye say?'

'A commanding officer of distinction, sir,' said the Captain.

'Ain't the 9th in the field?' enquired Cumberland.

'Not at the moment, sir.'

Caroline listened to this uneasily. Cumberland suspected something. But he surely could not suspect Captain Burnside was responsible for taking the letter, if he had discovered it was missing. Why should he? It must be something else. Perhaps to do with the unpalatable fact that the Captain was an imposter. No, not an imposter: a disgraced officer who had been forced to resign his commission and now lived by his wits. But if Cumberland was aware of that, then nothing would have induced him to sit down again at the card table with the Captain or even to acknowledge his existence. And he would have disowned the IOU on the grounds that he had been deceived into assuming he was gambling with a gentleman. So what did his sudden little inquisition of the Captain's military credentials mean if he did not suspect the one thing or the other?

He was dealing the cards now, and accordingly was silent.

'Caroline, Caroline, do attend,' said Cecilia, dark hair lush with a softly rich shine, powdered bosom delicately white within the revealing frame of her bodice. 'You are playing very sketchily, darling.'

'And I am playing hopelessly,' said Annabelle.

Caroline attended.

The four men murmured. Cards were given, stakes raised, losing hands thrown in, hopeful hands retained. The bank remained with Cumberland for a prolonged period. Robert revealed a queen and an ace at one stage, but Cumberland matched it and cleaned up. Lady Luck consistently favoured him, and even when he was eventually forced to yield the bank to Captain Burnside she still remained faithful, and he amassed further credits. Mr Wingrove, who had taken to playing with quiet dignity since being snubbed, staked modestly and kept modestly in credit. Robert, as usual, won some hands and lost others. He had never been known to rise from a card table excitingly enriched. Captain Burnside, having lost most hands while the bank had been with Cumberland, now found the Duke's hands still too good for him. Caroline, ears attuned to the men's voice, heard him say quite clearly once, 'Damn me, that's a painful leveller, Your Highness.' Was he taking her advice; was he taking care not to put himself on the wrong side of Cumberland? Cumberland's debt to him of almost a thousand guineas was a vast enough sum as it was, but it had only been a piece of paper when viewed in the context of a negotiation for the letter. Without the need for any negotiation, it represented something that would cause excessive irritation and annoyance to the Duke. To add to it tonight would be a dangerous mistake.

Captain Burnside was shuffling the cards when Cumberland clearly addressed him again. 'Ye're enjoying extended leave, Burnside?'

'After extended duty in Ireland, Your Highness,' said the Captain pleasantly.

'Ireland, b'God,' said Cumberland, and his blind eye, the colour of curdled milk, was a blankness that made his sound eye doubly penetrating. 'A land of papist rascals and Jesuit plots, ye'll allow?'

'A troublesome place, sir,' murmured the Captain. The cards having been cut, he began to deal, and the Duke, accordingly, ceased his further little inquisition. But it had increased Caroline's uneasiness.

The play terminated at midnight. Cumberland rose from the table the richer at the Captain's expense by seven hundred and ninety guineas, which reduced his debt to a mere one hundred and ninety. His smile was bleak. 'I'll let ye have a remittance, sir,' he said.

'Good of you, sir,' said the Captain.

There was a settlement of Mr Wingrove's modest wins and losses, which left him slightly down. Robert owed Captain Burnside twenty-five guineas, when all was totted up, and he also owed Cumberland seventy guineas.

'I'm short of the ready on my person,' he said, 'so I'll settle with you in a day or two, Captain.' To Cumberland he said with a cheerful smile, 'If you'll drop in on your way home, Your Highness, I'll settle with you at my place.'

'Ye can ride in my carriage, with Cecilia,' said Cumberland.

He said goodnight to Caroline, thanking her for her hospitality. He kissed her hand. He said goodnight to Annabelle, and in insolent provocation of her sister kissed her on the cheek. Annabelle blushed. The devil lurked in his smile.

To Mr Wingrove, he said, 'Goodnight, sir, ye may return to your potted figs and cabbages now.'

'I'm gratified, sir, to have your Highness's permission,' said Mr Wingrove, who may have been blooded but was, in his acerbic rejoinder, certainly unbowed.

'Oh, ye have it,' said Cumberland with royal indifference, and left with Robert and Cecilia.

Mr Wingrove, his handsomeness marred by a frown, stayed a while to offer his opinions on Cumberland's lack of decent graces. He expressed himself articulately and at length, finding a warm sympathiser in Caroline. Captain Burnside, seating himself again, leaned back and relaxed, expressing his own sympathy with the occasional nod. Annabelle, smothering a yawn, wondered how to get Mr Wingrove to go home. Caroline found the solution by taking advantage of an unexpected pause and telling him he had stood up very well to the Duke, that he could depart with his honour intact and that she would see him out herself. Which she did, although he bade her a very lingering goodnight at the door, and kissed her hand fervently.

Returning to the card room, she found Captain Burnside with his legs stretched out and his eyes closed.

Annabelle, on her feet, smiled. 'I fear, sister, he has fallen asleep.'

'The wretch,' said Caroline.

'You are surprisingly hard on him sometimes,' said Annabelle.

'He has no right to fall asleep when you and I have not yet retired.'

'But so likeable a man should be allowed some indulgence. He has endured hours of strain battling with the Duke at the card table. The Duke is always so formidable . . .'

'You have said that so often that I beg you to say it no more.'

'Then I shall at least say Charles sent the Duke home in the sweetest temper, for Charles lost heavily to him. Heigh-ho, dearest, I must go up, I vow myself asleep on my feet. Oh, but poor Mr Wingrove, the Duke set him down unmercifully.'

'His dignity was above Cumberland's rudeness,' said Caroline.

'Oh, yes, he is excessively dignified,' said Annabelle, and yawned. 'I won't wake Charles, and shall leave you to kiss him goodnight for me.'

'Ridiculous girl.'

With Annabelle gone, Caroline shook Captain Burnside awake.

'Faith,' he said, starting, 'is the house on fire, marm?'

'It is not.' Caroline seated herself beside him. 'I wish to say how wise you were to allow Cumberland to reduce his debt.'

'Well, a little manipulation of a card here and a card there . . .'

184

'I don't wish to hear about your talent for trickery, Captain Burnside. I prefer to believe you took risks too impossible to come off. But I am uneasy about the questions he put to you. I feel he suspects your standing. He won't lack to communicate with the commanding officer of the 9th Dragoons.'

'Damn me,' murmured the Captain, 'he's a very prying fellow considering he ain't common like the rest of us. It ain't decent, marm, for a royal personage to put his nose in advance of his dignity.'

'Cumberland makes his own rules,' said Caroline, green satin gown lustrous, auburn hair a crown of fiery magnificence. 'Was your regiment the 9th Dragoons?'

'Faith, I hope so,' said the Captain.

'You hope so?' Caroline flashed him an angry and troubled glance. 'I vow you a jackass to answer me so, and worse than a jackass if you've attempted to pull the wool over the eyes of a man like Cumberland. It's worrying enough to know he might find you had to resign your commission; it's worrying beyond anything to realise he may discover you've no connection with the 9th Dragoons.'

'Oh, Colonel Masterson's an old friend of mine,' said the Captain airily, 'and he don't have much feeling for Cumberland or any of the Hanoverians. He's a Jacobite, d'you see, an adherent of the Stuarts. He considers the Georges are usurpers of the throne. There, don't look so troubled, marm. Whatever obtains, I ain't going to have you put on the wrong side of Cumberland. You're an exceptional patron, and my feelings for you are respectfully affectionate – even loving . . .'

'Sir?' she said, a faint flush appearing.

'Respectfully loving, I assure you, and I beg you to take no offence,' said the Captain in haste. 'And should Cumberland find out I don't own a gentleman's credentials, I'll see no discredit attaches to you, dear lady. I'll not have Cumberland hire some bully boy to spoil your warm beauty, which he's capable of doing, despite his love for you.'

'Oh, tush, Captain Burnside,' said Caroline, 'Cumberland's avowed desire to bed me does not mean he loves me. He has no idea of what love is. And I have no idea myself of what respectful love is. Pray have the goodness to explain it.'

'Ah, yes,' said the Captain, and looked at the ceiling, as if the explanation lay there. 'H'm,' he said.

Caroline smiled. 'You have fallen into a trap of your own making,' she said. 'You cannot explain respectful love – no, I declare you can't, sir.'

'We're burning the candles, marm, but perhaps there's time for me to say it means my respect for you has a noble and unchangeable quality.'

'Noble?' Caroline laughed. 'What nonsense you do talk.'

'Well, I ain't always in my best form early in the morning, marm,' he said. For once during a conversation she had not mentioned Annabelle, so he murmured, 'I fancy your sister wasn't quite so taken up with Cumberland tonight.'

She frowned, finding herself unprepared for the comment. 'I fear,' she said, 'that Cumberland is still a dangerous excitement to her.'

'Oh, she's coming round,' said Captain Burnside, 'and I daresay it won't be long before she has eyes only for me.'

'Dear heaven,' breathed Caroline, 'was there ever a man in such vast conceit of himself?'

'It's professional self-confidence, marm. Shall we retire?'

She did not want to retire. She did not feel sleepy. She felt richly and newly alive. The years of Lord Clarence's betrayal of every sacred concept of marriage and the years of humiliation had almost destroyed her belief in herself as a wife and a woman. She had felt a failure as a wife and inadequate as a woman. Her emotions had become guarded and reserved. Now there was the wonderful sensation of re-awakening to life and all its sweet challenges. Now laughter had been reborn, and she felt young again, with every day a promise of excitement. What had caused such a change? Time, yes, time was responsible. The two years of widowhood had healed every wound and smoothed away every scar. Her body itself was

186

vibrant with life. Yes, time had been wonderfully healing, and sweetly so. She was even ready to consider marriage again. But the man must be unquestionably right; she must be in no doubt of him at all. Mr Wingrove, for instance: his principles were so sound, his integrity plain to see, his manliness entirely commendable. There was virtuous moral strength about him, and an eminent air of stability. And he was unfailingly agreeable.

'Oh, how boring,' she said.

'The thought of going to bed bores you?' said Captain Burnside.

'Oh, did I say that?' she asked in confusion.

'You did, marm, but I still think we should retire.'

'Yes,' she said a little reluctantly. 'It is very late. And we shall be late again tomorrow night, for it's Lady Chesterfield's ball.' She looked up at the Captain as he came to his feet. 'You will see Cumberland again.'

'So I believe. Well, I know my role, marm. I'm to pay the closest attention to Annabelle, and not to allow her to disappear with the Duke. I shall wear my uniform, and in it will make further progress in my task of sweeping her off her feet.'

Caroline said coldly, 'It will be self-satisfying to have her fall in love with you?'

'The situation being what it is, it'll be a certain way of—'

'Wait.' She rose in some agitation. 'Your uniform. It is the uniform of what regiment?'

'The 9th Dragoons, marm.'

Caroline rushed into an upbraiding of him. 'Oh, you creature, you wretch, only minutes ago you led me to believe, to infer, it was otherwise! What are you, sir, if not the most infuriating wretch?'

Captain Burnside bowed deferentially. 'I am, marm, your respectfully loving servant.'

And Caroline wanted to beat him, pummel him – and to laugh.

Cumberland, on arrival at the Humphreys' house, had alighted with them, and his coachman had taken the carriage back to the mews.

'Ye'll give me a bed for the night, Robert?' he said, as they entered the house near the Strand.

'Why, of course, Your Highness,' said Robert.

'A warm bed?' murmured Cumberland, and Robert cleared his throat and Cecilia grew dusky, for they both knew what that meant.

'As always, Your Highness, it's a pleasure to accommodate you,' said Robert. 'The settlement, sir, I must find the amount.'

'Seventy, I fancy, but ye may defer it until ye are more prosperously funded,' said Cumberland, but his glimmering smile was for Cecilia, not Robert.

'That's damned generous of you, sir,' said Robert.

'I cannot but feel that in return I must go up to warm the bed for you at once, Your Highness,' said Cecilia.

There was warmth indeed when Cumberland slipped into the bed later – the warmth of her fulsome body in her silk night shift. And he brought the warmth of his own body, masculine and rugged. His manipulative hands divested her of her shift, though in no rough way.

'Cumberland, oh, gentle you may be,' she breathed, 'but so disconcerting.'

She turned on to her side and he drew her naked body into his arms. Cecilia smothered her moans in his shoulder.

'By God, ye've a handsome shape,' he murmured, 'that ye have, and a beautiful belly.'

'Will you have me swoon?' she gasped faintly.

'I'll have ye attend on me for the moment, my beauty. Ye've known Caroline since she first met Clarence. Did ye also know that fellow Burnside?'

Cecilia, heated, breathed, 'Cumberland, I am expected to gossip with you?'

'For the moment.'

'Then no, I never knew Captain Burnside.'

'But ye've been a close relation and a close friend to Caroline, ain't ye?'

'She's a sweet woman and deserved better than Clarence gave her.'

'But ye never met Burnside until now?'

188

'No, but then I cannot claim to know her every friend and acquaintance. Cumberland, I beg you, if this conversation is to continue, hold me not so close, for I'm without a stitch and cannot endure my own nakedness.'

'It's warmly endurable to me,' murmured Cumberland, allowing her ardent breasts to cushion his chest. 'Now, since I've a personal interest, oblige me, sweet woman, by finding out precisely how and when Caroline first met Burnside. She'll confide in ye, though she'll ride her high horse at questions from others.'

'Cumberland – oh, heaven keep me from abandonment – are you jealous of the Captain? You see him as a rival concerning the favours of Caroline? But she will not offer or yield favours; she has an American puritanism, and Clarence was an offence to her.'

'I'm not here to have ye question me, but to have ye pleasure me and oblige me. Ye'll pleasure me as ye always do, generously, and oblige me by finding out how and when Caroline first met Burnside, and why she's hosting him in her house. Ye'll enquire as a woman can, innocently and innocuously?'

'How can I not when you are so good to Robert?'

'Ah, my obliging friend Robert.' Cumberland's murmurous voice was ironic. 'A position in the Quartermaster's commissariat in a month or so? Entailing little more than approving and signing indents and contracts, though the commission to be won is entirely unofficial and to be discreetly and quietly negotiated with the contractors. But there, y'see, his gift of cheerful good-fellowship should ensure he's consistently in profit.'

'Cumberland, I vow myself overwhelmed,' breathed Cecilia, 'and cannot deny you rapturous pleasure. And for the sake of my own needs, that you quicken so shamelessly in me, take your pleasure now, I beg.'

His muscular body was wholly the master of her fulsomeness, her groans stifled by his lips. The sheets whispered and rustled, and entwined bodies plunged, her belly fast to his loins.

# Chapter Sixteen

The ballroom, illuminated by a profusion of candlelight from an array of hanging chandeliers, swam with moving colour. Gentlemen richly dressed and officers in uniform complemented ladies dazzlingly gowned. The most renowned beauties of London's aristocracy shimmered and glided, and powdered bosoms floated past each other in the dance. They dipped and swayed, rose and fell.

Annabelle, gloriously arrayed in ultramarine blue, a perfect foil for her pale honey complexion and shining fair hair, was sitting out this dance and still fanning herself to relieve the warmth of the previous one. If the French had perfected the artistry of dancing, the English had given it an exhilarating liveliness. The exchange of kisses in some dances, such as the *Gavotte*, had come to an end in the stiff formality of the French court. Not so at the English court. And the *Cotillon*, the gayest of dances, was at its liveliest in a London where society took its inspiration from the irrepressible behaviour of the Prince of Wales.

Captain Burnside, in the uniform of the 9th Dragoons, his scarlet jacket tailored to precision, stood beside Annabelle's chair.

'Oh, I declare myself in heaven,' said Annabelle, pearly fan whisking. 'Such delicious fun, Charles, such sweet excitement, and see, there is the Duke of Cumberland deigning at last to participate, and with who else but his hostess, Lady Chesterfield. Oh, for sure, Lord Chesterfield will spend the whole time quizzing the behaviour of the Duke.'

'Or enquiring into the whereabouts of Lady Chesterfield,' smiled the Captain.

'And you are being quizzed,' said Annabelle, 'for you surely are cutting a superb dash. You are catching the eye of every lady here.' She felt she had the sweet advantage of all of them, however, because Charles was her own official escort for the evening, and no other man had the air he had. 'Even Caroline, who has become so cool and grand, sighed to see you looking so gallant and dashing.'

'I didn't remark it,' said the Captain, watching the *Quadrille*, commonly reputed to have been brought to England in its simplest form by William the Conqueror. Now it had many of the intricate graces of the *Minuet*. Caroline, partnered by Mr Wingrove, handsome in a dark blue coat and high-chinned in a lofty, starched cravat, was smiling and animated. Mr Wingrove moved with gallant assurance, his hand in hers, leading and guiding. Caroline, gliding, had chosen to adorn herself in pure, silken white, as if she had cast aside her widow's untrue mourning forever. She had worn black, in any case, only for the funeral, and none had reproached her for not wearing it again.

How wonderful it was to feel so much natural enjoyment of the occasion. Lady Chesterfield's annual ball was always a highlight of the London season, its brilliance and its popularity of a kind that left the uninvited grinding their teeth. One or more of the royal Dukes were always present, and usually the Prince of Wales. This year, however, he was in sulking absence, refusing to leave Brighton. Last year, Lady Chesterfield had firmly detached her sixteen-year-old niece from his scented, overpowering amorousness. If Cumberland took what he wanted in the fashion of an arrogant, omnipotent prince, the Prince of Wales helped himself in the fashion of a man so flattered and spoiled he thought no female could, or should, deny him. That Lady Chesterfield should coldly denounce him simply because he had been cuddling her swooning niece's breasts made him quiver with outrage. The chit was swooning out of pleasure, was she not?

Caroline, quite among the most beautiful women present, executed her steps with matchless grace and sweet enjoyment. Mr Wingrove was an excellent partner, so sure and so accomplished. The orchestra, composed of some of London's finest musicians, drew the dancers into rhythmic response. Jewels glittered in elaborately coiffed hair. Caroline had meant to wear her diamond-encrusted clasp, but had been unable to find it. She remembered when she had last worn it, on the evening when she had played cribbage with Captain Burnside, had fallen asleep and he had audaciously carried her up to her suite. But she could not remember taking it off or where she had put it. Helene had promised to make an industrious search for it.

The *Quadrille*, prolonged, came to an end at last. She placed a hand on Mr Wingrove's arm, and he threaded a measured and careful way through the throng to where Annabelle and Captain Burnside awaited them. Caroline seated herself beside Annabelle, and her fan went to work.

'There, I declare myself hot but enchanted,' she said. 'Mr Wingrove, how very enjoyable that was, and how very accomplished you are.'

'Oh, modestly so, Caroline,' said Mr Wingrove, 'although I confess that as a student I foresaw the social necessity of being able to partner a lady in well-versed style at a ball. Accordingly, I took instruction from Monsieur and Madame Campion at their school off the Strand and received their first-class diploma. If that has helped to make the *Quadrille* so enjoyable to you, I ask for nothing more.'

Caroline, glimpsing the lift of Captain Burnside's head and noting his familiar search of a ceiling, said winningly, 'But, dear Mr Wingrove, it was more than mere enjoyment. It was quite exhilarating, and have I not already declared myself enchanted?'

Mr Wingrove bowed in modest acknowledgement, and Annabelle was sure the Captain was thinking things he would rather not give tongue to. She was also sure he was in love with Caroline. He must be. His eyes followed her often, and he took on the whimsical expression of a man wondering in all good humour why she was so cool to him, perhaps. Annabelle thought it was all very well for

Caroline to be distant with men because one of them had not made her a very good husband, but of all things it was beyond anything to be cool towards Charles while gushing over Mr Wingrove. Well, perhaps not gushing, but warmly enthusiastic.

The crowded ballroom, a riot of dazzling satins and silks, hummed and buzzed with voices. Laughter bubbled and burst, and young ladies used their fans to peep at who was whom. Cumberland stood on the far side, gathering to him merely by being there a ring of people, mostly ladies.

Lady Chesterfield, handsome and extrovert, sailed in pink-gowned benevolence towards Caroline, who came up from her chair, as did Annabelle.

'Caroline, my dear, my niece Emma wishes to meet you. She has vowed you entirely the most beautiful vision. Emma, my sweet, come.'

A slim, willowy girl of almost seventeen floated up, dark hair shining, lashes lifting, her daffodil-yellow gown full-skirted and flowing. Her brown eyes smiled at Caroline, then glanced at Captain Burnside. Lady Chesterfield, to whom Captain Burnside had been presented on arrival and earned her approval, introduced her niece all round. Emma's smile was at its prettiest not for Caroline, but for the Captain.

'Delighted,' he said as she gave him her hand.

'Oh, I am too,' she said in girlish pleasure.

With most guests waiting for the next dance to be called, Lady Chesterfield said to Caroline, 'May I leave Emma with you for a while? And perhaps Mr Wingrove or Captain Burnside will be gallant enough to oblige, for she is longing to dance.'

'Caroline, I'm sure, will take the greatest care of her,' said Mr Wingrove, 'and I shall be entirely happy to accompany her in the dance of her choice.'

'So kind,' smiled Lady Chesterfield. 'There, Emma.' She sailed away, and Emma at once took two floating steps that put her beside the Captain.

How delicious, thought Annabelle, it isn't Caroline she was dying to meet, but Charles, and she has quite turned her back on Mr Wingrove.

The orchestra struck chords that were an invitation to the *Gavotte*.

'Miss Winthrop,' said Mr Wingrove, that being Emma's name, 'I am accounted reasonably—'

'Do you dance the *Gavotte*, sir?' asked Emma of the Captain.

'H'm,' he said. He smiled. 'Reasonably, young lady, reasonably.'

Annabelle gurgled. Caroline felt for the hurt Mr Wingrove.

'Oh, I think I can dance it reasonably too,' said Emma.

'Then shall it be my pleasure?' said the Captain.

'So kind,' said Emma breathlessly, and glowed as she laid her gloved hand on his red sleeve, cuffed in blue and piped in gold. Under the forgiving eye of Mr Wingrove, and the amused eye of Caroline, who felt the Captain for once was going to find it hard to come off best, he advanced with Emma to take up position for the dance.

Mr Wingrove was not sure now whether he should favour Caroline or her sister. One or the other must be left to kick her heels unless help arrived. It did, in the shape of Cumberland. Black-coated, with white pantaloons and a crisp, white cravat, he seemed to materialise silently out of a sea of colour. His shadow, cast by a huge chandelier, fell across Annabelle's white shoes. His bow was not perfunctory, but sweepingly deliberate.

'Good evening, my dear Annabelle. Ye're a delicious picture. And Lady Caroline, ye're queenly, b'God.' He ignored Mr Wingrove. 'Annabelle, I fancy ye'll excel in the *Gavotte*. So will ye favour me?'

'Sir – Your Highness—' Annabelle, startled by his sudden arrival, was flushed and uncertain.

'Excellent. Come, then.' He took her hand and placed it on his arm. Mesmerised, Annabelle advanced with him.

'Caroline, shall we be left out?' said Mr Wingrove. 'No, we shall not, if you will do me the pleasure of standing up with me again.'

'Thank you, Mr Wingrove,' said Caroline.

The orchestra soared into a rich extravaganza of

rhythmic music, and the *Gavotte* became an exhilarating performance. Its original capering movements had been developed into more graceful form, but it was just as active a dance. Gowns whisked to the quick turns of bodies, heads went back and laughing faces were turned upwards to partners.

'Oh, how famous,' gasped young Emma Winthrop, 'I am beside myself with joy.'

'I ain't precisely doleful myself, I hope,' said the easy-moving Captain.

'Oh, I think you quite beautiful,' breathed Emma, circling, 'I adore you.'

'Already?'

'At first sight,' said the precocious girl.

'An illusion, my child.'

'No, I am quite grown up.'

'You ain't, young madam, no, not at all, but that don't signify you aren't delicious, for you are, and therefore if you don't behave I'll throw you over my shoulder and carry you back to Lady Chesterfield for your own good.'

Head back, she laughed. 'Oh, should you take such hold of me, I'd die of bliss,' she said. 'When do you kiss me?'

'When the moment arrives I'll peck your cheek,' he said, and when the moment did arrive, the ladies glided and the men advanced to lay kisses on flushed cheeks, as was the custom.

Mr Wingrove kissed Caroline's cheek warmly, and ventured a light caress of her hand. Cumberland, using his own rules to improve on custom, kissed Annabelle on the mouth, and Annabelle prayed that in the great throng of dancers such audacious behaviour had not been noticed. Emma received the promised peck from Captain Burnside, which made her pout. But she continued to exchange provocative patter with him, and at the end of the dance begged to be allowed to pull several hairs from his head, which she vowed she would twist into a lover's knot and keep in her bosom by day and under her pillow at night. By way of response, Captain Burnside declared only a punitive measure could cure her of such fanciful notions, and that measure was to return her to her aunt. Emma laughed, her gloved fingers squeezing the firm hand resolutely leading her.

Caroline intercepted them.

'Oh, Lady Caroline,' said the breathless girl, 'such a magical *Gavotte*, and Captain Burnside has been adorable to me.'

'Then it will probably dismay you to part with him,' said Caroline, 'but detach him from you I must, for he is urgently required.'

Emma sighed. Catching sight of Lady Chesterfield, Captain Burnside gently pointed the girl at her. Emma sighed again, but went.

'Has something happened?' asked the Captain.

'Come aside with me, please, or Mr Wingrove will surely find us and I really don't wish him to know anything of the true relationship between us two.'

They stepped between alabaster pillars into an alcove.

'Now, dear lady, what is troubling you?' asked the Captain, noting the difference between a young and pert girl and a supremely beautiful woman.

Caroline said stiffly, 'You have done what you said you would not do: you have allowed Annabelle to disappear with Cumberland, and there are a hundred rooms in this house. She will be her giddy self, she will be excited and vulnerable. Did you have to allow that girl to take you away from my sister? Mr Wingrove was quite willing to accommodate her in the *Gavotte*.'

'I fancy I was swept away, for it seems to have been love at first sight.'

'Will you be serious, sir! Love at first sight? Tush. You are old enough to be her father.'

'If I were, I'd have been an infernally forward thirteen-year-old brat. Come, it ain't critical, Caroline—'

'I will not have a conversation with you! What are you about, standing there doing nothing? If anything happens to Annabelle, if Cumberland is even taking her at this moment back to his house, then God forgive you, sir, for I shan't.'

'No, no, it ain't like that, dear lady. They're in Lord Chesterfield's notable conservatory. It's true Miss Emma Winthrop detached me from Annabelle, but my eyes didn't forsake her. The conservatory, as you no doubt know, is beyond the ballroom. The west doors open on to it. I ventured a look earlier, with Annabelle, who sighed at its magnificence. I fancy she may now be firing an arrow on Mr Wingrove's behalf and acquainting Cumberland with Lord Chesterfield's potted greenery.' The Captain smiled. 'I doubt, certainly, if Cumberland is bedding her among the potted ferns.'

'That remark is not amusing, but in very poor taste, sir,' said Caroline, and stepped out of the alcove to glance down the length of the ballroom to the west doors. Captain Burnside joined her. 'You saw them?' she enquired.

'I did,' he said. 'Despite having the devil of a time holding Miss Winthrop in check, I managed not to lose sight of them. Cumberland don't make an insignificent figure, even at a crowded ball. Ah, re-enter the royal gentleman, with angelic Annabelle in tow. Do you see?'

The doors had opened. Annabelle and Cumberland had appeared. Caroline sighed with relief, her bosom subsiding, a diamond necklace gently settling.

'You should not let me judge you so hastily,' she said, 'although my fault only comes about from never knowing precisely what you're about.'

'In your concern for your sister, you have no fault,' said the Captain.

Cumberland and Annabelle approached, she with her hand on his arm, he escorting her in his majestic fashion, caring little for what people made of his relationship with her. Caroline feared everyone was whispering that Cumberland soon or late would have Miss Annabelle Howard, the pretty American girl, in his bed. The Duke brought her to Caroline, his smile faintly derisive, as if he knew their disappearance had caused concern and dismay.

'Egad, your delicious sister did excel in the dance, my dear Caroline,' he said, 'and so I return her to you unharmed and cooled. The conservatory has a moist air and

197

ain't as hot as the ballroom. Annabelle,' he said, 'ye have my compliments for favouring me.' He brought her hand to his lips. He then took Caroline's hand and pressed it, murmuring, 'I only regret I've won no favours from ye.'

'I am sure, sir, that you have won enough elsewhere,' retorted Caroline.

Cumberland laughed and looked at the Captain, and at his uniform. 'I wish ye joy in the rose of your choice, Burnside,' he said, and departed.

Mr Wingrove arrived in some haste, expressing anxiety that something might be amiss.

'Nothing is amiss, Mr Wingrove,' said Caroline, and they all had to withdraw a few steps at that moment as the orchestra, refreshed after a short break, invited participation in a *Cotillon*. Young ladies in high spirits advanced with their partners, for the *Cotillon* entailed the execution of an infinite variety of spins and pirouettes at this stage of its development, and none could deny its infectious excitements.

Mr Wingrove, not having partnered Annabelle so far and not wishing to be thought reluctant to dance with her, smilingly requested the honour. Annabelle would rather have danced the joyous *Cotillon* with Captain Burnside, who had captured his own place in her warm affections. But she could not refuse Mr Wingrove, and in smiling confidence he led her forward.

Caroline glanced at her hireling. He stood with his hands clasped behind his back, eyes on the gathering dancers moving into place. She began to feel dismay. Was he going to deny her the opportunity to enjoy the lively *Cotillon*? Was she to remain outside it, looking as if not a single gentleman of her acquaintance had cared to take her up?

Captain Burnside, catching her glance, said, 'Ah, Lady Caroline.'

'Yes?' she said.

'Ah, I ain't sure if you'll allow me the privilege of—'

'Captain Burnside, please don't be absurd. How can you not be sure?'

'Well, I ain't, dear lady, but all the same—'

'I shall strike you, sir, unless you offer to advance with me.'

He smiled at her refreshing American candour, and said, 'I assure you, it will be a delight to advance with Your Gracious Ladyship.'

Her hand placed itself on his arm, and they were just in time to join the assembled array. The orchestra struck the liveliest chords imaginable, and the *Cotillon* began. Within seconds, Caroline found herself carried away by the music, the intricate steps, and the sure hand of the Captain. Quite soon, she was vivaciously engrossed. The glittering ballroom, with its crystal chandeliers, its mirrors casting brilliant reflections, became a scene of whirling exuberance and gaiety. Shimmering gowns, flashing jewels and military uniforms became a kaleidoscope of vivid moving colours. Captain Burnside showed himself an adept guiding partner, and there was, for Caroline, a sense of giddy delight in the dance itself, and a feeling of wonder that her participation was totally joyful. Eyes a luminous green, lips slightly parted, ecstatic breath escaping, hand in the firm clasp of the Captain's, she danced, spun and pirouetted, as did all the ladies.

Full-skirted gowns and petticoats flew and swirled, affording delicious glimpses of the finest and most delicate white lace. Caroline displayed gossamer lace and pink ribbon so frothily delicious that Captain Burnside declared her dazzling.

'I did not catch that,' she said breathlessly, and spun about. Her gown swirled. She did not miss a little smile of masculine appreciation. 'I trust, sir, I am not disappointing you.'

'It's no disappointment, dear lady, to know limbs are fashionably to the fore in the *Cotillon*, and long may they be so.'

She caught all those words, and laughter hung on her lips. Mr Wingrove would have assured her his eyes were elsewhere. Not so Captain Burnside. Oh, how rapturous it was to dance like a girl again, to put aside her reserve and cast away all the painful memories of a disastrous marriage and all the inhibitions of widowhood. How simply lovely it was to turn and turn again, the guiding hand making her feel she was lighter than air, and leading her swimmingly into every intricate movement. The music took hold of her, and its infectious gaiety induced heady abandon to the dance; amid the revolving kaleidoscope of swirling colour she was a figure of flying white silk and delicate lace. She wished the dance would go on and on, and indeed it seemed to, only for its end to come with such apparent suddenness that she was sure she had been cheated.

Gentlemen were bowing to their partners. Captain Burnside was bowing to her. 'By my life,' he said in admiration, 'beg to inform you, Lady Caroline, that that was perfection.'

'Oh, I haven't danced like that since the early days of my marriage,' said Caroline breathlessly, her face flushed, her bosom quick in its rise and fall. 'I must surely thank you for making it perfection.'

'I meant,' he said, 'that the perfection was you. I was merely dancing attendance, as it were: doing my awkward best not to spoil the picture. It ain't my intention to trespass beyond the boundaries of our relationship, but permit me to say your perfection made the picture dazzling. Are you aware, dear lady, that you're a very beautiful woman?'

Such personal compliments were well beyond the boundary of what was permitted, but how could she rebuff him? She had not moved since the end of the dance, nor had he. People leaving the floor brushed by them as she looked up at him, into the warmth of his smiling eyes. Perplexingly, uncertainty took hold of her, and she experienced the oddest sensation of vulnerability.

Faintly she said, 'Thank you, Captain Burnside.' He offered her his arm and escorted her back to her chair. She seated herself, her knees suddenly weak, a little pulse fluttering in her throat, and she fluttered her fan to cool herself and to cover her confusion.

They were joined by Annabelle and Mr Wingrove, Annabelle declaring herself madly in love with the *Cotillon* as danced in London, and generously, and truthfully, announcing that Mr Wingrove had been an accomplished partner. Robert and Cecilia Humphreys put in an appearance, and both expressed admiration for the gowns of the American sisters. Robert said how young and lovely Caroline looked. Cecilia said it was all of satisfying to see her looking so happy.

'Oh, the *Cotillon* is responsible,' said Caroline, 'it's the most gay and infectious of dances.'

'One's partner can also be a help,' smiled Annabelle, who had not missed her sister's joyful commitment to her partnership with the Captain.

'I vow it's most important to ensure a lady's enjoyment of dancing,' said Mr Wingrove in his equable way, 'and to that end I willingly dedicate myself.'

'I ain't sure myself that I don't take two left feet into a dance with me,' said the Captain, which brought laughter from Annabelle and Cecilia, but which Caroline thought completely untrue. He was far more natural and free-moving than Mr Wingrove, who was all of correct in his style, and accordingly a little unexciting and conventional. No, no, I must not think like this, she told herself; I should not be critical of such a kind friend when comparing him with a man of Captain Burnside's background. I simply must not. Heavens, Annabelle *is* falling in love with him, her smile for him is very affectionate, and she parted from Cumberland without a single sigh. But how I dislike the thought of her in love with my scoundrel of a hireling. It can lead to nothing, nothing.

'Supper is being called,' observed Mr Wingrove.

'Shall we sup with you?' asked Cecilia, and Mr Wingrove gallantly gave her his arm and took her in. Robert escorted Caroline, and Captain Burnside looked after Annabelle. They joined a procession of guests to the banqueting hall, where a superb buffet was laid out. Doors were open to enable guests to take their chosen food into the garden and consume it at tables placed on the terrace, on the lawn or in candlelit alcoves. Wine of each guest's choice was poured by liveried footmen.

Supper at an alcove table for six was most enjoyable, and

the conversation was extremely sociable. Cecilia, always entertaining, with a fund of gossip interesting but unmalicious, dropped names with a laugh, Cumberland's among them. Cumberland, she said, was rumoured to be in ardent pursuit of a new love, but no one was sure which lady it was who would provide a conquest.

'I see,' murmured Captain Burnside, 'depending on how one regards Cumberland, no one yet knows who will be the fortunate lady and who the unfortunate.'

'There are two ladies involved?' said Mr Wingrove, relishing his slice of game pie. 'Then I should say both are unfortunate in catching his eye in the first place. Who are they, Mrs Humphreys?'

Cecilia, who knew they were Caroline and Annabelle, said, 'Oh, one should not name names that relate only to a rumour.'

'Well, Cumberland ain't such a bad fellow,' said Robert cheerfully.

'I count him a little short on manners,' said Mr Wingrove, and changed the subject by remarking, not for the first time, that the King's unfortunate illness almost certainly related to his mental decline. Demurely, Annabelle offered again the American opinion that the King had gone off his head at the shock of losing his colonies. Caroline thought that rather tactless, but Mr Wingrove took it in good part and began a dissertation on the pros and cons. Since this seemed to bring an air of boredom to Annabelle, Captain Burnside took her up in a conversation of their own. Cecilia, after a while, broke in sweetly on them to ask him exactly how long he had known Caroline, at which Caroline came out of a reverie to glance quickly at the Captain. He was smiling unconcernedly.

'How long have I known Her American Ladyship?' he said. 'All my life, I fancy, if you could say my life began seven years ago, when I first met her. That was the effect she had on me, for she was fresh from the Americas, d'you see, and came to my eyes like the first magnolia blossom of spring. Smitten but overlooked, I languished.'

Annabelle laughed.

Caroline said, 'Quite untrue.'

'He was not smitten?' enquired Annabelle.

'He did not languish,' said Caroline, 'for his interests fully occupied him. He always had his eye on some poor innocent or other.'

'It's true I didn't carry a languishing look on my person,' said the Captain, 'for it ain't the thing a gentleman should do. But I do recollect contemplating suicide when I heard she had promised herself to Lord Percival. Suicide seemed the only sure way to consoling oblivion.'

Caroline's laugh was involuntary. 'Either you made a deplorable hash of it,' she said, 'or you had second thoughts. Or it truly never entered your head at all.'

'I plead guilty to second thoughts,' smiled Captain Burnside. 'But there it is: my life seemed to begin with Caroline's arrival in England seven years ago, Mrs Humphreys, although I'm now recovered from my heartbreak.'

'We are all relieved, I daresay,' said Mr Wingrove equably.

'Captain Burnside, did you and I meet in those days?' asked Cecilia. 'I cannot myself clearly recall, but I suppose we must have.'

'I am sure you did,' said Caroline, and could not resist the temptation to add, 'He was in and out of every London house, leaving a trail of sighing innocents behind him, and was often at Great Wivenden, where he was much given to the pursuit of Clarence's prettiest maidservants.'

'So was Clarence himself,' said Robert, then coughed at his tactlessness.

'You were at the wedding, Captain Burnside?' smiled Cecilia.

'Alas, no,' he said. 'Caroline pressed me, but how could I have endured seeing her bind herself to another man? I buried myself in regimental headquarters for days.'

'Oh, dear,' said Cecilia. 'Were you also a close friend of Clarence's?'

'An acquaintance,' said the Captain, lying easily.

Cecilia pressed further questions with an air of smiling

innocence, and since he answered all of them with casual ambiguity, and, since Caroline made no further comments, she felt herself on sure ground in inferring they were not old friends but new. But if so, why should they want to pretend otherwise?

On the return to the ballroom, Cecilia said aside to Caroline, 'Come, darling, do tell me exactly why that exciting man is staying with you.'

'Captain Burnside?' said Caroline. 'Exciting?'

'I vow him so. Come, is he your guest because the two of you have an amorous understanding?'

'Cecilia, how absurd. Myself and Captain Burnside?' Caroline could think of nothing more impossible. 'We have no understanding of that kind at all. I am charitably accommodating him while he finds himself a suitable apartment, for his regiment is expecting to be in England for some time.'

'Ah,' murmured Cecilia, 'perhaps he favours Annabelle, for he's dancing close attendance on her, and giving her sweet cause to blush at times.'

'Really?' said Caroline, cool towards Cecilia for once.

They entered the ballroom, and the festive nature of the occasion was born again. Caroline and Annabelle had both occasionally stood up with gentlemen of their acquaintance during the first half, and there were promises to keep with other gentlemen during the second half. It was apparent to any observer that the American sisters, particularly Caroline, had acquired many admirers. But Annabelle had promised the first post-supper dance to Captain Burnside, and they joined many other ladies and gentlemen in the *Pavane*. This was the stateliest of dances, and something of a courtly procession that was the customary opening to the second half of a ball.

Annabelle, wholly given to the joys of the night, invested her stately glide with unsuppressed animation. Captain Burnside smiled as she improvised steps of her own.

'You're a sweet girl,' he said, 'if dangerously excitable.'

'Charles, I protest. I am of all things sensible, or I should not have broken my engagement to a man I did not love.'

'Well, it's a pleasure to see you in such enjoyment.'

'Oh, I declare London balls wholly blissful,' said Annabelle.

'But d'you not find London a little stifling after the lush openness of the Carolinas?' he asked.

'Oh, the Carolinas offer everything to gentlemen,' she said, 'but it's London that offers everything to ladies.'

'Not everything that is offered should be accepted.'

'I'm not so simple that I'm unaware of that,' said Annabelle, executing a graceful dip and then floating forward on his arm. 'I have resisted the Duke of Cumberland. Oh, and there is more than London: there is Caroline's estate at Great Wivenden. It is sweetly and softly beautiful there, and one does not droop in overbearing heat.'

'Cumberland now, what did he say to you?'

Annabelle glided and curtseyed to him. He bowed and took her by the hand, and they stepped on in the colourful promenade.

'Oh, he declared himself incurably attached to me, but said nothing of how that would advantage me. Truly, he is a mesmerising man and an exciting prince, but I don't wish to be merely his fancy. There were other people in the conservatory, and they at once left when Cumberland arrived with me. I trembled, Charles.'

'Very wise,' said the Captain.

Annabelle dipped and gurgled. 'Charles, you are surely the most amusing man. How can it be wise to tremble?'

'Why, it showed Cumberland you would scream if he attempted to loosen your bodice and avail himself of that which you would naturally wish to deny him.'

Amid the stateliness, Annabelle blushed fiery red. Her bosom itself turned pink. 'Charles! Oh, I declare! You are a shameless embarrassment!'

'Sweet girl, never lack to tremble or to show parted lips ready to scream, for Cumberland's devilishly short on niceties, and only a loud scream or two will pull him up.'

'All the same, I vow you devilish yourself to speak so of my bodice,' breathed Annabelle, 'for it surely was dreadfully disconcerting. And the Duke was quite gentlemanly, offering to drive us all home in his coach. I said how kind that was, but that you were taking Caroline and me in her carriage. He laughed and asked if you knew how to handle a pair.'

Captain Burnside laughed himself at that.

As the evening progressed, Caroline and Annabelle danced with various gentlemen to whom they were promised for certain promenades. In between, Caroline alternated with Robert and Mr Wingrove, while Annabelle was attended exclusively by Captain Burnside, who was playing his role to perfection. Annabelle declared to her sister that he was a delicious man.

'Your opinion is shared by Lady Chesterfield's precocious niece,' said Caroline, 'but really, it is all of flamboyant, attaching himself excessively to you and paying not a single compliment to Cecilia, who has been sociable enough to join us.'

'Oh, my, you're vexed,' said Annabelle. 'There, I will tell him he simply must partner Cecilia, that she is dying to stand up with him.'

'No, that is not the thing at all,' said Caroline, but Annabelle insisted on claiming the Captain's receptive ear, with the result that he partnered Cecilia in a most popular dance, a *Minuet*. Conversing with him during a slow movement, she asked him what he was doing in London, away from his regiment, and was the fact that he was staying with Caroline indicative of a romantic attachment?

'I've extended leave,' said the Captain airily, 'and couldn't for the life of me resist Caroline's offer of hospitality. Egad, if she ain't the most gracious and beautiful woman in London, then who is? Which ain't to say you don't make a magnificent picture yourself, dear lady, for so you do.'

Cecilia, her fulsome figure sheathed in crimson silk, accepted the compliment with the smile of a woman who knew it to be no more than the truth, for was not her figure a pleasure to the most majestic man in the land, Cumberland himself?

Gracefully, she went through the most complicated steps

of the *Minuet* with Captain Burnside before saying, 'In your admiration of Clarence's widow, are you confiding to me that you have hopes concerning her?'

'Assure you,' he said, 'my only hopes are that she won't turn me out before I've found a place of my own, for I'm living like a king. And ain't it true that it's Mr Wingrove who has promising expectations?'

Dear me, thought Cecilia, here is the most evasive gentleman I have ever encountered, for he sidesteps every question. I have gained nothing from either him or Caroline.

'Ah, is it Annabelle you favour, then?' she smiled.

'A sweet girl,' said the Captain, 'but I ain't set on trying to out-rival gentlemen of higher estate.'

Cecilia thought he had been trying to do that most of the evening, but she refrained from saying so.

The *Minuet* over, scores of jewelled fans came into play as ladies cooled their flushed faces, giving the impression they had attracted the attentions of a multitude of colourful butterflies. Everyone awaited the finale, a prolonged *Cotillon*. Mr Wingrove began to extol the merits of such a finale. Caroline came to her feet and drifted aside, standing to fan herself and to observe Cumberland saying goodnight to his hosts, Lord and Lady Chesterfield. She was at least grateful that he had not pressed his unwelcome self on her tonight. Indeed, he had given the impression that his interest had abruptly ended. It was typical of him to leave before the finale. It enabled him to avoid being caught up in the melee as everyone left at the same time. A melee to Cumberland was a mob, a rabble.

Mr Wingrove was at her elbow. She felt he meant, quite naturally, to establish his claim for the last *Cotillon*. If she had gone aside in order to avoid this, she must reproach herself for such unkindness. He began a preamble to what was obviously going to be the rhetorical question of a privileged escort, then turned his head as Annabelle called to him. She smiled and beckoned. He excused himself to Caroline, and she watched him rejoin her sister. Captain Burnside seemed to have disappeared.

'Your Ladyship?' murmured the Captain from her blind side. She jumped.

'You startled me,' she said.

'So sorry.' The Captain looked suitably apologetic. 'But Cumberland's departed, d'you see, and without carrying off Annabelle. She being safe, therefore, I thought . . . ah, I'm not sure, considering circumstances, that I ain't being importunate.'

'If you will tell me what you are about, sir, I will give you my opinion.'

'Well, marm—'

'Don't be ridiculous,' she said, and shook her fan at him.

'Well, Lady Caroline, concerning the final promenade, I fancy Mr Wingrove is already fretting to get back to you, and I ain't sure how long Annabelle can detain him.'

Caroline stared at him. He made an observation of her hair.

'Captain Burnside, Annabelle is detaining Mr Wingrove at your request?'

'I ain't going to deny it, for I can't. Now, though we've come to this friendly term in our relationship, I'd not want to take the privileges of friendship for granted, you understand.'

'Favour me, please, by coming to the point,' said Caroline, noting that Mr Wingrove had risen from Annabelle's side.

'I ain't sure, of course, whether or not Mr Wingrove hasn't already—'

'Oh, fiddle-de-dee,' she breathed in open impatience, 'I am astonished you cannot speak up.'

'Caroline?' Mr Wingrove was back. 'I thought the *Cotillon* should not be missed, not by any of us.'

'No, it should not and must not,' said Caroline, 'for it will cap a most magnificent ball. We must all participate. Captain Burnside has offered me his arm, and Robert, of course, will stand up with Cecilia. So if you have engaged to advance with Annabelle, I shan't mind in the least. You have been so agreeable all evening.'

'Ah,' said Mr Wingrove, a little taken aback. But gentlemanly and correct to the last, he made no quibble and attached himself for the finale to Annabelle, who had gurgled with delight when Captain Burnside confided to her that he would like to outdo Caroline's faultless and estimable gentleman friend.

'Oh, but poor Mr Wingrove,' she had said, 'he is so very agreeable – ah, isn't he?'

'Faith, he is, sweet Annabelle, and my fondest hope is that he'll enjoy a very agreeable future.'

The *Cotillon* marking the end of the ball was danced with great elan, becoming a spectacle of perpetual motion, wherein a multitude of whirling colours produced ever-changing patterns. Young ladies were in exaltation, for only at such a ball and in such a dance could they be so free-limbed and extrovert without being reproved for a loss of ladylike gentility and deportment. Led by the gentlemen, they pirouetted as if delight attended on their limbs. Gowns and petticoats swirled like foamy clouds dancing amid rainbows, and delicate, gauzy pantaloons flirted around silken-clad legs. If ladies' legs were destined to disappear during the Victorian era, no man was unaware of their existence when George the Third's son was Prince of Wales.

'Heavens,' murmured Captain Burnside.

Lady Caroline was superbly the vision. Enraptured again, she had capitulated to the infectious nature of the dance. The rhythm, the music and the gaiety of laughing voices, all induced headiness. Again, the pleasure was of a kind she had not known since the devastating disillusionment had killed her zest for life. There was no degenerate husband to shame her. There was only Captain Burnside with his firm handclasp and his whimsical awareness of her limbs showing amid swirling clouds of froth. Oh, it was sickening that a man who might have been a true gentleman should own such disreputable traits.

Her breath escaped blissfully, and there was the brilliance of life in her eyes and delight on her face. It was a prolonged finale, and when the end eventually arrived a concerted sigh rose from all the ladies, followed immediately by tremendous applause throughout the ballroom. The orchestra rose and bowed. Caroline drew deep breaths. Captain Burnside smiled.

'After that,' he said, 'perhaps I should apologise to Mr Wingrove for depriving him of so much pleasure. It was, I fancy, his entitlement.'

'No, he will simply accept he was a laggard,' said Caroline, 'and I did not mind standing up with you.' Slightly teasing, such was her animation, she added, 'One could not say you are less accomplished than Mr Wingrove, even if you do lack an academy diploma.'

'What one *can* say, Your Gifted Ladyship, is that you've few equals in the *Cotillon*. If it's agreeable to you, I'll now bring round the carriage, while you and Annabelle prepare yourselves for departure.'

'Thank you, Captain Burnside,' said Caroline.

Lord and Lady Chesterfield said goodbye to every guest at the open front doors. A positive tangle of coaches and carriages filled the street, grooms at the reins, but when Caroline and Annabelle emerged from the handsome house, their carriage, an elegant barouche, was immediately outside, Captain Burnside up on the box, Sammy beside him. Sammy jumped down to assist the ladies into their seats, gossamer shawls around their shoulders.

The barouche moved off, Captain Burnside at the reins. It was past three in the morning, and most of London was sleeping.

# Chapter Seventeen

Captain Burnside drove at a smart trot through the quiet streets, the following traffic from the ball dispersing at intervals. The darkness of the night was touched by the crescent moon's limited light. Caroline and Annabelle exchanged dreamy comments about the ball and its magnificence, and about guests who had made impressions on them. Annabelle vowed she would beseech their parents to accustom themselves to her preference for England. Then, to please her sister, she said Mr Wingrove's sociability had been all of civilised. Such a pleasant and personable gentleman could not fail to be a far better husband than Lord Clarence.

'I will surely hope, sister, that he will offer for you, since you are affectionately attached to him. Charles and I agreed he has a degree of culture that would make the two of you happily compatible.'

Caroline sat up. 'How dare he!'

'Caroline?' Annabelle was at her most demure.

'I don't require Captain Burnside to advise me on marital compatibility,' said Caroline. 'What does *he* know of such things? Or you?'

'Oh, dear,' said Annabelle.

'As for Mr Wingrove, it is ridiculous to suppose I see him as a husband. I do not. He is merely an agreeable friend.'

'Well, dearest sister, Charles and I both declared there is no gentleman more agreeable. Charles regretted that he himself did not own such pleasant characteristics, though I think he shouldn't be as modest as that.'

'Modest?' Caroline was finely sceptical. 'Modest? Captain Burnside?'

211

'He is adorable, don't you think so?' murmured Annabelle.

'Oh, fiddle-de-dee,' said Caroline. She sat up again. 'Annabelle, don't you dare fall in love with him.'

'Goodness me, I—'

'He is penniless except for his officer's pay.'

'Mercy, poor Charles,' said Annabelle. 'Oh, I do confess that wouldn't suit me at all. But how sweet and kind you surely are, putting him up until he finds an apartment he can afford.'

The carriage was slowing. They were only a hundred yards from home. Out from a side street, four horsemen had emerged, spurring to block Captain Burnside. They were dark figures, black-cloaked and black-masked. The handsome thoroughfare was quiet, and nor was there sight or sound of any night watch. Captain Burnside glimpsed long-barrelled pistols.

Sammy glimpsed them too. 'Blind me, it's flash nightingales, guv'nor—,' he gasped, 'highway coves in the middle of London, and the ladies wearing a mint of sparklers.'

The masked horsemen came at them, pistols levelled. One man issued an order: 'Pull up. Keep quiet. Get down.'

Captain Burnside had slowed, but had no intention of pulling up, not now.

He heard another man fling hissing words: 'Damnation, there's two on the box!'

The Captain, convinced it would be fatal to stop, whipped up the pair. Well-trained, and owning a great deal of mettle when a gallop was called for, the coach horses sprang forward and raced away. The barouche shuddered and jerked at the sudden, forceful pull, and inside Annabelle and Caroline floundered and gasped protests. The vehicle swept the horsemen aside as Captain Burnside burst through. A flurry of oaths and curses desecrated the warm summer night. The Captain, surmising those pistols would not be fired, gave the horses their heads and they ran with the vigour and power of their kind, exulting in the exercise. They reached a surging gallop in quick time. The four horsemen, recovering, elected for pursuit.

'Set up a hullabaloo, Sammy,' said Captain Burnside crisply.

'That I will, sir,' said Sammy, and began to shout and bellow.

The Captain made for the wide Strand, off which lay Bow Street and the headquarters of the Runners. The barouche travelled at alarming speed, and Caroline and Annabelle hung on to the handstraps for dear life.

'What is happening?' gasped Annabelle.

Caroline pulled down the window and shouted. 'Captain Burnside! What are you about? Halt this carriage, do you hear?'

'Hang on, Your Ladyship!' called the Captain.

Caroline heard Sammy bellowing. 'Thieves! Flash coves! Highway nobblers!'

The horsemen were up with them. Caroline caught sight of the shadowy figure of one galloping alongside the box before he reached out and dug the barrel of his pistol in Captain Burnside's ribs. The pair galloped on, their hoofbeats a drumming echo on the sanded road. The Captain's whip whistled and cracked, and the thong bit at the masked face of his assailant. He reeled in his saddle and dropped back.

'Thieves!' shouted Sammy. 'Bow Street, we're a'coming! Wake up, you Runners!'

The cursing horsemen pulled up. They turned and rode away, fast. Captain Burnside brought the barouche to a halt. He got down, leaving Sammy with the reins, and Sammy gentled the excited pair.

'Lady Caroline?' Captain Burnside appeared at the open window.

'Sir,' said Caroline, breathless but valiant, 'why has it been necessary to drive like a madman and to wake up the whole of London?'

Faces and lighted candles at the windows of houses offered proof that her question, allowing for exaggeration, was quite justified.

'We suffered a small alarm, no more,' said the Captain.

'Small? Small?' Annabelle found her voice. 'I thought

213

the carriage would overturn and break our bones. Charles, I'm in need of smelling salts for the first time in my life.'

'So sorry, sweet girl,' murmured the Captain, and Caroline compressed her lips at the endearment.

'Explain,' she demanded.

'We encountered a footpad or two. They're now dispersed. Sammy has a capital pair of lungs. Are you badly shaken up?'

'Captain Burnside,' said Caroline, 'I have been shaken up, I have been shaken about, and I have been shaken from head to foot. Sir, did you say footpads?'

'Much to my regret.' The Captain shook his head in sorrow. 'What is London coming to?'

'They were riding horses, were they not?' asked Caroline.

'Damn me, so they were,' said the Captain, as if that fact had only just occurred to him. 'There's a devilish development for you, footpads on horseback in the Strand. But all is well now, Lady Caroline, and I'll drive you home at a pace you'll find gentle and soothing.'

He was being evasive, but as people in night attire were peering from open doors, Caroline let it go for the moment.

'Yes, please take us home,' she said.

A thickset man in a neckerchief and bulky coat, and carrying a stout stick, appeared at Captain Burnside's elbow. 'What's to do, eh, what's to do?' he asked.

'Ah, you're a Bow Street officer?' enquired Captain Burnside.

'That I am, day and night I am, and werry conscientious, sir. So hearing what I did hear, I says to myself, hello and what's a-goin' on here? And what is a-goin' on here?'

'We're on our way home from Lady Chesterfield's ball,' said the Captain. 'This is Lady Clarence Percival. Our pair suffered a fright, but they've quietened down now.'

'Ah, hosses is nervous critturs,' said the Bow Street Runner, 'and werry like to shy at the flutter of a pigeon's ving.' Through the window, he regarded Caroline in the dim interior of the coach. It was not so dark that he was not at once aware of magnificence. 'Vell, them critturs of yours be standin' quiet enough now, as this gentleman and officer has pointed out, m'lady. So seeing there's no trouble requiring of my assistance, I'll see you safe on your way, then noses and fingers von't have anything to point at and can go back indoors.'

'Thank you, officer,' said Caroline. 'Goodnight.'

Captain Burnside returned to the box, took the reins from Sammy and set the pair in motion. He chose an alternative route back to the house. Sammy kept alert watch, but there were no signs of the aggressive highwaymen. The Captain doubted they were highwaymen. Being the professional he was, he felt the intended hold-up was of a highly suspect kind. No gentlemen of the road would venture into a salubrious quarter of London flourishing their barkers between three and four in the morning. They might be found haggling with greasy fences in the dim taverns of the riverside stewpots, but they did not carry on their trade in the residential areas inhabited by the Quality. Their pickings came from travellers on the post-chaise highways.

The Captain could only surmise that the four masked men had been engaged on a venture of a different kind. Something clicked in his active mind. Cumberland. Now why had Britain's dark prince offered to drive Lady Caroline and her party home? He would know she would be using her own carriage. Annabelle had confirmed this, and had also told Cumberland that he, Captain Burnside, would be driving. She had not mentioned Sammy would be in attendance. Something else clicked, something relating to an involuntary hiss of words.

*Damnation, there's two on the box!*

That related, quite clearly, to information that had been wrong. That, in turn, pointed to a prearranged ambush. The masked men had expected to see only himself on the box. Which fact led directly back to Cumberland and the information innocently given him by Annabelle. And what could be further surmised from that? The possibility, for some reason, that Cumberland was darkly interested not only in himself, but in Caroline and Annabelle too. He himself, of course, might certainly have been found suspect by Cumberland, but Caroline and Annabelle? Absurd.

A quiet word with Annabelle was required.

The house having been safely reached, it was left to Sammy to stable the barouche and the horses. Caroline disappeared only moments after entering the house, and that left Captain Burnside with Annabelle in the drawing room. Annabelle was already over the alarm and whatever fright she may have suffered, and sank in tranquil languor into a chair.

'Charles, such a beautiful ball,' she murmured. 'I have had an excess of delicious activity, and do declare I could have gone on until dawn. And never, since arriving in London, have I seen Caroline so happily engaged and so vivacious. Isn't it a little mournful that a ball has to come to an end?'

'It's extremely mournful to young ladies, for whom ballrooms are designed, and in which I've no doubt you could all happily live.' Captain Burnside mused. 'Let me see, Annabelle, on the afternoon when you came flying and flushed from Cumberland's house, had he upset you in any other way than trying to attempt kisses?'

'Why do you ask that? You aren't going to be in uncharitable consideration of the Duke, are you?'

The Captain, remarking that Annabelle had elected to make a study of her fingertips, said in his pleasantest fashion, 'Not if it will distress you, although I realise you were upset. Did he perhaps say something hurtful?'

'Charles, such a conversation is very dull after a ball.' Annabelle plucked at her gown. She was suddenly uneasy. 'Oh, I must tell you, I think,' she said, and in the little rushing fashion of one eager to confide, she recounted the conversation she had overheard between Cumberland and his secretary, Mr Erzburger. 'I vow it worried me,' she said. 'What do you think?'

'I think,' said Captain Burnside, 'that some hot tea would be welcome.'

'There are no servants up,' said Annabelle, 'and I cannot

think myself how tea came to be relevant: I surely do feel the Duke is mysterious in some of his ways, and much more of a concern than tea.'

'But not as refreshing. I'll go to the kitchen and prepare a pot.'

'But I don't need refreshing, I need to go to bed,' protested Annabelle, 'and you are being very cool about the Duke, you surely are. Nor have you said a word about those footpads and the dreadful alarm they put us in.'

'Oh, everything outside the ball and your enjoyment of it, Annabelle, is all of insignificant.'

'Oh, yes, who could deny it?' breathed Annabelle. 'Where is Caroline? Has she gone up?'

'I have no idea,' said the Captain, 'but should she appear, tell her I've taken the liberty of using the kitchen to make some tea.'

'Tea at this time?' Annabelle laughed softly. Having confided her worry to Charles, she was free of it. 'How funny you are.'

'Captain Burnside, what are you doing?' Caroline, still a figure of splendour and showing no hint of tiredness, swept into the kitchen.

'At this precise moment, marm, I am pouring boiling water into the kitchen teapot,' said Captain Burnside. 'I trust your staff will forgive my use of the available facilities.'

'Sometimes, I think you quite mad. On this occasion, I think you quite commonsensical. Tea sounds perfect. I hope you will allow me to share the pot. I'm of the opinion that simply going to bed after a ball isn't the most exciting thing.'

Caroline paused to make a thoughtful observation of her hireling. He seemed entirely at his ease, his military jacket unbuttoned, his attention concentrated on making the tea. 'I must congratulate you on your behaviour and performance tonight. Apart from your brief excursion into folly with Lady Chesterfield's niece, you were faultless. I'm quite certain Annabelle thought you the perfect escort,

217

and she spent very little time casting her eyes in search of Cumberland. She sang your praises with enthusiasm.' Caroline paused again, needing to choose her words carefully. 'So I must ask you, Captain Burnside, are you now able to tell me that Annabelle is no longer in danger of throwing herself into bed with Cumberland? Have you, in fact, completed your mission for me by seducing Annabelle from Cumberland's arms into your own?'

Captain Burnside poured the tea. He slid one cup and saucer over the surface of the long kitchen table until it was within reach of her hand. They stood on opposite sides of the table, his expression deferential, hers slightly challenging.

'There's lemon there, marm,' he said. 'Ah – did you say seducing?'

'I did, sir.' Caroline dropped a slice of lemon into her tea. 'What other word serves as well? Annabelle has just gone up to bed. On the way, she informed me she adored you. Therefore, answer me, have you won her?' Her calm voice suffered vibrations as she added, 'If so, then you must leave this house immediately after breakfast. That is what was agreed.'

'Ah,' said Captain Burnside.

'That is hardly an answer,' said Caroline, 'or even a comment. I wish to know, I *must* know, if Annabelle has transferred her infatuation to you. Do not attempt to make a secret of it, sir, while you worm your way deeper into her affections. So answer me: yes or no.'

'Then I must answer no,' said the Captain, at which Caroline did not berate him for his lack of success. She sat down at the table, poured her tea from the cup into the saucer, lifted it with both hands and sipped thirstily at it.

'So, you have failed,' she said. 'Her declared adoration of you is an affectation?'

'Failed?' said the Captain, and he sat down too. He gulped down tea from his cup. 'Assure you, marm, the game ain't yet been played to a finish. But there it is, danger from Cumberland still lurks. There's still a possibility he'll contrive to bring the sweet girl into his bed.'

'You promised me that such a possibility would never become a fact,' said Caroline. 'What are you about, sir? Are you playing a different kind of game? I have been speaking to Sammy, and I declare the incident on the way home was wrongly described by you as a small alarm. That four masked horsemen, all brandishing pistols, demanded you halt the carriage, that you get down and keep quiet, do not amount to anything small, Captain Burnside.'

'I'd no wish to frighten you, marm—'

'I have said you may call me Caroline.'

'I'd no wish to frighten you, dear lady, but since Sammy has painted the alarm in full for you, I must agree with you that Annabelle should be placed out of Cumberland's reach.'

Caroline gave him a critical look. 'Agree with me? But I've said no such thing.'

'Oh, I made a loose interpretation of your remark that possibility must not become fact,' said the Captain airily. 'I think a move to your country estate, Great Wivenden, would be just the thing. In London, Annabelle is permanently within reach of Cumberland. I don't doubt you both are. One wonders, indeed, if he came close to carrying off both of you tonight. He's bold enough to have attempted it.'

Caroline's green eyes opened wide in utter astonishment. 'That is absurd,' she said. 'Not even Cumberland would dare to kidnap or abduct us.'

'Cumberland is a man of strong passions, marm, and would dare much to bring you to his bed. It ain't too impudent of me, I hope, to suggest you're among London's most beautiful women. Faith and the angels, your magnificence and Annabelle's virgin sweetness are enough to provoke a prince of Cumberland's ilk into bedding both of you, willy-nilly.'

Caroline could not take him seriously. Laughter glimmered in her eyes. The ball had been a delight, re-awakening her love of music and dancing, and no matter that the hour was well advanced, she did not want to go to bed.

'What a curious mood you are in, Captain Burnside,' she said. 'Pray tell me, is my magnificence to be preferred to Annabelle's virgin sweetness, or vice versa?'

219

'By Cumberland?' enquired the Captain, remarking her resilience and staying power.

'I don't think you incapable of answering up for yourself,' said Caroline.

'Wisdom and the terms of our contract caution me against that. Would you care, dear lady, for more tea?'

'Thank you, yes. Tea is a stimulant, isn't it?'

'I ain't supposing four o'clock in the morning is the right time for a stimulant, and perhaps I should see you to your bed.'

'I can see myself to bed, sir,' said Caroline, undisguisedly animated. 'Be so kind as to refill my cup.'

Captain Burnside refilled both cups. The brown-walled kitchen might have made a hollow chamber for their voices had not the echoes wandered around the multitude of hanging pots and pans and been lost in them.

'It shall be Great Wivenden, then, for you and Annabelle?' he said.

'You are persisting in the absurd. You are suggesting Annabelle and I need to flee?'

'I am insisting,' said the Captain.

Caroline stared at him in disbelief. 'Insisting?' she said.

'I must.'

'Am I dreaming?' she asked, her chin up.

'It ain't the moment to indulge in dreams, marm, but to remove yourselves from Cumberland's reach.'

'Oh,' breathed Caroline, 'how has this change in our relationship come about? I am now expected to take orders from you, to do what you tell me to?'

'Why, of course not, marm,' said Captain Burnside, 'but if you could make preparations to leave tomorrow with Annabelle—'

'I will not, sir! You are above yourself.'

'You'll probably take a late breakfast, in which case you could leave after that.'

Caroline really did not know whether to laugh at him or retaliate. There was a natural feminine urge to rebuke, but just as natural an urge to laugh.

'Ridiculous man,' she said. 'I have said I won't leave, and I shan't.'

'Then I must tell you of a conversation Annabelle overheard. That is, part of a conversation.' Captain Burnside repeated Annabelle's account of the dialogue between Cumberland and his secretary Erzburger, which seemed to concern a person being held secure by Erzburger, and the secretary's strange reference to the importance of silence. It was, said the Captain, an unhappy fact that Annabelle was certain Cumberland knew she had overheard.

'Oh,' said Caroline in changed mood.

'There, marm, you'll concede the advisability of you and Annabelle leaving London? Cumberland is bound to believe Annabelle has confided in you, and to contrive in some unpleasant way to ensure silence in both of you. Perhaps the intended hold-up was an attempt at abduction. I'd say, from what Annabelle overheard, that Cumberland's engaged in one of his devilish plots. Great Wivenden will be far safer than London.'

Caroline, now worried, said, 'I see. Yes, very well. We will leave tomorrow, all three of us.'

'I'm unable to accompany you myself . . .'

'Captain Burnside,' she said firmly, 'you are still under commission to me, and I command your attendance. I declare myself roundly opposed to any specious argument from you, and under the circumstances, why, sir, it's your duty to protect Annabelle.'

'Quite so,' said the Captain, finishing his stimulating tea, 'but I've one or two matters in hand of a distinctly pressing kind. Be assured, however, that I'll follow later. In the meantime, I'll arrange for a friend of mine to escort you and Annabelle to Sussex and to remain with you until I arrive. He's a commendable gentleman, sharp as a needle, and as handy with his dabs as with a pistol.'

'A cut-throat?' said Caroline, disliking very much her hireling's intention to desert her, however temporarily. 'We are to be placed in the care of a cut-throat?'

'He ain't a cut-throat, dear lady, but a merry young gentleman full of stuff, and renowned for his chivalry.'

Caroline did laugh then. Sarcastically. 'I am to believe you own friends of a chivalrous kind?' she said.

'Life has its pleasanter surprises,' said the Captain, as suave and bland as ever. 'Now, I recommend you retire. It's almost morning. I must go out myself, to catch my friend before his day begins and puts him out of my reach.'

'You are going out now?' asked Caroline.

'In a little while. Much the best thing, the situation being what it is.'

'I trust,' she said a little bitterly, 'that during your absence we shan't be murdered in our beds.'

'Come, Lady Caroline, it ain't going to be as bad as that. I care excessively for your sweet sister, and won't lack to ensure her safety. Now I must go and change.'

They both rose from the table. Caroline showed a slight flush.

'Your excessive care for my sister is not preventing you placing her and myself in the hands of an escort we do not know,' she said. 'And if you remain in London, are you not putting yourself at risk? I have told you how dangerous Cumberland is.' Her lashes dropped and her voice became a little unsteady. 'You have shown many times that there is good in you, that you are not wholly worthless, and I – I should be distressed if anything truly unpleasant happened to you on my account, or Annabelle's.'

'Dear lady,' he said quite gently, 'I care excessively for both of you, and you have my word I'll take no risks, for I'm set on seeing Cumberland don't get the better of us. Allow me to go about my business, which is to do with ensuring your safety.'

'If I must, then I must,' said Caroline, but with some reluctance. She was worried, inexplicably, about his own safety.

'Is it possible you could use one of your tenants' cottages instead of your manor?' he asked. 'That would put you even more safely out of Cumberland's reach.'

'I cannot believe we are truly in that kind of danger,' she said, 'but I see you are sure we are. Yes, there is a cottage just fallen vacant, and we can use that.'

'Do so, Lady Caroline, and tell no one.'

# Chapter Eighteen

I dare swear Cumberland is the devil himself,' said the gentleman of impressive bearing, 'but I doubt he'd go so far as to abduct a lady of the Quality and her sister. A pretty serving wench of insignificance who won't come to heel, such a girl Cumberland might well carry off for a week, and then send her back without a thought for the consequences. But Lady Caroline and her sister? 'Pon my soul, Burnside, are you so convinced?'

'Fearful,' said the Captain.

'Fearful?'

'By reason of the overheard conversation, Your Grace. Nor would he leave proof of his own part, but ensure their silence in a way so devious as to escape any finger of suspicion himself.'

'Well,' said the gentleman, 'though I'd elect to say your fears are exaggerated, I ain't inclined to argue with you. Preventive measures shall prevail, even if they be unnecessary. So, then, proceed with your ploy and have Lady Caroline and her sister move to Great Wivenden.'

'I've spoken to our versatile friend, Jonathan Carter.'

'*Your* friend, I fancy,' said His Grace.

'He'll escort the ladies to Sussex and take good care of them.'

'He had better, Captain Burnside, he had better, or I'll have his head. And warn him to show none of his impudences. I shall, by the way, come close to hanging the pair of you if Lady Caroline and her sister come to any harm.' His Grace mused. 'I'm not sure it wouldn't be preferable if they were to return to the Americas.'

'H'm,' said Captain Burnside.

'What? What?'

'Assure you, Your Grace, it's a wise thought, but I ain't sure the ladies would agree with it. You'll be aware that Lady Caroline has a mind of her own, while Annabelle has a will of her own.'

'Find me any woman who has neither a mind of her own nor a will of her own, and you find me a phenomenon,' said the aristocratic gentleman. 'What of Mr Carter? Has the irreverent laggard made no progress at all with the Irish fellow?'

'The Irish fellow, sir, is proving uncommonly resistant. So far he ain't confided a single whisper, though Jonathan is willing to lend him as caring an ear as his own mother.'

'When I remark motherly qualities in Mr Carter, mountains will be flying as gracefully as larks. You still feel, do you, that all will come to light on the 29th?'

'It's a feeling,' said Captain Burnside.

'A feeling? Remarkable,' said His Grace drily. 'I had a notion we owned only suspicions. Now we have a feeling. Equatable with a woman's intuition?

'I ain't sure anything can equate with a woman's intuition, Your Grace. But my feeling prompts me to tangle with the Irish gentleman myself now that Jonathan is quitting his post to take care of the ladies.'

'If you intend to go fishing, sir, be sure your hook is baited,' said His Grace.

Captain Burnside ventured a smile. His Grace received it aloofly.

'The bait shall be sweet,' said the Captain.


'Your Ladyship?'

Caroline had only just finished dressing, although it was almost noon. But it had been five in the morning before sleep claimed her.

'What is it, Helene?'

Worriedly, Helene said, 'I've spent another twenty minutes looking, after searching for hours last night, but your hair clasp, milady, it still can't be found.'

'But it must be in my bedroom somewhere,' said Caroline.

'Yes, milady, but it still won't come to hand.' Helene's worry increased, since she knew it would be all of unpleasant for suspicion to fall on one of the servants, or even on herself. The clasp was priceless. It adorned Lady Caroline's auburn hair as brilliantly as a tiara.

'Tush, Helene, don't look so worried,' said Caroline. 'I vow it must be somewhere in my bedroom. There, you can turn the whole room over in the most thorough way after Miss Annabelle and I have left this afternoon.'

'Yes, Your Ladyship,' said Helene. She would have liked to accompany Lady Caroline to Sussex, but had not been asked.

Caroline entered her bedroom and sat down at her dressing table. She mused on her reflection and thought about the hair clasp. She had last worn it on the night she fell asleep at the card table, and Captain Burnside had had the audacity to carry her up to her suite. Helene had reported it missing the following morning. A sudden little shock disturbed her, and cold tingles ran down her back. Captain Burnside. The oddest kind of man, with a penchant for getting his hands on trinkets.

The shock wave increased, spreading numbing coldness. A feeling of terrible unhappiness became trapped by ice and could not escape. She came to her feet with an effort. Her legs trembled. She made her way into the corridor, to the door of the Captain's room. There she hesitated. Then she turned the handle and entered. The bedroom was tidy. His bed had not been slept in. It occurred to her that the reason he was not going to Sussex with herself and Annabelle was simply because he had not intended to. He had already decamped, no doubt, taking with him the clasp and the small fortune it represented. But no, he would not have left his many clothes and personal possessions behind. He was too smooth and self-assured not to be able to put on a face of innocence. She must search his room, she must, and if she found the clasp then no one else need know he had taken it. She could give him a chance to confess and

225

explain. He might, perhaps, have been motivated by heavy debts, debts that could mean imprisonment unless they were settled. No, she must not find excuses for him. He was a wretched thief of a particularly despicable kind.

She looked around, her unhappiness a cold, leaden thing. Already the bedroom seemed to bear his imprint. It was as well-ordered as his appearance. A leather razor holder lay on the dressing table, with hair brushes and a little box of toothpicks. The wardrobe beckoned, as did the drawers of a tallboy. But she could not bring herself even to begin the search. And perhaps she should not condemn him as guilty before giving him an opportunity to prove himself innocent.

Something else occurred to her. She rushed to her library, to her desk there. The drawer in which she kept ready money was always locked. It was locked now. She turned the key and pulled open the drawer. What money there was there lay undisturbed. That at least gave her great relief. She went back to the bedroom, but still could not bring herself to search it. Wait. If he returned this afternoon, bringing his friend with him, she would search in his presence. Oh, why did such a man laugh at the virtues of honesty and integrity? Why could he not be as trustworthy as Mr Wingrove? She walked slowly from the room, wondering why she was so much more unhappy than angry.

Betsy bobbed along in her approach to Horse Guards Parade. Sometimes there were handsome officers with time on their hands. She favoured being set up by a handsome officer, who would buy her presents and also make her an allowance.

'Why, there you are, sweet puss,' said a pleasant and friendly voice, and Betsy, startled, found her gentleman friend walking beside her.

'Oh, sir, you be springing out of nowhere again,' she said, but her smile was bright with pleasure and her bobbing walk became sprightly.

'Not to bite you, Betsy. How very pretty you look.'

In her dark blue servant's gown and white cap, Betsy's prettiness was neat.

'Mr Burnside, sir, some gentlemen flam a girl, but it be a pleasure to hear you call me pretty, even if it's only just to sweeten me.'

'Come, come, Betsy, ain't I been bowled over by your pretty looks since I first met you? Shall we go on to Collins? Yes, I think we will, for I can't buss you here.'

'Oh, you be passioning to buss me?' asked Betsy, delighted at the thought that he was.

'Not in public, puss. It don't do to passion in public. Now,' he said, as they began to proceed in the direction of Collins, 'when do you have your next free Sunday?'

'This coming one, sir.'

'Capital. We shall go out, then, you and I. We have our Lord Chancellor's permission.'

'Sunday out with you, sir?' Betsy's walk became even sprightlier. 'Oh, I aren't never had any gentleman more kind to me. But your wife—?'

'Heavens, it won't do to let my wife know.'

'Oh, I won't say a word.' Betsy pulsated. The thought of spending Sunday with her exciting and pleasuring gentleman was bliss. 'I'll spit on silver that I won't even whisper.'

'Silver, yes,' murmured Captain Burnside. 'Well, you shall have a few shillings, pretty pussy, for you're a dab hand at holding your tongue.'

Inside the private room at Collins, Betsy waited until coffee and confectionery had been served, then drew herself close to the Captain.

She lifted her pursed mouth. He indulged her. Betsy exhaled moist sighs against his lips.

'There, I be ready to be bussed like I can hardly bear,' she said. 'I never did know any gentleman who made my pretty ones shyer.'

'Quite so, my pretty kitten, but go and sit down and drink your coffee.'

Betsy complied. She sipped coffee, nibbled at the confectionery, and eyed him sighingly. 'You be sweetly exciting to a girl,' she said.

227

'Faith, you're a precocious temptation, Betsy, but there's my wife and our Lord Chancellor. But a kiss or two here, another there, and a few on Sunday – that shouldn't upset either of them.'

'But that Lord Chancellor, he be more fond of hanging than kissing,' said Betsy.

'A stern taskmaster,' said the Captain, 'but he's come to look kindly on you. I've sworn ferocious oaths on your reliability. Now, you haven't forgotten you're to let me in on the 29th?'

'I'm all a-tremble every time I think on it, but I'll do it, sir.'

'Splendid puss. Is Mr Erzburger still going out each afternoon?'

'Most afternoons, yes, sir.'

'Good. Now, let me in this evening, Betsy.'

'Oh, lor',' said Betsy, and perceptibly quaked.

'Between nine and ten.'

'Oh, must I, sir?'

'Damn it, Betsy, I'll get hanged if you don't. So will you.'

'Oh, that Lord Chancellor,' breathed Betsy, 'he be a terrible hanging gentleman, like I never did dream of.'

'Well, I can't deny it, he is,' said Captain Burnside, 'but hanging a few from time to time ensures that the rest of us remain willingly conscientious. He don't encourage backsliding, my young beauty. But come, cheer up, I'll wager you're as conscientious as any of us.'

'What's conscientious?' asked Betsy.

'Why, obeying orders. So, you'll let me in this evening.'

'Oh, lor',' said Betsy.

'Good,' said Captain Burnside, 'I'll be waiting between nine and ten, which means you can pick the time that's safest during the hour. Now, purse your rosy lips and I'll deliver a partner's true kiss.'

'Oh, but there be time for loving kisses,' said Betsy. She jumped up, swooped, and plumped herself down on his knees. Her bottom wriggled ecstatically and secured its warm place in his lap. She put her lips to his and brought his hand up to her bosom. She sighed and kissed, she murmured and kissed, she quivered and kissed. Her breathing was sweetly rapturous. 'Oh, I be going to swoon,' she said.

'Well, that won't do at all, puss,' said Captain Burnside, and came to his feet.

Betsy spilled to the floor with a gasp. She sat up, lifted her face and laughed. 'Oh, I hardly ever knowed a more blissful gentleman,' she said, 'and there be silver coins as well, didn't you say, sir?'

'Yes, I fancy I did,' he said. He extracted some coins. She cupped her hands, held them up and he dropped the coins into her palms. Her eyes sparkled and she came to her feet. 'This evening, then, sweet puss.'

'I won't mind my quiverings and tremblings, Mr Burnside, sir, but I'm begging you'll be as quiet as a mouse.'

'We'll be as quiet as two mouses, Betsy.'

'Two mouses be mice, sir.'

'Egad, you're right, my kitten. Ah, kindly tidy yourself up.'

'Your Ladyship,' said William Anders, Caroline's quiet, studious-looking secretary, 'Thomas informs me there's a person asking to see you.'

Thomas, the footman, was presently holding the person at bay at the front door.

'A person?' Caroline spoke absently. Her mind could relate to little except her missing hair clasp. 'Oh, is Captain Burnside with him?'

'No, milady.'

'I see.' Her heart was sinking. 'Never mind. Show him in, please.'

The person was shown in. A young man in his mid-twenties, he doffed his brown top hat and bowed.

'I have the honour, Your Ladyship, to present myself: Mr Jonathan Carter. At your service. I am informed by a friend of mine that I am to escort you to Sussex, with your sister, Miss Annabelle Howard; that I am further to guard and protect you both, and to lay low any miscreant whose

229

intentions towards you don't look too friendly. In the interests of your well-being, I can offer—'

'Wait, please.' Caroline held up a hand. She studied the young man, finding him pleasant of face, broad of shoulder and cheerful of smile. His blue eyes were alert, his legs and thighs strong. He wore a brown velvet coat, green waistcoat, a neat white cravat and brown knee-breeches. His dark brown hair was tidily brushed. He exuded self-confidence. 'Your friend is—?'

'Captain Charles Burnside, Your Ladyship. He—'

'Where is Captain Burnside?'

'At the moment, I ain't sure,' said Jonathan, 'but he hopes to be here to see us off. You're ready, Lady Clarence? That's your coach and four outside, with luggage? Shall we depart, say, in ten minutes?'

'We shall depart, Mr Carter, only after I have seen and spoken to Captain Burnside.'

'Eh?' said Jonathan. 'Captain Burnside was very precise. Away by three o'clock, he said. So three o'clock it is, don't you see.'

'No, I do not see, sir,' said Caroline, stiffly upright and almost haughty. 'I repeat, we shall not depart until I have seen and spoken to Captain Burnside.'

'Well, he ain't going to like it, Your Ladyship. He's an exacting gentleman and—'

'He's a gentleman of a kind, no doubt,' said Caroline, clad in a green travelling gown. 'Mr Carter, it is no use muttering and scraping your feet. Captain Burnside may order your comings and goings, but he does not order mine. How long have you known him?'

'Since he pulled me out of the river seventeen years ago,' said Jonathan. 'Fell in. Set up a hullabaloo. Damn cold, Your Ladyship, and deep. He pulled me out and carried me home over his shoulder. To my mother. My mother boxed my ears and Charles stayed for tea. 'Pon my dear soul, a friend he is and always will be, but if we ain't away by three-fifteen at the latest, I'll get my head cracked.'

'You share the same way of life?' asked Caroline, face set and stiff.

230

'Common interests, Your Ladyship.'

Caroline gave him a cold look. Annabelle entered the drawing room at that moment, looking her prettiest and fairest in a gown of dark blue. She regarded the visitor coolly, for she guessed who he was, the friend who was to escort Caroline and herself to Sussex, and she was by no means reconciled to going.

'Good afternoon,' said Jonathan briskly. 'I fancy you're Miss Annabelle Howard.'

'I surely am,' said Annabelle. 'And who are you, pray?'

'Annabelle, this is Mr Jonathan Carter,' said Caroline, 'the gentleman recommended by Captain Burnside.'

'How interesting,' said Annabelle.

Jonathan bowed. 'I hope, Miss Howard, that things ain't going to get as interesting as that. Though I can box, fence, lay an accurate pistol and kick the wind from a footpad's bread-basket, I'd favour a peaceful journey and a tranquil Sussex. But if that don't come about, I'll break a few heads with pleasure, but beg to suggest you and Lady Clarence stand quietly aside with your smelling salts. When dealing with things ugly, it don't do to have ladies screaming and swooning, you understand.'

'Well!' breathed Annabelle. 'Sir, I declare you the sauciest and most impudent scallywag I have ever met. My sister and I are proud Americans, and don't suffer the swooning vapours of the fragile English.' She tossed up her chin. 'Do not address me further, sir. Caroline, are we to go now?'

'We are not,' said Caroline. 'I am determined to see Captain Burnside before we depart.'

'But we may not see him at all today,' said Annabelle.

'Then we shall not go today,' said Caroline.

'Oh, gad,' said Jonathan, 'here's a pretty dish of nettles.'

'Jonathan, damn it, why ain't you up and away?' Captain Burnside spoke from the open door. Caroline turned with a swift rustle of her gown, her emotions a sudden turmoil of relief and anguish. 'Ladies, where are your bonnets and jackets?'

'Captain Burnside.' Caroline swept towards him. 'Come

231

with me, sir. I wish to speak with you. At once.' She swept past him, into the hall and towards the staircase. She turned her head. He was still in the doorway, looking at her, and even daring to frown at her. 'Do you hear me, sir?' She ascended the staircase, gown hitched. Captain Burnside followed. She went up to his room and entered it. She turned. He appeared. 'Close the door, sir.'

He closed it.

'Marm, it's a four-hour journey—'

'I do not care to discuss that.' Caroline's breathing was agitated, her eyes darkly green. 'I wish to be frank. My jewelled hair clasp is missing. It's been missing since the night I fell asleep playing cribbage with you. I must ask you, Captain Burnside, do you know anything of it?'

He regarded her in some puzzlement for a moment, then in comprehension. He coughed. 'I fancy, marm, you mean did I filch it?' he said.

'I am sorry,' said Caroline, voice unsteady, 'but yes, I do mean that.'

'Quite understandable,' said Captain Burnside, 'but beg to inform you it ain't a principle of mine to take advantage of a patron, dear lady. I fancy you've made an exhaustive search?'

'Several exhaustive searches have been made,' said Caroline, desperately wanting to believe him. 'But not in this room, *your* room.'

'Well, that ain't going to unearth a single jewel, marm. I recollect you were very tired that night, but you had sent your servants to bed. Ah, did you undress yourself?'

'Yes. I always do, although Helene puts my clothes away.'

'And the gown you were wearing, marm, was that put away or left out for cleaning? I assume it was attended to by Helene the following morning.'

'Captain Burnside?' Her hand was at her throat.

'If it was put away, marm, shall we take a look at it?'

Caroline trembled, stared at him, came to and rushed to the door. She opened it and hurried to her suite, to the wardrobe in her dressing room. The Captain, following, watched as she drew out the red gown she had worn the night they had played cribbage. She removed it from its frame, and as she did so the jewelled hair clasp fell through it and dropped to the carpet. She stared in utter dismay and mortification at its glitter. Her knees trembled. 'Oh,' she said.

'Quite so,' said the Captain. 'All is well, marm. So, then, shall you and Annabelle put on your bonnets and jackets? It ain't favourable to linger.'

Caroline had a horrifying feeling she was going to cry. Cry? She had not known the foolishness of tears for many years. She had suffered most of her humiliations bitterly but without crying. She hated crying. But she was mortifyingly close to it now.

She turned away, the gown sagging in her hands. 'Captain Burnside, I – I – oh, I am sorry. Please forgive me.'

'Wouldn't dream of being so pompous, marm. Nor is there anything to forgive. Your assumption was all of natural. Except I ain't so far made a monkey out of a patron. It wouldn't do, d'you see. I'll go down and advise Annabelle to make herself ready. I'll give her five minutes. You've confidence in Jonathan, I hope.'

'I . . .' Caroline turned again, but he was already out of the room. Her mortification had brought a flush to her face and moisture to her eyes. Yet, above all, she felt relief almost rapturous. It exhaled from her in a long, long breath.

When she entered the drawing room several minutes later, Annabelle was facing up to the Captain in pretty, pouting protest.

'But, Charles, it's of all things ridiculous, leaving London to hide ourselves at Great Wivenden. Why, as if those footpads would dare to show themselves again. I don't wish to go, not when the season is so exciting—'

'And Cumberland is even more so?' Captain Burnside shook his head at her. 'No, it won't do, sweet girl, and your sister's mind is made up. Your bonnet is on, the coach is waiting, the horses petulant with impatience. So off you go,'

'Oh, you wretch!' cried Annabelle.

Mr Jonathan Carter intervened breezily. 'Say the word,

Charles, and I'll carry her out,' he said, and Annabelle turned fretfully on him.

'Go away, you creature!'

'Can't do that,' said Jonathan cheerfully, 'I promised to see you and Lady Caroline safely to Sussex. It's all one to me, carrying you out or escorting you.'

Annabelle gasped in outrage. 'Oh, you all are a varmint and scallywag!' she cried.

'Well, I ain't noted for being a die-away popinjay, I'll give you that, Miss Howard,' said Jonathan. 'I'm firm as a rock, quick with a punishing blow, and a defender of virtue.'

'Charles,' said Annabelle, 'are we truly to go with this brutal beast?'

'Favour me by bearing with him,' said Captain Burnside, and took her arm. Sighing, Annabelle went with him. Caroline and Jonathan followed.

Outside the house, Caroline's travelling coach-and-four stood waiting, Sammy gentling the noses of the leading pair. Jonathan mounted the box and took up the reins. Sammy climbed up beside him. Annabelle, assisted into the coach by Captain Burnside, gave him the reproachful look of a young lady who really could not see why she had to fly from the summer season of London, especially under the escort of Mr Jonathan Carter, who had already made it evident he was going to be boringly unlikeable.

Caroline, about to follow her sister into the coach, looked up at Captain Burnside a little uncertainly. 'You have promised to join us as soon as you can,' she said. 'We may rely on that?'

'Indeed you may,' he smiled, then murmured, 'I believe my venture for you is still unfinished.'

'Yes. Yes.' It was a restless affirmative. She felt she did not really care any more about the second part of the venture. She whispered, for his ears alone, 'Please reassure me, please tell me that in misjudging you I haven't spoiled the friendliness of our relationship.'

'Sometimes one's relationship with a patron moves out of the businesslike and ordinary,' he said, and kissed her gloved hand in farewell. 'I hope to be with you tomorrow.'

'Please take care,' she said.

'The cottage, where is it?' he asked.

'Half a mile west of the manor. It stands by itself in Birchwood Lane, and is called Pond Cottage.'

'Capital,' said Captain Burnside, and Caroline entered the coach.

# Chapter Nineteen

Caroline, standing at the gate of Pond Cottage, filled her lungs with the pure country air. Why it was called Pond Cottage no one seemed to know. The nearest pond was in Wychling village, a mile away on the other side of Great Wivenden. Its bricks were mellow with age, its slate roof adorned with a cluster of red chimney pots. It stood alone in the lane that led to Pond Farm, the lease of which was owned by herself. Two other cottages lay farther west. They housed farm labourers and their families.

This was farming country, and at this time of the year the pastures were still lush, the fields rich with summer growth. The hedgerows, to Caroline, were singularly English. They divided fields and they bordered every rutted track and dusty lane. Honeysuckle sprang from them, and wild roses, and in the fall, which the English in their peculiarity called autumn, blackberries plump and ripe glistened with morning dew.

Visible, the rising green folds of the South Downs were soft with evening light, the air caressingly warm. A single fleecy cloud, tinted by the sun to pearly pink, drifted westwards through the heavenly ocean of blue.

The landscape presented every shade of green to the eye, and every shade had its own variability in the ever-changing light of an English day. No one could say the Carolinas did not hold their own beauty, but the greens of Sussex always made Caroline feel that nature had come to rest here in the quintessence of tranquillity.

She loved her Sussex estate, and Sussex itself. Had she been blessed with an affectionate husband and loving children, it was here she would have lived, not London. But as a childless widow, Great Wivenden, for all the pleasure she took in it, made her feel incomplete. She had neither husband nor children. She was almost twenty-five – twenty-five! – and was without children.

Great Wivenden's manor house cried out for the laughter of children, and for their scampering feet. How could she live here by herself, with only servants to keep her company? She must marry again, she must. She must have children. Three, four, five, oh, even six. Then the quietness of the house would burst into the joyful, hurly-burly noises of children growing up. But whom could she marry? Was there a man she wished to bed with? Should she consider Mr Wingrove? He would surely make an affectionate and thoughtful husband, and looked manly enough to bring her to motherhood. She reflected on what this would entail. Simply, the act of physical union. The reflection brought no quickening to her body, no excitement. Mr Wingrove was a very good friend, and a gentleman all of upright, but she had lately come to feel he was a little wordy. As his wife, she would have no escape from his informative dissertations. One did not always want a conversation to be informative. There was a deal of pleasure in taking up a challenging dialogue, in giving tit for tat, as with . . .

Caroline bit her lip. How unkind, how wrong, to think of comparing Mr Wingrove's honest conversation un-favourably with Captain Burnside's devious use of words. Mr Wingrove was a gentleman, a pleasant English gentle-man. His integrity as a husband would be much to her liking. It was only recently she had begun to think of marrying again, although she could not imagine why. Consequent upon her wretched life with Clarence, she had found widowhood an equable state. Why had she suddenly become restless, even worse than restless? Her present state was a starved one. She really must consider encouraging Mr Wingrove to propose. Yet why, if her body felt starved, did the thought of being bedded and loved by Mr Wingrove not excite her? Should not the thought of being loved by any personable man arouse some quickening of her blood? London was full of handsome, athletic Corinthian bucks, and it was ridiculous she could think of none who might be responsible for inducing this restlessness in her.

Her deeply introspective mood brought her to the realisation that she wanted a husband she was in love with. To conceive children in the arms of a cardboard husband did not excite the imagination at all. To conceive in the arms of a husband she loved would be a joy. Was that not what most women dreamed of, loving, giving and being loved? Was it not what even some widows dreamed of?

In coming to know Clarence, it had seemed to her that some men could take physical pleasure of a woman without being remotely in love. Clarence had never been capable of loving anyone. She supposed Captain Burnside . . . No, she could not think so ill of him as to place him in the same degenerate mould as Clarence, but she supposed he had bedded infatuated young ladies without any consideration of love. If not degenerate, it was wretchedly immoral to seduce a young woman of her honour and her trinkets. Captain Burnside was . . .

She found herself trembling then, a strange wildness afflicting her at the thought of her unprincipled hireling even now in the company of some woman he intended to seduce. She thrust the thought from her. But she still trembled, her agitation a physical thing.

Inside the cottage, Jonathan was removing dust-sheets from the furniture. Annabelle, coming down from one of the bedrooms, was greeted with a brisk smile and an unwelcome suggestion. 'Perhaps you'll lend a delicate hand, Miss Howard? Sammy's dusting the kitchen, and you might care to do this room.' This was the living room, with an ingle-nook fireplace, comfortable furniture, and a dining table and chairs in the bay window. The cottage had a pretty character, a cosiness, and a polished wood flooring. 'Sammy will find you a duster.'

'I beg your pardon?' said Annabelle.

'Why, there's dust, don't you see. But it won't do, working in your pretty gown.' Jonathan, his coat off and his shirt sleeves rolled up, was in a practical mood, albeit cheerful. 'I presume there are kitchen smocks somewhere.'

'Are you addressing me, sir?' Annabelle was as haughty as a young lady of Charleston could be.

'Well, Sammy ain't present, and I fancy your sister is still outside . . .'

'Sir, you all are a bare-faced impertinence,' breathed Annabelle. 'One more word and I shall box your ears.'

'Wouldn't recommend it,' said Jonathan, 'I'm quick to counter. However, I ain't known to be heavy-handed with young ladies, and it won't come to more than a light slap on your derriere.'

Annabelle gasped. How could dear and delightful Captain Burnside have delivered her and Caroline into the hands of an oaf? 'Oh, if I were a man, sir, I should call you out and knock you down,' she said.

'Well, you ain't a man,' said Jonathan, 'you're a pretty young thing with her nose in the air.' He picked up the pile of folded dust sheets and offered them to her. 'Could you find a place for these while I see what Sammy and I can do about lighting the kitchen stove?'

'Mr Carter,' said Annabelle with delicate aloofness, 'I am not your paid servant, and I don't wish to be smothered with dust.'

'Servants, yes, that's a point,' said Jonathan. 'There's only Sammy. I put it to you, Miss Howard, he ain't expected to do all the work, is he?'

'How should I know? I did not ask to come here. Nor did I ask to be escorted by a creature utterly beastly and boring.' Annabelle pushed past him and swept out of the cottage to join Caroline at the gate. 'Caroline, I do declare we are in the hands of a ruffian and a boor, and I vow myself capable of striking him.'

'Mr Carter?' Caroline shook herself free of brooding introspection. She smiled. Annabelle had been at odds

239

with their escort from the start, perhaps because he had been far too casual for her liking. 'Well, perhaps he doesn't have the same whimsical ways as Captain Burnside, but I think he may prove resolute in our behalf, and one can't deny he's a cheerful young man.'

'He is too vainglorious by half,' said Annabelle. 'He expected me to clean and dust, would you believe, and was offensive enough to threaten me with a slap.'

'He could not have been serious.' Caroline frowned, wondering if Mr Carter, a crony of Captain Burnside's, had no more scruples than the Captain. 'Annabelle, isn't the evening beautiful? Leaving London is not really too bad, though I disliked the reason for coming here.'

'It's a ridiculous reason, all to get me away from the Duke of Cumberland,' said Annabelle. 'I thought Charles was on my side.'

'I should hope he wasn't,' said Caroline firmly. 'Come, you know very well by now that Cumberland has no intention of marrying you.'

Annabelle fidgeted. 'But there's nothing to do here except sit and look at vegetables. I shall turn into a turnip, and I know I shan't ever be able to put up with the incivilities of the odious Mr Carter. Why don't you bring a servant over from Great Wivenden?'

'Because, sister dear, it is better so.'

'But who is to cook and clean and dust?' asked Annabelle in horror.

'*We* are, all of us,' said Caroline, and in truth she did not mind busying herself domestically. It would be an antidote for her restlessness.

Annabelle gave a despairing sigh. 'We cannot go out, we cannot drive to Great Wivenden or even to the village?' she said. 'And I am to cook and clean and dust? I shall die of boredom and peevishness. It would not be so bad if Charles were here. He is such amusing and affectionate company, and would surely never make a kitchen maid of me. Already I am missing him.'

Caroline, the dark auburn tints of her hair enriched by the sun, turned to look at a copper-beech. It held her gaze. 'Charles – Captain Burnside – means more to you now than Cumberland, Annabelle?' she asked.

Annabelle, who thought the less she said of her feelings concerning Cumberland the better, replied, 'But, Caroline, you surely do agree Charles is a sweet and exciting man, don't you?'

'Is it necessary for me to agree?' asked Caroline, looking as if she found the magnificent beech somewhat imperfect.

'I cannot think why you all are so cool towards him,' said Annabelle, then drew herself up warily as Mr Carter showed himself at the open front door.

'Beg to report, Your Ladyship,' he said, 'that there are no beds made, nor bed linen unpacked. Beg to report also that Sammy has the kitchen stove going, and that boiled potatoes will be served with cold ham for supper. Beg further to report there are mice in the harpsichord, playing tunes.'

'Mice?' cried Annabelle, and instinctively clasped close the skirt of her gown. 'Why do you tell us? Am I to remove them?'

'Beg to suggest, Miss Howard,' said Jonathan, 'that while I take the harpsichord to pieces, you peel the potatoes.'

'Potatoes? Peel them?' gasped Annabelle, thinking of what it would do to her hands. 'Oh, you abominable creature!'

Caroline, smiling, said, 'As you see, Mr Carter, my sister is not too much in favour of peeling potatoes. But you have made your point. There is work for all of us. Come along, Annabelle, let us see what we can do to help.'

'I vow myself utterly despairing,' said Annabelle.

She was sure, as she found herself flicking a duster some minutes later, that in some awful way she had become the victim of a conspiracy, that she had been brought here to keep her away from the Duke.

If Annabelle was fretful, Jonathan was cheerful and adaptable, Sammy a willing workhorse, and Caroline a quiet, efficient preparer of the supper, which proved to be somewhat more attractive than mere ham and boiled potatoes.

The high, square house within its perimeter of iron railings showed only ground floor lights. Captain Burnside, unobtrusively lurking, saw the glimmer of a lamp as the side door opened a little. Outside the front door stood the usual sentry, an infantryman, the butt of his rifle resting on the stone step. Out of the soldier's sight, Captain Burnside moved to the railings at the side of the house, opened a latched gate and advanced. The side door opened wider, and from around it Betsy peeped, curls frisky under her cap as she bobbed a little curtsey.

'Oh, there you be, sir,' she whispered, 'but I hardly knows what I'm at I'm so beset with quakings.'

Slipping into the passage, Captain Burnside murmured, 'God's life, puss, you'll quake yourself into a quivering jelly one day and get served for supper.' He quietly closed the door. 'All is clear, my pretty?'

'His Highness be out with his officers, sir, but Mr Erzburger be in bed with the colic or summat, and groaning fit to throw his stomach up.' Betsy's nervous and very low whisper counselled the utmost caution. 'But he be a spry listener, so I beg you won't rummage about nor clump on floors, sir, or we'll be took in the act. And you best not be no more than five minutes.'

'Good puss, sweet kitten.' Captain Burnside patted her shoulder, and Betsy at once snuggled herself up against his, seeking comfort for her quaking bosom. Then she led him up the back staircase, and they both ascended with considerable care and deliberation. He heard only the faint murmur of servants gathered together below stairs. She took him into the secretary's study, dim with dusk. He turned up the wick of the desk lamp, and its thin streak of light grew to a small flame. Betsy, ears twitching, watched him as he took out the royal diary from a drawer, opened it and leaned over it. She had closed the curtains.

He scanned recent entries quickly, looking for something,

anything, that might offer a constructive pointer, although he knew it was highly unlikely he would find positive information. He found nothing at all other than official and innocuous entries concerning engagements. He leafed his way then to the day of 29th July, to take a look at the entry that had interested him before.

What had that entry been?

'3 pm. Geo. Pn. from Lady K.'

And below it: '3.30 pm. Fd, Wm & Ed also. Concerning poss. marriage to Lady CP. Bty *and* riches.'

That had been in Cumberland's own hand, and smacked of Cumberland's own contempt for the eyes of posterity. But was it a contemptuous flourish of his quill, that reference to beauty *and* riches, or was it to emphasise the subject of the meeting and leave no doubts in the eyes and minds of others?

Captain Burnside found the relevant page.

'3 pm. Geo. Pn. from Lady K.' In Erzburger's hand.

'3.30 pm. Fd, Wm & Ed also. Concerning betrothal to Frederica of M-S.'

The Captain peered in astonishment. That entry too was in the secretary's hand. The former entry was gone, and without any sign of erasure. He ran his hand over the page, feeling it with fingertips. He felt the next page. He could detect no difference, each felt the same as the other. There could be no possible doubt, however, that there had been extraction and substitution, something that could be easily effected by a skilful bookbinder.

'Sir, oh, lord, be quick,' breathed Betsy, 'I be nigh on dying.'

Captain Burnside closed the diary, replaced it and turned down the lamp. Betsy drew back the curtains. Outside, the July dusk had turned into night. The Captain stood in silence for a moment. That new page and new entry meant, for a start, that the former entry could be considered never to have existed. It meant, further, that Cumberland assumed Lady Caroline would be a permanent absentee from London and England by 29th July. Perhaps a permanent absentee from life. It also meant Cumberland did not wish to cancel his meeting with his elder brothers. He now intended to place before them his possible marriage to the Duchess Frederica of Mecklenburg-Strelitz. She was his natural choice. Yet he had, perhaps, in his sense of self-omnipotence, considered he could exercise a princely right to choose a commoner. A commoner who was exceptionally uncommon. An American woman, undoubtedly among the most beautiful in London, and undoubtedly rich. It was typical of his darkness that he was now willing to dispose of her because . . . ah, yes, what was it?

Because of something that now pointed to his meeting with his elder brothers, all of whom stood between him and the throne.

Captain Burnside's smile was a faint gleam. 'Come, Betsy,' he murmured, and in relief Betsy led the way back to the stairs. At the top, she stiffened, then shrank back against him. A handbell was being rung in a vexed, erratic way. She drew a breath. 'Erzburger?' he whispered. She nodded. They stayed where they were for the moment, poised to fly to a dark corner for shelter. Although the sound of the repeatedly shaken bell came from a room on the other side of the house, it was penetrating enough to induce caution and stillness. It stopped.

Betsy waited a few seconds, then tiptoed her way down the stairs and reached the passage to the side door in a breathless burst of new relief. There, close to the door, she turned and snuggled herself up to the Captain again. 'Oh, I be shaking to my every bone,' she breathed.

'Ah, well, though it's your every bone,' he murmured, 'you shake as deliciously as a peach tree blown by the wind.'

Betsy snuggled her palpitating bosom closer. 'Oh, I be that gone on you, Mr Burnside, sir—'

'Hush. No names, puss.'

'No, sir, but you fair melt me all over, you do. We be meeting on Sunday, like you said?'

'Sunday it is, Betsy. Ten-thirty, outside the Theatre Royal in the Hay Market. Prettiest gown, mind, and your Sunday bonnet.'

'Oh, my Sunday pantaloons too,' whispered Betsy ecstatically, 'they be so pretty, with ribbons and all. It'll be a loving Sunday? I'll blush fit to die, sir, but I don't know how I can hardly say no.'

'Have no fears, innocent puss. My wife will say no for me as well as for you, and you shan't spend the day quaking, quivering and blushing.'

Betsy smothered giggles against his shoulder, then lifted her head as he touched her hand. She felt him press a coin into her palm. 'What be this, sir?'

'A golden guinea, pussy poppet. You're a brave partner and a deserving one.'

Delighted, Betsy flung her arms around his neck and kissed him rapturously on the mouth.

'Betsy! Where are you, wench? I'll deal thee a thump come you don't show a quick pair of feet!' A demanding voice echoed and the echoes rang in the passage.

'Oh, that be Job Cuffley, second footman,' whispered Betsy, and opened the door. Captain Burnside slipped out. 'Sunday, then, sir, and I be all agog already.'

Captain Burnside went on his way, thoughful on account of the diary, smiling on account of Betsy. She was an endearing puss, and invaluable.

Sammy put his head into the cottage kitchen. His mistress, Lady Caroline, had been astonishing him today. She had set about domestic chores without a single note of fuss, helping to bring a clean and cosy glow to the cottage. Mr Carter had worked with her, while Miss Annabelle had wandered from room to room, trailing a brush and pan, and giving vent to despairing sighs, much to Mr Carter's amusement. Lady Caroline was now unpacking preserved foodstuffs from a large wicker basket that had travelled with them from London yesterday. She wore a calico white apron to protect her gown, and a white mob cap on her head.

'Your Ladyship?'

'Yes, Sammy?'

'Cap'n Burnside's a-coming, Your Ladyship. A-coming down the lane, he is, on his tod.'

There was no response from Her Ladyship for a moment. Then, her back to him, she said in a busy way, 'Really? Captain Burnside? Dear me, are you certain?'

'Certain positive, Your Ladyship,' said Sammy. 'I told Miss Annabelle and she's gone a-running to meet him.' Sammy essayed a little grin. 'She said heaven be praised, Your Ladyship.'

'Really?' Her Ladyship sounded offhand. She dipped into the basket and brought out a jar of preserved figs, which she placed on a shelf in the pantry. 'Thank you, Sammy.'

'Yes'm,' said Sammy, and disappeared.

Caroline heard her sister's laughter then, laughter from the open front door, followed by the sound of Captain Burnside's voice. 'Faith, here's a charming place.'

'Charming?' Annabelle made herself heard. 'But, Charles, it's so poky. Caroline calls it a cosy retreat, but there's hardly room to pass each other by, and no room at all to avoid each other. And, oh, I declare, you have burdened us with such an uppity varmint. How could you?'

'You're referring to the estimable Jonathan?' murmured the Captain.

'He is not at all estimable; he's unfeeling.'

'Where is he?'

'In the back yard, chopping wood for the kitchen stove.'

'Back yard?' said the Captain, and Caroline realised Annabelle had yet to understand a back yard was a garden to the English.

'Yes,' said Annabelle, 'and would you believe, he expects me to carry in a basket of logs. And Caroline is in the kitchen, working with pots and pans. Charles, look at my hands. Already they are ruined. Mama would swoon to see them. Oh, but now that you are here, I shall go and change into a fresh gown, then beg you to protect me from that boring bully, Mr Carter. Do go and say hello to Caroline.'

'Of course. And I'll acquaint myself with her pots and pans.'

A moment later, the kitchen door, ajar, was pushed open and he came in. His beaver hat was in his hand, his boots a little dusty, his hair a trifle ruffled by the country breeze. His smile arrived in friendly fashion.

'Oh, it's you,' said Caroline, attempting a casual attitude while putting her back against the pantry door. Alarmingly, she was in need of its support, for her legs felt ridiculously weak. The Captain bowed. Faint colour flushed her.

'Lady Caroline? My compliments. How very domesticated.'

'I was not sure you would come,' she said, almost faltering. 'I am afraid we finished our midday meal some time ago, but if you are at all peckish, there is food you can have. See, do you care for these?'

She turned, hiding her flush, and opened the pantry door. Without knowing exactly what she was doing, she took out the jar of figs. She looked at it, then showed it to him.

'Figs?' said Captain Burnside, and regarded her in curiosity, for she was quite unlike her usual composed self. Her lashes were flickering, her eyes looking everywhere except at him, and the jar was actually unsteady in her hand. 'That's an extremely kind offer, dear lady, but I ain't all that partial to preserved figs.'

'Oh, there are other foodstuffs, I assure you, and can declare all of them to be very palatable. See, the hamper is full of them. Meats in aspic, fruit in syrup, and – and . . .' She did falter then.

'Heavens, are we stocked to endure a siege?' smiled the Captain.

'Yes. That is, I don't know.' Caroline examined the jar of figs, then lifted her eyes to him. 'Oh, I am so glad to see you.'

'Are you?' His curiosity deepened.

'Yes, of course I am. We have been worried about you, about Cumberland.'

'Oh, Cumberland's his usual self, his head high in clouds of self-esteem and feet running with the devil's.

And I'm safe and sound, as you see, having caught a morning stage coach to Lewes, and a cart to this side of Wychling.'

'A cart?'

'Farm waggon. Devilishly bumpy. But I'm delighted that you and Annabelle are safe and sound yourselves, though Annabelle don't seem too taken with Jonathan.'

Caroline, steadier of limbs now, said, 'Oh, she has met her match in that young man.'

'While you are getting the better of the pots and pans?' Captain Burnside eyed her white cap and apron with a smile. 'Respectfully, marm, I'm compelled to say you look uncommonly fetching in a mob cap.'

'Among pots and pans and potatoes, Captain Burnside, one must dress for the part,' she said. 'We have no servants except Sammy, which is putting Annabelle into fits of despair. In South Carolina, it's considered most indelicate for any young lady to do anything for herself.'

'Every family owns another family, a family of negro servants?'

'Yes.'

'Well, Annabelle will come round.' The Captain dipped into the hamper and came up with a jar of creamy mussels. He broke the red wax seal with a kitchen knife, prised up the large cork and smelled the contents. Caroline watched as he spooned out mussels and popped them into his mouth. 'Delicious,' he said, and sat down at the table with the jar and spoon.

'Please, if you are hungry,' said Caroline, 'I'll prepare a proper meal for you.'

'We ain't come down to having you set a table,' said Captain Burnside. 'No, not the thing at all.'

'But without servants, we are all doing something. Do you think I could not set a table?'

'I ain't allowing it,' said Captain Burnside, eating mussels.

The challenging light appeared in Caroline's eyes. 'I declare you out of order, sir.'

'Marm, you may declare night is day, but I still ain't allowing you to set tables.'

'Captain Burnside, if I will, I will, and there is no more to be said on the subject. And please do not call me marm.'

'Your Ladyship—'

'Nor that,' she said. 'We are surely friends now, aren't we? And there is some good in you, I know there is. So you may call me Caroline.'

'No, it won't do,' said the Captain, 'except in front of Annabelle, or your friends. It would never do to become familiar with a patron. No, it shall be businesslike between us all the way, and when all is over, done and settled, marm, I shall depart in the agreed fashion, taking no advantage of Annabelle – and you, I hope, will be free of problems and worries, though lighter of two-fifty guineas and expenses.'

Caroline stared down at him, appalled by such unfeeling matter-of-factness. 'Captain Burnside, I can scarcely believe my ears,' she said. 'I have never required our relationship to be as businesslike as that.'

'Marm, I fancy you made it clear at the beginning, which was wise and sensible of you.'

Caroline made an angry gesture. 'Will you stop calling me marm?' she breathed. 'I detest the word, it is unctuous and unappealing. The beginning is irrelevant. It is the present that counts. Oh, I vow you a miserable and difficult man to put me in such annoyance and irritation with you, for you know very well things have changed. I won't have you speak of being businesslike, no, sir, I will not. Was it businesslike to dance as you did at the ball with Annabelle, and make it such a joyful and exhilarating occasion for her?'

'Surely, dear lady,' said Captain Burnside, frowning at the mussels, 'that was only as I was required to.'

'Oh, you wretched man, was it also required of you to stand up with me in the *Cotillon*? Was that an act of business you felt obliged to effect?'

'That, Your Ladyship, was perfection, but it still won't do, d'you see, for a patron to offer more than the terms of the contract.'

249

'Oh!' Caroline's be-aproned bosom surged in an excess of stormy emotion. 'Go about being miserably businesslike, then, for if you have no friendly regard for Annabelle and me I shall return to London, taking her with me, and Cumberland may do his worst!'

Captain Burnside stood up. 'Cumberland will,' he said, 'so you shan't.'

'Shan't?' Caroline was fiercely glad he was on his feet. On his feet, he was easier to challenge, better to confront, to stand up to. 'Who are *you*, sir, to say what I shall or shan't do?'

'Lady Caroline,' he said firmly, 'there's no use your stamping your foot and waving your arms about, for you ain't going back to London, and that's flat.'

Electrified into incensed action, Caroline did what she had done before. She slapped his face. She had to, or else feel reduced to a spiritless creature only able to say yes or no to him.

Captain Burnside received the slap with frank surprise. 'Damn me,' he said.

'Yes, you may well be damned, Captain Burnside, for your miserable lack of simple affection and your provoking excess of outrageous impertinence.'

'Simple affection?' he said, rubbing his tingling jaw.

'Yes!' Caroline was beside herself, and the more so because her angry emotions did not make sense. But there it was, she was unbearably wounded by his declared intention to depart and disappear once the venture was over. 'Annabelle has been sweet to you and sung your praises to our friends, and I have taken your welfare to my heart, worrying myself dreadfully that you may end up being hanged or transported. We have both earned some little affection, and it is of all things hateful of you to speak so coldly and unfeelingly.'

'Oh, ye gods,' said Captain Burnside, and eyed her in utter consternation, for his proud and magnificent patron was in stormy upset. 'May the devil himself claim me if I've offended you. Marm – Caroline – not for the world would I consciously do so.' In his contrition he took her

250

hand and lifted it to his lips. 'I beg your sweet for-giveness.'

Caroline, head bent, eyes hidden, said unsteadily, 'I will forgive you if you will promise never again to suggest Annabelle and I cannot be your friends. And you must also promise to give the most serious consideration to letting me help you live an honest and commendable life. It is in you to live very commendably instead of wasting your talents.'

'Well, I shall even consider taking a rosy-cheeked Sussex wife,' said the Captain quite earnestly, at which she cast a shocked look at him. What was he about now in speaking of wedding a simple country girl? Such a wife would never do for him. Then she remembered it had been her own suggestion. How could she have been so absurd?

'You may consider that,' she said, 'but need not pro-mise.'

'Then I shan't,' he said with a smile, 'for if I did I'd be committed, and it ain't quite the sort of thing on which to commit oneself. Now, may I hope you'll forget what you said about returning to London? I don't wish to be guilty of further impertinence, which I will be if you don't re-consider, for you can take it from me I ain't going to let you go, nor Annabelle.'

Caroline said in a low voice, 'I have been graceless again. You have come all this way to see if we are safe and sound, and I have only given you a quarrel.'

'Oh, a few spirited words,' he said, 'and there were also some excellent mussels.'

Caroline smiled then, although a little uncertainly. She could not make head or tail of her recent emotions and tempers, nor why he aroused them so quickly in her.

Annabelle reappeared, wearing a fresh gown of blue, her face newly-powdered. 'Caroline, isn't it all of a pleas-ure to have Charles here?' Her blue eyes sparkled. It dismayed Caroline intensely, the certainty that Captain Burnside had succeeded with her sister. 'It isn't nearly so boring now,' said Annabelle. 'All the same – oh!' The

251

door bumped her back as it was pushed open by a basket of logs. The basket preceded Jonathan, who was carrying it. 'Oh, you unmannerly brute,' cried Annabelle, 'must you throw doors bruisingly open?'

'Humble apologies, my infant,' said Jonathan cheerfully.

'*Infant*?' gasped Annabelle.

'So sorry,' said Jonathan. He placed the basket down on the stone hearth of the stove. In his shirt sleeves and minus his cravat, his hair damp at the roots, he looked warm from the sun and from the toil of splitting logs. 'I trust you ain't uncommonly bruised, Miss Howard? Beg to say hello, Charles.'

'H'm,' said Captain Burnside.

'I shall discover myself black and blue,' declared Annabelle hotly. 'Charles, see what a ruffian you have attached to us. Oh, I meant to ask you, have you come to take us back to London?'

'No, he ain't,' said Jonathan, 'it can't be done.'

'I was not addressing you, Mr Carter,' said Annabelle, and looked proudly pretty in her haughtiness.

'It still can't be done,' said Jonathan.

'Well, it's true it wouldn't be wise to return yet,' said Captain Burnside, and Caroline thought how cool and collected he always was. Such redoubtable assets for a man of his kind. Oh, why did he have to be a trickster?

'But, Charles,' protested Annabelle, 'I'm sure the Duke of Cumberland can't be a danger to us. I'm sure you are wrong about him, sweet though you are.'

'Bless us,' said Jonathan, 'is my hearing faulty? Sweet, did you say, Miss Howard?'

'Captain Burnside is a gentleman, sir, which you are not,' said Annabelle.

'Well, I ain't sweet, and that's a fact,' said Jonathan. He looked at Captain Burnside. 'Sweet, oh, egad,' he said, and laughed.

'Kindly go away,' said Annabelle.

'Shall we go together?' suggested Jonathan. 'Will you come and help me split logs?'

'Oh, I declare! You all will provoke me into flying back to London.'

'In which case,' said Jonathan, 'I'd have to fly after you and carry you back here. Orders from Charles, don't you see. He ain't quite as sweet as all that.' And Jonathan departed whistling.

'I vow I shall scratch that creature's eyes out,' breathed Annabelle.

Caroline said to the Captain, 'You have given Mr Carter orders to restrain Annabelle forcibly in certain circumstances?'

'Caroline, such a question,' said Annabelle. 'Charles would never allow anyone to lay rough hands on me, would you, Charles?'

'Ah,' said Captain Burnside and made a critical inspection of pots and pans.

'And did such orders embrace me?' asked Caroline.

The Captain, studying an iron pot as if it were grievously suspect, cleared his throat and murmured, 'Do excuse me while I look around.' His exit from the kitchen was effected smoothly.

'Mercy me,' laughed Annabelle, 'I do believe he has elected to be stern and masterful.'

'Your sweet gentleman has only elected to be evasive, sister,' said Caroline.

'Yes, he isn't at all like your agreeable Mr Wingrove,' said Annabelle, and eyed Caroline a little teasingly. 'He would surely make a delicious husband, don't you think so?'

'For whom?' asked Caroline, resuming her unpacking of the food basket.

'Why, dearest, for you, of course.'

'That is not very amusing,' said Caroline.

'Then for me,' smiled Annabelle, and Caroline thought that even less amusing.

# Chapter Twenty

Captain Burnside, having established that the cottage was no citadel, that it was a safe retreat only while the presence of its occupants remained unknown to Cumberland's hirelings, decided for his own peace of mind to investigate the situation at Great Wivenden. He needed to find out if Cumberland had come to the natural conclusion that Lady Caroline and Annabelle had fled in fright to Great Wivenden. If so, his cut-throats might be in the vicinity already. It would be as well to know.

The Captain decided to investigate after supper. Meantime, he had taken over the task of splitting logs. The kitchen stove was huge and ravenous, and Lady Caroline insisted that a constant supply of hot water be available. He had asked Jonathan to turn his hand to the lighter chore of preparing supper, with Annabelle's help. Annabelle, quite unused to kitchen work, or any kind of labour, had scarcely been able to believe he could command this of her. Moreover, there was the entirely repellent aspect of having to share this domestic ordeal with the utterly horrid Jonathan. For his part, Jonathan accepted the situation cheerfully.

But it provoked a further altercation between Caroline and the Captain, though not such a stormy one as the first. She elected to confront him in the little wooded area that bounded the back garden, where he was splitting the logs in a clearing. With his coat and cravat off, his shirt sleeves rolled up, he looked a man of lean, strong sinews.

'Captain Burnside?' There she was, before him, tall, proud and challenging.

'Marm? Ah – Caroline?'

'Mr Carter and Annabelle have taken over my kitchen.'

'Have they? Yes, I believe they have.'

'It happened while my back was turned,' she said.

'Well, since they offered to prepare supper—'

'No, Captain Burnside, they did not offer. They were commanded by you, and Annabelle is horrified that you insisted on incarcerating her with the ruffianly Mr Carter. And I am very vexed, sir, that preparation of our supper has been taken out of my hands behind my back.'

Captain Burnside examined the cold chisel and said, 'Assure you, not consciously, no, not at all.'

'Very consciously,' said Caroline, the confrontation a compulsive thing. 'Will you kindly explain?'

'You'll not mind that I've set Sammy peeling potatoes outside the woodshed?'

'No, I do not mind that at all, though your question neatly avoids your giving an answer to mine.'

'H'm,' said the Captain, and wedged the chisel in a log.

'I have remarked to my sister that you can be very evasive,' said Caroline. Sunlight filtering through the trees dappled her hair with fiery glints. 'Do you intend to explain why you frustrated my wish to prepare the supper myself?'

'Oh, it was merely a matter—' The Captain broke off to give the chisel a light tap with the hammer. Insecurely wedged, the chisel jumped free. Caroline hid a smile. She moved forward, her feet entering a pile of chips and splinters. She stooped and retrieved the chisel. She wedged it again and held it firmly. She was down on one knee in the chippings.

'Strike again,' she said.

'Faith, no, not with your hand there,' he said, looking down at her like a man uncertain of their relationship.

'Well, you were saying, Captain Burnside?'

'Ah, yes, that it was merely a matter of establishing what was right and proper.'

Caroline laughed, her hand still around the wedge. Again there was this enjoyment of being in challenging dialogue with him. 'You are not a man to worry about what is right and proper,' she said. 'I can prepare a meal and set a table, and there is nothing wrong about that.'

'So you have said,' conceded the Captain, 'but I ain't having it.'

'Sometimes, sir,' she retorted, 'I have the greatest difficulty in convincing myself that what I have heard is what you have said. I am my own mistress. Do you understand?'

'Perfectly,' said Captain Burnside, 'but it's still a question of what's right. I ain't having you sweep floors, scrub pots and pans, and peel potatoes. Jonathan and Sammy can attend to all that, with Annabelle's help.'

'Captain Burnside, you are not to order my comings and goings, nor what I will do or won't do. Will you strike this chisel or not, sir?'

'I'll not strike while you're holding it, marm . . .'

'Oh, if you call me marm once more, it will be you who will be struck, sir!'

'Then let go of the chisel, Caroline, or the strike will bruise your fingers.'

She let go. He struck, and the chisel bit into the wood. It quivered and rang. She watched as with blows he split the log. Perspiration glimmered on his forehead, dampening his hair.

She stood up, brushing chips from her gown. 'Captain Burnside, I have been thinking about your regimental commander, Colonel Masterson,' she said. 'You spoke of him as if you were on excellent terms, that Cumberland would get nothing from him. Yet when I first saw you, you told me he forced you to resign your commission on account of your dishonourable behaviour. Were you lying to me?'

'God forbid I should ever give you less respect than I should,' he said.

'That is not an answer, sir. That is more taradiddle.'

He wiped his brow and made a thoughtful observation of his patron.

If she was not a woman to suffer shyness, she could not

deny she was becoming uncommonly sensitive under his eyes. But it was of all things ridiculous to feel herself colouring up. Revealing décolleté had been fashionable for years, and even the politest gentleman quizzed the feminine enchantment of a gown. One was used to it. Oh, how unfair that Captain Burnside could make her colour rise.

'Lady Caroline,' he said, 'you're a most unusual patron. I've known none with a warmer heart or with such tender regard for my welfare. It's a privilege to serve you, and to anticipate the lucrative connections you may be able to manufacture for me by recommending me to any of your friends who come to be in need of my professionalism.'

Coming to, Caroline said, 'That, sir, is a farrago of nonsense, designed to confuse me concerning what is true and what is not true. Be assured I shall examine you more keenly from now on, for I feel you have taken me in on many counts. If I find you sadly wanting, sir, I shall have your head.'

'Well, it ain't the most deserving head in the world, that's true,' he said.

'I agree,' said Caroline, and walked away in a mood that took her up to her room to write an immediate letter to her father-in-law.

'Dearest Father-in-law,

'I am at present in Sussex by reason of certain developments that I shall explain another time. I must tell you that Captain Burnside has not been a disappointment so far, and although he is undoubtedly as devious as you warned, I have discovered some good in him. In your loving regard for me, do please favour me with as much further information about him as you can. I assume that in finding him for me you acquainted yourself thoroughly with many details concerning his background.

'I shall be most grateful if you are able to let me have his full history, and beg you to send your reply to my London address with all speed. I am most anxious to know all there is to know about Captain Burnside, for I have his future in mind and would like to do what I can to ensure it is more estimable than his past.

257

'I send you my love, and please give my most affectionate greetings to my dearest Mother-in-law.'

She sent Sammy sneaking out with the letter a few minutes later. He was to take it to the carriers in Wychling, and to avoid being seen by Captain Burnside.

'Yes'm,' said Sammy, well up to such discretion in his devotion to her.

'No, I won't,' cried Annabelle, looking with horror at the round, crisp onions in the earthenware bowl.

'Heavens, I ain't asking you to take 'em to bed with you,' said Jonathan, 'only to peel 'em. Baked onions with stewed rabbit make for a gourmet's repast.' Sammy had snared a couple of rabbits. 'There now, you can manage to peel a few onions.'

'Oh, you all are surely a brute and a bully.'

'No, I ain't,' said Jonathan, 'or I'd have made you skin the rabbits, my pretty one.'

'I am not your pretty one,' said Annabelle, gazing at the shining onions with utter distaste. 'Oh, how Captain Burnside came to regard you with any favour I cannot think.'

'Oh, I ain't as bad as all that,' said Jonathan, placing the prepared rabbits in the oven. 'I fancy we need more water, by the way. The bucket's there.'

The wooden bucket stood near the stove. It was empty.

'I shan't, nor won't,' said Annabelle. 'I shan't peel onions, and I won't draw water. My Pa would whip you for making me.'

'Well, it's all hands to the pump if we're going to keep the lifeboat afloat,' said Jonathan. 'Here now, you need only half-fill it.' He picked up the bucket and offered it to her. Annabelle boxed his ears. He dropped the bucket in his surprise, and Annabelle kicked it across the stone floor.

'Oh, egad,' he said, and he sat down, reached swiftly and pulled her over his knees. Annabelle screamed in outrage.

It brought Caroline hastening into the kitchen. She

258

stared at the sight of her sister over Jonathan's knees and kicking furiously. 'Mr Carter! What are you doing?'

'Nothing yet,' said Jonathan breezily, 'but it won't take long once I make a beginning. Beg you'll stand aside, Lady Caroline.'

'I will not! Release her, Mr Carter, do you hear!'

'Beg to suggest it would be wiser to paste her, Your Ladyship,' he said, but Annabelle gathered herself and sprang free. Suffused with rage, she boxed his ears again. 'Well, damn my forbearing soul,' said Jonathan, and laughed in cheerful appreciation of her spirit.

Annabelle seized his hair and yanked at it. 'Odious, odious beast!' she cried.

'Annabelle!' Caroline was shocked. 'Annabelle, stop this!'

Annabelle let go. Jonathan looked up at her, then leapt to his feet. Annabelle gasped, retreated and fled out of the back door into the garden.

'Can't make her out,' said Jonathan. 'Won't peel onions, won't draw water.'

'Then you shall draw the water, Mr Carter,' said Caroline, 'and I will peel the onions.'

'Beg to inform you, Your Ladyship, that Captain Burnside won't allow that,' said Jonathan.

Her Ladyship presented him with her coolest look. 'Mr Carter, you are mistaken if you think I live in fear and trembling of Captain Burnside,' she said.

'Eh?' said Jonathan.

'You may so live. I do not. I accept he is better-versed than I am in dealing with the kind of unpleasantnesses he assumes are facing us, but as to other things, whether he will allow or won't allow, I shall peel the onions while you draw water.'

'Your Ladyship, it's more than my head's worth to let you,' said Jonathan. 'He'll fetch me a rattler that will curdle my brains.'

'Mr Carter, I declare you ridiculous. Kindly do as I ask, while I do as I wish.'

Jonathan drew the water from the well, and Caroline

peeled the onions. She did so in cool defiance of their pungency, wondering the more why the need to marry again had taken such a hold on her.

Annabelle had sought refuge with Captain Burnside. 'Charles, oh, I have been bruised and battered by that dreadful ruffian,' she informed him breathlessly. 'How can such a scallywag be a friend of yours?'

The Captain, hammer and chisel in his hands, and perspiration on his brow, examined her searchingly. True, she was flushed and her gown slightly dishevelled, but he remarked no bruises.

'Come, sweet girl,' he said, 'I fancy you've only suffered another argument with Jonathan. And all it has done is given you a tender flush to your prettiness. I ain't remarked you looking prettier, indeed I ain't.'

'Charles, you are such an angel I could kiss you,' said Annabelle, always responsive to compliments. 'You are going to stay here with us until we return to London?'

'I have to catch the dawn stage from Lewes tomorrow, but will be back the day after, on Monday.'

'We are to spend all day tomorrow with that fearful brute, Mr Carter?'

'Alas, yes, dear young lady. But if he brings further tender flushes to your prettiness, accept them, for they become you.'

That brought Annabelle to laughter.

The supper of baked onions and roast potatoes with the rabbit stewed in a delicious sauce concocted by Jonathan, was eaten hungrily and with much appreciation. Over the meal, Caroline asked the Captain if it was true that he intended to go to London tomorrow and return on Monday. He replied that it was quite true. She asked his reason for going.

'Cumberland,' he said.

Her eyes levelled with his across the dining-table. 'If you intend to put your head in the lion's den, please don't do so in our behalf, for neither Annabelle nor I would want you to.'

'We surely would not,' said Annabelle. 'Let Mr Carter go. His head is out of our consideration.'

'It ain't out of mine,' said Jonathan.

'I vow that if *my* head were made of thick wood, I should not care whether I lost it or kept it,' said Annabelle.

'Precisely what are you going to do in London concerning Cumberland?' Caroline put the question challengingly to Captain Burnside.

'Do?' he said.

'Yes, do, sir,' said Caroline, and Annabelle smiled. How they fenced, these two, much as if their long-standing friendship held little secrets.

'Well, Cumberland ain't to be ignored, d'you see,' said the Captain ambiguously.

'Faith, who don't see him these days?' said Jonathan. 'He's a ubiquitous gentleman, with a nose in every pie.'

'The Duke of Cumberland is also mannerly,' said Annabelle, 'which you are not.'

'Well, I ain't too much like him, that I ain't,' said Jonathan affably.

'Captain Burnside?' said Caroline, persisting.

'Yes, quite so, I think I should go,' said the Captain. 'One needs to keep up with Cumberland's unprettier activities. It don't do to be in ignorance of what he's about. Jonathan, Annabelle, allow me to compliment you on the baked onions.'

'You may compliment me,' said Caroline, 'for they were prepared by me and nursed to perfection by me.' She smiled as the Captain cast a frowning look at Jonathan. 'No, it's no use your fetching Mr Carter a rattler, for what I wish to do I will do. I cannot sit idle and let Mr Carter and Annabelle do all the work.'

'Oh, she don't do more than she can contrive,' said Jonathan, 'but then she's a dainty chit and don't care a great deal except for looking pretty, which I ain't disposed to quarrel with, for she does look pretty, the more so when her dander is up and she's boxing my ears.'

Caroline laughed.

Annabelle turned a scornful look on Jonathan. 'No, I never did meet such a bore and a scallywag as you,' she said.

'There,' said Jonathan, 'ain't she delicious?'

It was a while after supper, at twilight, that Caroline stepped from the cottage into the back garden. Previously, the place had been occupied by one of her farm labourers and his family. With the arrival of further children, twins, she had been able to house him in a larger cottage on the other side of the farm. She was the owner not only of Great Wivenden but many cottages both on the estate and outside it.

The garden was being tended temporarily by the labourer, who came once a week to hoe the flower and vegetable beds, and he was allowed to harvest the vegetables.

She walked along the path that fronted the garden and made her way to the stable, where Sammy was keeping her coach and four.

Sammy appeared, 'Ah, Sammy,' she said, looking around.

'Yes'm?'

'Have you seen Captain Burnside? I think he came out here a little while ago.'

'Oh, he's a-gone walking, Your Ladyship, that way.' Sammy pointed in the direction of Great Wivenden. 'He asked me which way it was over the fields.'

'It?' said Caroline.

'Great Wivenden, Your Ladyship.'

'He took the path over that field, Sammy?'

'Yes'm.'

'Thank you, Sammy.' Caroline went back to the cottage and re-emerged only moments later, wearing a light summer cloak of dark green, its hood thrown back and her head bare. She made her way at a quick, gliding walk to the field beyond the garden and the little wood. She pursued a fast course, and it was not long before she sighted the Captain, a hundred yards ahead. She kept to that distance.

## Chapter Twenty-one

'What's that ye say?' asked Cumberland.

'Our man,' said Erzburger, sickly and sallow of face from a stomach upset, 'has again been advised that Lady Percival and her sister are not at home, Your Highness.'

'Well, their absence or their presence don't signify any longer,' rasped Cumberland, 'nor do heard or not heard. Ye ain't supposing, are ye, that a twittering, feather-brained American cuckoo can put together a few words of yours and mine and make sense of 'em? Ye ain't supposing I'm incapable of making her memory look vague and bird-like if she elects to quote us, are ye? Ye panicked, man.'

Erzburger might have remarked that, if that were so, His Highness had shared the panic. Instead, he said, 'You are suggesting no further action, Your Highness?'

'I ain't making a suggestion. Ye are being told to do as I've done. To give yourself time to think. She ain't of the stuff to stand up and blow trumpet blasts. Call off the hounds. Maintain the watch on your Irish friend.'

Erzburger might also have said the Duke shared that friendship.

The twilight cast its softness over the land as the blue faded from the western sky. Fields lay peacefully at rest, offering undisturbed grass to nibbling rabbits. The green slopes of the South Downs lay in shadow. In little woods, dry leaves rustled and stirred to the advent of creatures that foraged only after the sun went down. Beeches, chestnuts and oaks stood in quiet contemplation of the air from which they drew their oxygen.

From the edge of a wood, Captain Burnside viewed the manor house of Great Wivenden grandly rising from the top of a gently ascending slope, its windows surveying a landscape undulating and magnificent. It was built of Sussex stone, three storeys high, its many gables creating lines of architectual handsomeness. There was nothing to suggest it had known enquiring strangers that day. But there existed the possibility that Cumberland, finding the birds flown, would have lost no time in investigating the country coop. Captain Burnside considered Cumberland wholly the dark prince.

A figure appeared, a sturdy figure in coat, breeches and leather leggings, striding up from the parkland that the house overlooked. Captain Burnside emerged from the wood and walked to intercept him. The man, spotting him, checked for a moment, then came on. They met in the fading twilight, their feet in lush grass.

'Good evening, sir,' said Captain Burnside, and from under bushy grey eyebrows, Caroline's steward, John Forbes, regarded him in grave enquiry.

'You've the advantage of me, sir,' he said, a Sussex burr to his voice.

'Well, no, I haven't,' smiled the Captain, 'for as much as you don't know me, I've not the foggiest notion who you are.'

'I'd say whoever you are, sir, you're on private land.'

'I don't dispute it, for it belongs to Lady Clarence Percival, who prefers to be known as Lady Caroline.'

'It does,' said John Forbes, economical of speech but a loyal and efficient steward. 'My name is Forbes. I'm steward to the estate.'

The Captain nodded and smiled, showing a countenance as pleasant and open as the most honest of men. 'I'm a friend,' he said.

'That's as maybe,' said Mr Forbes.

'Be assured.'

'It doesn't suffice.'

'Quite so,' said the Captain, taking no offence.

'Her Ladyship's friends don't appear out of a wood,'

said Mr Forbes, 'but present themselves at her front door. When she's here, which she's not at the moment.'

'Well, it's circumstances, d'you see.'

'No, sir, I don't see,' said Mr Forbes, standing up square of shoulders to the lean-looking stranger.

'I've called,' said the Captain, 'to enquire if you've had any visitors today.'

Mr Forbes could not deny the openness of the man. But he still asked, 'Why?'

'Favour me, Mr Forbes, by believing I ask on behalf of Her Ladyship,' said the Captain, and the steward looked him in the eye.

'We've had no visitors,' he said.

'None?'

'None. Save you, sir.'

'Thank you, Mr Forbes, I'm obliged. Goodnight to you.'

The twilight was dusky as the Captain made his way back through the wood towards the fields and paths. Midway through the wood, he checked as he heard a rustling sound a little way behind him and to his right. He turned but saw no one. He went on, took a bend in the woodland path and turned off it to lose himself among trees. From there, a few moments later, he heard the rustling sound again, faint but perceptible. He waited. He thought of masked men. The rustling increased, as if someone had begun to hurry. He supposed himself to be the quarry, a quarry that had disappeared. A shadowy figure flitted through the gloom. He pounced, and Caroline emitted a startled gasp as an arm whipped around her waist from behind and pinned her.

Captain Burnside, as surprised as she was startled, said, 'God's life, it's you. May the angels forgive you for hazarding yourself so recklessly.'

'Forgive me? Me? Let me go, sir!' Caroline turned inside the encircling arm, and this put her for a brief moment in his embrace. Her firm, healthy body was warm against his. His own firmness, masculine, was not the same as hers. The difference, the momentary closeness,

265

brought a sense of devastating weakness to her. Then his arm dropped away and he stepped back, looking dark and forbidding in the dusk. 'Sir,' she said huskily, 'I am appalled you could fall on me like a footpad. Shame on you.'

Because of many things, Captain Burnside could not rid himself of thoughts of those masked horsemen and the conviction they boded no good for Lady Caroline and Annabelle. He was, however, prepared to believe he may have exaggerated the dangers, and there was the thankful fact that the manor house had received no enquiring visitors. Even so, he was not in approval of Lady Caroline's excursion.

'Madam,' he said sternly, 'you should not have left the cottage.'

'Madam?' she breathed in affront. 'Madam? I am to be addressed as if I were being served in a shop?'

'It was foolish of you to wander.'

'Sir, you are taking my breath with your impudence. I will not be addressed as if what you are and what I am are the other way about. I left the cottage, yes, but so did you.'

'My excursion was for a purpose.'

Caroline could barely believe her ears. He was actually daring to show sternness and disapproval. Oh, the gall of the monster. 'I declare you out of all conceit, Captain Burnside, if you think you can make one rule for yourself and another for me. What are you about in taking on such objectionable airs? And what were you about in going to meet my steward?' Caroline was carrying the fight to the opposition, and, let it be said, with no lack of fire. 'Do not think to give me the lie, sir, for I saw you. I might have shown myself, but did not, because you wished our presence here to go unnoticed. What of your presence? Is that to be advertised to one and all?'

'I did not arrange to meet your steward, nor did I know who he was until I spoke with him.' Captain Burnside, much to her vexation, was still disapproving. 'I thought to discover if Cumberland had sent anyone to enquire if you

266

were in residence with Annabelle. Fortunately, the answer was no.'

'Oh, I will come at you with both fists in a moment, I surely will,' breathed Caroline. 'I will not be spoken to in such a surly way, nor looked at so crossly. Sammy advised me you had gone walking. I confess I followed you, for the things you do sometimes make me uneasy.'

'You lack trust in me?'

'I lack being consulted,' said Caroline. 'You go here, you go there, you do this and you do that, and all without ever confiding your purposes to me. Yes, you may well mutter, you may well stand on shifty feet, but that won't help you escape the shame of knowing you have unfairly bullied me.'

'Angels of light,' declared the Captain, 'was there ever such a punishing patron?'

'I am minded, sir, to send you packing,' she said. The advancing dusk was bringing dark patches to the wood, but she was in no hurry to curtail this cut-and-thrust. She knew no man who provoked her tongue more than he did. It enlivened their every dialogue. 'Why are you looking askance? Am I showing my petticoats again?'

'It's my contention, marm, that pretty petticoats ain't to be regarded lightly – especially yours.' He delivered this ridiculous comment with such gravity that she could not help her sudden little rush of laughter.

'You are singularly absurd,' she said, 'but my temper is sweet again. Please escort me back.'

'Willingly,' he said, 'or darkness will catch us.'

They walked together, emerging from the wood on to a field path.

'I think you must be wrong about Cumberland,' she said.

'True, I might be, but recommend you still lie low for a few days.'

'Very well.' A thought occurred to her. 'Your widowed mother, Captain Burnside, are you a sympathetic son to her?'

'My mother?' he said.

267

'Your widowed mother. How often do you visit her, and where does she live?'

'Oh, I visit her from time to time in her grace-and-favour lodging in Winchester.'

'I know Winchester,' said Caroline. 'A lovely city. When you arrive in your mother's presence, do you wish you could show her an honest face?'

'Good God,' said Captain Burnside, listening to the whisper and rustle of her garments.

'Do not take God's name in order to dissemble, sir, but answer me,' said Caroline, her thoughts taking a positive turn.

'My mother, dear lady, has never mentioned I arrive looking dishonest.'

'Perhaps because you've an exceptional talent for hiding your deviousness,' said Caroline. 'Annabelle failed to re-mark your true self, and so you have won her over. She is in love with you, is she not?'

'Ah,' he said, 'I am now due for the whole of my fee?'

Caroline's intoxication with their exchanges received a sobering drench of cold water. 'How petty you are, sir. Is Annabelle in love with you?'

'She ain't said so, Your Ladyship.'

Caroline made an impatient gesture. The sky was dark-ening fast, and the scarcely visible quarter moon began to acquire shape and light.

'Apart from the professional self-satisfaction you feel whenever you entrap trusting innocence, I presume it is all one to you whether Annabelle or any woman is in love with you?' she said.

'Well, it don't do to let my feelings get in the way of my earning ability,' said the Captain reasonably.

'Really, Captain Burnside, to indulge your predilection for knavery at the expense of becoming a human being is a deplorable thing in any man. You will not always show presentable and personable, not always find it easy to dupe young women.'

'Faith, I know it,' said the Captain, 'and can only hope a rich heiress will come my way and solve all my problems.'

'You have said that before, or something like it,' said Caroline. 'I could have wished—'

'The stile, Your Ladyship, there's no gateway.'

They had reached the only exit through a hedgerow.

'I am quite aware of the lie of the land hereabouts,' said Caroline. 'Kindly precede me, sir, and keep your back turned.' The Captain negotiated the stile with the ease of an active man, and waited for Caroline to follow, his back to her. There were the most telling whispers of silks and lace brushing feminine limbs. A questing fox barked. A young vixen responded in her startlingly strangled and suffering way, and Captain Burnside turned involuntarily to lend Caroline what kind of helping hand was necessary. None was necessary. Neither fox nor vixen had startled the resilient young widow from South Carolina. She was in perfect negotiation of the stile, presenting a picture of bewitchment, not helplessness. Lace glimmered, legs glimmered, and silk-covered ankles shone. She stepped down. Her hands let go. Skirts floated and fell into place.

'Delightful,' said the unabashed Captain.

'You are speaking of my athleticism?' enquired Caroline coolly.

'Oh, that as well, marm.'

Exactly how could one deal with so specious a rogue? 'Continue walking, sir,' she said, 'for I do not wish to give Annabelle or Mr Carter any wrong impressions about us. I was going to say I could have wished someone might have saved you from yourself in the years before you took up a life of duplicity and perfidy. How sad your mother must be that you have chosen to live by your wits instead of exercising yourself in a worthier way. She the widow of a man of God, and you his son – oh, my heart goes out to her.'

'Don't distress yourself, marm: she ain't a woman to hold me in too much dismay, nor quote the Lord at me.'

'Then her Christian tolerance is much to be admired,' said Caroline, thinking about Winchester, sixty miles from Lewes, and about Captain Burnside's absence tomorrow.

The Captain departed well before dawn the following morning, Sammy driving him in the coach to Lewes, where he caught the six o'clock stage to London.

Over breakfast in the cottage, Caroline and Annabelle discussed the possibility of going to church. Jonathan stepped in to say it couldn't be done, for on no account were they to show themselves to people.

'Mr Carter, you are as absurd as Captain Burnside,' said Caroline. 'He has allowed his opinion of the Duke of Cumberland to exaggerate his fears of what the Duke might do. Although my own opinion equates with his, I have not allowed it to affect either my commonsense or my intuition. And my intuition shares with my commonsense a certainty that Cumberland would not dare to do us any harm.' If her intuition served her well in her certainty, Captain Burnside's suspicions had served him equally well. Erzburger, acting for his master, *had* contemplated means of ensuring silence. Cumberland had called it off, thereby putting Caroline's intuition in credit. 'However,' she went on, 'since there is still a very faint chance that Captain Burnside is right, and I am wrong, we will continue for the moment to be discreet. We will stay away from church.'

'I'm much obliged,' said Jonathan, and Caroline gave him the sweetest smile.

Not long after breakfast, she called to him from the little landing. Going up, he found her at the open door of her bedroom.

She pointed at the casement window. 'Look,' she said, and Jonathan entered the room and crossed quickly to the window.

Caroline at once shut him in by closing the door and locking it from the outside. She hastened down the stairs, where she was joined by Annabelle, who helped her into her cloak. They darted from the cottage, and Sammy, hearing a call, brought the coach round from the stables. Sammy was a willing accomplice, for in his eyes Lady Caroline could do no wrong, and he had secreted a travelling trunk aboard the coach thirty minutes ago. The sisters entered the vehicle.

'Winchester, Sammy,' said Lady Caroline.

'Yes, Your Ladyship, and relying on a change of hosses at Petworth. Yes'm?'

'Yes, away you go, Sammy, and no dawdling.'

Sammy whipped up the four and went. Jonathan, head out of the casement window, gave a shout of outrage. Annabelle laughed in triumph.

'What sweet bliss, Caroline, we have done the creature down.'

## Chapter Twenty-two

Betsy waited in barely-concealed impatience outside the Theatre Royal in the Hay Market. There were not too many people about on this warm Sunday morning, and Betsy scanned each new face in the hope of alighting on the countenance of her exciting gentleman friend. She was dressed in the lightest and thinnest gown of pink taffeta, having purchased it in a fit of delicious extravagance, extracting the necessary money from her precious hoard. Her summer bonnet was a matching pink. She wore no under-skirt or petticoat, and filmy white pantaloons were a faint, gossamer blur beneath the light taffeta. She – or they – had already caught the eye of passing gentlemen, but Betsy, faithful to her own special gentleman for the day, prettily turned her nose up at all of them from under her parasol.

He appeared, clad in blue coat, blue trousers and a dashing top hat. He was not there one moment, he was before her the next.

Betsy glowed. 'Oh, sir, you be nigh on almost late.'

'I am late, my poppet. My stage was a lumbering ancient. But there you are, and looking, I see, as pretty as a posy of June rosebuds.'

'Oh, I be fair set to swoon with ravishing excitement, sir, you speak so lovingly to me. Where will you take me for pleasuring?'

'Business first, Betsy,' said Captain Burnside, 'pleasuring later.'

Betsy pouted. 'But it's Sunday, sir, and you never said not one word about business. You're not set on business I won't like, are you?'

'Betsy, come, come,' smiled the Captain, placing her hand on his arm, 'I ain't ever disposed to have you do things you won't like. Could I be so unkind to so pretty a girl?'

'But I be mindful of all them quakings you put me in before, and more than once,' said Betsy. 'Oh, you're not going to make me quake today, are you?'

'God's life, puss, never. You shall only quake deliciously, from pleasuring. Come, we'll find a carriage and I'll tell you what the Lord Chancellor requires of us today. As you say, it's Sunday, and just as you and I know it, so does he, which is a gracious thing in any Lord Chancellor. Therefore, all will be quite easy and simple.'

'Oh, lor',' said Betsy, 'easy and simple sounds like I won't like it a little bit.'

But she proceeded with him along the Hay Market in tripping, bobbing pertness, her flimsy gown fluttering. Captain Burnside hailed a cabbie and his carriage, and it pleased Betsy that it was a closed vehicle, for such a conveyance permitted a girl to snuggle up to a gentleman. And if her own gentleman was going to instruct her on a matter of business, a cuddle or two would make the business more bearable. He gave the driver his destination, Aldgate South.

Betsy snuggled up as soon as her gentleman seated himself beside her.

'By all means make yourself comfortable, Betsy,' he said.

'I can't say no to you, sir,' she murmured, and he looked down into her upturned face. Her lashes fluttered coyly. She was a sweet minx. 'What be the business about?'

'It's what the Lord Chancellor requires of us, puss. By the way, he's further impressed with you, and I fancy the gibbet is a lot farther from his stern mind than it was. Now, you and I are going to a house in which an Irish gentleman resides.'

'Yes, sir, that be simple enough,' said Betsy, 'and I shan't mind if you want kissing first.'

'The moment you understand the business procedure, kissing shall be seriously considered.' Captain Burnside applied a fond squeeze, and Betsy sighed. 'I shall want you to go up to the lodging of the Irish gentleman, knock on his door and ask him if he's acquainted with Mr Henry Bullivant.'

'Who be Mr Henry Bullivant?' asked Betsy.

'Your affectionate gentleman friend.'

'But he aren't, sir; I never heard of him.'

'Heavens, sweet chicken, when you skipped out in your delightful gown this morning, did you leave your clever little mind behind? Simply convey to the Irish gentleman the fact that you've come in search of your loving beau, extract from your enchanting bosom this piece of paper which bears his address and show it.'

'What piece of – oh, sir.' Betsy almost blushed as Captain Burnside tucked a scrap of paper into the warm valley of her bosom.

'Now, as you move to show him the address, contrive to trip over his feet and to fall. Contrive further to become – ah, delicately disarranged, shall we say?'

'Disarranged?' Betsy's eyes opened wide. Quaking began.

'Quite so, Betsy. I did venture to point out it would be easy and simple. You will scream at this happening, and your affectionate gentleman, Mr Henry Bullivant, will appear.'

'Oh, Lord help me,' gasped Betsy, 'I be all a-tremble already, nor don't I still know this Mr Bullivant.'

'Come, come, Betsy, that will be me, and everything can then be left to me. There, I'll allow you to tremble a little now, but not when you're at the business with the Irish gentleman. I shall expect an excellent performance.'

'But disarranged? Oh, I can't, I couldn't. I'm a good girl.' Betsy was bargaining.

'Damn me,' said Captain Burnside, 'there's no can't or couldn't. You'll get me drawn and quartered. We ain't going to be excused failure, Betsy, nor shilly-shallying. The Lord Chancellor won't tolerate it.'

274

'Oh, lawks,' breathed Betsy, 'he's terrible hard on us. Did he say how much, sir?'

Her roundness bobbed as the carriage jolted over cobbles, but the bargaining light in her eyes remained undisturbed.

'How much?'

'Guineas, sir,' murmured Betsy. She went along with the maxim that if a labourer was worthy of his hire, so was a girl.

'Ah, so you ain't brought an empty head with you,' said the Captain. Well aware of how the mere sight of a golden guinea could cure her every qualm and quake, he drew one from his pocket. In the shaded light of the cab, it gleamed as brightly as Betsy's eyes. 'That, my fluttering partridge, is a single guinea.'

'And it be a sweet thing in its own right,' said Betsy.

'Four more would be even sweeter, I warrant,' said the Captain.

'Five in all, sir, five?' Betsy glowed. 'For asking and showing, tripping and disarranging?'

'And screaming.'

'Oh, you be very fair, sir.' Betsy snuggled closer. 'But I won't think about it until I'm doing it, that I won't, or I'll give myself terrible frightening turns. I never did know any gentleman more of a pleasure to me, nor more set on making me shiver all over. And when you've done with the Irish gentleman, sir?'

'Then, Betsy, to Vauxhall Gardens, to the love nest of a bowery alcove and refreshments of your choice.'

'Vauxhall Gardens?' Betsy sat up and sparkled. 'With all the lords and ladies?'

'And with the Lord Chancellor's permission,' said Captain Burnside, and the carriage swayed, creaked and jolted over the cobbled streets.

They reached Aldgate and passed through it to a quarter by no means salubrious. Betsy, a country girl, had an inherent distaste for the grime of cities and for people who let poverty render them sluttish. The run-down look of this district came very unappealingly to her discerning eye, making her turn her nose up. The children seen from the carriage appeared to be urchins and ragamuffins. Shabby men sat on doorsteps, doing nothing about littered gutters, and shawled women, neglecting their homes, stood gossiping. Betsy was sure, even with the carriage windows closed, that the streets exuded a smell like boiled cabbage. But there was one street at the end of a cobbled lane that was an improvement on the rest. The doorsteps looked swept, there was only a little refuse in the gutters, and the windows of the houses seemed actually clean. As the cab passed the street, Captain Burnside rapped on the roof and the driver brought his horse to a stop.

'Oh, lor', it's here we be getting out?' enquired Betsy nervously.

'Yes, here, clever puss,' said the Captain. He alighted and gave her a hand down. The dainty delicacy of her new Sunday gown accentuated for Betsy the grimy condition of the surroundings. The Captain asked the cabbie to wait, perhaps for twenty or thirty minutes. He would be paid for the waiting time. The cabbie, recognising a gentleman of potential generosity, declared himself willing and trusting.

'Come, Betsy,' said the Captain, and walked back with her to the corner of the street. 'Now, my fine accomplice, it's the third house on the right. The Irish gentleman is lodged on the first floor. Go up the stairs, turn left on the landing, and his door is immediately opposite you.' The Captain had received this basic information from Jonathan, though the latter's gift for making people talk had availed him nothing in the face of the tight-mouthed Irishman. 'Knock with anxious gentility, Betsy, and then proceed as arranged. But don't come to your scream as if you needed to bring down the Tower of London, for we don't want the whole city to be roused. I shall be near enough to hear a little ladylike scream.'

'Lord help us, already I hardly knows if I'm coming or going, sir,' breathed Betsy, 'but seeing you said five minutes ago that it's all for the sake of His Royal Highness, I aren't going to lay down and die of fright, not considering you're going to give me ten guineas.'

'Four, puss.'

'Oh, you promised five,' protested Betsy, neatly tricked.

'Five it is, then. Now, when I arrive to enquire into the reason for your agitation—'

'My which, sir?'

'Your ladylike squeak of distress equals agitation, puss. I shall need to address you in front of the Irish blackguard. It won't do to call you Betsy. Who knows how quickly your name might reach ears it shouldn't reach? Like Mr Erzburger's ears.'

'Oh, save us, not his, sir,' begged Betsy. 'Or Mr Pringle's.'

'I shall address you as Polly.'

'You be a thinking gentleman, sir, and understanding. I'll do the scream very ladylike.'

'Good puss. Off you go, then.'

The terraced house had a fairly neat look, its curtains threadbare, perhaps, but clean. The front door was not locked, for it yielded as Betsy turned the handle. On the ground floor lived a solicitor's poorly-paid clerk and his family. They were at Aldgate church for the Sunday morning service. Betsy, hitching her gown, climbed the stairs.

The Irish gentleman, answering a light knock on his door, found himself looking into the hopeful eyes of a young lady in summer pink. 'Oh, begging your pardon, sir,' she said a little breathlessly, 'be you sharing this lodging with Mr Henry Bullivant?'

'The divil I'm not,' said Mr Joseph Maguire, 'nor did I ever hear of him.' He made to close the door, for he was not encouraged to talk to strangers, male or female. Betsy, however, simulating appealing anxiety, pushed forward, and the door was forced to stay open.

'But I were to meet him here,' she said worriedly, 'and I daresn't like to think I be at the wrong address, for close

277

by it aren't a respectable neighbourhood to look at. Mr Bullivant's my gentleman friend, and tall and handsome, with—'

'So he might be, that he might,' said Joseph Maguire, who was small and wiry himself, with curly black hair, 'but it's sure I am I don't know him, nor where he lodges.'

'But, sir,' said Betsy, expression worried and gown whispering anxiously, 'it be this address I were given by him, I'm sure. I'll show you, and beg you'll help a girl.' She dipped her fingers into her cleavage, drawing Mr Maguire's eyes to her bosom, and extracted the piece of paper. She unfolded it under his reluctant but mesmerised gaze, and in what seemed like an eager wishfulness to secure his help, she moved forward. Her foot struck his, and she tripped and tumbled, executing the manoeuvre with all the credibility Captain Burnside had anticipated she would. As a preliminary to a scream, she uttered a little cry as she fell, though her tumble was a gentle one, for she feared for her new gown. The tumble took her to her knees. She then collapsed, and when she turned over and sat up, her bodice was so disarranged that the startled Mr Maguire was confronted by the alarming sight of a bare breast. The scream came then, a brief ejaculation, and she followed this by gasping, 'Oh, I be in for ravishment!' The scream was just loud enough to be heard in the passage below. At once, someone came bounding up the stairs, and the astonished and bewildered Joseph Maguire was further confronted, this time by a tall and slender gentleman carrying a cane and wearing an expression of anger and disgust.

'By God,' breathed Captain Burnside, 'you damned scoundrel!'

'Henry, oh, it's you,' cried Betsy. 'Look what he's done to me!'

'Twice damned satyr,' said the Captain in fury, 'you shall be brought to capital account for laying your perverted hands on a young lady dear to me.' He closed the door smartly to guard against possible interruption, and put his back against it. Betsy came to her feet, turning aside to adjust her bodice with the trembling agitation of a young lady whose modesty had been grievously wounded. Nor did she forget to breathe noisily.

The room, the Captain noted, was furnished only with essentials, a little table, a chair, a crude chest of drawers and a truckle bed. But it was neat and tidy, and so was the Irish gentleman himself. He was also pale and aghast. 'Yer Honour, ye're mistaken—'

'Mistaken?' Captain Burnside looked dangerously outraged. 'My young lady floored, her gown savaged, her bosom uncovered? Offspring of Satan, if you've escaped the hangman before on like counts, you'll not escape him this time.' He gripped his cane as if determined to use it. 'Polly, as soon as you feel less distressed, go and find a boy who will bring a Bow Street Runner here, while I keep this fiend detained.'

'Yer Honour, for the love of God, don't do that,' gasped the fearful Ulsterman, 'for I swear I niver laid a single finger on the young lady, nor would I, not if the divil himself was at my back and in my ear. Ask her, sir . . .'

'Oh, you terrible man,' breathed Betsy, 'tripping me up, putting me on the floor and spoiling my gown to make me show – oh, Henry, I be so thankful you were close by.'

'Hush, don't cry,' said the devious Captain tenderly, 'I'll wager you'll never be at such risk again with this libertine. Nor will other young ladies, for I'll see the law has him dangling at Tyburn within a week.'

'Yer Honour, I beg your belief in me own true self,' gasped Mr Maguire, appalled at what was overtaking him. ''Tis the way it looked, not the way it was. 'Tis circumstantial, so it is, and may I niver receive the blessing of my Protestant faith if I had any wish to harm the young lady.'

'Damn my eyes and ears,' said Captain Burnside ferociously, 'I heard and I saw. You are damned and doomed: there, you villain, see what you have run yourself up against in your unbridled depravity.' He whisked a card from his coat pocket and thrust it under Mr

279

Maguire's nose. Mr Maguire, further appalled, read the printed words.

*HENRY J BULLIVANT*       *Attorney-at-Law*
*No 25 Cheapside, London*

'Yer Honour, ye'll not see a God-fearing man hanged by reason of the way it looked . . .'

'I'll see you hanged, be sure I will,' said the Captain. 'In my profession as a servant of the law, I find no villains worthier of Tyburn's gibbet than those who subject innocent young ladies to carnal abuse.'

Joseph Maguire's thin, dark face paled with fear, though not with guilt. 'Sir – Yer Lordship – 'tis meself that's as innocent as a babe new-born,' he breathed.

Betsy, shrewdly guessing that her gentleman wished to have the Irishman eating out of his hand, said with credible protestation, 'Oh, if you be innocent, then I be guilty of bawdiness, which I never could be. Henry, I be ready now to find a boy and send him for the Runners.'

'If you are recovered enough, dear Polly, then between us we shall deliver this licentious miscreant into the arms of the law,' said Captain Burnside, and the panic-stricken Orangeman paled to whiteness.

'I swear, 'twas the way it looked, no more,' he said desperately. 'If Yer Honour hands me over to the Runners, it's meself, me own mother's innocent son, that'll swing at Tyburn, and not inside a week, oh Lord, but a day.'

'You're Irish,' said Captain Burnside, as if he had only just deduced this.

'So I am, sir, but no papist. I'm an Orangeman, and swear there's none more loyal to the King. 'Tis God's truth.'

'A likely story,' said Captain Burnside sternly. 'I'll bandy no more words with you, but send my young lady to—'

'Yer Grace, ye'd not do that which would hang an innocent man, Joseph Maguire meself, who's a faithful subject of His Protestant Majesty, King George.'

'Faithful subject?' said Captain Burnside scathingly.

'Do you dare to suggest His Majesty would accept a libertine as faithful?' He was wearing Mr Maguire down. 'You may mock me, reptile, and make your case no better than it is, but you mock His Majesty at your peril.'

'Henry,' said Betsy, 'am I to go?'

'No, I beg,' gasped the unfortunate Mr Maguire, 'carry a message to His Protestant Highness, the Duke of Cumberland, for me. His own royal self will speak for me.'

'His own royal self will watch you topped,' said the Captain. 'Go on your way, Polly.'

'No!' gasped Mr Maguire. ''Tis meself that's a boon and a blessing to the Royal family, and can prove it, so I can.'

'What's that you say?' asked the Captain curtly.

'True it is, sir, I swear.'

'Is it possible there's something in your favour that may mitigate your heinous sin of attempted ravishment?' asked the Captain, frowning.

'No sin was in my mind, Yer Honour, but if it will make Yer Honour forget it looked like sin, and Yer Honour being a servant of the law and His Majesty accordingly, I'll give ye that truth, though I've been sworn to silence.'

Captain Burnside took on the look of a servant of the law giving due and fair consideration to the plea, while the unhappy Mr Maguire looked at him in hope.

'Polly, my dear,' said the Captain eventually, 'pray wait outside.'

'Oh, I'll be glad to,' said Betsy fervently, 'I be all of a quiver in here.'

'I'll not keep you waiting long, I hope,' said the Captain, and Betsy went out to wait on the landing, leaving him alone with the Orangeman who, psychologically bruised and battered, seemed to be in hope that he could save his neck. It was all of a puzzle to Betsy, save that she knew by now that her gentleman friend worked in ways mysterious, and she could not but admire his performance.

Among other things, Mr Maguire confided he was being guarded and watched by a man lodging in the house immediately opposite. Mr Erzburger had said it was for his own protection. Accordingly, when Captain Burnside emerged into the street with Betsy, he glanced casually about. If there were eyes watching him, he could not determine them. But as he and Betsy approached the corner of the street, a man carrying a jug of ale appeared. He turned into the street. He gave the Captain and Betsy an interested look. The interest was mainly in Betsy's gauzy gown. He was full of drink, his face mottled with it. The Captain and Betsy turned into the lane. They saw their cabbie waiting, standing beside his horse. The Captain stopped, retraced his steps to the corner of the street, and took a discreet look. The man with the jug entered the house opposite that in which Mr Maguire was lodging. Luck, thought the Captain, had played its part. While he and Betsy had been with the Orangeman, his watchdog, deserting his post for a spell, had been in a tavern.

The cabbie drove his passengers to Vauxhall Gardens, where he was generously paid off. There, Betsy took refreshments with her audacious and pleasurable gentleman in the pavilion. She was almost too breathless to pay proper attention to her food, though she drank wine thirstily. She was breathless from her own performance in helping to reduce that poor little Irishman to a frightened wreck, breathless in her intense curiosity to know why it had had to be done, and breathless, finally, in being in these Arcadian surroundings with her gentleman, and among members of the Quality. Her gentleman assured her that what had had to be done to Mr Maguire was for the good of the King's realm and also for the good of Mr Maguire himself. It was not necessary for Betsy to know more than that; it was sufficient for her to understand that their arrival in Mr Maguire's life had probably saved it.

'Saved his life?' Betsy gulped more wine. 'Oh, it's all razzle, dazzle and fourpenny ones to me, sir.'

'You have my permission, and His Majesty's, to forget all about it. Not a word, puss.'

'His Majesty?' Betsy looked awestruck. 'Oh, I never did know a gentleman more flummoxing than you.' But

282

since she could be the essence of discreet silence when silence was so gainful, she declared an oath of dumbness. Her fine gentleman was as rewarding as the golden goose. 'You be giving me the guineas now, sir?'

'Now, Betsy? Here?' Captain Burnside shook his head at her. 'Do you wish the lords and ladies to see you accepting money from me across the table? It would at once change you in their eyes from a shy young lady of sweet innocence to a trollop.'

Betsy was so overcome by her *faux pas* that the blush mantling her cheeks was a true one. The bright, colourful pavilion was full of ladies and gentlemen spending as much time quizzing their neighbours as pecking at their food.

'Sir, I'm a good girl, liking pleasuring, that's all.'

'Why, of course,' said the Captain kindly, 'and I shouldn't have been allowed to make an accomplice of a trollop. Eat your food now, and drink up your wine.' He refilled her glass, and not for the first time. 'The wine, pretty kitten, will bring you to well-being. You have my fond regard, you deserve well-being, and I shall see that you come to it.'

'Nor don't I mind coming to kissing with you,' said Betsy, 'for I never did meet any gentleman more kind, or who said nicer things to me.' She filled her mouth with food and washed it down with more wine, all under her kind gentleman's encouraging eye.

After the meal, he took her to a restful alcove in the Gardens, leafily screened from prying eyes. The strains of orchestral music reached their ears. Betsy, in wine-induced languor, reposed in pretty sleepiness amongst the cushions on a long cane *chaise-longue*. Well-being had arrived. But if her lids were heavy, her lips, still dewy from wine, were wakefully expectant of kisses.

'Your guineas, Betsy,' murmured the Captain, and that caused her to lift her lids in delight. Five golden guineas spilled into her eager hand.

Saucily, she drew her gown up to her waist, uncovering

her Sunday pantaloons, their delicate lace frills threaded with pink ribbons. She slipped the coins into the waist pocket of the pantaloons, then wound her arms around her gentleman's neck and kissed him dreamily on the mouth. 'Oh, you be a delight to a girl,' she whispered.

'The gold given was gold earned, Betsy,' he said, and he drew her gown back into place, covering up her limbs.

Betsy's sleepy lids blinked. 'But I don't mind,' she said, 'not if it be a pleasure to you to look.'

'I'm sure you don't mind, puss, but pleasuring ain't encouraged in the Gardens, d'you see. I ain't inclined to let you be disapproved of.'

Betsy, reclining in the dreaminess of well-being, gazed up at him. He smiled, waiting for the wine to send her to sleep. Betsy, with her fondness for cuddling and kissing, would be less of a problem asleep.

'Sir,' she murmured, 'I be full of sweet feelings.' A little true colour touched her again. 'It's not the guineas, nor that you be such a pleasure to a girl; it be you, sir. Even if you go hammer and tongs together, you and your lady wife, like married couples do sometimes, I be certain sure she be glad to be your wife. Sir, you don't mind I've come to love you?'

'Betsy, you're dreaming. But dream on, puss.'

Betsy sighed, her eyes closed and she stretched. The warmth of the day and the wine she had taken drew her into bliss. People sauntered by on the other side of the leafy screen. The Gardens were murmurous with the faint sounds of music, the soft laughter of ladies and the lazy hum of July.

She fell asleep. Captain Burnside smiled. The wine had taken care of Betsy.

# Chapter Twenty-three

The George Inn at Winchester, a highly respectable and most comfortable hostelry, was noted for the excellent service it offered to ladies and gentlemen of the Quality. That afternoon, it received Lady Clarence Percival and her sister, Miss Annabelle Howard, with much courtesy, providing for them adjoining rooms well-appointed and welcomingly cool. Supper, mine host ventured to say, was at six-thirty, and there was to be a music recital in the guests' lounge later in the evening.

With Annabelle taking a little rest after the long journey, Caroline went in search of Sammy. She found him in the carriage yard. She required him, she said, to find the location of the grace-and-favour residences in which lived retired members of the clergy or their widows, and to discover which one housed Mrs Burnside, widow of a deceased bishop.

'Right, Your Ladyship, very good,' said Sammy, asking no questions.

'Convey the information only to me, Sammy.'

'That I will, yes'm,' said Sammy.

He did not take long. He was an intelligent youth.

After a most satisfying supper, during which Caroline with her superb looks and Annabelle with her vivacious prettiness received many glances of interest from other guests, Caroline advised her sister she was going out on a little matter of business.

'Business, sister? Here, in Winchester?'

'Yes, here, Annabelle, in Winchester. I will join you in the music room later. I did say there was a person I wished to see.'

285

'Yes, but I thought we were to visit the Cathedral and enjoy the shops,' said Annabelle.

'We will do that tomorrow morning,' said Caroline, 'before we depart at midday.'

'I vow I shall be dreadfully bored if I have to sit and listen to music by myself,' said Annabelle.

'And I vow, dearest sister, it is time you stopped being bored unless Cumberland is within reach. Be thankful you are not within *his* reach. Now, I am sure I shan't be long, but, if you become truly bored, then pray entertain yourself by writing a letter to our parents.'

A middle-aged lady, servant and companion to Mrs Honoria Burnside, answered Caroline's knock on the little white door of the apartment near the Cathedral.

'Good evening,' said Caroline.

The servant, recognising Quality, dipped a knee and said, 'Good evening, madam, may I help you?'

'I am Lady Clarence Percival, and I should consider it most helpful if you would present my compliments to Mrs Burnside and ask her if she would be kind enough to give me a few moments of her time. If she has visitors, then perhaps I might venture to call again, say tomorrow morning?'

'Madam has no visitors, Your Ladyship,' said the servant. 'Will you please step in, and I will ask her if she will receive you.' She took Caroline into a charming little sitting room, delicate with light colours and graceful furniture. She begged Her Ladyship to seat herself, then went to speak to Mrs Burnside.

Mrs Burnside entered the room a minute later. Caroline had rather imagined she would be stately of form and carriage, but Mrs Burnside was petite and still with a hint of girlish prettiness. In her early fifties, she wore a widow's cap on her brown hair, and a black silk gown graced her slim figure. She advanced in brisk fashion, a smile on her face, her hazel eyes clearly showing interest. Caroline came to her feet.

'Mrs Burnside?' she said, and Mrs Burnside, who might

have been a ladyship herself had her husband not passed away while still in office, regarded the widow of Lord Clarence Percival with distinct approval. In an evening cloak of emerald silk and a feathered turban, Caroline did not look less than her usual magnificent self.

'Yes, I am Mrs Burnside, Mrs Honoria Burnside. I am advised you are Lady Clarence Percival.' Her voice was a sweet lightness. 'I am intrigued by your visit.'

'You must forgive me in that I gave you no notice,' said Caroline, 'but, finding myself in Winchester for a brief stay, I felt I should like to see you.'

'Please, do sit down,' said Mrs Burnside, and both ladies rustlingly seated themselves.

'I have, you see, recently made the acquaintance of your son Charles,' said Caroline.

'Charles?' Mrs Burnside looked most intrigued. Young at heart, she had a liveliness about her. 'Charles?'

'Yes,' said Caroline, slightly tentative.

'Dear me, dear me,' said Mrs Burnside, which Caroline at once took to mean Captain Burnside's mother was well aware he could not be considered England's worthiest citizen.

'Oh, I assure you, madam, I have found much good in him,' she said, and her warm voice, with its lingering Southern lilt, came delightfully to Mrs Burnside's ears, although the implication of the comment somewhat puzzled her.

'I cannot refrain from asking if that means you have also found him a little wanting,' she smiled.

'Oh, do believe me, I am not so critical as to expect perfection in any human being,' said Caroline earnestly, 'for I cannot find perfection in myself, nor ever will.'

'As to that,' said Mrs Burnside, 'my dear husband, the Bishop, always declared that while perfection may be coveted, a lack of it in some people can be quite endearing. Weakness is very human.'

'Alas,' sighed Caroline.

'Alas?' Mrs Burnside was even more intrigued.

'It is all too true, is it not, Mrs Burnside, that some

ladies find the weaknesses of some gentlemen foolishly endearing?' said Caroline, thinking of herself and Lord Clarence, and of Annabelle and Cumberland.

'Oh, dear me,' said Mrs Burnside, 'I would hope not to be so foolish myself as to value any gentleman more for his weaknesses than his virtues.'

'That is of all things a most sensible outlook,' said Caroline. 'It is far wiser, I am sure, to help a man set aside his failings and to encourage development of his better self.'

'My dear Lady Clarence,' said Mrs Burnside with a smile, 'is it the failings of my son Charles we are discussing?'

'Oh, not at all, no, no,' said Caroline in haste. 'Indeed, such are his good points that I have offered him a position as assistant to my steward on my Sussex estate.'

Mrs Burnside's eyes opened wide. 'Goodness me,' she said, 'oh, my goodness.'

'You are surprised?' said Caroline, wishful to have Captain Burnside's mother as an ally in her campaign to turn him into a man of honest endeavour.

'I am fascinated,' said Mrs Burnside.

'I must confess I have an earnest desire to see him with an untroubled future in front of him,' said Caroline.

'Untroubled? Bless my soul,' said the sprightly Mrs Burnside. 'May I ask how he responded to your offer?'

'Not at all seriously,' said Caroline. 'It is to my great regret, Mrs Burnside, and I say this in all respect to you, his mother, that he is serious about few things and approaches most with alarming levity. Of course, I am only a friend, a new friend, but his lack of concern for his future is very worrying.'

'It has not been too worrying to me,' said Mrs Burnside, 'for he has always managed to emerge safely from his scrapes. Um – do I recall that I have heard something of Lord Clarence Percival, your husband?'

'Lord Clarence died two years ago,' said Caroline. 'I am a widow, as you are.'

'Not quite as I am, I venture,' said Mrs Burnside, a

288

ittle perplexed, a little amused. 'You are young and extremely attractive, and I am a little elderly and a little faded. But I am sorry, of course, that you suffered such a grievous loss while still young.'

'Thank you,' said Caroline, and added quietly and frankly, 'However, as you see, I do not wear mourning black.'

'That may offend people unchangeably attached to the custom,' said Mrs Burnside, 'but not all of us lack understanding. I am sure your reasons are reasonable, and the wearing of black don't always signify sincere mourning. So, you are your own mistress, Lady Clarence, and wish to help my son approach his future in a serious way. You do not feel his present occupation ensures a commendable future?'

Caroline did not want to comment specifically on that. It was bad enough for Captain Burnside's mother to know her son was a ne'er-do-well. 'Oh, I hardly think it an occupation,' she said.

'Myself,' said Mrs Burnside, 'I am never quite sure what he is at or what he is about. It is either one vague thing or another, here or there or elsewhere, and I am sure my dear husband would have allowed himself to say that even God does not move in more mysterious ways than Charles.'

Caroline felt a surge of relief that this charming lady was obviously ignorant of the true nature of her son's way of life, which accounted for the calm and almost amused fashion in which she spoke of him. It was also a relief not to have made the mistake of being specific.

'I have, perhaps, been mistaken in feeling his mysterious ways point to an unsatisfactory future, Mrs Burnside. It led me to think his many talents should be directed into clearer channels, and that perhaps was an impertinence on my part. Being in Winchester, I could not resist calling on you and to suggest that you and I together might persuade him to take up my offer. I declare myself quite out of order, and beg your indulgence of my misguidedness.'

'La,' said Mrs Burnside lightly, 'pray don't consider

yourself out of order, Lady Clarence, for I don't. I only
wonder if – um – what you are offering Charles is what he
would think suitable.'

'Suitable?' said Caroline, who could only think that any
kind of honest work might save Captain Burnside from
himself.

'I don't say Charles is the worthiest man in the world,'
said Mrs Burnside, 'but unlike those who eschew any kind
of work, feeling it is not what gentlemen are born to, my
son has always liked to turn his hand to something or
other. My only complaint, as his mother, is that he says so
little about his activities.'

It was a point in his favour, thought Caroline, that he
had refrained from distressing his mother by keeping her
blissfully ignorant of his sins and omissions. It would
surely shame such a sweet woman to know that her son
had deceived young ladies and made off with their
jewellery, never mind how dubious his activities had been
in behalf of the patrons he talked about. Caroline felt very
relieved indeed that Mrs Burnside was entirely vague
about his reprehensible ways. She had thought her
meeting with his mother might be a little painful and
embarrassing. She had intended to be completely
sympathetic and reassuring, to declare herself determined
to bring about a change in him, and with Mrs Burnside's
help. Now, however, she must discontinue implying that
he was an unworthy son.

'I was constrained to feel my offer might advantage
him,' she said.

'And he himself did not share that feeling?' murmured
Mrs Burnside.

'Perhaps, as you say, he did not feel the work would be
suitable for him,' said Caroline, still quite sure that anything was preferable to that which might lead him to
transportation or Tyburn. 'But there, I shall not take up
any more of your time. It has been so kind of you to
receive me, and I am happy to have met you.' She rose,
and Mrs Burnside followed suit. 'When do you expect
next to see Charles?'

Mrs Burnside laughed lightly. 'Oh, when he is next disposed to visit,' she said, 'and then I shall tell him that his newest friend is entirely delightful. Goodness, how very fortunate he is.'

'Fortunate?'

'Indeed,' said Mrs Burnside, smiling.

The following morning, after a most comfortable night and satisfying breakfast, Annabelle was preparing to go to the shops with Caroline, and to visit the Cathedral, when there was a very peremptory knock on her door. Opening it, she found Mr Jonathan Carter there.

His look was severe. 'Damn my eyes if you didn't make a fool of me,' he said.

'I cannot be blamed for nature's handiwork,' said Annabelle, and tried to close the door. Jonathan put his foot in the way. 'Pest, go away,' she said.

'Can't be done,' said Jonathan. 'Beg to inform you you're leaving. At once. Kindly pack your dainty where-withals, while I speak to Lady Caroline.'

'Oh, such impertinence,' breathed Annabelle. 'My sister and I are to shop, sir, and to visit the Cathedral.'

'No, you ain't,' said Jonathan, 'you're going back to the cottage. If that's why you've led me such a dance, to visit Winchester Cathedral and go shopping, may the saints preserve my patience.'

'The gentlest saint would pay no heed to you, sir,' retorted Annabelle. 'You are an interfering creature. What does it matter whether my sister and I are here or at the cottage? The cottage is boring. So are you. How you found us, I do not know, but you are welcome to return as hurriedly as you like. My sister and I will do so at our leisure. And I vow, sir, that if you do not remove your foot, I shall kick your leg.'

'In which event, Miss Howard, I shall—'

'Mr Carter? Mr Carter?' It was Caroline's astonished voice. 'What are you doing here?'

Jonathan eyed her with the kind of disapproval she would have considered an impertinence in any man. 'Beg to inform you, Lady Caroline, that that question should be asked of you, and in the sternest way. The orders—'

'Orders?' said Caroline warningly.

'Innocence don't signify, Your Ladyship . . .'

'Mr Carter, kindly favour me by entering this room, for I don't wish to quarrel with you in the corridor,' said Caroline firmly.

'After you, Your Ladyship,' said Jonathan. Caroline entered Annabelle's room and he followed, closing the door.

'Now, sir,' said Caroline, 'you may apologise, if you wish, and so avoid a quarrel.'

Jonathan flourished the beaver hat in his hand and bowed. 'My sincerest apologies, Lady Caroline,' he said, 'but it don't alter the fact that orders were for everyone to remain at the cottage.'

'Orders?' said Caroline again. 'Are you referring to instructions given by Captain Burnside, and if so, are you under the impression that my sister and I accept these as orders? It may please you to do so, but my sister and I are not to be ordered by any man, whether he be a gentleman of the highest quality or a lord of the highest esteem. And Captain Burnside is neither.'

'All the same, Your Ladyship, beg to request you and Miss Annabelle allow me to escort you back to Sussex immediately, or there'll be the devil to pay. Charles ain't going to like this escapade, no, not a bit. It was no easy task climbing out of that window and getting myself to the ground. Nor was it easy finding a horse to hire and then riding the suffering nag all over Sussex to look for people who had spotted your coach. Egad, persistence is a wearing thing, but it took me to Petworth in the end, and to the inn where you changed horses and announced your destination. It was near to midnight when I arrived here, and not before this morning was I able to discover where you were staying.' Jonathan shook his head in sorrow. 'It's a sad thing, Your Ladyship, to have been done in the eye by so fine a lady as yourself, for never did I think you capable of duplicity. Your sister, Miss Howard, yes, there's no telling what she might get up to . . .'

'Why, you objectionable wretch, I do not get up to anything,' said Annabelle. 'If you have been done in the eye by Caroline, I am overjoyed.'

'Well, I ain't even pleased about it myself,' said Jonathan. 'However, now that all's been said and done, I propose an immediate return to Sussex.'

'Annabelle and I will be returning first thing this afternoon, when we have seen the Cathedral, finished our shopping and enjoyed a midday meal,' said Caroline. 'Really, Mr Carter, you must see we are just as safe here in Winchester as at the cottage. It can make no difference whether we return now or this afternoon.'

'Charles still ain't going to like it,' said Jonathan, 'and he'll like it even less if he gets back before we do and finds all of us missing. He'll think Cumberland's bullies have carried us off, which ain't going to make him dance for joy.'

Caroline frowned, then smiled coolly. 'I have left him a note, telling him of our excursion,' she said.

'Thoughtful of you, Lady Caroline,' said Jonathan, 'but unless he has the key to the front door, I fancy he ain't going to have the consolation of reading your note.'

'Oh, dear,' said Annabelle, and Caroline frowned again and bit her lip.

'Bother it,' she said. 'Very well, Mr Carter, Annabelle and I will pack and depart with you as soon as possible. Perhaps you will ask Sammy to get the coach ready.'

'Yes, we cannot put Charles into a fret,' said Annabelle. 'Charles is a gentleman. It is not the same with Mr Carter, Caroline. One cannot help being indifferent to his sensibilities.'

'Well, I ain't a ruffian for the fun of it,' said Jonathan, cheerful again, 'I'm noted for being as hard as iron. I'll go down to the carriage yard and find Sammy.'

'Was there ever such an uncaring brute?' said Annabelle when Jonathan had gone.

'I must confess he seems uncaring of how sweet and pretty you are, dear sister,' said Caroline gravely. 'All other gentlemen of our acquaintance esteem your looks.'

'I vow Mr Carter an oaf, not a gentleman,' said Annabelle.

'So,' said the gentleman of distinguished bearing, 'here we have the very devil of plots and plots. Pelion is piled on Ossa. A plot to assassinate Wales and Cumberland, topped by a plot of silence from Cumberland. He's made not a single move against the papists, nor informed on them. His own informant is under a peculiar kind of restraint, and sworn to silence. By God, Burnside, your method of breaking his silence was also of a peculiar kind. Using an innocent serving wench in such a way don't commend itself to me. Too damned unsavoury by half. You're a blackguard, sir.'

'Means to an end, Your Grace,' said Captain Burnside.

'You're a fine pair, you and the irreverent Mr Carter, but there it is, and for the sake of His Majesty's realm I must practise being blind and deaf on occasions. Well, sir, what now? Precisely what is Cumberland up to?'

'I fancy, sir,' said the Captain, 'he may be set on an attempt to bring himself closer to the throne.'

The dignified gentleman fixed him with a piercing look. 'Kindly be more exact,' he said.

'Cumberland's four elder brothers stand between him and kingship, Your Grace. They will all be present at Cumberland's residence on the 29th, by his special request. He has all the details of the papist plot: a window broken . . . a smoking bomb tossed in, a bomb capable of blowing to smithereens every person in the room – Wales, York, Clarence, Kent and Cumberland himself. Except that, when the bomb explodes, it's my belief Cumberland will have found a credible pretext to absent himself for a moment or two.'

'Madness,' said His Grace.

'Cold calculation, sir.'

'Hear me, Burnside, I meant your *conjecture* was madness.'

'It is your privilege, sir, so to describe it.'

'Not even Cumberland would devise so unspeakable a

294

scheme. It would make him the quintessence of a modern Macbeth.'

'I venture to suggest Cumberland could wear the mantle very comfortably,' said Captain Burnside.

'I grant you his silence on the papist plot is extraordinary, but put from your mind any possibility he can be arraigned on a charge of complicity concerning the restraint imposed on – what was the fellow's name?'

'Joseph Maguire, sir.'

'Damned odd, damned peculiar,' said His Grace. 'Well, one thing is certain, Burnside. Cumberland will never be hanged, for whatever he's about he'll never so design events as to incriminate himself. There will be no proof, no positive evidence. There may be whispers, but whispers are chaff in the wind. Now, be so good as to see to what is necessary. Further, continue to ensure the safety of Lady Caroline and her sister. I'll have no consideration for your person if you fail there.'

'Nor, I judge, will Lady Caroline, Your Grace.'

His Grace allowed himself a faint smile.

# Chapter Twenty-four

Captain Burnside hired a curricle and pair to take him back to Sussex and Pond Cottage. The curricle was in splendid order, and the pair pulled in well-trained concert. The condition of the roads, poor in parts, was not the impediment to the curricle that it was to heavy vehicles. The Captain gave the pair a break at Redhill, when he stopped at a coaching inn for a meal and a tankard of welcome ale. An ostler rubbed down the pair and supplied them with fodder, and they took the Captain along at a steady pace for the rest of the journey.

He stabled the horses, noting that Sammy was not in evidence. Nor was Lady Caroline's coach and four. And the cottage seemed ominously quiet. There was no answer to his knocks on either the front or back door, and both were locked. There was, however, a casement window open at one side of the cottage. He felt distinctly alarmed. Jonathan would not have gone unless compelled to. Had he used the coach as a means of escape for all of them? Had Cumberland's hirelings been sighted?

He searched for a ladder and found one behind the stable. It was long enough to reach the open window. He climbed up and eased himself into the room that had been occupied by Lady Caroline and Annabelle. The look of the room was innocuous, offering no evidence of a hasty and forced departure. He moved to the door. It was locked. Disturbingly curious. Had they all retreated to this room, locked out intruders and then escaped by the window? Impossible for the ladies without the help of the ladder. Jonathan would have managed, and Sammy too, but not the sisters. Yet Lady Caroline by no means lacked resolution, and Annabelle was spritely.

He looked out of the window and studied the landscape. Sussex lay bathed in afternoon sunshine. A spread of fields and woods afforded a vista of rural quiet. A herd of cows moved slowly into view over a distant pasture. A winding ribbon of light brown caught his eye. It was the road that led to Wychling. A coach, emerging out of green folds, traversed the visible ribbon and disappeared again.

Captain Burnside climbed out of the window and descended the ladder. He went round to the front of the cottage, sat down on the doorstep and waited. It was several minutes before he heard the coach. It was travelling down the lane towards the cottage. It rounded the bend. Jonathan and Sammy were on the box. Jonathan, at the reins, brought the coach to a halt outside the cottage gate, gave the reins to Sammy and jumped down. He opened the door and Lady Caroline descended, a turban on her auburn head, her summer cloak over her gown.

Annabelle followed. Doffing his beaver hat, Jonathan acknowledged her descent from the coach with a sweeping bow. Annabelle floated disdainfully past him. She was not in the happiest mood. The Duke of Cumberland was a dark, worrying image in her mind, despite her ardent wish to believe him innocent of truly harmful intentions. Then there was the boredom of the cottage to endure, and the possibility of uncomfortable moments with Captain Burnside if he had already returned to find them absent and himself locked out.

She came to a sudden stop with Caroline at the gate, for there he was, sitting on the doorstep and waiting for them. They advanced along the path and he came to his feet.

Behind them, Jonathan spoke in a murmur. 'Egad, the game's up, ladies.'

From beneath the brim of his top hat, Captain Burnside regarded Caroline frowningly. She stared haughtily at him. He stared sternly back. Green eyes clashed with grey. The green were aloof, the grey accusing.

'Who has the key to the cottage?' he asked.

'I have,' said Caroline, and took it from her reticule. Electing for offence as the best defence, she said loftily, 'You may open the door, sir.' And she handed him the key. He accepted it silently, and opened the door. He stood aside. Caroline entered.

Annabelle hesitated and said, 'Charles, you are not going to be vexed, are you?'

'Please go in,' he said. Annabelle made a little face at him and went in. Sammy appeared, bearing the trunk on his strong young shoulders. He took it into the cottage, and the Captain turned to Jonathan.

'It's my belief you're going to roast me,' said Jonathan.

'Explain,' said the Captain, 'slowly and concisely.'

Jonathan began to explain at length.

Up in their room, Annabelle said to Caroline, 'Oh, dear, I have never seen Charles looking so cross.'

'Cross?' Caroline removed her turban. 'I should hope he won't take it on himself to be cross with me.'

'But I do declare, it was very unthinking of us to leave him locked out. He has been so gallant concerning our welfare.'

'He has no right to be cross,' said Caroline, simmering because of the way he had looked at her. How dared a man of his background look at any lady like that?

'All the same,' said Annabelle, 'I vow I shall be sweet and contrite. Charles is an adorable man.'

'I think your adorable man is presently subjecting Mr Carter to a most discomfiting ordeal,' said Caroline.

'Good,' said Annabelle, 'that will give the brute's interfering nose a pinched look.'

When they ventured downstairs a little later, Annabelle was eager to make amends and Caroline prepared to stand her ground. However, Captain Burnside was absent. Jonathan was in the kitchen, examining the contents of the larder. His nose was questing, not pinched. He seemed quite cheerful, his mind on supper.

'Where is Sammy?' asked Caroline.

'Rubbing down the horses,' said Jonathan.

'And where is Captain Burnside?'

'Gone,' said Jonathan briskly, 'gone to—'

'Gone?' Caroline experienced unhappy shock. 'Gone?'

'To pull carrots and dig potatoes,' said Jonathan.

'Oh, Captain Burnside is not a field hand,' said Annabelle indignantly, 'you should be doing that.'

'Well, I ain't,' said Jonathan. 'I'm set to scrape the carrots. You're set to peel the potatoes.'

Annabelle's tongue leapt furiously at him. Caroline slipped out. She found the Captain in the vegetable plot, using a fork.

'Oh, really,' she said.

He looked up, the sun a warmth on his face. 'Ah, the Lady Caroline disapproves?' he said.

'You are ridiculous,' she said. 'Sammy will willingly dig potatoes.'

'The lad is attending to your horses.'

Caroline fidgeted. 'I won't have this,' she said.

Captain Burnside unearthed potatoes and placed them in a trug. He looked up again, his expression mildly enquiring. 'Precisely what won't you have, marm?' he asked.

'I won't have you venting your vexation by cold-shouldering us,' she said.

He laughed. Caroline's eyes smouldered.

'You're standing on the carrots,' he said.

Caroline's feet, white-slippered, were buried in ferny green carrot tops. 'They are my carrots,' she said.

'Faith, so they are,' he smiled, 'but you'll allow me to pull a few? And I ain't vexed, no, not at all.'

Hating the thought that he might have been, and yet feeling any vexation on his part was an impudence, Caroline bit her lip, then chose to be reasonable. 'I did leave you a note,' she said, 'and I did think we would be as safe in Winchester as here. I declare myself penitent in forgetting you could not get into the cottage. Truly, I am sorry. We – Annabelle was most upset to see you looking so dark and forbidding.'

299

Captain Burnside seemed to find that amusing. In truth, he was vastly relieved that she and her sister had come to no harm, that their absence had been nothing to do with Cumberland. 'Dark and forbidding?' he said.

'Yes . And you were.' Caroline smiled faintly. 'I am not sure how it has come about that you can permit yourself to look at me as if I were a naughty child and you were my stern guardian. I declare, sir, it was in your mind to put me over your knees.'

'Good God,' said the astonished Captain.

'There, I knew it. It was in your mind.' Caroline felt she had turned the tables. His stunned look captivated her. She was coming to revel in crossing swords with him, and to feel frankly delighted whenever she was able to outdo him in any battle of words. His very presence keyed her up. With Mr Wingrove receding into the background as a prospective husband, she went on compulsively. 'Had we been alone, sir, you surely would have attempted it, for your mood was savage.'

Captain Burnside ran a helpless hand through his hair. 'I'm accused because of my looks of an intent to put you over my knees?'

'Yes. You are accused by me. And do not bother to give me the lie, sir.'

'Madam, I am speechless.'

Caroline laughed in pure exhilaration. 'Captain Burnside, if I have truly rendered you speechless, I have achieved a miracle. Come, sir, find your tongue and confess that in your growling and muttering mood you would have laid brutal hands on me.'

'God forgive you, Lady Caroline, my tongue ain't up to confessing any such thing. I ain't given to brutalising any woman, least of all you. You are—' He checked himself and frowned at the fork.

'Yes?' said Caroline, and her pulse was suddenly erratic. 'Please go on, Captain Burnside. I am. . . ?'

'My most respected patron.'

'Coward,' declared Caroline.

'Marm?'

'I am not your most respected patron. That is all over.'

'Is it?' Captain Burnside ventured a smile. 'Well, I ain't been paid.'

'Oh!' Caroline stamped a foot and crushed a carrot top. 'Sir, I vow your pecuniary self is the worst part of you.'

'Alas, marm, poverty's the undoing of many a gentleman.'

'I wish, sir, you did not own so knowing a tongue or deliver such ready answers,' said Caroline. 'I cannot think why your gentle mother regards you as sweetly as she does, with never a suspicion of your true mode of life.'

'Request you enlarge on that, Lady Caroline,' said the Captain.

'You spoke to Mr Carter, I think,' said Caroline.

'I did, and he explained everything.'

'And so you realised it was ridiculous to be so vexed,' she said. 'But, of course, he did not tell you I called on your mother in Winchester.'

'Heaven preserve us,' murmured the Captain, 'was that why you chose Winchester?'

'Yes, and you may well shift on your sly feet, sir, for you are an unworthy son of so good and trusting a mother. I wished to meet her, to assure her you had your good points, but found she exists in sublime ignorance of your tricks, deceptions, card-sharping and even thievery. To her, your activities are a respectable but vague mystery. Shame on you. I could not disillusion her, and only went as far as telling her I had offered you a position at Great Wivenden as assistant to my steward.'

'Saints and angels,' breathed the Captain, 'my poor mother. I ain't ever supposed that she, too, would find herself confounded.'

'Confounded, sir?' enquired Caroline.

'Lost for words, d'you see.'

'Ridiculous man, your mother was most articulate, and all her words were a sweet reflection of her loving nature.'

'She expressed herself sweetly at your willingness to make an honest clerk of me?'

'Please do not think I spoke to her as your patron,' said

Caroline, hugely enjoying herself. 'I made no mention of that aspect of our relationship. I advised her I was a new friend of yours who wished you to become a man of straightforward endeavour instead of a dubious mystery. Your mother was excessively charming, declaring how fortunate you were to have acquired such a delightful new friend.'

'Ah,' said Captain Burnside, and looked at the sky. 'Delightful,' he said, and rubbed his chin. 'Ah,' he said again.

Caroline, quite willing to prolong the fencing, said, 'You don't share her opinion?'

'Indeed I do, marm. You are as delightful a patron as any professional could wish.'

'Fiddle-de-dee, sir, to marm, and to patron. I am speaking as a friend willing to discount your regrettable past and help you enjoy an honest and commendable future.'

'I fancy, Lady Caroline,' said the Captain, 'that your friendly willingness will yet turn me into a country bumpkin with hay in my hair and a straw between my teeth. A man as simple as I am, d'you see, ain't a match, nor even half a match, for a woman as determined as you are.'

Caroline wanted to laugh again, for his absurdities were richly entertaining. Controlling herself, she said in her cool way, 'I am pleased to hear I may save you from yourself, though I shan't fall into the trap of accepting you as simple. However, for now, sir, you may dig the potatoes and pull the carrots. That is very honest work. Bring them into the kitchen, and Mr Carter and Annabelle will see to their preparation. Oh, and hay in your hair will suit you very well.'

This was all of singularly provocative, and she knew it.

'Quite so, marm,' said Captain Burnside. He laid the fork aside and dusted his hands. He stooped, swiftly. Caroline gasped as he lifted her off her feet. Tall, and with a figure that made no lightweight of her, she was swept up with an ease that told her he was far stronger than a man of his kind had any right to be.

'Captain Burnside! Put me down! Put me down, do you hear!'

'You'll pardon me for lifting you off the carrots,' said the Captain, 'but they don't take kindly to being trodden on.'

'Put me down! At once!' Caroline kicked. The skirt of her gown showered. Oh, the impudence, he was daring to carry her. '*Put me down!*'

He set her on her feet, quite gently. She could not think why she felt so exhilarated, for she was not a woman who liked being subjected to horseplay. She was close to him for a moment, very close, and strange agitation arrived to confuse the exhilaration.

Captain Burnside stepped back. 'Recommend Jonathan slices the carrots, then steams 'em,' he said. 'It keeps 'em sweet.'

'Apologise!' she demanded, her face visibly flushed. 'Never, sir, have I been treated so discourteously.'

'Assure you, Lady Caroline, I acted only in defence of the carrots.'

'You seized me, sir, you brutalised me!'

'Marm, I handled you as tenderly as I could.'

'Handled me?' Caroline looked outraged, but did not feel so. 'Did you say in defence of the carrots?'

'Beg you to agree that's how it was,' said the Captain.

It came then. A rush of laughter from Caroline. 'Carrots?' she gasped helplessly. 'Oh, Captain Burnside, what am I to do with such an absurd man as you?'

'Throw me to the lions one day, I fancy,' he suggested. 'But there it was, Your Ladyship, you were—'

'No, I beg you, please don't mention carrots again, or I vow I shall die of hysteria. Pray proceed with your honest work of pulling them.' And Caroline picked up her skirts and hastened away, for she was sure that if she stayed some kind of disaster might eventuate.

Disaster? Truth made its fiery strike.

She stopped, and her hand flew to her throat. Oh, merciful heavens, it can't be, it can't be!

# Chapter Twenty-five

It was midnight, and the villages of England were asleep. Sussex lay quiet. Sammy, however, was awake. He was on a four-hour watch until two in the morning. Captain Burnside had spoken to him and Mr Carter, and Sammy had offered his services. He patrolled up and down, and round and about. The moon, a bright crescent, cast silver light. Captain Burnside had said that if any unpleasant characters turned up, it would probably be at a time when they might expect the occupants of the cottage to be asleep and unprepared. So Sammy, willing and conscientious, was keeping watch.

Caroline was also awake. She simply could not get to sleep, cosy though the room and the bed were. She was in emotional turmoil, the impossible making its claim on her mind and restlessness afflicting her body. At times she felt almost feverish. She knew herself to be physically healthy. Too healthy. It was nearly six years since she had denied Clarence access to her bed. Now her feelings appalled her. She wanted to, she needed to, lie in the arms of a man. Not any man. A particular man, a singular man, a man of such dubious activities that one could only pray for him.

In dreadful dismay at her longings, she turned on to her stomach, buried her face in the feather pillow and even bit on it. Oh, dear heaven, how wretchedly true it was, the weakness some women had for scoundrels and adventurers. Clarence had been a degenerate scoundrel, and Captain Burnside was a philandering adventurer. But she knew now why she had worried about him, why she had come to hate the thought of Annabelle in his arms, and why she had been so wishful to reform him.

She must conquer her weakness, she must. She did not doubt that, given the encouragement, he would marry her for her money and make her as unhappy in the end as Clarence had. She turned again and sat up, her silk night-gown slipping off her shoulders. Her breasts were taut and sensitive, her mouth dry, her thirst acute. There was water in a large terra-cotta pot in the kitchen. The coolness of the container and its contents, crystal-clear spring water, drew her from the bed. On her bare feet she left the bedroom. She heard no sounds from Annabelle, or from the room that Captain Burnside was sharing with Mr Carter. The cottage was quiet, and filtering moonlight saw her safely down the narrow stairs. Her bare feet moved over the polished boards of the passage, and she entered the kitchen. There, a brass oil lamp gave light. She took a pewter drinking mug from the dresser, lifted the lid of the water vessel and dipped the mug. She drank deeply. The water still had a sweet, re-freshing coolness to it.

'Stay quite still, whoever you are – oh, ye gods, Caroline?'

She dropped the mug in startled fright. It fell with a splash into the container, the lid of which was still in her left hand. She turned. Captain Burnside, in shirt and breeches, re-garded her like a man mesmerised. The light of the all-night lamp bathed her face, neck and shoulders. Her splendid body was a pale, shimmering shape amid the silken delicacy of her nightgown. She was as much mesmerised as he was, though her limbs were trembling and her blood rushing, wayward and burning. She put a hand to her throat. Other than that, she could not move. And he, it seemed, could find none of his ready words.

She felt the lamplight was uncovering her. Her whole body trembled, causing the lightest of ripples to disturb her nightgown. It hung quivering, so it seemed, from the curved ledge of her breasts.

'I – Captain Burnside, I beg you.' Her voice was a strained huskiness.

He came to. He turned his glance aside from the revealing silk. 'So sorry,' he said, 'but I was on the couch in the living room and heard a noise.'

'Yes. I came down for water. I was dreadfully thirsty.' Emotion shortened the lingering vowels of South Carolina. 'I am sorry to have disturbed you. I did not know you had chosen to sleep in the living room.'

'A precautionary measure, marm.'

Marm. That stupid appellation. So discouraging of friendship. Did he want nothing from her except, perhaps, her fortune? He even had his back to her now. It was true, because she felt the light was disrobing her, that she had made the plea of modesty. Now, made perverse by her wayward blood, she wanted him to look at her. No, what was she thinking of? There must be no encouragement, none, for if he touched as well as looked, she would lose her head.

With an effort, she said, 'I do not think precautionary measures at all necessary – I think your fears and suspicions exaggerated.'

'I am beginning to think so myself. But I'll stay in the living room. Meanwhile, go back to bed.' He was curt, brusque. He had never been so before. It should have helped her in her intention to conquer her weakness, but it was no help at all. It wounded her.

'I will go when I will; I will not be told,' she breathed, and still he kept his back to her.

'Well, you are your own mistress,' he said.

'And you would always rather quarrel with me than not!'

He swung round, and it wounded her again, unbearably, to see how stiff and unyielding he was.

'You are well aware,' he said, 'that I can't command the privilege of either quarrelling with you or equating myself with you. If I—' He broke off, his uncharacteristic harshness falling helplessly from him in the face of her revealing, night-clad splendour. She was wholly the woman, the white silk bestowing lustre to the visible glimmer of her body. The moment was fraught with im-

306

possibility in what it demanded of the man. It demanded the self-denial of a saint. What did it demand of the woman? A gesture that would save him from committing the unpardonable, a simple, quick retreat that would remove her from his eyes. But she made no gesture, none at all. She stood before him, as if compulsively inviting the unpardonable, her limbs trembling again. He made an effort by saying in a strained whisper, 'God help you, Lady Caroline, and God help me too if you don't go up to bed.'

Faintly she breathed, 'Have you no affection—'

'Cap'n Burnside?' The momentous interruption came from outside the back door. It was Sammy's voice.

Caroline gasped, and she did move then, just as the door began to open. She fled from the kitchen. Sammy looked in. He saw Captain Burnside.

'Sammy?' The Captain forced himself out of his own emotional turmoil.

'Oh, it ain't no alarm bells, guv'nor, except there's a tinker. Comes here reg'lar, he says, and sleeps in the stables and gets fed in the mornings. I thought best you know, sir.'

'Yes, best I do, Sammy, and I'll come and inspect the gentleman.'

'In case he ain't a tinker?' said Sammy. 'Well, I ain't seen one more like. Hairy as an old goat, he is, with a cart full of tin kettles and suchlike, and smelling of onions, guv'nor.'

Even so, Captain Burnside went to inspect the itinerant pedlar. Satisfied, he returned to the cottage. He retrieved the pewter mug from the water container. He took a drink himself, to ease the dryness of his throat. Images danced in the lamplight.

'Here is the lid, Captain Burnside.' The warm voice of South Carolina reached his startled ears. The voice was calmer, and it owned a forgiving softness. Caroline was unable, quite unable, to go back to her bed without trying to ease the tension between herself and him.

'Oh, my God,' he breathed, and turned, expecting to

307

see an irresistible vision again. But she had put her cloak on, and there was even a slight smile on her face. Her hair, unbound, was a tumbling, fiery cloud. In her hand was the lid of the terra-cotta container.

'I am sorry,' she said, and he had no idea how much it had cost her to reduce her emotions to a controllable level.

He took the lid from her and replaced it. 'Sorry?' he said.

'I declare myself to be the one at fault,' she said. 'If either of us was quarrelsome, it was I. Please forgive me.'

His look was rueful, as if he felt her too beautiful for her own good, which she nearly had been. He chose a safe, self-calming rejoinder. 'You aren't at fault,' he said. 'By the way, you've a guest in your stables. A tinker. You're expected to supply him with breakfast. That, it seems, has been the custom.'

'He need not fear we shall break it,' she said. 'What would England's countryside be without its tinkers?' Needing to re-establish the singular nature of their relationship, she went on lightly. 'Are you sure he's a tinker? Are you sure he isn't Cumberland?'

Captain Burnside recognised her own kind of raillery. Much to her relief, he laughed. 'Whatever else he might do, Cumberland ain't the man to dress himself in a patched coat and ragged breeches that smell of onions, nor sport enough hair to stuff a pillow.'

Caroline's responsive laugh was born of her relief. 'When all is over, when Cumberland is no longer in fits at us for one reason or another, we – you and I – need not be such bad friends, do you think?' she said, still keeping to a light note.

'Assure you, I ain't ever parted from any patron on unfriendly terms.'

'You should not speak of parting from Annabelle and me.'

'Your Ladyship—'

'I won't allow it. Nor will Annabelle.' The challenging note was back. 'And I am not Your Ladyship. I am your friend. I shall go back to my bed now.'

She went. Her resolve to keep herself at a distance from

him, to fight her weakness, had had no more substance than a dry and withered straw.

The rest of the night was without incident. The morning brought clouds and a touch of humidity. Captain Burnside reflected on the possibility that Lady Caroline had not been wrong in her conviction that Cumberland, for all his majestic indifference to people, Parliament and certain laws, would not go so far as to have her and Annabelle silenced by an act of murder. And why should he? It would be Annabelle's word against his, and there was no certainty Annabelle would testify against him. Even if she did, she could not name her sister, or anyone else, as a witness. Her word would never stand up against Cumberland's in the event of an official enquiry into incidents planned to take place on 29th July. And since those incidents were not going to be quite as planned, an enquiry was doubtful. Cumberland did not know that. But he did know Annabelle could never be as convincing as himself. Perhaps those masked horsemen had related in no way to Cumberland's machinations.

Captain Burnside wondered if he had not made somewhat of a fool of himself, in which case he must blame his emotive weakness for overturning his reasoning. Wryly, he conceded a man in love was not a man of cold logic. His first thought, his only thought, had been to contrive the removal of Annabelle and Lady Caroline from the immediate reach of Cumberland.

He stopped pacing the garden and entered the kitchen by the back door. The aroma of frying ham had a delicious effect on his sense of smell. The large iron pan was on the stove. In it were sizzling slices of ham and thick round pats. Lady Caroline was turning the ham with a long frying fork. Her kitchen smock guarded her gown. Jonathan was making coffee. Annabelle entered from the living room, having just finished laying the table.

Captain Burnside gave Jonathan a testy look.

'Egad, don't blame me,' said Jonathan. 'Her Ladyship had a stand-up with me, and I lost.'

'It is my kitchen,' said Caroline, who had decided her relationship with the Captain was at its most enjoyable when she stood up for herself.

'Jonathan,' said the Captain, 'you're required to see to it that Lady Caroline don't wait on us.'

'Well,' said Jonathan, 'I ain't supposing—'

'Captain Burnside,' said Caroline, 'kindly don't interfere. Breakfast is almost ready and you may take your place at the table.'

'Mercy me,' said Annabelle, 'we are going to have such a trying day, Charles. Caroline is in a haughty mood.'

Captain Burnside let a smile come and go. He peered at the contents of the frying pan. He took up a fork and poked one of the round pats. 'What, may I ask, are these?'

'Go away,' said Caroline, and lightly rapped his knuckles with the frying fork. She had enjoyed a beautiful sleep after going back to bed, and she had woken with a feeling of sweet determination. Captain Burnside must be reformed. And he must be made to fall in love with her. She would not let emotion weaken her, but proceed calmly along the path to success, matching his impertinences in her own kind of way. 'These are American browns,' she said.

'Potato pats,' said Jonathan. The pats were crisply browning on either side.

'There, ready,' said Caroline. 'Who is going to take breakfast to Sammy and the tinker?' Plates sat warming on the stove. She filled the top one with ham and browns. Jonathan took it up. She filled another.

Jonathan offered both plates to Annabelle. 'There, my girl, you take 'em while I finish making the coffee.'

Incensed, Annabelle cried, 'Oh, I cannot believe this. Do you hear him, Charles? Do this, do that, and calling me girl . . . Where did you find such a coarse, common creature?'

'Come, Miss Howard,' said Jonathan briskly, 'it ain't much to ask.'

'I shan't, I won't,' said Annabelle. 'Why, you beast, you know that Sammy says the tinker has fleas.'

'I'll take them,' said Captain Burnside, and relieved Jonathan of the filled plates.

When he returned, the others were sitting at the table, breakfasts in front of them.

'I will get yours, Charles,' said Annabelle, and came to her feet in sweet willingness.

'Captain Burnside is quite capable,' said Caroline.

'Yes, sit down, sweet girl,' said the Captain, and fetched his breakfast.

The ham was delicious, the crisp-sided potato pats equally so. Caroline accepted all compliments graciously.

'After breakfast,' she said, 'we shall go to Great Wivenden.'

'Shall we?' asked Jonathan.

'You need not come,' said Annabelle, 'you can help the tinker mend kettles and catch his fleas.'

'That won't do, he'll pass them on to us,' said the Captain.

'Oh, is there nothing the horrid varmint wouldn't do to us?' said Annabelle.

'I ain't any more partial to fleas than you, Miss Howard,' said Jonathan, 'though I daresay you'd be a plumper meal than I would.'

Annabelle gasped a muffled little shriek of outrage. 'Oh, you all are lower than a snake!' she cried.

'Mr Carter, don't tease her so,' said Caroline.

'Great Wivenden?' mused Captain Burnside.

'Yes,' said Caroline. 'I have decided that as we're so close, you and Mr Carter may come and look at my house. And it is no use your arguing.'

'I'm entirely happy about it,' said the Captain, 'and will agree to a return to London tomorrow.'

'Oh, you are a dear man, and should be kissed,' said Annabelle.

'Not by me,' said Jonathan. 'He ain't at all kissable in my eyes.'

'No one, sir, is interested in your opinions,' said Annabelle. 'I vow you are at your most bearable when you are dumb.'

'Ain't she a pretty wag?' said Jonathan to the coffee-pot.

The clouds were breaking apart, and shafts of sunshine warmed the stone bulwarks of the manor house. Caroline and Annabelle stood on the paved terrace with Captain Burnside and Jonathan. Steps led down from the terrace to the lawns and gardens. Beyond stretched the broad vista of the parkland, prolific in places with mighty oaks, copper beeches and stately poplars. In the distance rose the undulating slopes of the Downs.

'I do declare, God has given us a beautiful world,' said Annabelle, always affected by the unspoiled enchantment of Great Wivenden's vistas and landscapes. 'Could anything be lovelier?'

'Well,' said Jonathan, never lacking in cheerful boldness, 'I fancy God ain't above being proud of Lady Caroline, and nor ain't you less than pretty, my infant.'

'*Infant*?' Annabelle seethed. Jonathan smiled. She did look pretty, ravishingly so in her gown and bonnet. But her blue eyes gave him angry contempt. 'Sir, be so good as not to address me,' she said.

'Oh, silence don't signify,' he said; 'it don't alter the facts.'

Caroline smiled. She glanced at Captain Burnside. He was taking in the soft magnificence of the greens, all changing their tints so swiftly as racing clouds continually edged the sun. He had been unusually quiet, as if Great Wivenden was having a sobering effect on him. Was she making a mistake? Did he feel she was in conceit of herself by showing him that all this belonged to her? But would that not appeal to his acquisitive nature, her wealth of ownership? Was it not something he would marry her for, in his calculating way? Dear heaven, she did not want that.

He had not been quite his usual debonair self since last night. Last night. The sun caught her and cast warmth over her, but her thoughts brought little shivers.

'You would like to see the house, Jonathan, wouldn't you?' she said. 'And you too, Captain Burnside?'

312

Goodness, thought Annabelle, how odd she is, calling the odious Mr Carter by his first name and still calling our entertaining Charles nothing but Captain Burnside. How strange was this old friendship of theirs.

The interior of the house was altogether imposing, yet had the distinct appeal of being warm and welcoming. A multitude of windows allowed the light to dance in every room, brightening the colours of tapestries, carpets and pictures. As for the pictures there were so many that the beautiful main hall, the dining room, the private reception room and the two drawing rooms had the entrancing look of furnished galleries.

On the ground floor, the steward, John Forbes, had his office. Caroline introduced him to her visitors. Jonathan shook his hand breezily. Captain Burnside did so with a reminiscent smile. 'I am, as you see, a friend,' he said.

'I was in no doubt by the time you left me,' said Mr Forbes.

Coming out of the office a few minutes later, Jonathan said, 'Shall we look at the kitchen?'

'Kitchens,' said Annabelle. 'Cooking kitchen, dairy kitchen, meat kitchen, fish kitchen, and so on. I declare you'll be at home there. The servants will show you where the potatoes are stored, and the turnips. I shan't come, unless Charles wishes to meet Caroline's cook and kitchen boy.'

'Well, I'll take you, all the same,' said Jonathan, 'if Lady Caroline don't mind.'

'I find it distinctly intriguing to have a gentleman interest himself in kitchens,' said Caroline.

'Charles has expressed no interest,' said Annabelle, 'and he's the only gentleman present.'

'Oh, I'm sure Mr Carter won't disgrace himself, so do go with him,' said Caroline, 'while I show Captain Burnside the library.'

'There, come along, Miss Howard,' said Jonathan. It was in his mind to give Lady Caroline and the Captain a little time together. 'Lead the way, my infant.'

'Oh, I shall box your ears again in a moment,' said Annabelle. 'And I am not interested in the kitchens.'

'Well, you should be,' said Jonathan. 'Prettiness alone

313

ain't going to be enough when you're some gentleman's wife. You'll have to know how to run the household. Come along now.'

'Oh, you wretched thing,' said Annabelle, but Jonathan took her by the hand and she perforce went with him.

Caroline took Captain Burnside to the splendid library. He looked around in silence.

'I am sorry if Great Wivenden does not impress you,' she said.

'I can't recall saying so,' murmured the Captain.

'Your silence, sir, is quite sufficient.'

'My silence, marm, is a homage. What can be said about beauty and splendour that can't be better expressed by reverential silence?'

'Fiddlesticks,' said Caroline.

'Assure you, marm—'

'If, sir, you still persist in calling me marm, I shall have Mr Forbes and two gardeners lock you in the estate stocks and throw bad eggs at you. I shall throw some myself. I am Caroline, and you shall call me so. What must my sister think that you don't?'

'Faith, I ain't supposing Annabelle gives it any thought.'

'Oh, yes, Annabelle . . .' Caroline took her bonnet off and let the light fire her hair. 'See what you have done for her. She rarely mentions Cumberland now. I declare myself entirely satisfied with your accomplishment, and the moment we return to London you shall be paid all you have earned.'

Captain Burnside grimaced. 'It ain't a pressing matter,' he said.

'It must be very pressing to a penniless man,' said Caroline firmly, watching him as he inspected the spines of several weighty-looking tomes. She moved closer to him. 'Are you distressingly penniless?'

'Marm—'

'Do you wish me to strike you, sir?'

'Caroline—'

'There, that did not hurt, did it? You should not be so proud.'

314

'It ain't pride,' said the Captain, keeping his eyes off her, 'it's principles.'

'I won't allow them,' said Caroline.

'Them?'

'Principles. Not your kind. They are a ridiculous nonsense.'

'No, they ain't, they're necessary,' said the Captain, examining titles, his top hat in his hand. He found it better not to look at her.

'I should hope, sir, that our friendship is not to suffer the continual pinpricks of your tendency always to argue with me.'

'God forgive me if I ever do. Egad, it ain't the thing at all, arguing with a patron. It's a principle of mine not to, nor to be familiar.'

'Why, you deplorable villain,' said Caroline, 'you have subjected me to a hundred familiarities.'

Captain Burnside coughed. 'Only, you might say, in the exercise of my accepted role,' he said. 'Heaven forbid, Your Ladyship, that I should ever, in normal and conventional circumstances, offend you with even the smallest familiarities.'

Delight danced in her green eyes. Oh, was there any more adorable man? All his sins were insignificant compared with Clarence's heinous aberrations. They were all forgivable. Oh, that he might turn over a new leaf and give up all scheming and philandering.

'I forgive you your absurd principles,' she said. 'I am a sweet-natured woman, as you have no doubt noticed. In my sweetness, and in my gratitude for what you have done, I am utterly determined to help you, despite yourself.'

'Oh, ye angels,' sighed the Captain.

'What was that, sir?'

'Ah, a passing comment of no significance.'

'Caroline.'

'A passing comment of no significance, Caroline,' he said, and her eyes swam with laughter and love.

'There, we have come to sincere friendship, though I

315

fear it may still be some time before I can cure you of your provoking moments. Tell me truthfully, do you like Great Wivenden?'

'One can't merely *like* such an estate, one can only stand in silence and worship,' observed the Captain, who had still not taken his eyes off the library shelves.

'Worship?' enquired Caroline.

'I've a romantic nature, Your Ladyship . . .'

'Romantic? Can it be true of a deceiver of innocents?'

'Oh, I am touched and affected by beauty, Caroline.'

'Well, I declare,' said Caroline, vastly amused.

'Merely to like is to be a Philistine. What man owning any kind of discrimination could merely like the magnificent Alps, the English Lakes, a purple sunset or a beautiful woman?'

'I have never heard of any man worshipping a purple sunset,' said Caroline. 'A beautiful woman, yes, he might worship her. How many have you worshipped recently?'

'Recently,' he said, 'I've had pressing business to attend to.'

'Yes, mostly my business. And thank you, Captain Burnside, for attending to it so efficiently. But that, of course, is the last of any such business. I am glad you agree on that.'

'I don't recall—'

'Please don't interrupt, or I shall lose my way. Now, you have formally met my steward, Mr John Forbes. He is one of England's sturdiest and finest yeomen, and I am sure you cannot help but like him. That will make things very pleasant for you, liking him, and I am convinced your many talents will stand you in good stead as his assistant.'

'Oh, the Lord Harry,' sighed Captain Burnside, 'and have you also determined which of your rosy-cheeked dairymaids I'm to marry?'

'Marry? A dairymaid? Don't be absurd. Really, whatever put such a foolish idea into your mind?' Caroline, wholly aware of his refusal to look at her, or even glance at her, felt the moment could not be more delicious.

When we return to London, please favour me by winding up any little dubious business affairs you may have on hand. I shall be happy to reimburse you for any losses this might incur. You will need funds in order to equip yourself with suitable country clothes. Silk cravats and pearl-buttoned waistcoats won't do at all. I shall be here most of the time to give you advice and encouragement.'

'Oh, ye gods,' said Captain Burnside.

'Was that another comment of no significance, sir?'

'It was a cry for help.'

'But as I have just said, I shall give you help in the way of advice and encouragement. Because I know you have many good points, I shall spare no effort in assisting you to become an honest and industrious citizen of our lovely England. I have decided to take up residence here, at Great Wivenden, and visit my house in London only occasionally. So if becoming honest and industrious presents difficult moments for you at times, I shall be here for you to turn to, and I shall never be less than sympathetic.'

Oh, his expression. It was one of utter helplessness. Caroline hugged her exultation.

'Your Most Gracious Ladyship—'

'Please don't thank me,' she said. 'I could not do less for you when you have done so much for me. Why, with your abilities, I can envisage you stepping into my steward's shoes when he retires in a few years. I vow my faith in you is all it could be.'

'Beg to point out—'

'Also, I have decided I must marry again.' In her exultation, Caroline was sweetly relentless. 'Great Wivenden is a place for a husband, wife and children.'

'I fancy so,' said Captain Burnside, and frowned at a biography of Julius Caesar.

'I am still only twenty-three,' she said, taking off a year or two.

'Ye gods, you married as a tender young girl?'

'I married in mistake, sir.'

'Then I earnestly hope your new choice won't be another mistake,' said the frowning Captain. 'Mr

317

Wingrove springs to my mind as a faultless prospect, though it ain't for me to name names. But if you care for my advice. . . ?'

'I don't care for that advice at all,' said Caroline. 'Mr Wingrove? Really. Do you wish me to live in faultless boredom?'

'Since I own a fair line in boring patter myself, I ain't in any position to cast doubt on Mr Wingrove's ability to be entertaining.'

'Heavens, are my ears deceiving me?' said Caroline. She could have stayed in conversation with her delicious love all day, all week, all month, all year. For ever. 'I declare that what you own, sir, is a singular line in taradiddle.'

'I ain't denying you've a healthy American awareness of English taradiddle,' he said.

'Nor should you,' said Caroline. 'I own I am sharp to spot it, and have had cause to accuse you countless times. I am acutely perceptive of nonsense, piffle and taradiddle, especially yours.'

Looking pained, Captain Burnside said, 'I'm un-acquainted with piffle, madam.'

'Madam yourself, sir. And you're not unacquainted at all. Your piffle is of the highest quality. But no one could say it was boring. And I shall not marry Mr Wingrove. There is Cumberland, of course . . .'

'What?' Captain Burnside looked her in the face at last, his expression glowering. Caroline tingled. 'Mr Wingrove, yes. Cumberland, no.'

'I beg your pardon?'

'Cumberland, never. I ain't going to allow that.'

'Friends should not get above themselves, Captain Burnside. I am not to be told what man I may have and what man I may not.'

'You ain't going to marry Cumberland, except over my dead body, and you can take that as final and unalterable from your most respectful friend.'

'Heavens, such arrogance,' said Caroline, and her most respectful friend looked positively grim. She smiled

318

weetly. 'You must know I shall marry by my own
dictates, sir, not yours.'

'Damn all my patience if I don't end up putting you
over my knees.'

Her eyes locked with his. Heavens, he meant it.

'Attempt it, sir, and I will scratch your eyes out,' said
Caroline, tingling with rapture at the sparks that were
flying.

He sighed. 'Then I beg you'll dismiss Cumberland from
your list,' he said.

'Ridiculous man, do you think I would ever seriously
consider Cumberland? I have told you I never would. I
shall choose an adorable husband, one who can make me
laugh, tease me into tantrums and love me for myself.'

Captain Burnside quizzed her searchingly. 'Then you
can choose from the whole of London,' he said, 'for I
don't doubt the whole of London loves you for yourself.'

She examined her gloved hands. 'The whole of
London, Captain Burnside?'

'From which I hope you'll choose the best and most
deserving man,' he said.

'The whole of London?' she reiterated.

'Oh, gentlemen and beggars, merchants and princes,'
he said.

'And ruffians and blackguards?'

That visibly startled him. 'They won't offer a worthy
choice,' he said.

'But you will allow me to make up my own mind?' she
said.

'No, not if it points you at the wrong man. I admire you
too much, marm, to let you—'

'Caroline. Must I keep reminding you?'

'Damn it, I can't forsake all my principles.'

'I thought, sir, we had already dismissed your principles
as fiddlesticks.'

Downstairs, in the main kitchen, Jonathan examined a
long copper cooking pot. 'That, Miss Howard, is for
steaming a fish, a fine salmon, say.'

319

'How boring,' said Annabelle.

'Now, now,' said Jonathan amiably, 'food ain't boring, nor are the ways of cooking it.'

'Oh, tush,' said Annabelle.

'It ain't wise for a young lady to come ignorant to marriage,' said Jonathan, his cheerfulness undaunted by all rebuffs.

'Precocious and detestable beast, do you think I wish to marry a kitchen?' said Annabelle. 'Why are you so interested?'

'I like food,' said Jonathan, 'don't you?'

'I do not gobble,' said Annabelle, fidgeting.

'Or wine?'

'Nor do I guzzle,' said Annabelle.

Jonathan laughed. From the other side of the kitchen, Mrs Hetty Simmons, the well-upholstered cook, smiled at the young couple. Miss Annabelle had found herself a very amiable gentleman, although she was playing him up a bit. Usually, whenever she appeared at Great Wivenden, she was sweetly engaging. Such a pity she and Lady Caroline did not come more often. Most of the time one was only cooking for the permanent staff. Lady Caroline was an exceptionally gracious lady, even if she was American. She had more style than some English duchesses.

'Do you know what that is?' asked Jonathan.

Annabelle regarded a peculiar-looking machine with the mystification of a young lady who had rarely entered a kitchen. 'Oh, do, I pray, inform my ignorance,' she said.

'Well, in the first place, it's a singularly secretive device,' said Jonathan confidentially. 'It ain't every household that owns one. Come closer. I don't want to shout.'

Annabelle, warm body gowned in muslin, kept her distance. 'Oh, you are so boring,' she said, 'and who cares what the thing is?'

'Who cares? Well, you should, because if I bundled you into it and turned that handle, you'd come out as mincemeat. But keep it to yourself, or terrible things will happen to young ladies pretty enough to be eaten.'

320

Mrs Simmons hastily muffled giggles. Annabelle stared at Jonathan as if he represented all that was pitiful.

'Sickening beast,' she said.

He moved to inspect a long iron spit mounted on the hearth. 'That,' he said, 'would take an ox . . . Hello, hello, where are you, infant?'

'Miss Annabelle slipped out, sir,' said Mrs Simmons, hiding a smile. 'She went through that door.'

'Egad, ain't she a contrary madam?' he said. He found her on the terrace, at the rear of the house, its handsome facade rising to command the countryside, its many windows blinking in the sunlight. 'This won't do,' he said.

'It will do for me,' said Annabelle. 'You may go.'

'No, I ain't supposed to let you go wandering off into trouble, though I don't know who would want to harm a sweet little girl like you.'

'Little girl? Oh,' breathed Annabelle, 'never did I meet such a baboon. I would have you know, you odious specimen, that I am admired and favoured by a gentleman of high and noble majesty, beside whom you are low and common. Go away.'

'Can't be done,' said Jonathan.

'Tiresome creature,' said Annabelle, 'I did not know what misfortune truly meant until you appeared to take charge of me.'

'Bless you, my infant,' said Jonathan, 'tomorrow when we return to London, misfortune will depart at speed from your life, for I shall be gone in a puff of smoke.'

'Choking to death, I hope,' said Annabelle, and Jonathan laughed aloud.

Caroline and Captain Burnside appeared. Caroline looked as if she had found the atmosphere of the library entirely elevating. The Captain looked as if he had found it all of mystifying.

'We are taking dinner and supper here,' said Caroline, 'and also staying the night. We can bring our luggage from the cottage this afternoon. Captain Burnside has been sweetly reasonable.'

'I've known Charles to be fairly reasonable,' said Jonathan, 'I ain't ever known him sweetly so.'

'And I,' declared Annabelle, 'have never known him to be less than sweet in all things. Charles is adorable. You are a baboon.'

'Ain't she delicious?' said Jonathan. 'Beg to suggest, Lady Caroline, we all take a saunter around your gardens before dinner.'

'How lovely,' said Caroline.

'Beg further to suggest Charles gives you his arm,' said Jonathan, 'while I take care of our delicious infant.'

'Oh,' cried Annabelle, 'I vow myself utterly despairing.'

# Chapter Twenty-six

They were back in the London house the following afternoon. Caroline's first thought was for a bath, a warm, soapy and cleansing bath, wherein she could relax and dream while ridding herself of the dust of the journey.

Jonathan bowed himself out, saying goodbye first to Caroline and then to Annabelle. Annabelle expressed a polite and slightly distant farewell.

'Shall you be returning home to Charleston and the family bosom?' he asked.

'I do not think I have ever discussed my home and family with you, Mr Carter,' she said, 'nor whether or not I intend to return.'

'Well, you ain't, no, that's a fact,' said Jonathan.

'And I've no wish to detain you by discussing them now. You surely have many things to hurry to, such as kitchens and pots, brooms and dusters. Goodbye, sir.'

'Ain't you a mettlesome young filly, egad?' said Jonathan, and departed as cheerfully as he had arrived.

The moment Caroline was in her bath, Captain Burnside excused himself to Annabelle, advising her he had a little matter of pressing business to attend to.

'Oh, bother everything,' said Annabelle to herself. With both men gone, she felt unaccountably flat.

H'm,' said His Grace, as distinguished a figure as ever.

'Quite so, sir,' said Captain Burnside, 'a little matter of flying too high. I exaggerated the probable, and took off at the expense of the logical. I overlooked the obvious, which was that Miss Annabelle would refuse to stand up against Cumberland, and that even if she did, Cumberland would reduce her to a total lack of credibility.'

'Myself, I'm not so sure,' said His Grace. 'Cumberland, fearing his back was to the wall, could be as wickedly lethal as Macbeth.'

'Ah, Lady Macbeth?' suggested the Captain.

'Woman deadlier than the male, eh?'

'Except Cumberland's capable of living with his ghosts, sir.'

'True, true. So you've brought Lady Caroline and her sister back. Well, I trust they'll come to no harm. I also trust Lady Caroline don't discover the truth about you. If she does, I'll have you packed off to India in the employ of the East India Company. How does that fancy take you?'

'It don't have irresistible appeal, Your Grace.'

'Well, I'm not quarrelling with you yet, since I'm not too dissatisfied with results.' His Grace permitted himself a slight smile. 'Damned if I wouldn't like to see Cumberland's face when he discovers nothing comes out of tomorrow except an empty silence. There's no chance he knows the four papists are under lock and key?'

'Not unless he's put his nose inside the Tower,' said Captain Burnside.

'And you are sure the Protestant fellow will hold his tongue? While he remains at Aldgate South, there's the risk he'll wag it whenever Erzburger calls on him.'

'He ain't without wits, sir. It wasn't too difficult to guide his mind into taking hold of the strange fact that Cumberland hadn't had the papists apprehended. Acting in my assumed capacity as a guardian of the law—'

'You've a talent, sir, for making yourself sound damned self-important,' said His Grace brusquely.

'So-so, when required,' said the Captain. 'I assured him as a guardian of the law, that I knew no such arrests had been made. On our behalf, he'll hold his tongue. He sees the danger he's in without our help. But to have moved him would have alerted Cumberland, and I believe what you believe, Your Grace, that Cumberland deserves the chagrin and discomfiture of the empty silence.'

'So he does, damn him. By this time tomorrow his plot will have collapsed like an empty sack.' His Grace paused to make a thoughtful study of the Captain. 'So then, you now have no need to continue your association with Lady Caroline. You may pack your bags, sir, and leave tomorrow, counting yourself fortunate she has not found you out.'

Captain Burnside rubbed his chin. 'I thought to ease myself out of her life in more kindly fashion,' he said, 'coming to it gradually.'

'Kinder fashion, sir? What's this, you blackguard, what are you up to with Lady Caroline?'

'I can only tell you she is frankly not in the mood to allow me a sudden departure.'

'Not allow you?' His Grace's countenance darkened. 'What the devil does that mean?'

'Ah – she considers friendship has obligations.'

'Friendship?' His Grace simmered. 'By God, sir, have you permitted yourself the damned liberty of rising above your role?'

'My role, sir, and my accomplishments—'

'Accomplishments?'

'I am quoting Lady Caroline. They have resulted in arousing her excessive gratitude, and a wish for an enduring friendship.'

'Good God,' said His Grace.

'And I repeat, sir, she considers friendship has obligations. Beg to point out she's American and owns the proud blood of the founding fathers of the United States. She don't take friendship lightly.'

'Don't she, by God. Well, sir, you'll take it in no wise. You'll pack your bags and leave tomorrow, first thing. I'll not have you risk the inevitable by lingering. She'll come to have her suspicions, if they ain't already stirring in her mind now, and you'll come to a confession. I'll not risk having that lead to me. You'll depart, by God, without a single word of confession.'

Captain Burnside looked as if self-dislike had come to plague him. 'I ain't precisely happy about it,' he said, 'but

325

at least, while she's still unaware she's been deceived, I'll escape without having her take my head off.'

'Be in no doubt, Lady Caroline would not forgive either of us,' said His Grace, frowning. 'This evening, by the way, you and your atrocious friend Carter will see to it that a sergeant and a corporal are placed with Maguire to ensure his safety, for the first thing Cumberland will do, when he finds nothing has come out of Maguire's information, will be to send an executioner to Aldgate South. Oh, and put the fear of death into the man who's watching Maguire.'

Caroline, restless, was standing at the drawing room window that gave a view of the street. She conceded her feeling of upset might be unreasonable. She really had no right to expect him to ask permission of her whenever he needed to go out. But where had he gone? And on what little business matter? Was he conducting one of his affairs with an innocent young lady who owned a few trinkets? He was always coming and going without ever being specific about what he was up to.

The palms of her hands were hurting. Her fingers were clenched, her nails biting. Dear heaven, her feelings bore not the slightest resemblance to those she had experienced when infatuated with the handsome and amusing Lord Clarence Percival. She understood now the difference between what was the shallowness of infatuation and what was the torment of love. But after Clarence, how could she have come to love a smooth and plausible trickster?

She saw him then, coming along the street, walking slowly, top hat at a slightly rakish angle and a cane in his hand. He nearly always carried a cane. It complemented his debonair facade. But beneath that facade, he was surprisingly strong. As a man who engaged in such disreputable fashion with life, he had no right to be so physically fit.

He turned in at the house.

Caroline was seated when he entered the drawing room

326

a minute or so later. He did not know the giddy turn he gave to her heart when he smiled at her.

'Why, there you are,' he said.

'And here you are,' she said lightly. 'Where have you been?'

'Oh, a little business appointment.' He was as light as she was.

'Really?' Caroline did not want to make the mistake of examining him censoriously, but she could not refrain from asking, 'What would have happened if we had not returned today?'

'I should have disgraced myself,' said the Captain, looking down at her. She was gowned in rich peach, fashion dictating the revealing lines of her décolleté, and the application of comb and brush had burnished her hair. He acknowledged her peerless looks with another smile. 'I should have been considered unreliable. Extremely damaging to a professional's reputation. I did inform Annabelle I had to go out. Where is the dear girl?'

'The dear girl is in her room, resting from her exertions in Sussex and basking in relief now your friend Mr Carter is no longer around to badger her.' Caroline forced a smile. 'I'm afraid that until supper you will have to put up with me. Do you remember we spoke yesterday of how you were to wind up any outstanding business affairs?'

'I think there was a suggestion that honest endeavour should take the place of dubious activities,' he said, standing with his back to the tapestried fire screen and making an abstract survey of the carpet. 'I was deeply touched.'

'You surely were not,' said Caroline, 'you spent much time wriggling. It made no difference, of course. I am uncontradictably determined. May I ask if you have just come back from winding up an affair?'

'Is that a shot fired in the dark, or a question emanating from acute perception?' he asked. 'I was indeed engaged, and still am, Your Ladyship, in—'

'Caroline, you wretch.'

'I am attempting, Caroline, to wind up the affair

327

concerning Cumberland,' he said. 'It's one thing to have taken the edge off Annabelle's infatuation, it's another to put an end to Cumberland's pursuit of both of you. Although Annabelle may no longer wish to be drawn into his bed, nor you—'

'I have never wished that,' protested Caroline.

'But who can tell how Cumberland may contrive seduction of the unwilling? I intend to ensure he leaves both of you permanently alone.'

'You are jesting,' said Caroline. 'We are not going to have another conversation full of absurdities, are we?'

'No, much too dull,' he said.

'But they aren't.' Caroline shook her head at him. 'I am addicted to absurdities. They are very engaging. But were you serious about Cumberland?'

'Indeed I was, and am.' Captain Burnside looked sober. 'After supper, you'll permit me to go out again?'

'Again? You are going to desert us again?'

'Only to continue my campaign to take Cumberland out of your private lives.'

'You can do that? To Cumberland?' Caroline was disbelieving. 'He in his devious majesty will give you best?'

'Oh, a devious professional, Caroline, ain't always less than devious majesty.'

'You surely do hold your accomplishments in—' Caroline checked. 'Wait, you are not going to put yourself in danger, are you? I beg you won't. Cumberland is wickedly omnipotent, and Annabelle and I will quarrel bitterly with you if you intend to run recklessly at him. You are quite up to forcing a duel on him, I know, whether he is the King's son or not. I won't have it, nor permit it.'

'I ain't going to be reckless,' said the Captain, 'I've all the virtues of a coward and never place myself in danger.'

'I do not believe you,' said Caroline. 'The virtues you do have are those that most appeal to Annabelle and me.'

'Saints and angels, what virtues are these?'

'The virtues of never being boring,' said Caroline, wishing he would sit with her, close to her. 'I shall let you go, but please take care. When you return, I shall have a promissory note ready for you. It will be drawn in your favour on my bank, and for the agreed amount in respect of your accomplishments.'

Captain Burnside looked distinctly unhappy. He grimaced. 'Perhaps, under the circumstances, we should agree it was all accomplished in the name of friendship,' he said, 'and it was really very little.'

Caroline stared at him. He had haggled at the beginning, he had bargained, and he had made it very clear he was short of funds. 'You are asking for nothing?'

'I am happy to have been of service, and am glad you agree no payment is necessary. I should now like to have a bath, if I may.'

'Not yet, sir. I do not agree. You have proved an invaluable help and a protective friend. You must not put me down unfairly by refusing to accept what you have earned so well. Your purse is threadbare. You have said so, and I won't have it.'

'Your Ladyship—'

'And I won't have that, either.'

'Caroline, allow me to say that in coming to know you and Annabelle, I've been adequately rewarded for my insignificant endeavours.'

Caroline said softly, 'That is very sweet of you, dear Captain Burnside, but how can I not pay you? It was an honourable contract. Why do you look so uncomfortable about it?'

'I ain't too keen on discussing money with friends,' he said.

'Very well, I shall say no more. I shall simply pay you.'

'I'll take my bath,' he said. 'Ah, I must return to my lodgings tomorrow, of course.'

'Lodgings?' Caroline felt shock. 'That is ridiculous. Annabelle will tell you so at supper. You are our friend and our guest. Why, we need you here, to stand between us and Cumberland. And we – we hold you in affection. How could we not when you have been so caring in our behalf? And you have a little affection for us, don't you?'

He moved to the door, looking as if he found it difficult to respond. Then he said, 'Why, of course.'

His swift exit gave her no time to say more.

After supper, when he had gone out again, Caroline was quiet, Annabelle fidgety.

'Annabelle, what is the matter with you?' asked Caroline eventually.

'I am bored. Nothing is happening.'

'What should be happening, pray?'

'Oh, something, anything,' said Annabelle, getting up and swishing about. 'Charles isn't here, no one is here. It is all dreadfully dull and quiet.'

'Well, there is Lady Repton's reception tomorrow, and your visit to Almanack's with Lily de Vere the day after.'

'But there is nothing this evening, not one gentleman in sight,' sighed Annabelle. 'Oh, I surely do wish for company.'

Caroline wished for Captain Burnside to return, and unscathed. 'I wonder if I should have asked Mr Jonathan Carter to stay on?' she murmured.

'Merciful heaven,' breathed Annabelle, 'that low, trashy creature? I don't wish his kind of company.'

'I think he thought you quite sweet and amusing,' said Caroline.

'He is bumptious, conceited, patronising and boring,' said Annabelle. 'He is also a brute.'

'All that? Dear me. Annabelle, shouldn't you think about returning home? Mamma is anxious you should marry and settle down.'

'Oh, I declare,' said Annabelle fretfully. 'Mamma is just as anxious about you. She said in her last letter she hopes you won't remain a widow for ever. She would just as much like you to return home. Oh, dear, I am sure she has found husbands for both of us.'

'Annabelle, my roots are here now,' said Caroline. 'I will pay a visit home next year, perhaps, in the spring, but only a visit. I have come to love England.'

'But to live alone, Caroline, that is so dull. Don't you wish to marry again?'

Caroline hesitated, then quietly said, 'Yes.'

'Oh.' Annabelle quickened with interest. 'Caroline, are you in love?'

Again Caroline hesitated, then again said, 'Yes.'

'Mr Wingrove?'

'Such an agreeable gentleman,' said Caroline with a faint smile.

Thomas, the footman, knocked and entered. He announced that a young person had called and was asking to see Mr Burnside.

'I think he must mean Captain Burnside,' said Caroline. Young person, she thought. That suggested Thomas did not consider him a gentleman. An ill-visaged gambling associate of Captain Burnside, perhaps? 'He is not a gentleman, Thomas?'

'Not as I can make out, Your Ladyship,' said Thomas. 'It's a young woman.'

Caroline had a sudden, dreadful suspicion the caller was either a trollop or the latest in the long line of Captain Burnside's infatuated young victims. And in some way or another, she had discovered he was living here.

Suppressing the wretchedness of suspicion and jealousy, she said calmly, 'Show her in, Thomas, and I will see if I can help her.'

Thomas brought the young woman in. She was quite prettily gowned, even if the muslin material was cheap, and her equally cheap bonnet sat not unattractively on her brown hair. Her bosom had a buxom fullness, and she was as pretty as Annabelle.

Normally, Betsy's eyes were pert and inquisitive. Now they bore a perceptible look of anxiety. She stared at the elegant splendour of Caroline's drawing room, her mouth agape. 'Oh,' she said, then hastily dropped a curtsey, for the haughty footman had told her to.

'Good evening,' said Caroline, and rose, while Annabelle looked on in curiosity.

'Oh, good evening, madam,' said Betsy, and because Caroline was all of a queenly vision, she dropped another curtsey. She stared around again. 'Oh, be this the Lord

Chancellor's house? Be you the Lady Chancellor, madam?'

'I was advised that you were enquiring after a Mr Burnside, not the Lord Chancellor.' Caroline was distant, having quickly made up her mind that the wench was pretty enough and bosomy enough to be a trollop. 'This is my house.'

'Oh, yes, it be Mr Burnside I wish to see,' said Betsy, and glanced at Annabelle. At once her eyes fluttered into innocence. 'Only to ask his advice, madam.'

'Come with me,' said Caroline, who realised she did not want Annabelle to hear anything that might point to the fact that the Captain was not quite the gentleman her sister thought he was. She took Betsy to a semi-circular room with glass-panelled doors that opened on to a small conservatory, which in turn led to the garden. 'You may sit down.'

'Thank you, ma'am – Your Ladyship—?'

'I am Lady Clarence Percival. Who, pray, are you?' Caroline's tall magnificence intimidated Betsy.

'Oh, I be Betsy Williams, Your Ladyship.'

'What is Mr Burnside to do with you?'

Betsy, seated, looked at her peeping slippers. The situation was not one she favoured. Gentlemen were easy to deal with. Ladies were shrewder, and didn't give a fig for the way a girl could use her eyelashes. Also, they were terrible hard on their own sex. 'Mr Burnside, Your Ladyship?'

'Yes. Does he bed you?'

Betsy lifted her face and showed the genuine blush of shock. She didn't mind kissing, cuddling and petting, but she was keeping herself for a nice gentleman who would set her up. She would willingly give herself to Mr Burnside if he would do so. 'Oh, Your Ladyship, I be a respectable serving girl, and never would let Mr Burnside—'

'Wait.' Caroline remembered. 'Did you say your name was Betsy?'

'Yes, Your Ladyship.'

'And do you have a position on the household staff of His Royal Highness, the Duke of Cumberland?'

'Yes, except His Royal Highness—'

'So you know Captain Burnside very well.'

Betsy's brown eyes opened wide. 'Captain Burnside? He be a captain, Your Ladyship?'

'Yes,' said Caroline, and wondered if she really knew precisely what he was. 'You have been intimate with him?' The accusing question was compulsive.

'Oh, Your Ladyship,' protested Betsy.

'Has he seduced you? Is that why you have called to see him? Answer me.'

Betsy quivered. Oh, what a fierce lady this Ladyship was, green eyes on fire, body vibrating, hands clenched. 'Oh, I daresn't hardly know what I'm at, I'm that upset,' she gasped. 'Your Ladyship, I never would, and there be his wife and all.'

'His wife?' Caroline became rigid. 'His wife?'

'The lady in the other room, is she his wife?' asked Betsy. 'She be so like her, the lady he pointed out to me one day. Only she were on the other side of the street, and I never did see her close.'

Caroline stood in torment. Oh, to have done this to her. To make her love him out of all reason, and then utterly to destroy her. Such anguish was not to be borne. She spoke mechanically. 'No, the lady in the other room is not his wife, but my sister. What is it you wanted of Captain Burnside?'

'Oh, just to see him, thinking he be kind enough to give me advice on a matter, Your Ladyship. I be in a little trouble, and him being as kind as he is, I thought it be best to come and see him.'

Through her pain, Caroline said, 'I will tell him you called.'

'Thank you, Your Ladyship,' said Betsy, wondering at the strange paleness of this beautiful woman. 'Could you ask him to meet me tomorrow morning, if he could? I'll wait outside Collins Coffee House from ten o'clock. It be important, and he'll know I wouldn't say it was if it wasn't.'

'I will give him your message.'

'I be that grateful, Your Ladyship.'

It took Captain Burnside and Jonathan some time to
secure the services of a Guards' sergeant and corporal, to
take them to Aldgate South and into Mr Joseph Maguire's
lodgings under cover of darkness. At this stage, Mr
Maguire was thankful to see them. Jonathan procured a
huge jar of ale from the tavern for the benefit of the
soldiers and the Ulsterman. Captain Burnside took upon
himself the responsibility of putting the fear of God into
the man who lodged opposite, the man who had been
keeping an eye on Mr Maguire. He left him shaken and
palsied. Should Erzburger arrive to check on both men
the following day, it was certain neither would say the
wrong thing, while the soldiers would hide themselves.

It was close to midnight when Captain Burnside arrived
back at Caroline's house. A sleepy Thomas let him in.

Caroline and Annabelle had both retired, but Caroline
had left a sealed note for the Captain.

'Dear Captain Burnside,

'Your friend Miss Betsy Williams called, saying it was
important for you to meet her outside Collins Coffee
House tomorrow morning. She will be there from ten
o'clock onwards. She advised me, while she was here, that
you had a wife. I understand now why you were never in a
position to marry one of your middle-class young ladies.

'As you once said, when all was over and done, you
would prefer to go your own way. I cannot think now why
you should not, and as I am sure you would not favour a
tedious goodbye any more than I would, perhaps you
would be so kind as to leave before I am up. I shall not
rise before nine. I write my goodbye now, and enclose the
remittance that is a settlement of what I owe you. C.P.'

Captain Burnside read the note twice, and a deep sigh
escaped him. Then he made use of a quill and paper at the
desk in Caroline's library, where they had first met, and
where her peerless looks had created for him an unequalled image of beauty and pride.

# Chapter Twenty-seven

Helene did not wake Her Ladyship until nine-thirty, as requested. Caroline, actually, was already awake. And there were faint but perceptible shadows around her eyes, as if she had not enjoyed too much sleep. Helene expressed concern.

'I am quite all right, Helene, thank you.' Caroline hesitated a while before asking if Captain Burnside had left.

'Yes, milady. Thomas said he left last night. He addressed a letter to you. There's also another one, by delivery.' Helene handed both letters to Caroline, who sat up and spoke casually.

'Helene, would you bring me some tea, please?'

She tore open Captain Burnside's letter the moment Helene had gone.

'My dear Lady Caroline,

'Your note has been read. I quite understand, and shall depart as soon as I have finished this letter and packed my bags. It's to my regret that I feel I have hurt you in some way. I am not the most perfect of men, but of all things affecting my life, the one I would have most wished to avoid would have been that of causing you any hurt whatsoever. Sincerely, I beg your forgiveness.

'I am afraid I gave Betsy the impression I was married in order to convince her I was too faithful a husband to set her up in a stylish love nest. But she has truly been invaluable as an accomplice respecting a certain majestic gentleman, and I would consider myself even less than I am if I failed her in a moment of trouble, for I suspect she is in trouble. Accordingly, I will meet her as she requests.

335

'Permit me to ask you to remember me to Annabelle, for I hold her in affection and wish her well. In saying goodbye to you, I do so in the conviction that I have had the pleasure and privilege of serving a lady entirely gracious and exceptionally endearing, of whom America can be proud. The days have been momentous. I would not have changed them for any others. Forgive me that I cannot accept the promissory note. It is impossible to accept payment for what has been a privilege.

'I am, most sincerely, Charles Burnside.'

Tears came to mortify and scald her. She turned and buried her face in the pillows, her hand crushing the letter.

Oh, what had she done? Her note to him, so cold and unfeeling, and so ungrateful. What must he think of her? What did it matter that he had the faults she most disliked in a man? He had countless good points, and of all things was a joy to be with and to talk to. How could a man who had contrived so well in her behalf be given in the end only a cold, bitter note of dismissal? And he had not taken the bank draft, he had refused all payment. Oh, dear heaven, what had she done?

But there was still some pride left, and when Helene came in with the tea Her Ladyship was sitting up, opening the second letter, head bent over it.

'Thank you, Helene. I shan't require breakfast.'

'Milady—'

'No breakfast, please. Is Miss Annabelle taking hers in her room?'

'No. She was up early, and Thomas is serving hers now, downstairs.'

'I see.' Caroline cleared her eyes and scanned the second letter. It was from her father-in-law, the Duke of Avonhurst, but in its brevity was hardly a letter at all.

'My dearest Daughter,

'I regret I have no further information to give you on Burnside, and recommend you have nothing more to do with him. Dismiss the blackguard if he has served his purpose.

336

'My fondest love. A.'

It was not good enough. It hid something. But what? That Captain Burnside was even worse than a blackguard? Had he committed an act so godless that he was liable, if caught, to be hanged? If so, she would save him and reform him. She could save him by persuading him to go to South Carolina with her. There he would be far removed from Tyburn Tree, and there she would reform him. He had done so much for her. He had done even more, by not having a wife.

First, she must call on her father-in-law, and beg from him the full extent of Captain Burnside's sins and omissions, and where his lodgings were.

Annabelle spread another finger of toast with marmalade. Introduced to English marmalade on arrival at her sister's house, she had acquired a passion for it.

'Miss Annabelle?' Thomas appeared. In his arms was a magnificent bouquet of long-stemmed red roses.

'Thomas? Mercy, how beautiful. Who are they for?'

'I was asked, Miss Annabelle, to present them to you.'

'I am overcome,' said Annabelle, eyes alight. 'Who has sent them? Is there a card?'

She received the bouquet in its open white box. She could see no card.

'The gentleman, Miss Annabelle, asked me to say as he would follow the bouquet in.'

'I follow at speed,' said Jonathan, entering the breakfast room, which was bright with morning light. 'Good morning, Miss Howard. Why, that looks good. I've a weakness for toast – and do I see marmalade? Thank you, Thomas, I'll help myself.'

'Very good, sir,' said the footman, and departed gravely, leaving Annabelle in round-eyed, tongue-tied speechlessness at the cheerful effrontery of the visitor, who was all of unwelcome. He sat down at the table with her. His buff-coloured coat was trim, his cravat neat, his hair formally brushed. But his devil-may-care jauntiness was no different. He helped himself to toast and peered into the marmalade pot.

337

'Bless us, dear girl, you ain't eaten it all, have you?' he enquired.

Annabelle came to, laying the bouquet aside. 'Well, I declare,' she said. 'What do you mean, you audacious scallywag, by coming here and inviting yourself to breakfast?'

'Important business,' said Jonathan. 'Thought I ought to let the roses precede me. Young ladies should be sweetened first.'

'I don't wish to be sweetened by you, sir,' said Annabelle forthrightly. 'What is your business? Is it with my sister?'

'Lady Caroline? Egad, no.' Jonathan spooned marmalade on to his toast. 'I fancy it's the encouraging hand of sweet fate that has enabled me to catch you alone.'

'It is not sweet to me, it's a painful start to my day.'

'Well, I ain't going to beat about the bush,' said Jonathan, 'so I put it to you here and now, Miss Howard. Would you allow me the pleasure of becoming a suitor?'

'A suitor?' Annabelle could not believe her ears. 'A suitor?'

'Marriage being the objective, don't you see. I'll be frank, dear girl. I ain't met a prettier or more mettlesome young lady than you.'

'Well!' gasped Annabelle. 'Such outrageous nerve. You are actually daring to propose?'

'Giving it thought,' said Jonathan. He sampled the toast and marmalade. 'Delicious. So, in fact, are you, and I ain't going to quarrel with your tendency to bite my head off. You look good enough to eat when your dander's up.'

'Why, you bumptious beast,' said Annabelle, 'I wouldn't marry you if you were the last man on earth.'

'Positive?' said Jonathan.

'Utterly,' said Annabelle.

'Ah,' said Jonathan, and eyed her with a rueful smile. 'Well, I ain't surprised. I thought it might come to an uncompromising negative. I ain't the best catch in the world.' He rose to his feet. 'Beg to reassure you I ain't going to pester you. I don't favour harassing a young lady after she's administered a positive no.' His smile was more rueful. Annabelle, looking up at him, felt oddly discomfited. 'Bid you good morning, Miss Howard, and long may you adorn life.'

He walked to the door.

Impulsively, and quite without making sense to herself, Annabelle called to him. 'Come back!' He turned, shaking his head. 'Come back!' He came back. Annabelle searched for sense. 'You haven't finished your toast.'

He smiled and shook his head again. Annabelle, in wonder, felt she knew then why yesterday evening had been so dull.

'No matter,' said Jonathan, 'toast don't signify now. Fare thee well, sweet girl.' He bent, he kissed her goodbye, on the mouth. It was a light kiss, but it lingered a spell. Breathless, Annabelle fell in love.

'Oh,' she said faintly, and took a deep breath. 'You kissed me,' she said.

'Sorry,' said Jonathan, 'couldn't help myself. Had to kiss you just once.'

'I was afraid you wouldn't,' said Annabelle, and turned pink.

'Eh?'

'It was very ungentlemanly of you, sir, to take such advantage of me.'

'Eh?' said Jonathan again, and eyed her suspiciously. Her lashes fell demurely, hiding her blue eyes. 'You're confusing me,' he said. 'Now I ain't noted for kissing every girl I meet . . .'

'I should hope not,' said Annabelle. 'I am simply surprised you can kiss so sweetly. Heigh-ho, how perplexing it is not to know if you really are an unmannerly ruffian. Are you?'

'Not always,' smiled Jonathan. 'Can I take it I ain't precisely out in the cold, after all?'

'Well, perhaps you might have the makings of a fairly acceptable gentleman,' said Annabelle, feeling a little giddy. 'Perhaps it isn't your fault that you still have some way to go. Perhaps you were brought up by a ruffianly father and unsympathetic mother. Who are your parents, and what are they like?'

'I think I'd better go and see them and talk to them about you. Under the circumstances, I think I'd better arrange for you to meet them and let you find out for yourself what they're like. I'll dash off in a moment.'

'Jonathan, under what circumstances?' asked Annabelle, giddier.

'These, Annabelle,' said Jonathan, and kissed her again, warmly and lovingly. The images of Cumberland and dark, towering majesty slipped for good from her mind.


'Now, Betsy, what ails you?' asked Captain Burnside in a private room of the coffee house. Betsy was gulping coffee agitatedly, and disregarding the confectionery.

'Oh, sir, that were a terrible proud lady I saw last night at your house – no, it were her house, she said.'

'Never mind whose house it was,' said Captain Burnside, his mood very sober. 'Or how proud the lady was.'

'There were another lady there too, and she made me quake a mite, for I thought her your wife.'

'Never mind her, either. Betsy, you were to let me into the Duke's house this morning.'

'Oh, I know.' Betsy sighed in her worry. 'That were one reason why I had to see you, for I can't let you in now. Oh, lor', you'll not be hard on me for that, will you, sir?'

'Well, I'd have been there, as arranged, but only to tell you it was no longer necessary. His Royal Highness is presently as safe as you might wish him to be.'

'I don't wish him,' said Betsy. 'There's been a terrible rumpus, and they've thrown me out, along with others. The Duke's soldier staff, they said there were damnable rogues and vagabonds serving His Highness, that someone's been at his private desk and suchlike, that someone's pocketed a letter. Oh, them high-tailed soldier officers, giving some of us such a going-over, sir, and

340

twisting my arm near to pulling it off. And saying I be too often where I shouldn't be in the house, and light-fingered as well, which made me kick one of them. Sir, I'd hardly know how to pray in church if I were given to lifting and pocketing and nipping.'

'Betsy, you kicked one of His Highness's staff officers?' said the Captain.

'He were at me something wicked – oh, the Lord Chancellor won't top poor Betsy just for a kick, will he, sir? You'll speak up for me, won't you? I never did know a kinder gentleman, and it's not just them guineas you give me.'

'No, you shan't be topped, Betsy. But you've been dismissed, is that it?'

'And not even given wages, sir, nor a character writing,' said Betsy, moist-eyed and woebegone. 'I be in black disgrace, and daresn't hardly know how I can get another position, or how I can add little bits to my savings. I daresn't write and tell my parents I been dismissed from the Duke's household, they've been that proud of me. I be the rosy apple of my father's eye, and he'll be like to fall down and die if he hears they threw me out without a character writing. And I don't have lodgings, sir. I stayed with Mr Pringle's kind sister last night, but she didn't dare let Mr Pringle know.'

'Dry your eyes, puss,' said Captain Burnside, 'you shall have lodgings at least, and a promise to see what can be done about another position. It won't do to have you out of work in London, and trying to find yourself a gentleman, for I fancy you might mistake a smiling and helpful face for one of gentlemanly kindness, and it won't be kind at all.'

'Oh, you'll help me, sir?' asked Betsy, eyes swimming with hope.

'Of course, puss.'

'Sir, you be a true gentleman, even if you didn't tell me you were a captain. I hardly knows when I cared more for anyone.' Betsy regarded him with warm, sentimental affection, then with a little worry. 'Sir, be there anything wrong?'

341

'Wrong?' he asked.

'You look sad, sir, and I never saw you sad before.'

'Sometimes, Betsy, one day isn't quite as good as another.'

'Well, if loving be . . .' Betsy found it difficult for once to be flirtatious, to offer consoling kisses and cuddles. 'Sir, it's just that you be a very special gentleman.'

Captain Burnside regarded her swimming eyes. For all her acquisitiveness, she had proved a loyal partner, her word as good as her bond. 'And you, Betsy,' he said, 'shall become a very special girl with a very special appeal to some young man who is as yet unknown, but exists somewhere. You ain't going to be set up by any sensuous gentleman. Come, let's find lodgings for you.'

## Chapter Twenty-eight

The Duke of Avonhurst received his American daughter-in-law in his study. He had no option, for having been admitted and told where he was, Caroline swept there at once.

Aged sixty, Avonhurst had the distinguishable air of a born aristocrat, although he considered it more of a privilege to have simply been born to God's world than to be born the first son of a duke. He was tall, and there was silver in his hair. For all that, he had the physical fitness of an active and temperate man. His affection for his daughter-in-law was constant and unchangeable, and his most melancholy regret was that his wastrel son Clarence had given her neither children nor happiness.

'Caroline? My dear young lady.' He rose, came round from his desk, took her hand and kissed her on the cheek.

'I am very glad, father-in-law, that I am always your dear young lady, for I sometimes feel the years are running away with me.' Caroline might have exchanged a variety of affectionate greetings with him, but such was her obsession with one matter alone that she came at once to it. 'Yet how unkind you were to send Captain Burnside to me.'

'Unkind?' The Duke's glance, usually steadfast, wavered a little, and he fingered his white lawn cravat. 'He hasn't been up to my recommendation?'

'More than you suggested he might, more than I expected he would, and more than he himself boasted he would.'

'Even so, he's been a disappointment to you?' enquired the Duke.

'Grievously, father-in-law, in one singular respect,' said Caroline, her calmness a deceptive mask. But if she could confide her feelings to anyone, it was to the understanding Duke of Avonhurst, always a comforting father figure. 'It was unkind of you, was it not, to send me a man so attractive to women that I was bound to fall in love with him?'

His brows drew together. 'I might have thought a weak woman would come to hold him in foolish affection,' he said, 'but not you, Caroline.'

'Foolish affection?' Caroline's little laugh was hardly mirthful.

'Infatuation?' ventured the Duke.

'You are thinking of what I felt for Clarence?' Caroline shook her head and seated herself. 'No, this is nothing like that. This is far, far worse, and makes love a desperate thing. And you are to blame, father-in-law, for sending him to me.'

'Am I so?' The Duke's frown advanced.

'Oh, that was not said in reproach, only in wryness. Father-in-law, what is this terrible thing called love? You are wise in your maturity, and in the service you have given to your Government and its people. Your wife, the Duchess, is still handsome and much to be admired. Do you in your wisdom and in the endearing wife you have, know what love is? Is one in love when one cannot sleep and can scarcely eat? Does love give one no peace, only heartache?'

The Duke sighed. 'Only when it is not returned,' he said.

'And if returned, what then? I have known infatuation, but not love, which is new to me, even at almost twenty-five. So if it is returned, what then?'

'Caroline, it is, when returned, the sweetest of God's gifts to a man and a woman.'

Caroline, eyes dark, smiled wryly. 'I vow, then, that I am deprived of this gift, for Charles Burnside shows not even affection for me. I suffered humiliation as Clarence's wife, as you know. You were sad for me and in shame for your son. But that humiliation cannot compare with the dreadful, wounding misery of feeling myself unloved by a man I cannot live without.'

'I am immeasurably distressed,' said the Duke, moved beyond anything by the calm way in which she was offering up her very soul for inspection. 'You have truly come to find life unbearable without this damned fellow?'

'Father-in-law, I shall quarrel with you if you call him a damned fellow.'

'Damn him, all the same,' said His Grace.

'You are not to say that. My life is unbearable, because I *am* without him. He has gone. It is in that way that he has been a grievous disappointment.' Caroline bit her lip. 'Oh, why did he not stay to talk to me? You would never believe how many conversations we have had, and all such a joy to me. I can't, I won't, let him disappear or do nothing about helping him. A man will fight for what he wants, and I shall fight fiercely for what I want. Father-in-law, am I not a woman a man could love? Clarence did not love me. He saw me only as a new toy, because I had come young and untouched from America. And Charles Burnside has walked away from me.' Caroline could not bring herself to say that she herself had asked him to quit her life.

'He may not have walked away out of indifference,' said the Duke.

'Then could it have been because he knows himself for what he is, a wastrel? And perhaps worse? I am terrified there is something worse. I am sure you would know. So tell me, please, even if the truth is like to shatter me. I beg your frankness, and ask you to take no heed of my sensibilities, but to tell me if he has been guilty of anything which, if caught, would put him in danger of being hanged.'

'Hanged?' The Duke looked aghast. 'My dearest Caroline, never think I'd send you a man with a noose hovering over his head.'

Caroline breathed in relief. 'Then he is merely faulty, but no more than many men? He is not a murderer or arsonist or highwayman?'

'No, but he's a damned scoundrel for laying his

345

impertinent hands on my daughter-in-law, for feeding you sweet nothings, I don't doubt, for giving you sly smiles that have caressed you . . .'

'Father-in-law, I declare you out of order,' said Caroline. 'He has done no such things. He has never laid such hands on me or caressed me in any way. That has been no consolation to me. He has been so much the polite gentleman and put me into such perverse moods that I could have wished him to – to . . .'

'Caroline?'

'No,' she breathed, 'I cannot express my shamelessness to you. But how ruinous to a woman's self-respect is the kind of love that makes her want a certain man to be no gentleman at all. You must never think Captain Burnside behaved towards me in any way that would have offended you. He has been of all things protective towards Annabelle and me. He and a friend of his, Mr Jonathan Carter, were determined that Cumberland in his malice should not harm us.'

'Ah, yes, Mr Jonathan Carter, the irreverent son of General Sir Laurence Carter,' murmured the Duke.

'Father-in-law?' said Caroline in curiosity. 'How did you come to know of Mr Carter? And do you say he's the son of a Sir Laurence Carter? Annabelle will burn at the things she said to him. Why, he was with her when I left to come to see you, but I was in too much of a hurry to speak to him. Father-in-law, what is going on?'

'Ah, yes,' said the Duke ambiguously, and at once reminded Caroline of how evasive Captain Burnside was whenever faced with awkward questions. 'Ah, Burnside reported to me when his – ah – work for you had come to an end. I instructed him to, for I naturally wished to know if he had come up to expectations.'

'Which he had,' said Caroline, eyeing her father-in-law with some curiosity still lingering, 'and proved himself to have many good points. Truly, he has much to commend him. I must find him. If I had stopped to think instead of letting my mind run so wildly, I could have found him this morning by being at Collins Coffee House at ten o'clock.

Father-in-law, do you know where his lodgings are? If he lives in some cheap, unsalubrious quarter of London, be in no fear for me, since I will take Sammy and other servants with me, and shan't therefore lack protection. I must and will find Charles, for I mean to remove him from London, from the temptations he falls prey to, and take him to Great Wivenden, where I shall insist he learns how to plough a hard but straight furrow.'

'Take him?' asked the Duke in slight shock.

'My servants shall persuade him,' said Caroline firmly. 'I should not want to fail him through lack of purpose and audacity, and I would fail him if I left him to his weaknesses.'

'I pray you aren't serious,' said His Grace, alarmed.

'I have never been more serious. Heaven knows how he will end up unless I am brave enough to reform him. Unhappily, he has an exceptional talent for seducing middle-class girls into parting with what little wealth they have in the way of jewellery. One day an aggrieved father may catch up with him and force him to marry the deceived girl. He must be saved from such a dreadful consequence as that.'

'Caroline, I cannot approve your intentions,' said the Duke earnestly. 'It is not the kind of thing a lady should do. It would shock the whole of London.'

'I do not propose to inform the whole of London.'

The Duke, thoroughly alarmed, said, 'You cannot use your servants to remove from London a man who has his obligations and responsibilities.'

Caroline, surprised by her father-in-law's alarm, which was not at all the same as disapproval, said, 'Obligations and responsibilities? Do you know more of Captain Burnside's activities than you have told me? Is it not true that in his wretched indulgence of his weaknesses he is only irresponsible?'

'Ah – not quite,' said the Duke, and Caroline suddenly found him suspect.

'I vow it very odd,' she said, 'that an adventurer like Captain Burnside can claim close friendship with a man whom you say is the son of a baronet. Would a gentleman of Mr Carter's background not only become extremely friendly with a professional trickster, but also obey his orders? When I first met Jonathan, I thought him no less dubious than Captain Burnside. Am I wrong? Is he an undeniable gentleman? Father-in-law, are there things you should have told me, but have not? I declare myself uneasy with sudden suspicions.'

His Grace sighed in resignation. 'Some men don't hold with thinking women, feeling they already own acute perception and intuition,' he said. 'It ain't in the interests of most men to have women thoughtfully reflecting on the faults of all men, for those faults are legion. I see now that if I don't give you the truth, you'll come to it in time. In telling you precisely why I sent Captain Burnside to you, I pray it won't destroy your regard for me, nor cause you to give him furious death—' The Duke allowed himself a slight smile. 'For that is what he fears you will do. This, my dear daughter-in-law, is the way of it.' And he proceeded to give Caroline the facts of the matter.

Captain Burnside had originally been sent to her by Avonhurst in order to relate to that which concerned the machinations of Cumberland, with whom she was in contention. Yet she was also inside his circle of intimates, mainly because he had designs on her. Captain Burnside was to enter that circle, to watch Cumberland and to study him. The Captain had lately been in troublesome Ireland, where he had come upon rumours concerning a possible assassination plot. This was at once the subject of investigation in London, particularly when the rumours took a curious turn. Cumberland, it was said, had become aware of the plot, and intense curiosity was aroused by the fact that he had not made his awareness known. Who could not have been intrigued when Cumberland himself was threatened? The assassination attempt was to be aimed at him and his eldest brother, the Prince of Wales, heir to the throne. But Cumberland kept his silence. Nor did he demand protection for himself and Wales.

Captain Burnside's task was to breach Cumberland's

citadel as discreetly as he could, and to look for anything that might point to the reason for the Duke's silence. There was, of course, a very real danger of being discovered in the act. In this event, he was to declare his clandestine entry was motivated by a wish to recover a letter sent to Cumberland by a certain unhappy lady, a letter that any true prince or gentleman would have returned on request, not used to make the lady unhappier. The Captain would also declare he was acting for the lady's closest friend, Lady Clarence Percival, who could not have denied it. He had thought, indeed, to gain entrance to Cumberland's residence with her help, since it was known Cumberland was in love with her and that she had been entertained by him, with other guests. Captain Burnside had thought, in fact, to ask her to contrive at the unfastening of a suitable window, and to leave it unfastened, so that he might enter after she had gone.

'A suitable window?' Caroline, already icy, interrupted. 'Do you mean a window in Cumberland's bedroom?'

'Not so, not so,' said her father-in-law. 'Any upstairs window . . .'

'But that was what Captain Burnside had in mind, did he not? Cumberland's bedroom? How dared he think or assume or suggest I was ever disposed so?' Caroline was coldly bitter. 'You may continue, father-in-law.'

Caroline was meant to assume this ploy was solely for the purpose of gaining access to the letter, but it was also to give Captain Burnside an opportunity to examine Cumberland's appointments' diary for July. However, during the course of conversation with her, the Captain realised that if she had ever engaged in meetings of an encouraging kind with Cumberland, she no longer did so.

'I am grateful for that conclusion,' said Caroline fiercely.

'Alas, this is not a happy confession,' said His Grace, and went on. Her relationship with Cumberland at that time was wholly concerned with how that letter might be retrieved and how to divert Cumberland from his obvious intention to seduce Annabelle. So Captain Burnside looked elsewhere for the help he required, and took up an acquaintanceship with a minor member of Cumberland's civilian staff, a servant girl called Betsy. Not only was she able to let Burnside into the house, but she reduced the danger of discovery, for she knew who was in, who was out, and how to get him safely to Cumberland's personal suite and his secretary's room adjacent.

He had the good fortune to find the letter and also to discover a diary entry that was both interesting and mystifying. He left, taking with him food for thought. Subsequently, residing as he was in Lady Caroline's house, he was within easy reach of his helpful confederate, Betsy, and of Cumberland. He continued his investigations in the comfortable guise of an officer and gentleman enjoying extended leave. He was most suitably circumstanced to be attentive to Annabelle, to play his agreed role with her. He found her a charming girl, well worth saving from Cumberland's devilish designs, although he had no reason to believe he could win her over, for his reputation as a ladies' man had no basis to it.

'The basis lay on his tongue,' breathed Caroline, 'which is so forked it could deceive even a Cherokee chief.'

'If you have a mind to cut it out,' said His Grace, 'that will not be less than he expects.' He continued, saying Captain Burnside was only too aware he had conveyed a false picture of himself to Lady Caroline, and had recently been existing in the alarmed state of a man certain she would find him out.

During his excursions and investigations, he acquired information that justified the belief in the existence of the plot. He was led to the assumption that Cumberland was engaged in an adjunctive plot of his own. An Irish Protestant was located. He provided many details of the conspiracy designed to blow Cumberland and the Prince of Wales to pieces. Incredibly, it seemed from a peculiar entry in Cumberland's diary that his other three elder brothers would also become victims. Obviously, of course, Cumberland would place himself out of danger at the right moment, and so survive to become heir to the throne. However, certain steps had been taken, and other steps would also be taken, all to ensure the would-be assassins enjoyed no gain and the Royal family endured no loss. Cumberland's intentions, the devil's own, if true, would be thwarted. His apparent attempt to secure silence from Lady Caroline and Annabelle, because Annabelle had overheard part of a conversation between himself and his secretary, Erzburger, added weight to the suspicions of what he was about. It was perhaps a little in Captain Burnside's favour that Caroline and her sister had emerged safely from a crisis, but he knew his deception of Caroline would be an outrage to her.

'As for my own part,' said Avonhurst, 'it was not the best thing I have done, nor will I seek to excuse myself, save to point out I did not anticipate anything would be of greater consequence to you than the recovery of the letter and the saving of Annabelle's honour. The venture over, I assumed you would be only too happy to see the back of Captain Burnside. I did not think the impudent fellow, who is only the son of a bishop, would so rise above himself as to ingratiate himself with you to the extent that he has.'

'No, he did not ingratiate himself,' said Caroline palely, 'he is not that kind of scoundrel. He is simply worthless.'

'Our heads are on the block, his and mine,' said Avonhurst sombrely, 'and you shall take up the axe and strike at a moment of your own choosing.'

'I do not want your head, father-in-law,' said Caroline, 'or even his.' She felt betrayed. Captain Burnside had stripped her of all pride and robbed her of all self-respect. His every word had been false, his every smile a mockery. He had never once thought of taking her into his confidence, of trusting her with secrets. She must have meant very little to him. From first to last he had made a fool of her. From beginning to end he had treated her as a simpleton. How he must have been laughing at her. He had taken her in with such ease that he no doubt saw her as a naive and credulous idiot. Her visit to his mother –

oh, dear God, what a fool she had made of herself there. And he had let her speak hundreds of stupid words about her willingness to help him become an honest and industrious man. She would not be a true Howard if she did not cast him out of her life for ever.

'Caroline?' said His Grace, perturbed by her silence, by the glitter in her eyes. She came to her feet, and he felt a deep fatherly love for her in the way she held herself, her back straight. She was as much of an aristocrat as any woman he knew.

'In the light of what you have told me, father-in-law,' she said, 'I know I have not suffered at your hands what I have suffered at his. I understand your motives, your need for secrecy, and your immense concern about plans and plots. And there is too much affection between us for me to quarrel with you. But Captain Burnside is a man who lacks all human feelings, and I shall not trouble myself to see him ever again.'

'Caroline, I am distressed beyond words to have you so unhappy, and cannot forgive myself for my part in it.'

'You are forgiven by me,' said Caroline, and gave him her cold cheek to kiss. Then she left.

'Caroline?' Annabelle entered her sister's bedroom. Caroline, standing at her window, averted her face.

'Yes?' she said. She had been riding around London for hours in her carriage, Sammy driving her and wondering what was wrong with her that she would not let him take her home. It was ages before she did, and neither he nor she had had a bite to eat in all that time.

'Caroline, where have you been all day?' asked Annabelle. 'You left in such a hurry.'

'I have been to see Avonhurst, my father-in-law.' Caroline sounded lifeless.

'Oh, yes, such a lovely father-in-law.' Annabelle was too heady to note her sister's lack of interest. 'Caroline, I have such sweet news.'

'Have you? What news, pray?'

'You will never believe it, but I've discovered I'm

suddenly head over heels. Oh, I can scarcely believe it myself.'

'You are in love? Again?'

'Caroline, don't be so unkind, I was never in love with Cumberland,' said Annabelle. 'I am dreadfully set on being proposed to – oh, I think he has already done so in a way.'

Caroline's icy body stiffened, and she turned to look at her sister. 'You are in love with Captain Burnside?' That was the only name in her frozen mind, the only man she could think of. If he could be called a man. 'If so, you are more stupid than I thought.' The ice around her heart tightened its grip at the thought that he had proposed to Annabelle in some oblique way. It caused unbearable pain. 'You shan't marry him, he is even more unsuitable than Cumberland.'

'Why, Caroline, how could you possibly think it is Charles? You know he has eyes for no one but you – oh, is he the one you are in love with? You said you would like to marry again. Is Charles the one?'

'No, he is not!' said Caroline fiercely. 'Who is the man you are talking about?'

'Oh, what a mood you are in,' said Annabelle.

'Who is he?'

'Why, Jonathan,' said Annabelle.

'Jonathan?' Caroline's icy stiffness relaxed a little. 'Mr Carter?'

'Yes,' said Annabelle. 'Caroline, you aren't going to be as fretful and unsympathetic about Jonathan as you were about the Duke, I hope. You will upset me terribly if you are. I confess he may not be comfortably off, but I should think from his dashing style he isn't actually penniless, or without the makings of a gentleman. And he's such fun. I shall die if he neglects to propose formally, but I am sure he will, for when he left this morning it was to see his parents and arrange for me to meet them. Shall you disapprove if his father is only a tradesman or what the English call a country yokel? I should—'

'Miss Annabelle?' Helene looked in. 'A gentleman has called and is asking to see you. Mr Jonathan Carter.'

Annabelle's eyes danced. 'Caroline, oh, do excuse me,' she said.

'There you are,' said Jonathan, as Annabelle, bewitching in flimsy blue organdie, floated into the drawing room.

'Why, it's Mr Carter,' she said. 'Good afternoon, Mr Carter.'

'Oh, that's the way of it now, is it?' said Jonathan. 'I'm out in the cold again? Then good afternoon, Miss Howard.'

'I am not Miss Howard, I'm your love,' protested Annabelle. 'You said so when you left this morning.'

'So I did,' said Jonathan, 'but I ain't having any shilly-shallying.'

'But, Jonathan, I want to be your love.'

'Bless you, my angel,' said Jonathan, and pressed a chaste kiss on her forehead. Annabelle cast a demure glance. 'I ain't sure I won't finish up eating you.'

She laughed and she sparkled. 'Jonathan, you are such sweet fun,' she said.

'Egad, and ain't you a sweet shape?' said Jonathan, eyeing her figure with appreciation.

She blushed in pleasure. She did not feel, as she had with Cumberland, the shivers and palpitations that related as much to fright as excitement. She felt warmly and lovingly responsive. Cumberland's dark eye had regarded her rounded prettiness wickedly. Jonathan regarded it with the frank, healthy pleasure of a frank, healthy young man. However, a certain amount of decorum was called for.

'Jonathan, do turn your glance, I beg, or I shall go pink all over.'

'All over?' he said. 'Well, I'll not ask you to prove it here and now. We're not married yet.'

'And I shan't prove it even then, you disgraceful sauciness – oh, Jonathan, am I to receive a formal proposal? I do declare it's only fair, and in return I shall give it fair consideration.'

'You're a teasing witch,' said Jonathan.

'Witch? But I am divinely fresh and innocent.'

'Agreed,' said Jonathan, 'though your innocence don't prevent you running rings round me. Well, I shall have my own back and come to the sweetness of unlacing you with bold adventurousness once we're married . . .'

'Oh, you all are a dreadful sauciness! Have you no consideration for my blushes?'

'Not as much as for marrying you, kissing you and loving you,' said Jonathan. 'So will you say yes now or in ten minutes? I ain't able to endure longer than ten minutes.'

'I think you should suffer a little for being so brutal to me at the cottage, don't you?' said Annabelle, giddily happy but eternally feminine. 'You shall endure five minutes of waiting for my answer. There, five minutes, that's not too bad – Jonathan!' She muffled a shriek as he swept her up and deposited her along the *chaise-longue*. He sat on its edge, leaned forward, and kissed her lovingly and decisively on the lips. And he slipped his hand into her bodice. Annabelle became a flurry of kicking legs and cloudy petticoats for a few moments, then collapsed into sweet, yielding bliss, colour suffusing her as his adventurous hand caressed her. Again, there were no fearful palpitations, only a healthy, loving enjoyment of his touch. But her legs strained and stretched, and she blushed vividly, as her pink buds became erect. 'Jonathan, oh, I declare! Don't do that! Oh, mercy me, am I to be seduced before you have pledged yourself a loving husband? And someone will come in – Jonathan!'

He withdrew his hand and sat up. He was laughing in delight. 'Ain't you a dear and delicious girl?' he said. 'Now will you say yes, or shall I ransack you?'

'Oh, I must say yes,' she gasped, 'I cannot risk being ransacked in Caroline's drawing room.'

At which Jonathan kissed her again, tenderly. 'There,' he said, 'never think I don't recognise how sweet you are and how lucky I am.'

'We will have such fun, won't we?' said Annabelle. 'But shall we be desperately poor?'

'Eh?' said Jonathan.

'Oh, I shall still love you, but as you aren't a bang-up, slap-up, fancy gentleman . . .'

'Eh?' said Jonathan again.

'You don't understand the language of persons of the Quality?' said Annabelle. 'Oh, I suppose not.'

'Bang-up, slap-up and fancy is the language of the Quality?' enquired Jonathan, hiding a smile.

'Of course. I am very up with Corinthian terminology. But never mind if you aren't comfortably off. I shall receive a dowry from my father, and you can invest it in the East India Company, which I'm told is a most recommendable way of making a fortune.'

'You'll give me your dowry? You won't.'

'But I want to,' said Annabelle.

'Well, I ain't going to take it,' said Jonathan. 'I fancy we won't starve. Now, I've seen the P.P. and She Who Must Be Obeyed, and am taking you to meet them tomorrow. Put on your best bonnet and I'll call for you at ten-thirty in the morning.'

'What do you mean, "the P.P. and She Who Must Be Obeyed"?' asked Annabelle, reclining in the fashion of a young lady happy to prolong these moments.

'The P.P. is my Paternal Parent, and She Who Must Be Obeyed is my Maternal Parent.'

'Oh, they sound dreadfully formidable. Am I to fear they won't approve of me?'

Jonathan laughed and kissed her yet again. She gave her lips very happily. 'Approve of you? They'll give you Burleigh Court. Well, they'll give it to both of us. It comes to me when I marry.'

Annabelle's eyes opened wide. 'Jonathan, what is Burleigh Court?' she asked.

'A little estate in Sussex, not too far from Great Wivenden. It's one of our family properties, and you'll find the house owns a commendable kitchen.'

Her eyes became huge. 'Jonathan, oh, I declare, you've been keeping things from me,' she said. 'Who is your father?'

'General Sir Laurence Cheviot Carter. Fought your American rebels years ago, and got dished with Lord Cornwallis at Yorktown. He'll dip you in brimstone when he discovers you're American. I fancy you'd better not blow the gaff. I've told him you come from China.'

'Horrid beast.' Annabelle laughed. 'I vow you wicked – you haven't told him any such thing. And I am really very vexed with you that you made me think you were poor. It has been very worrying today, feeling I'd have to exist in rags.'

'I don't recall making you think—'

'Oh, Jonathan!' Annabelle exclaimed in delight. 'Do you realise you're not a common ruffian, after all, but a bang-up, slap-up, fancy gentleman?'

'Oh, so-so,' said Jonathan cheerfully.

# Chapter Twenty-nine

The Prince of Wales was, as Beau Brummell subsequently observed, becoming a fat fellow, and the Dukes of York, Clarence and Kent were all traditionally pear-shaped Hanoverian princes. Cumberland alone had a chest in advance of his stomach, which was a firm and flat terrain, and was apt to make a mistress feel that her belly would never regain its curve.

The Prince of Wales was also becoming pettish. Once handsome, generous and charming, rich food was now making him soft and plump; extravagant debts caused him to tighten his pockets, and flattering sycophancy had spoiled him, leading him to imagine he was the wittiest prince in Christendom.

His brothers bored him. He also bored them. It could not be said that the sons of George the Third were too compatible. Each did what he could to avoid the others socially, restricting contact in the main to State occasions or family conferences. Typically, there was little pleasure or satisfaction to be derived from this conference at Cumberland's town residence, but it had not been easy to say no to him. It was never easy to say no in any manner to Cumberland, whose powerful personality put its limits on brotherly hedging and procrastination.

Wales was fidgeting irritably. In his pale pink coat, yellow breeches, white waistcoat, and high, fussy cravat, he resembled a popinjay when compared with the majestic Cumberland clad in sober hues. Wales had already evinced boredom, and even fatigue, at Cumberland's private meeting with him. The latter had produced a petition from a certain lady in respect of the compromising of her honour by Wales. He had taken the petition in graceless fashion, crumpling it up and thrusting it into his coat pocket. Now, with York, Clarence and Kent also present, he had had to listen to Cumberland's request for family consideration of his potential marriage to a German duchess. As far as Wales was concerned, Cumberland could marry any duchess he liked. But Cumberland enunciated difficulties. There were no difficulties Wales could see, and his other brothers considered their opinions counted for nothing. It would be their kingly father who would say yea or nay.

They were all seated, except Cumberland, who remained on his feet, giving vent to certain exasperations by stalking about. He dominated the atmosphere as he expounded on consequences, good and bad, advantageous or disadvantageous. From time to time his stalking came to a halt before a window. There he seemed in brooding reflection, looking out of the window and directing his gaze downwards. The window overlooked the gravelled area on the west side of the house. Perhaps Cumberland was expecting four men to appear, four men garbed as building workers, and carrying long ladders that would enable them to climb up and inspect the gutters. One man would have a forged paper on his person, a paper giving them the authority to carry out the inspection, and to make good gutters that were faulty. And two would have bombs secreted in workmen's tin containers, together with tinder boxes to light the fuses. Perhaps it was fatefully important for Cumberland to note their arrival and to take careful heed of the moment when the ladders were erected against the wall of the house. That would be the moment he would have to absent himself. He needed a good reason for doing so. He had one.

Wales paved the way by making a testy comment. 'All this don't signify, Ernest. Ye've no mountains to climb, nor even molehills. Ye're painting pictures of what don't exist. Unless' – Wales put a sly smile on his face – 'unless ye're looking for an excuse to set aside a plain duchess in

359

favour of a ravishing commoner. I'm told she's the coveted American commoner.'

'The devil she is,' said York.

'I ain't denying I do favour her,' said Cumberland, 'nor that she's suitable in all ways.'

'She ain't in the least suitable, if she's a commoner,' said Kent.

'I've quizzed her a time or two,' said Clarence, jovial by nature, 'and swear her bosom at least ain't common.'

'Allow me,' said Cumberland, 'to inform ye all I've details of her family tree.'

'Have ye, b'God,' said York. 'I assume ye're speaking of Lord Percival's widow, Lady Clarence?'

'Ye assume correctly,' said Cumberland, glancing out of the window again.

'I ain't acquainted with the lady's antecedents,' said Wales, with a mincing laugh, 'but I'm acquainted with her magnificence. But she won't do, not for His Majesty.'

'I've papers with details, the details drawn up by Erzburger and authenticated,' said Cumberland.

'Papers? Authenticated?' said Kent, destined to be the father of Victoria. 'Authenticating what, precisely?'

'We've arrived at a point meriting the most serious consideration,' said Cumberland, sound eye fixing Wales in mesmerising fashion. 'Lady Clarence Percival's own family, the Howards, can trace their tree back to William of Orange, and Erzburger has done so.'

''Pon my pitiful soul,' said Wales, 'ye'll be informing us next that Lady Clarence is the rightful Queen of England.'

Cumberland picked up a sheaf of papers from a table and took them to the window. Inside a flood of bright light, he leafed through the papers, his blind, cloudy eye blank, his seeing eye very searching.

'The papers don't seem to be among these,' he said. 'But ye have my word, they exist and the details exist. So I require from all of ye serious consideration of a situation which ain't now unfavourable to a rejection of the proposed alliance.'

'The papers,' said York impatiently.

'I fancy they're in my study,' said Cumberland. 'In a moment or so, I'll fetch them.'

'God in heaven,' said Clarence, wondering if his sardonic brother had a touch of the mental weakness that periodically afflicted their father, 'ye're expecting us to consider how ye might marry Percival's American widow?'

'And why not?' said Cumberland, dark and lowering.

'I ain't considering a damned thing until ye've produced those papers, Ernest,' said Kent mutinously.

'I will,' said Cumberland, 'but first give me a few moments to suggest to ye how I might put my case to our tetchy Majesty, who ain't always able to make an agreeable listener.' He mused. He was at the window again. His brothers fidgeted, Wales in irritable fashion, but Cumberland began to describe how Lady Clarence Percival compared advantageously with the German duchess. She was endowed with wealth, health and beauty, and with a lineage that could not be discounted.

'Orange lineage,' said Wales disdainfully. 'It's a dull thing, and originated in a medieval French farmyard.'

Cumberland removed his gaze from the window to turn a black scowl on his eldest brother, and Wales slumped and muttered. Cumberland was an Orange adherent, a powerful figure in the Order that inspired and dominated the lives of Ulstermen, who sternly kept at bay the popery of the Catholic Irish.

He continued to outline the pros and cons, but it was a pointless exercise if he really was expecting four men to arrive in the guise of building labourers. His every glance could draw only a blank. He grew darker; his eye glittered. He could not fetch papers, for there were no papers, not of the kind he had mentioned. There did not need to be under certain assumed circumstances. He had established the pretext of going to his study to fetch them, but by the time he returned the Irish bombs would have done their work. Irish bombs were always lethal.

The useless conference was brought to an abrupt end by

the refusal of his brothers to prolong further a meeting that had no sense to it, and Cumberland was seen to be in a dark mood for the rest of the day. Erzburger had a problem concerning Mr Joseph Maguire. He might have thought the best way to deal with a man who may have laid a trap for His Highness was to hand him over to Irish papists as an informer.

Then there was the hireling who had Maguire under surveillance.

Whatever steps were decided on and by whom, the fact remained that a capable-looking man arrived at the lodgings of the hireling. Finding him not at home, he crossed the street and went up to Maguire's modest abode. His knock on the door was answered by a British Army sergeant, whose comrade, a corporal, stepped smartly out and cut off the visitor's retreat. They took him into custody, but neither they nor any other representatives of His Majesty's Government secured a jot of information from him. He kept his mouth tightly shut throughout. He was sentenced to be transported, along with the lookout and the four papist conspirators. And Captain Burnside had the satisfaction of knowing the interests of the loyal Mr Maguire were well looked after. It did not, however, make him feel any better about the abrupt and uncompromising termination of what he considered was his precious relationship with the equally precious Lady Caroline.

'So,' said the Duke of Avonhurst later that day, 'Cumberland endured a negative afternoon. With bad grace, I'll warrant.'

'We shall probably never know the extent of his implication. Even so, I fancy he ain't enjoyed the best week of his life.' Captain Burnside looked as if his own week had not been the happiest. Nor was His Grace in his best mood. The Captain knew him for a perfectionist, a demanding one, but he was always fair. Something was gnawing at him now. 'He discovered Lady Russell's *billet-doux* was missing. I gathered from Betsy that his household staff were made to run the gauntlet of an abrasive interrogation. Some were dismissed on the spot, including Betsy. I've found lodgings for her until she gets another position.'

'Have you formed an attachment for that wench?' asked His Grace disparagingly. 'Ain't it time, sir, you gave thought to the honourable estate of marriage, and with a lady of grace, a lady somewhat of an improvement on a flirtatious wench?'

'I ain't immune to the prospect,' said Captain Burnside, 'but as to Betsy, I simply ain't too keen on seeing a girl like her thrown on to the streets. Her nature's far too friendly.'

Avonhurst frowned. 'Concerning Lady Caroline,' he said, and Captain Burnside's grimace did not escape him, 'I have to tell you that she called on me this morning, and such were the circumstances that I was compelled to confess to her.'

'Oh, my God,' said the Captain.

'You need His help,' said His Grace, 'as I do myself.'

'I must go and see her.'

'I don't advise it. She'll have her servants horsewhip you, and she won't receive you, nor give you a salve for your scourged back.'

'I'll risk the horsewhip,' said the Captain, set of face.

# Chapter Thirty

'I has to inform you, sir, that Her Ladyship is not at home,' said Thomas, standing squarely at the open door.

'Do you mean she is out?' asked Captain Burnside.

'I mean, sir,' said Thomas regretfully, for he liked the Captain, 'that she is not at home.'

'She won't see me, is that it?'

'Her Ladyship is not at home,' said Thomas.

'I see. Then would you ask Miss Annabelle to receive me?'

'Miss Annabelle Howard, sir, is not at home.'

'Damn me, Thomas, do you want me to black your eye?'

'No, sir. Not as it'll do you any good. Miss Annabelle is at Lady Repton's evening reception. Being it's my duty, I'll now close the door.'

'Do so,' said the Captain, 'then kindly carry a message to Lady Caroline, advising her that if her door stays closed to me I'll break it down.'

'Ah, has I heard you correct, sir?' asked Thomas.

'You have.'

'Very good, sir,' said Thomas, and closed the door. He carried the message upstairs to Helene, passing over the fact that Lady Caroline was pecking at her supper in the dining room.

Helene, about to go down to join the servants at supper in their hall, received the message in startlement. 'He is not serious, Thomas?'

'Well,' said Thomas, 'I didn't like the look in his eye, I tell you that.'

'Oh, poor Captain Burnside,' said Helene. 'At the first blow on the door, Lady Caroline will have him arrested. She'll send Sammy for the Bow Street Runners. I had better go down and talk to him.'

Captain Burnside looked at her as she opened the door. 'I hope you bring reasonable news,' he said.

'Sir, I hope myself you will be reasonable and go away,' said Helene.

'Yours is a vain hope, Helene, for at the moment I ain't a reasonable man.'

'I regret that won't help,' said Helene. 'Lady Caroline will not see you under any circumstances, whether you are reasonable or not. Nor am I sure if it would profit you if she did see you. She is making plans to return to America.'

'Oh, ye gods,' said Captain Burnside. 'Well, tell her to unmake them.'

'Captain Burnside,' said Helene gently, 'it will be more than my life is worth even to tell her I've been talking to you.'

'Oh, the devil,' he said, 'is she so out of sorts?'

Helene looked quite sadly at him. She had hoped Her Ladyship would find enough integrity and character in Captain Burnside to marry him. 'Sir, what have you done to her?' she asked quietly. 'She is more than out of sorts, far more. She is suffering. She endured her bad days with – oh, I should not say so, but Lord Clarence caused her much unhappiness. She bore it all with pride. What have you done to her to make her say she wishes she were dead?'

'Let me see her,' said Captain Burnside.

'I beg you won't force yourself on her,' said Helene. She hesitated, then whispered. 'I am breaking a confidence, which I never have before, but tomorrow she is going to Great Wivenden, to spend her time there until she sails for America. I can speak no more with you now.' And Helene closed the door.

Caroline saw him. She saw him from the window of her

bedroom in the manor house. The August day was glorious, laying gold on the wheatfields and brightly defining his figure as he rode up the long sandy drive to the forecourt of the house. His demeanour seemed thoughtful, his back slight bent, eyes downcast, and his horse was only ambling. It was a slow, deliberate ride to the great front doors of her country residence.

The freezing sensations returned to her body. She watched him, hating him, and she felt disgust that he should have come here, to the place she loved most. In such a place, he was an obscenity. She turned and pulled on the bellcord.

Helene came in. 'Milady?'

'That man is here.'

'Your pardon?' said Helene, although she guessed.

'Captain Burnside. I am out, do you hear? I have gone to Brighton.'

'He will ask—'

'Do as I say. Tell him. Answer no questions.' Caroline was pale, shadows around her eyes. Whenever she was able to sleep, it was only fitfully, and for the last few hours, exhaustedly. 'Send him away.'

The front door bell sprang its peal.

Helene hurried down, intercepting Mr Frederick Jarvis, the head servant of the household. 'I will answer it, Mr Jarvis, I know who it is,' she said.

It was Helene whom Captain Burnside saw again when one of the double doors opened. He seemed calm but determined. He raised his beaver hat to her. 'Good afternoon,' he said. 'I wish to see Lady Clarence Percival.'

'I am so sorry,' said Helene, making an effort to look him in the eye, 'but Her Ladyship is in Brighton.'

'No, she ain't.'

'Captain Burnside—'

'It won't do,' he said. 'Be so kind as to advise her that I'm here, and that I ain't going to depart until I've seen her. Further advise her that if she don't give me a chance to talk to her, she ain't as sweet-natured as I thought she was. Nor is she fair.'

366

'Oh, Captain Burnside,' gasped Helene, 'I can't tell her that. She *is* sweet-natured, and fair . . .'

'She ain't. Not if she won't allow me a hearing. Advise her so.'

'Sir, I simply cannot. And she's in Brighton.'

'Oh, you insist, do you, Helene?' Captain Burnside was grim. Helene quivered, certain he was in a mood to sweep her aside and force his way into the presence of Her Ladyship. 'Very well. Where in Brighton?'

'I really don't know,' said Helene, a little desperate.

'Quite so. Why should you know? Why should anyone know? She ain't in Brighton. She's here.'

'Captain Burnside, you must go about things in your own way, but I cannot let you in, and beg you won't have me side with you against Her Ladyship, only tell you that I wish you well, which I truly do.'

'Then at least acquaint Her Ladyship with the fact that I ain't going to depart until she sees me. Also tell her she ain't going back to America except over my dead body.'

'Oh,' said Helene. The faintest smile came. 'You love her.'

'Of course I love her,' said Captain Burnside. 'Who couldn't? But if it comes to putting her over my knees, damned if I won't do it.'

'Oh, dear Lord,' gasped Helene, and hastily closed the door. Captain Burnside, his horse tethered, sat down on the step.

'Your Ladyship?' Helene was tentative.

'Well?' Caroline, at her window again, swung round, eyes glittering.

'He—'

'He hasn't gone,' said Caroline, 'for I haven't seen him ride away.'

'I beg Your Ladyship's forbearance, but he was so determined.'

'Really?' Lady Caroline was icy. 'His determination does not match mine. Did you not tell him I was in Brighton?'

'Indeed, yes, I did. Twice.' Helene took the plunge. 'I am afraid he did not believe me.'

'That would be amusing if it weren't so wretched. How dare a man like that give the lie to anyone?'

'Milady, what has he done?' asked Helene bravely.

'What does that matter? It is enough for you to know him an utterly worthless creature. When Mr Forbes returns to his office, ask him to come and see me. If you are unable to persuade Captain Burnside to go away, I shall ask Mr Forbes to intercede.'

'Your Ladyship,' said Helene, brave again, 'Captain Burnside asked me to advise you he won't depart until you consent to see him.'

'Oh, I declare myself ravaged and racked by his importunities!' Caroline was fierce, tearing herself apart in her bitterness. 'Let us discover just how importunate he will be when Mr Forbes and the gardeners have locked him in the stocks.'

'Oh, Lady Caroline, no, you cannot!' gasped Helene. 'Not Captain Burnside.'

Caroline's glittering eyes fixed her devoted servant. 'Well,' she breathed, 'is this what it has come to? You, whom I trust more than any other, are making sheep's eyes at Captain Burnside like an infatuated wench or a covetous trollop?'

'Your Ladyship,' said Helene quietly, 'you know that is not true.'

Caroline shivered. 'Oh, I am sorry, Helene. Forgive me. But I won't see Captain Burnside, ever. Do you understand?'

'Yes,' said Helene. But her next words were forced from her because of Captain Burnside. 'He said if you won't give him the chance to talk to you, you – you aren't as sweet-natured and as fair as he thought you were.'

'Oh, I vow that man's arrogance unbearable, and he himself despicable!'

Drawing breath, Helene said, 'He also assured me you are not going back to America except over his dead body.'

'Oh!' Caroline put her fingertips to her eyelids and pressed them in anguish. 'Go away! Please go away!'

'Ah, Sammy,' said Captain Burnside.

Sammy was in the stables, about to shoe a horse. He looked young but workmanlike, and his eyes lit up to see the Captain, whom he considered a rare dab hand at dealing with life. 'Why, it's you yourself, guv'nor. I'm that pleased to see you, sir. You've come to stay a bit?'

'I'm staying, yes, you can say that,' said the Captain, and gave Sammy a friendly pat on the arm. 'Here's my horse. Can you rub her down and stable her?'

'Willingly,' said Sammy. 'And oats, Cap'n Burnside?'

'I'll rely on you, but let me know how much she's taken between now and the time I go. I'll need to reimburse Her Ladyship.'

'D'you mean pay, sir?' asked Sammy, askance. 'Lady Caroline won't go much on that, guests paying for their 'osses oats.'

'It's a question of principle, d'you see,' said the Captain in pleasant and confiding fashion. 'Her Ladyship and yours truly are presently in argument.'

'Oh, lor',' said Sammy, 'that's a stiff one to take, sir, you and Her Ladyship on an up-and-downer. And her being such a fine lady, and all. But it ain't too serious, guv'nor?'

'Well, critical at the moment, I must confess,' said Captain Burnside. 'In fact, I ain't actually allowed into the house.'

'Lord help us, that's a blinder, sir,' said Sammy, shaking his head and dislodging a stray straw from his hair.

'We shall arrive in calmer waters eventually, though it's stormy today. Young fellow, I ain't proposing you should be disloyal, and I know you won't be, but you can tell me, I hope, if Her Ladyship is regularly out and about.'

'Ah,' said Sammy, and examined his loyalties. Captain Burnside, he reckoned, had taken a fancy to Her Ladyship, and Her Ladyship, being in the kind of mood she'd never been in before, wasn't making it easy for him. And she was talking about going back to America. 'Well, guv'nor, I can tell you she ain't one for sitting indoors

369

when she's here, that she ain't. She's been out riding several times, and bringing her 'oss back lathered.'

'I'd like to be tipped the wink when she next rides out. Can I rely on you, Sammy?'

'You can rely on me if she don't tell me not to tell you,' said Sammy. 'If she says I ain't to, then I ain't a-going to, begging your pardon and all, sir.'

'Quite right, Sammy. What she tells you you mustn't do, you won't do. What she doesn't tell you to do, you can do. Excellent. You're a capital young fellow.'

'Guv'nor, I think you've just put me on the ropes,' said Sammy.

'It will help the calmer seas to arrive,' said the Captain. 'I shall be within hearing distance.'

He took a stroll in the gardens below the terrace. From a drawing room, Caroline saw him again. She clenched her hands and gritted her teeth. There he was, meandering, in his beaver hat, and idly swinging his cane, as if all was well with his world. His presence was confining her. She would not, could not, go out while he was here. To meet him, to come face-to-face with him, would do her no good at all. Oh, how dare he put himself back in her life, how dared he have the effrontery to come and to stay? She had fared very badly. First Clarence, wholly decadent, and now this man, wholly spurious.

John Forbes appeared, walking in his deliberate way. He came up from the parkland, and she saw him turn and advance on Captain Burnside.

'Captain Burnside?' said Mr Forbes.

'Good afternoon, Mr Forbes,' said the Captain.

'You're visiting?' asked the steward.

'I arrived an hour ago. I'm now taking in the tranquil effect of these gardens.'

'You must thank George Cutts for that. He's head gardener. Good afternoon to you, sir.' Mr Forbes had no idea Captain Burnside was presently in argument with Her Ladyship, though he was well aware Her Ladyship was not at her best. He had no sooner reached his office a minute or so later than she appeared.

'John,' she said, 'you have just been speaking to Captain Burnside. What did he say to you?'

Mr Forbes, thinking she looked unwell, said, 'He remarked he was taking in the tranquil effect of your gardens.'

'He has arrived uninvited,' said Caroline coldly. 'He has refused to go. Will you please prevail on him to take himself off? I am receiving no visitors, none.'

'Your Ladyship, he's refused to go?'

'He has. I declare him unwelcome. Therefore, please see to it that he departs.'

Mr Forbes, a grave man, gave himself time to reflect. 'Your Ladyship,' he said, 'am I being asked to intervene because you've quarrelled with Captain Burnside?'

'How dare you!' said Caroline.

'It was put respectfully,' said Mr Forbes.

'Ask him to leave, please. Call the gardeners if he proves objectionable, and have them carry him off the estate.' And Caroline turned and swept away.

She watched again from the drawing room. She saw Mr Forbes speaking to the Captain. The Captain nodded, cut off a dead rose bloom with a swish of his cane, lifted his hat to the steward, and strolled away. She lost sight of him as he made for the stables. Mr Forbes returned to the house, and reported that Captain Burnside had consented to go.

'Thank you, John,' said Caroline, 'and forgive me if I was too demanding of you.'

So, he had come and he had gone. The ice around her heart turned leaden.

Captain Burnside rode back to the house under cover of darkness that night. He stabled his horse, removed his hat and coat, made a bed of a great mound of dry straw, settled himself down, composed his thoughts, and went to sleep.

'Oh, save my soul,' said Sammy. Captain Burnside was at

the pump, shirt sleeves rolled up. He was dousing his head in the cold water. 'Sir, you're a hot potato, that you are. The word's out. You ain't permitted nowhere near the place. I'll get stoned if I don't see you off.'

Captain Burnside shook the water from his hair. 'Well, there it is, Sammy, stormy as a raging south-wester,' he said. 'Be a good young fellow and find me a razor. I ain't half my usual self when I'm unshaven. And a crust or two would be very welcome.'

'Oh, lor', that's another blinder,' said Sammy. 'Guv'nor, you'll get me topped.'

'Sammy, I ain't as much in need of a few crusts as I am of a friend. Just a razor, then, how will that do?'

Sammy gave a huge grin. 'Seeing you ain't short of nerve, guv'nor, I'll risk getting topped.'

'In that case,' said the Captain, freshened by the cold water, 'you won't lack a consoling companion. We'll get topped together. But not a word out of place; can I rely on that?'

'Her Ladyship ain't yet told me what I mustn't do today,' said Sammy, and sidled off.

The warm breeze blew in her face, and the sunlight danced ahead of her. The side-saddle was firm, and she was expertly at home in it, her black gelding a flyer. She galloped to take out of her heart and mind everything except the glory of the August morning. The speed of the gallop was an antidote to cold, crushing anguish. And it helped her to reject the persistent intrusion into her mind: the thought that she was in blind, obsessive martyrdom of herself.

The boundary brick wall of the estate appeared in the distance. She turned her horse, continuing her reckless gallop as she made for Wivenden Wood, its trees profuse with summer leaf. She heard a sound behind her. She looked back. A horseman, fifty yards away, his head bare, was racing up on her. She went rigid in her saddle, and her frisky gelding pulled on the bit. Her body shivered and she clenched her teeth, digging with a spur.

He had come back, he was behind her, and the suffering was a torment. She raced over the thick grass alongside the wood, heading back to the house. He raced after her. He did not attempt to catch her up. He knew that at the pace she was going, and had been going, she would run her mount to a standstill long before she reached the house. He stayed within twenty yards of her, watching her ride like a madwoman. He did not call, or shout. He let her gallop on. She looked back, more than once, and she did not open her mouth, either.

Her gelding began to flounder, to falter, at which point Captain Burnside came up beside her.

'Kindly stop,' he said.

'Never! Never for you!'

'Gently, marm, gently,' he said.

'Oh!' she raged, and struck at him with her riding crop. It caught him across his jaw. Her gelding, blown and lathered, stopped, head hanging, flanks heaving. Captain Burnside pulled up and dismounted. She slapped wildly at her horse, but it was too winded to respond. The Captain reached for her with long arms. She struck him again. He pulled her from her saddle, her fury almost hysterical as she tumbled into his arms, her top hat falling off. He held her, and she kicked in his arms.

'It won't do, marm, it won't do at all,' he said.

'Let me go!'

He set her on her feet. Bitter, glittering and utterly outraged, she struck at him yet again. His arm came up, warding off the blow. He shook his head at her.

'I ain't ever put a woman over my knees before,' he said, 'but I fancy if I don't do it now, you'll never come to your senses.'

He bent low, he wound an arm around her, and he straightened up. Caroline screamed as she found herself hanging over his shoulder, his right arm wrapped around her skirted legs. Her hair came loose. Frenziedly, she beat at his back. He carried her into the shelter of the wood. In a clearing, he found an ideal tree stump. He seated himself, and Caroline screamed again as he brought her down over his knees. The indignity was paralysing, and horror rushed to suffuse her with fiery colour as her riding skirt and underskirt were whirled upwards over her back, uncovering her pantaloons. Oh, dear God, he really was going to do it!

'No,' she gasped, 'no!'

'Shall we talk, then, Your Ladyship?'

'Yes – yes.'

He released her. She escaped her indignity, her skirts falling into place, her brown coat awry, her hair disordered, her face burning.

'This ain't an inconsequential matter, marm,' he said, 'it's life and death.'

'Your death,' she said, but her bitter look was gone, and so had the misery of feeling locked in numbing ice. In its place was a swamping, surging tide of reborn gladness at simply being alive. What had happened to her that she had become a grey, cold, self-pitying and unproud shadow of herself? Why, here he was, the torment of her being, and she could not be called a true woman if she did not stand up and fight him. 'Sir,' she said, 'before I catalogue your infamies, I must congratulate you on your bravery in dragging a helpless woman from her horse and assaulting her.'

'Helpless?' he said, fingering his tender jaw.

'You shall pay dearly for subjecting me to such indignity. I have discovered all your sins. You are a fraudulent wretch and a worthless deceiver.'

'I thought, Your Ladyship, you were aware of that from the beginning.'

'In the beginning, you led me to believe you were a professional adventurer, an unprincipled rogue and a shameless blackguard. This beginning itself, sir, was an act of contemptible fraudulence.'

'I agree, marm, and confess it so, humbly,' declared the Captain, 'but I'm no more than an ordinary blackguard, such as you may come across every day in London. But as things were—'

'Ordinary?' said Caroline, spirited now. 'Did you not

374

declare you would commit any crime short of assassination or murder? There are few men so lost to all grace and decency as to deliver lies of such magnitude as you did, and to one as kind and trusting as myself.'

'Quite so, marm, but the circumstances, d'you see—'

'You are not an adventurer, a rogue or a thief, but you are a man of deceits,' said Caroline. She had grasped the nettle and seized the initiative. She was in her element, finding entirely new exhilaration in standing up to him instead of denying him access to her presence. 'Why, you are not even a professional card-sharp.'

'I'm a professional soldier, though not of the usual kind,' he said. 'I execute uncommon commissions for His Majesty's Government.'

'As I have discovered to the cost of my self-respect. The Duke of Avonhurst, my father-in-law, confessed all your deceits. Do you now say, sir, that you did not compromise your adjutant's wife or decamp with the trinkets of young ladies who thought you would marry them?'

'God forbid I should even dream of it,' said Captain Burnside, 'and God forgive your father-in-law for spilling the beans.'

'My father-in-law does not spill beans, sir. He is a gentleman of honour, and in honourable fashion he—' Caroline broke off as Captain Burnside coughed. 'Sir?' she said haughtily.

'A cough ain't always significant, Your Ladyship.'

'My father-in-law, as a matter of honour, felt impelled to acquaint me with all the miserable details of your two-faced activities. I have forgiven him his own part. Your part, sir, will never be forgiven. I detest myself for being a naive, trusting and sweet-natured simpleton, thinking of your professed sins not with scorn but with Christian pity.'

Captain Burnside eyed her with due gravity. Chin high, she stared him out, showing not a sign that this final confrontation had her in a state of resurgent challenge.

'Allow me, marm, to confess myself abject, penitent and contrite,' he said, 'and to offer myself up for execution. But while I am all of a piece, I beg your consideration of the plight of the maidservant Betsy, so invaluable in the matter of the letter. The sweet puss—'

'The pretty trollop?' interjected Caroline bitingly.

'She's been dismissed following an investigation into the letter's disappearance. While allowing you ain't charitably inclined at the moment, due to my regrettable abuse of your trust and self-respect, I know you to have natural compassion and I thought, therefore, you might find her a position here at Great Wivenden. Sussex, d'you see, offers her less temptations than London, she owning too much of a weakness for gentlemen of a suspect kind.'

Caroline could not believe her ears. Merciful heavens, was the ground she had newly won to be swept from beneath her feet? Were there no limits to his outrageous audacity? Was there ever a more presumptuous villain, or a more endearing one? Her resolution trembled on the brink.

'Sir, your impudence is breathtaking,' she said. 'I am to consider employing your trollop? Oh, sir, I vow you of all things conscienceless. I have found you out, discovered your perfidy, and the first thing you do is beg me to take up your fallen baggage. I am lost for words, sir, lost.'

'Ah,' said the Captain, and coughed again. 'I ain't noticed it,' he said.

Caroline could hardly contain her swamping tide of re-charged spirit. There he was, standing before her, his expression that of a man being entirely reasonable. Oh, that she had denied herself this exultant confrontation until now.

'You are shifting about, sir,' she said. 'You may have no shame, but you are surely not such a coward that you can't face your deserved death bravely. But I declare myself unvindictive. I am returning home to Charleston at the end of this month.'

'Only over my dead body,' said the Captain.

'Sir?'

'You ain't going,' he said.

'This conversation is over,' said Caroline.

'It ain't properly begun yet. Beg to suggest, Your Ladyship, that you stop playing games.'

'Games?' Her head came up.

'It's affecting my well-being,' said the Captain.

A breeze came drifting from the Downs and lightly kissed the leafy trees. Caroline stood still, yielding nothing. The Captain was poised, however, to cut off her probable, darting flight.

'Your well-being, sir, is not my concern. I am selling Great Wivenden—'

'No, you ain't,' he said.

'Captain Burnside, there is a suspicion in my mind that you're threatening me.'

'Quite right,' said the Captain, 'I am. Declare yourself permanently attached to Great Wivenden, or take the consequences.'

'Declare those consequences, sir.'

'Abduction, confinement, and bread and water. Sammy is presently at Pond Cottage, with your coach. Unless, marm, you come to your senses, I shall carry you there, bundle you aboard, and get Sammy to drive us to a place where I shall lock you up and feed you bread and water, which won't necessarily be the least of it.'

'Lock me up?' Caroline could scarcely restrain her joy. No woman could have failed to perceive what lay behind this outrageous threat. He loved her. He wanted her, and meant to have her whether she would or no. Merciful heavens, was ravishment included? Not for him the timid words of a fainthearted swain, but the calculating and uncompromising approach that carried the implication of a fate worse than death. A fate worse than death? At his hands? Oh, joy. He did love her. But she would not give in, never, until he told her so. 'Am I dreaming?' she asked. 'Am I among phantoms and fantasies? Abduct me? Lock me up and feed me bread and water?'

'Which my estimable mother always prescribed as the most salutary cure for the sulks of rebellious boys and pettish girls.'

'Pettish girls? Pettish girls?'

'Alas, Lady Caroline, that you should have come to girlish sulks, you who adorned Lady Chesterfield's ball like a magnificent goddess,' said the unblinking Captain.

'Oh, that disgraceful tongue of yours will bring you to a

377

miserable end, Captain Burnside,' she said, 'and your ridiculous threats will avail you nothing. Sammy and my coach indeed—fiddlesticks, sir, fiddlesticks. You could never make a confederate of Sammy. He would never go against me.'

'He is under the impression, Your Ladyship, that you and I are to elope.'

Caroline was further entranced. Oh, the audacious villain. 'Elope? With you? I should leave Sammy in no doubt that you were engaged in forceful abduction, for I should fight you tooth and nail. You deceived me, lied to me, mocked me, humiliated me and made a fool of me. Have you no thought of what that did to me?'

'Your Most Precious and Endearing Ladyship,' said Captain Burnside, 'what do you think it did to me, loving you hopelessly as I did from the moment I first saw you?'

He had said it at last. It took all breath from her. Dizzy rapture overtook her. Henceforward, the confrontation could only offer unparalleled delight. But all she could say for the moment was, 'Hopelessly, Captain Burnside?'

His expression became wry. 'I ain't supposing you've any great regard for me,' he said, 'but all the same I'll not stand aside and let you go back to America.'

'So,' she breathed, 'you would abduct me, imprison me and starve me until I let you have your dreadful way with me? Why, you would never even get me into the coach, for I should make it plain to Sammy that you were attempting brutal abduction, no less.'

'Unfortunately, marm,' he said smoothly, 'Sammy won't be there, nor the coach. One plays a hopeful hand to see what it will achieve, and when it don't bring forth the right results, one plays the ace. The ace is Pond Cottage. I shall carry you there, muffling all your cries for help, and keep you captive until you give up your unacceptable notion of running off to America. America won't do, Your Ladyship, and it ain't going to do.'

Caroline's eyes were luminous with bliss. Joy upon joy, he was no sooner shorn of one bluff than another sprang from his facile tongue. Oh, what a divinely talkative marriage they would have.

'Why, you disgraceful braggart,' she said, 'I am no weak and wailing woman, or an incapable one. I should escape the cottage with ease.'

'I should discourage that by removing your clothes,' said Captain Burnside, as straight of face as she was scornful of smile.

'Removing my clothes?'

'Ah – most of them,' he said.

Caroline was almost delirious with inner laughter. 'Sir, I declare you unspeakable,' she said.

'All is fair, marm, in love and war,' he said.

'Your villainy is breathtaking, sir, your love utterly suspect,' she declared. 'Do you think I would let you remove a single stitch of my clothing, or allow you to carry me all the way to Pond Cottage with my screams muffled?'

'I consider you a bearable armful, Lady Caroline, and the walk ain't beyond me, nor the muffling of your tantrums.'

'*Tantrums*?' Caroline felt that every leaf of every tree was laughing. 'Is it a tantrum, sir, to fight for my honour? Show me how you will muffle me. There, you have given me threats, I now give you a challenge. Show me, sir, that you are as good as your vaunted boasts.'

'H'm,' said Captain Burnside.

'Don't shift about, sir, but show me. Yes, show me precisely how you will carry me and muffle me.'

'Very well, Your Ladyship,' he said, and swept her up into his arms, much to her delight. Carrying her, he began to walk, bearing her through the trees. She did not kick, nor did she scream.

'I am, as you see, free to cry for help,' she said, settling herself blissfully and comfortably in his arms, her hands locked around his neck. 'So, will you come to the muffling? How is that to be done?'

'Alas, there is only one way,' said the Captain. 'This way.' And he kissed her. His lips were firm and determined, making their claim and taking possession of hers, and hers broke apart. The summer breeze brought the lightest of whispers as the surging tide of love engulfed Caroline. In his arms, she drowned in warm seas of ecstasy. He carried her from the wood into the golden sunlight, and still she was muffled, each kiss more prolonged. She sighed when at last he freed her mouth. He said nothing, but he stopped, his expression that of a man not now entirely sure of himself. The responsive ardour of her mouth had bemused him.

'Pray continue,' said Caroline, her voice a little throaty.

'No, I shall set you down here, having shown you how it will be done,' he said, and he set her down.

'Continue,' said Caroline, her warm body breathing close to his. 'Take me up again. You have not shown me all you intend to do to me. Continue, therefore, and when we reach Pond Cottage, show me how you will go about undressing me.'

'Ah, I think not,' he said.

'I think yes,' said Caroline, eyes loving him.

'Why?' he asked, wanting her.

'Why? Why?' Caroline laughed in rich joy. 'Because you are my most audacious and adorable villain, because I am your willing Caroline and your sweet pleasure, and because I love you, love you, love you. Oh, dearest, dearest Charles, you will be true to me, won't you?'

Captain Burnside, not ignorant of the reputation Lord Clarence Percival had earned for himself, said, 'What kind of a true man would any man be if, having been gifted with the love of such a beautiful and endearing woman as you, he could not be faithful to her?'

'Oh, how glad I am to know you aren't going to end up on Tyburn Tree,' said Caroline, 'and how very glad I am that you love me. I really don't mind going on to Pond Cottage.'

'For what purpose, Your Ladyship?' he smiled.

'Darling, to fight for my honour, of course,' said Caroline. 'I have a dreadful feeling I shall lose, for you are a man of such singular accomplishments and I such a weak and helpless woman . . . Dearest, what are you laughing at?'

Captain Burnside was laughing indeed. Richly. She saw the delight he had in her, she saw the love he had for her, and she knew that this time she had made no mistake.

I am at my beginning.